The Evil Thereof

By the same author

Man on the Crater's Edge
The Omega Factor
The Assassination Run
The Treachery Game
The Whitehall Sanction
The Back of the Tiger
Death's Head Berlin
Death Squad London
Death Watch '39

The Evil Thereof

Jack Gerson

PIATKUS

For my friends, Maggie and Donald MacAskill

Copyright © 1991 by Jack Gerson

First published in Great Britain in 1991 by
Judy Piatkus (Publishers) Ltd of
5 Windmill Street, London W1

*The author hereby asserts his moral rights
and Piatkus will observe the moral rights conferred by
the Copyright Designs and Patents Act 1988.*

British Library Cataloguing in Publication Data

Gerson, Jack
  The evil thereof.
  I. Title
  823[F]

ISBN 0-7499-0080-6

Phototypeset in 11/12pt Linotron Times by
Computerset, Harmondsworth, Middlesex
Printed and bound in Great Britain by
Mackays of Chatham PLC, Chatham, Kent

Prologue 1976

Coming down from the hill. Edron Hill. *The* hill. In the darkness that seemed the absolute negation of light; a clouded starless sky, a dead unseen moon. Guided only by custom and instinct, he'd known the path since he'd been a child, wandering there both night and day; playing hookey from school so many days; climbing from his window so many nights, parents asleep, or about their own affairs. A time ago, that was, forty years or more, when he'd been learning the beginnings of it all. All he knew now and would use. If they allowed him to use it.

A chill wind came up from the flat land below, across Mallen's Meadow and up the gentle slope. A coldness that iced the flesh and reached inwards to the bone.

He thought, How calm I am, considering . . .

A darker patch in the black dark. The split oak, it would be, lightning split a hundred years before and still standing, solid dead wood looking towards petrification. He could sense it, knew it was there, he knew everything, on and off the path, despite the dark. And the oak would be shaped like a hunchback with long arms raised to heaven in supplication.

They would want him to do that; lift his arms to the sky and beg. To their moon-shaped faces, stupid with unquestioning obedience. He would not do it. In all his fifty-seven years, he'd begged for nothing, neither food nor coin, the favours of women, the approbation of men. Nor the easing of pain. And pain he *had* endured. So much pain to reach where he was.

They were on the hill behind them. Following. They would be on the meadow below. Waiting. And somewhere, the

1

others who knew that if he survived this night, they were lost.

If he survived . . .

And if he did not, there would not just be death, but something worse, something unknown, but sensed. As he could sense the familiar in the darkness, he could sense too the fate that would await him. He didn't fear death, he barely feared the pain of death, but there was this other, an aftermath of damnation that would last through an eternity of shadowed horror. If one believed in damnation.

The problem was, *he* believed.

The foot of the hill now. The smell of hay in his nostrils. Grass underfoot. And to the left the gorse bushes. He was moving fast now across Mallen's Meadow and towards the village. Once in the village, a few steps to his cottage, and they wouldn't be able to touch him. Around the cottage he had set up his own safeguards.

A rustling sound from the direction of the gorse bushes. Darker shapes in the night, moving shapes, twisting and turning, drifting towards him then fading away, as if fearful of coming too close. They wouldn't come too close singly, but only as a body. And he was approaching the edge of the meadow. By the solitary old ash tree and then but steps to the road.

He stopped. Frozen. Feeling the chill spread from his feet up his legs into his body, a paralytic cold, the icy grip of the symbols of hell. In front of him, the ash tree. At his feet, ancient symbols in the grass, twisted out of hanks of corn and human hair and wood and iron, all dampened with water, barring his way. Around him the rustling increased, the shadows closed in.

They were strong.

They were too strong for him. Now he knew . . .

. . . and knew he would be defeated. Could feel too the cold of steel in his throat, driven through the flesh, severing arteries, filling his throat and mouth with great gouts of blood . . . he could feel his death, anticipate it, taste the salt of the blood spilled in the act . . .

. . . was able now to move forward, but slowly, towards the ash tree, where he would sit, back against the bole of the tree . . . and would wait . . .

2

. . . and would wait . . .
. . . at their pleasure . . .
. . . accepting his defeat . . . weary with the driving out of elation . . . left only to accept . . .
. . . and fear the horror that would come later . . .
. . . after he had been killed.

Braden 1988

Chapter One

Winter in the air, he thought as he left the apartment in Chiswick: the slight haze, a trace of mist, a minuscule lowering of the temperature . . . he could sense it every year, and feel a chill in the bones, waiting for the tube-train at Gunnersbury Station. Waiting, alone.

He frowned. Three months now, he'd been taking the tube into the centre of the city alone, and he could not yet say he was used to it. He should be able to say so now, he told himself. After all, they'd only been together eighteen months before the big walk-out, the final slamming of the door. He'd tried to tell himself at the time he was glad. He was free of emotional entanglement, he again had his Chiswick apartment to himself, had a decent job, his health, no money worries, thirty-two years of age and, he told himself, passably good-looking.

It wasn't working. Judy's absence was a perpetual ache somewhere at the back of his consciousness, a dead zone in the soul. He wanted her back and knew it would never happen. He needed her back and knew his need would have to be endured. Time would heal, so his friends told him, with a superior kind of commiseration. They'd all been through it (had they?) . . . there were plenty more fish in the sea . . . how lucky he was to be free of emotional entanglements, they'd give their eye teeth (did people have any eye teeth left?) . . . any moment now another nice girl would come along . . . at his age, he should know better . . . Oh, hell, did everyone live in a world of cliché?

Your fault, old man, Hammond would say, you work in Fleet Street. You pen-pushers create the clichés, we merely spout them. Hammond was a chartered accountant and spoke his own language and, like all accountants, would eventually rule the world. Somebody should have told Hammond it was rarely Fleet Street these days, not any more, but ugly new buildings on the bank of the Thames, or on some sullen side street, south of the City. Except for the paper Braden worked on, which clung to Fleet Street as if to preserve a kind of claim to respectability. The *Comet*, like its celestial companions the *Sun* and the *Star*, was a tabloid of sensational attributes. To call it a newspaper would have been to bestow on it a great compliment. It was famous, or notorious, not only for its page three girl, but for its page four, five and six girls, not forgetting its back-page boy, for sports enthusiasts and the other two sexes. Horoscopes occupied an entire page, as did Ruthie Cornford's advice to the lovelorn. Jane Crook ran the two pages of society and 'pop' gossip which titillated the less fortunate, and occasionally wrote a patriotic (but not uncritical) article on the younger members of the Royal Family. Jane was known to her colleagues (and to the younger members of the Royal Family) as Jane *Pluke*, but never to her face.

It was to this national institution that Eric Braden contributed several articles a week as principal features writer. What he really wanted to do was write penetrating and perceptive articles on world affairs for the Sunday *Observer*. What he *did* do was write revelations on movie and television actors; exposés of 'porn' rackets in Soho, Southend and Southampton; and a dubious six-part series called 'The Secret Sex Lives of Soviet Agents'. His work was seemingly dominated by sibilants. In fact, sibilants held a strong fascination for his editor, Louis Jordan, who believed in the mystical power of the hissing sound on his readers.

'The sibilant gets them every time,' Jordan insisted. 'It's sexy and sensational!'

And thus, thought Braden, as he entered the Fleet Street monolith, was the language of Shakespeare and Chaucer, Byron and Shelley, reduced to a hiss at the reader.

The building did not look quite as much like a black juke-box as did the old *Daily Express* building. Rather, as one wit had said, it resembled a giant one-armed bandit, with its three great windows staring down on to the street, with perhaps half an eye on Ludgate Hill.

The newsroom echoed to the whisper of word processors. Gavin Bentley, the racing correspondent, looked up from his desk. Bentley, the best-dressed man on the paper, was clad in elegant grey flannel, Savile Row cut. It was rumoured he trebled his salary on various courses by gambling against his own tips.

'Jordan's been screaming for you, Eric,' he informed Braden. 'Either you're fired or he's had another inspiration from above.'

Inspirations came from the Lord . . . not the one cele-brated in church, but the one who owned the paper. Also owned three papermills, ten thousand acres in Scotland, twenty thousand in England and a number of forests in Canada. Also a seat in the House of Lords, a clutch of seats on boards of numerous companies, and various country seats in the Home Counties.

Braden by-passed his corner desk and put his head around the door of the glass-walled oblong that was Jordan's office.

'You want me?' he said.

'Come in!' Jordan deliberately retained vestiges of a York-shire accent which he believed gave him an earthy quality which might indicate a direct line to the average reader of the *Comet*, whoever that might be. Braden went in.

'Got it last night,' Jordan said. 'The idea . . . '

Braden knew he'd been dining with the Lord the previous night.

'Oh, yes?'

'Run it for a week. Centre page. Blood and gore. Shots of the bodies if we can get them . . . '

'Bodies?' Braden said uncertainly.

'Aye, bodies. The idea is one a day: "Famous Unsolved Murders".'

Christ, thought Braden.

'It's been done,' he said.

9

'Not showing the bodies, it hasn't! And in colour. We don't usually show the bodies in this country.'

'Not the bodies – the idea. It's been done some time or other by every paper in the business.'

It was the wrong thing to say. Jordan scowled at him.

'Not the bodies,' the editor insisted. 'Not the angle I'm giving you . . . *is the killer still alive?* Has that been done?'

'Maybe.'

'Not with the bodies, if we can get them. Hogan's got a connection. Might just get photos of the bodies . . . '

There was a gruesome thought.

'And,' Jordan added, 'if the killers are known but dead long enough, we might even name them.'

'Didn't know the Lord was interested in old murders. Thought he was only into slayings on the stock exchange.'

'Some day you'll say that, he'll walk in that door as you're saying it, and you'll walk out for good. Anyway, this wasn't his idea. It was mine.'

Which was surprising as Jordan didn't usually have good ideas for features. A good editor, but not a good ideas man.

'Want you to dig up five, six murders. All unsolved, mind. Do one. Complete research. Interview survivors. Could start with that one in Scotland: "Who Killed Oscar Slater?"'

'Eventually, God, I believe. Slater was wrongly accused of being the killer. The victim was a Miss Gilchrist.'

'Just testing you, boy. How about, "Is the Gilchrist woman's killer still roaming the streets of Glasgow?"'

'Gilchrist was murdered in 1908. Not a bad headline. "Tottering Centenarian Killer Stalks City".'

Jordan's face wrinkled into a contour map. 'I sometimes wonder, lad, whether you 'ave the right frame of mind for this journal. Now, go find one good unsolved homicide. Read it up. Interview survivors. If it works, you do a series. If it doesn't work, you're back as junior reporter on the *Chipping Sodbury Weekly Advertiser*. Or should it be the *Fertiliser and Manure Monthly*?'

Braden was at the door now. 'I thought I was working on that one. But . . . your wish is my command.'

'Foocking well better be!' said Jordan, and turned to consider various page three girl photographs in front of him.

Braden took the lift down to the basement which housed the vast clipping library. The man in charge was a thin figure in his fifties known only as Alec to the editorial staff.

'Alec!' said Braden.

'Mister Braden,' said Alec who was rumoured to have an encyclopaedic memory. He sat at a tiny desk in a recess surrounded by filing cabinet upon filing cabinet. The library was halfway through the process of being put on to microfilm, and Alec had often been heard to express his disgust of this process. It was indeed rumoured he was quietly sabotaging the process. Rarely was anyone referred to the viewer and a segment of microfilm. Alec would furnish the original paper or clippings from his multitudinous cross-reference files.

'Unsolved murders,' Braden said. 'Preferably in our time, for now. Readers don't like history lessons.'

'That one,' said the librarian. 'Someone's always doing that one.'

'Now it's our turn. And my job.'

'Every five years, somebody does it. Regular as clockwork. Over and over. You can pinch it from all those True Crime magazines.'

'I don't want to pinch it. Not yet anyway. I'd like to see if there's a new angle . . . '

'Never is,' Alec said mournfully, and then wheezed, his version of laughing. 'Knew one fellow used to make up his own murders. Set them so far away nobody could check up on them. Y'know the kind of thing: "Jack the Ripper of the Tasmanian Bush". Or "The Yukon Multiple Wife Murderer". That kind of thing. Let his imagination rip. 'He fed her to the husky dogs. Did it for her gold mine." Great! Never happened. Who was to know?'

'I think mine had better be real.'

'Please yourself. What is reality? Whatever it is, it's not the stuff appears in the papers.'

Braden leaned on the back of an upright chair which stood in front of an ancient table, its surface scarred with the impatient etchings of generations of researchers. Like a schoolboy's desk, he thought.

'All right, where do I look for unsolved murders?' he asked. 'Under "M" for murder, or under "U" for unsolved?'

11

Alec shrugged, his thin arms like elongated matchsticks.

'"M" is the biggest file in the building. "Matrimony" to "Murder". Everybody at it, for one or the other. You say you want your murders unsolved?'

'The killer still stalks the streets. What Mr Jordan wants.'

Alec looked thoughtfully at the ceiling. 'Plenty of them.'

'I'd like a selection,' Braden said, feeling suddenly as if he were ordering an assortment of chocolates.

'I'll do you that. But you'll want a good one to start with. Calderon . . . that's it.'

'Calderon?'

'Calderon. Greater Calderon and Lesser Calderon. Villages in Warwickshire.'

'Oh, yes?' The name recalled nothing.

'Twelve years ago. Murder. Never solved. What did they say? "The last witchcraft murder in England." Witchcraft and black magic. Now that's a nice one for you.'

Everything has a beginning. For others the beginning had been twelve years before. For Braden, it was now.

Chapter Two

Three minutes later he was sitting at the scarred table, a file of yellowing clippings in front of him.

'Enjoy these,' Alec said. 'In a few months they'll all be put on micro-bloody-film, and you'll mess up your eyesight peering at them. As if you was looking at television. As if there wasn't enough of that. We'll all end up with square eyeballs. And who's job won't they ruin next?'

He shuffled off into his dim alcove, picked up a large mug, emerged and disappeared into the corridor in the general direction of a tea-dispensing machine. Braden addressed his attention to the clippings. Starting at the beginning of October, 1976. Headlines, he noted, for two days on the front pages.

WITCHCRAFT IN WARWICKSHIRE
RITUAL MURDER IN VILLAGE

He read on.

The body of farm labourer Joshua Gideon was discovered in a field between the villages of Greater and Lesser Calderon yesterday morning. Gideon was found impaled to a tree by a pitchfork and surrounded by what the police described as 'ritual objects used in the practice of witchcraft'.

Then, the next day:

13

BLACK MAGIC MURDER IN SILENT VILLAGE.
LOCAL POLICE BAFFLED

For the next few days the story was consigned to inside pages.

FARM LABOURER KILLING — STILL NO ARREST

HOUSE TO HOUSE QUESTIONING
IN WARWICKSHIRE VILLAGE

INQUEST VERDICT ON FARM LABOURER.
MURDER BY PERSONS UNKNOWN

Then, a week after the first reports of the crime, a box headline, again on the front page:

WITCHCRAFT MURDER — SCOTLAND YARD CALLED IN

Superintendent Jack Harkness of Scotland Yard's CID has been called in by the Warwickshire County Constabulary to take over the investigation of the ritual witchcraft murder of farm labourer Joshua Gideon. Superintendent Harkness, one of the Yard's top detectives, was the man who achieved fame some months ago when he headed the squad responsible for the smashing of the East London Swanson gang which resulted in gang leader Ronnie Swanson being sentenced at the Old Bailey to a twenty-year prison sentence. Harkness was commended by Mr Justice Openshaw despite allegations of police brutality made by the defending counsel.

There then followed another story some two days later.

CID ACE TAKES OVER WITCHCRAFT CASE

Superintendent Jack Harkness arrived today in Warwickshire to take over investigation of the murder of Joshua Gideon. The Warwickshire police announced developments are expected shortly. It is understood that Superintendent Harkness has recruited into his team,

14

local police constable Harold Drewitt, twenty-four, who was born in the village of Lesser Calderon.

For two weeks after this, the rest seemed to be silence. Except for one brief report, no stories, no developments, shortly or otherwise. Simply a confirmation of the lack of progress.

The killer of farm labourer Joshua (Josh) Gideon is still at large. Despite calling in an ace detective, Superintendent Jack Harkness, Warwickshire Constabulary report no further progress in the murder hunt.

A demand for action came from local MP George Arnold, who issued a statement from Westminster. Mr Arnold said: 'This murderer is still among us and must be apprehended. Lurid publicity about witchcraft and black magic will not have helped the police in their investigations. Nevertheless we are not in the Middle Ages and superstition must not cloud the fact that a sadistic killer is still at large.' Superintendent Harkness's office had no comment to make on the MP's statement.

Braden smiled to himself. The local member had done his duty and then closed his mouth. No further recorded comment from George Arnold. If memory served, he'd lost his seat in the 1979 General Election and disappeared into that limbo inhabited by defeated and undistinguished Members of Parliament.

There were two further clippings.

ACE DETECTIVE TAKEN ILL

Superintendent Jack Harkness, the man who put Ronnie Swanson behind bars, collapsed yesterday while engaged in a murder investigation in Warwickshire. It is understood that Superintendent Harkness is now on sick leave and the investigation of the murder of Joshua Gideon has been returned to Chief Inspector Blakelock of the Warwickshire CID.

There are no further developments in what has been described as 'the last witchcraft murder in England'.

The final clipping, a small paragraph on an inside page, made no mention of the murder of Joshua Gideon.

TOP DETECTIVE RETIRES

Superintendent Jack Harkness of Scotland Yard, the man who put Ronnie Swanson, notorious East End gang leader, behind bars, and who solved the Camberwell Slasher murders, has retired on the grounds of ill health. Superintendent Harkness, a Scot, joined the police in Glasgow in 1946, later transferring to the Metropolitan force. He is fifty-nine years of age.'

There was nothing else. Except for a page of indecipherable shorthand. No further stories on the murder of Joshua Gideon. The unsolved murder of Joshua Gideon. 'The last witchcraft murder in England'. Unsolved. And therefore forgotten by the press. A slightly longer than nine days' wonder, twelve years ago. Very possibly, the murderer would still be alive.

'Nice one, eh?' Alec was standing behind him, mug of tea in one hand, paper cup of tea in the other. He placed the paper cup on the desk top beside Braden. 'What you want, eh?'

Braden looked up. 'I like it,' he said, and at once felt uneasy. Alec's manner, probably; a combination of unctuousness and morbidity. Perhaps one got like that, living in a newspaper morgue.

'Thought you might,' he said.

'Never heard of it before. One I missed. Wasn't working on a national twelve years ago.'

'Just a boy, eh? It crops up now and then. Here and there. By the specialists in murder, and the occult. All that witchcraft and black magic stuff, grist to somebody's mill. Otherwise it's forgotten.'

'Why forgotten?'

The matchstick shoulders shrugged again. 'Dunno. Dunno anythin', 'cept what I read in the papers. And that's mostly fiction, in't it? Anyway, no killer, no news.'

16

'Could the killer have died and the police knew about it? Just let it go?'

'Could be. Have to ask the police.'

'Can I get photo-stats of this stuff?'

'I'll do it for you. On your desk in fifteen minutes.'

'Fine. Not a lot there though. Have to do some digging.' He found himself using Alec as a sounding board. 'Still, it'll be meat and drink to Jordan. He has an unhealthy mind. Not just murder but black magic thrown in. And that name . . . Joshua Gideon.'

'What about the name?' Alec said, eyes narrowing in puzzlement. 'Perfectly ordinary name.'

'Josh Gideon – I almost don't believe it. If it wasn't Josh, it would have been Seth or Reuben. Like something from *Cold Comfort Farm*.'

The allusion was lost on Alec. He blinked.

Braden went on: 'And skewered to a tree, with a pitchfork . . . Nasty.'

'Bloody,' Alec contributed. 'Blood and gore. Whatever gore is.'

'A stake through the chest and we might have had an odd vampire thrown in. These witchcraft symbols around the body . . . now what would they be?'

'Straw dolls. Corn dollies, they call them. And symbols – the old symbols – from the *Cabbala* . . . '

Braden stared again at Alec in surprise. 'You're well informed.'

'You get like that, down here. Place is full of bits of useless information, you could say. Gets into your head.'

Braden turned back to the clippings. 'Josh Gideon. Farm labourer. Bachelor o' the Parish. But why? Why murder? What had he done? No indication of motive. Apart from all this witchcraft crap . . . '

'And by whom?' said Alec. 'Isn't that what you'd really be after?'

'Be something if I could solve it, without getting sued to kingdom come. Still, Jordan wants unsolved murders and this is a good one. I wonder if this Superintendent . . . what-shisname? . . . Harkness is still alive. Retired at fifty-nine . . .

17

he'd only be seventy-one. Of course, if he's dead I'm out of luck. And he didn't sound too great when he had to retire.'

'There's one thing you might have missed, Mister Braden. This uniformed constable Harkness used . . . Harry Drewitt. Born in one of the Calderons. He was only twenty-four. Make him thirty-six now.'

'Yes, I could talk to him. Poor bugger's probably still pounding a beat in Warwickshire.'

Alec grinned. Crevices deepened on the contour map of his face.

'Ah, now, there's where my cross-reference system comes into play. See this?' He handed Braden a clipping, not yellowing but comparatively recent. 'Only two weeks old.'

Braden took the clipping and read:

WARWICK BANK ROBBERY – TWO CHARGED

Within five hours of the robbery at the East Street branch of the Midland Bank, Detective Inspector Harry Drewitt, Warwick CID, announced the arrest of two men . . .

Braden didn't have to read any more. 'Alec, you're a gem and I love you.'

Alec frowned, unused to such flattery. 'I know I'm loveable, but nobody else does.'

'Mind you, with my luck, it might not be the same Harry Drewitt.'

'You're a worrier, Mr Braden. It's not so common a name. Not too many Drewitts strewn around.'

'Easily found out. One phone call. If it is the same man, it's a beginning.'

Warwick County Constabulary, as with most regional forces, and indeed most large organisations in this media-conscious society, had its own public relations department. It was necessary in this twentieth century to assure the honest citizens of Warwickshire that their police force was a benevolent organisation whose only aim was to protect their bodies and their possessions from predators . . . and to guard the wealth accumulated by large companies and corporations from such predators; the latter being more important than the former, although this was never admitted.

Braden was eventually connected to a Chief Inspector Dowling, in charge of Public Relations. At first, at the end of the phone, Dowling sounded young, enthusiastic and affable.

'Always willing to help the Press, Mister Braden . . . Detective Inspector Drewitt? Yes, I'm sure he'd be pleased to be interviewed. Did a marvellous job on a bank robbery we had up here a couple of weeks ago . . . '

'I'm interested in doing a series of articles on unsolved murders.'

A mistake, Braden realised at once. Dowling became guarded, the tone of voice changing, becoming less affable.

'We don't have many of these in this county. We have a high rate of arrest in the matter of murder. And I'm sure any emphasis on unsolved cases would be counter-productive, to say the least.'

Braden knew he had to restore the affability, and quickly.

'The aim is not to denigrate the police. Indeed, it is to show that, in the few cases unsolved, you never close your books on murder.'

The affability was partially restored. 'Well, of course, that's true.'

'And certainly Inspector Drewitt's recent success makes him an ideal subject. If an interview could be arranged as soon as possible?'

The interview was duly arranged for the next day in Warwick. And affability fully restored.

'Warwickshire?' said Jordan, later that day. 'Why do you want to go to Warwickshire?'

Braden told him.

'Can't you get everything you need from the library?'

'Old press clippings don't tell me who killed Joshua Gideon. And, after all, it was your idea. See if we could find the killer.'

'All right, all right, take a couple of days and go,' Jordan said testily. 'But come back with something decent we can print. Otherwise there's always the *Fertiliser and Manure Weekly*.'

19

'I told you I thought I was already working for that,' Braden replied, moving quickly from the office.

That evening he settled in front of a silent television set in his apartment in Chiswick and re-read the photo-stats of the old clippings. He then picked up a book he had borrowed from the Chiswick Public Library. *The Encroaching of the Occult* by Charles Watson contained a chapter on the 'last witchcraft murder in England'.

Whether witchcraft is a reality or not, belief in it still exists. Wicca is considered by many as an alternative religion to Christianity and can possibly be traced back to the worship of Diana, or the White Goddess of antiquity. These adherents would consider themselves white witches, seekers of the Good, followers of the 'right hand' path.

But there are those, practitioners as well as believers, who hold to the concept of witchcraft as being a cult of the Devil. The late Aleister Crowley was certainly a believer and a practitioner and was believed to have conducted ceremonies to raise certain demons.

Certainly, too, the so-called 'last witchcraft murder in England,' the killing of a farm labourer in a field in Warwickshire in 1976, exhibits all the signs of being a ritual murder committed by followers of the 'left hand' path. The body, skewered to a tree by a pitchfork through the neck, was surrounded by symbols from the *Cabbala*, and while it may well have been a revenge killing, the indications are that it was some kind of ritual sacrifice.

Although the subject was taboo to the villagers of Greater and Lesser Calderon, there were rumours that the victim, Joshua Gideon, a man in his fifties, was himself an Adept and therefore a worthy and considerable sacrifice. Despite the investigations undertaken by a Scotland Yard detective, Superintendent Harkness, no one was ever apprehended for the murder.

20

It is interesting to reflect that this part of War-wickshire has always been a centre of superstition; legends abound, and among those legends there are many stories of witchcraft. This murder may well repres-ent an intrusion of medieval practice into the twentieth century.

Braden put the book aside, smiling. The author had made his name as a writer on esoteric subjects, and always with the suggestion that he himself believed in the reality of his themes. Perhaps he really did believe. The world, Braden thought, is full of cranks and eccentrics. They would be willing to ignore the all too human hand that drove the pitchfork into Gideon's throat. And the all too human motive that probably inspired the homicidal act.

He went to bed early. He had one appointment before catching the train to Warwick. He preferred travelling by train and, if absolutely necessary, hiring a car at the paper's expense. Which gave him some vicarious pleasure.

In bed he fell asleep almost at once.

He found himself, in sleep, wandering through a vast plain, the horizon broken only by squat grey stone cottages. They seemed to be uninhabited, the few windows like dark eyes glazing sightlessly on to the plain. Yet every time he turned away from the cottages, it seemed as if, at the corner of his eye, a suggestion of a face appeared behind the glass. When he turned back, there was only the dark glass. He wandered, in his dream across the plain, always with the feeling that there was someone behind him, a follower, elusive to vision, but there, existing in the senses. Eventually he turned and waited, standing alone, a cold wind rising. And then, in the distance, he glimpsed something, a hazy, indistinct figure at the edge of the horizon, approaching and yet getting no clearer. The follower was coming, looming larger and yet never distinct. Finally, as the amorphous figure came closer and closer, he found he was forcing himself from sleep, upwards, away from the plain, the cottages, the figure, up and up to wakefulness.

He awoke, naked as always – he never wore pyjamas – drenched in perspiration, the cold sweat of nightmare soaking pillow and sheets. He was filled with a very real terror, indefinable, unless only as a result of his dream. Thinking too much about the murder of Joshua Gideon, about Watson's pretentious prose. What was it Ebenezer Scrooge had said of his nightmares? The result of a piece of undigested pork, of a segment of overripe cheese. Had to be something like that. He was relieved to see from his luminous alarm clock that he had been asleep barely an hour. The rest of the night was still his.

Some time later he slept again and, when he awakened, was aware only of some vaguely erotic images, remembering nothing else.

Chapter Three

Cresswell was sixty-two and had been the *Comet*'s chief crime reporter for thirty years. As he informed everybody frequently.

'Of course I heard of the Calderon business, but I never covered it. Well, it was in the sticks, wasn't it? It was done by the stringer in Warwick. That would be Charlie Huston. Drank himself to death five years ago, silly bugger. Rotten reporter too. No help there.'

Braden forced himself to give the expected smile. But he could never get used to Cresswell's assumed cynicism and practised arrogance. At least, he hoped it was assumed. He accepted the arrogance. He could do nothing else. They were drinking luke-warm coffee in a well-known Fleet Street coffee house, and he wanted Cresswell's help.

'If you don't know anything about the Calderon business, what do you know about Harkness?'

Cresswell, who was overweight and overflowing from the narrow chair at the table, shrugged. Braden thought, The world is full of shrugging people. Shrugging everything off made it all seem simple.

'Harkness was a pretty good detective,' Cresswell said. 'But he was a lousy policeman.'

Illogically Braden thought of Judy. She'd been a great lover but a lousy mistress. God, did his mind have to bring her into everything?

'Tell me about that,' he said.

'He had the detective's instincts. Knew what to look for, and the luck to find it. Had a kind of dedication too. In the end, he burnt himself out. Nervous breakdown . . . all that business. Poor sod couldn't take thirty years of concentration.' A small, smug smile. 'Just as well some of us can.'

'How was he a lousy policeman?'

'Didn't like the rules. Wouldn't play by them.'

'What does that mean?'

'Take the Swanson case. Oh, Ronnie Swanson was a real villain. Sadistic bastard too. Harkness went for him, no holds barred. Nearly ruined the case against Swanson doing it.'

'How? He was commended . . .'

'Read about it, transcript of the trial. Swanson's brief claimed his client had been beaten up by the police. Specifically by Harkness. By the time Swanson went to the Old Bailey most of the scars had healed. But when he was brought up the first time before the beak, he looked as if he'd been run over by multiple express trains. Oh, Harkness beat him up all right.'

'And got away with it?

'Sure. The usual thing: prisoner resisted arrest, fell downstairs, all that. Mind you, it looked as if Harkness was as sadistic as Swanson.'

'Was he?'

A pause. Cresswell contemplated his coffee on the table in front of him. Then the massive body moved, a major exercise, and he picked up his cup and sipped the now barely warm liquid.

'I liked Jack Harkness. He was honest. Can't stand bent coppers. But he had a kind of anger in him. Maybe he'd been around too long, seen too much that people shouldn't see. He once said as much to me. The world was a cesspit, he said, and he was one of the cleaners. But when you clean up filth, you get dirty. Of course, Swanson was dirtier than most. Ran the East End for years on fear. Made a fortune on fear and violence.'

'I don't really remember much about that.'

'Why should you? Twelve, thirteen years ago. You were a college boy. Cambridge, wasn't it?' Braden ignored the strong suggestion of a sneer. Cresswell went on, 'He was worse than his predecessors, the Krays and Richardson. Sure, there was all the same stuff. Nailing to the floor by the kneecaps, beatings, killings . . . a few castrations. Swanson liked that. Used to do it personally.'

'Nice fellow.'

'Also he's read *The Godfather* and fancied himself in the part. Harkness went for him for murder, GBH, extortion – you name it, it was a thick book. And when he lacked part of the evidence, that's when he beat it out of Swanson. Not that Swanson was a coward, but that kind of beating, not many can take. That's why the brief went for Harkness in court.'

'But he got away with it?'

'The book was too thick, and everybody in London knew about Swanson. Harkness could prove most of it . . . and some of that came from the beating. The judge, old Openshaw, accepted the resisting arrest story. Of course, he was a reactionary old bastard. Would have personally hanged Swanson if he could. So the trial went on and Swanson was convicted. We had a field day reporting it, even though some of it was too ugly to print. Openshaw commended Harkness. He was the blue-eyed boy. And the police ordered an enquiry and damn' near suspended him.'

Braden was puzzled. 'But he'd done what they wanted him to do. He'd got Swanson.'

The large cheeks creased into a smile. 'Sure, he had. And the big boys at the Yard wouldn't have minded the beating if it hadn't showed. But it did, and they reckoned it was a near thing that Swanson got sent up. They reckoned, because of Harkness, Swanson nearly got off. And the Home Secretary thought it wasn't good for the Yard's image. It wasn't the first time Harkness had used third degree methods. Before Swanson an accused rapist got off because Jack Harkness became . . . over-enthusiastic.'

'They censured him?'

'When he did up the rapist. But after Swanson, they didn't dare. He was Fleet Street's Bright Blue Harold too. But I got it from one of my sources at the Yard. He was a superintendent – he'd go no further. That was a blow to Harkness. He had ideas about combatting crime . . . as I've told you, not exactly orthodox ideas. He wanted to go to the top, Commander at least, so as he could try his ideas out. They wouldn't have it. You stay, they told him, and you stay as superintendent until you retire.'

'Not a lot of thanks.'

'They were afraid of him. They don't like wild men. Then the Calderon case came up, Warwickshire asked the Yard for help, and they had a chance to get Harkness out of town for a while. Out of sight, out of mind. Also it was a funny case, as you know. The attitude was, let him solve that one. And they hoped it would take him some time. Then he had his crackup. Even if he'd wanted to come back afterwards, they didn't want him. Retirement because of ill-health.'

'What happened to him?'

'How do I know? Yesterday's news. He should have written his memoirs. Others did. But not Jack Harkness. He just faded away . . . '

'Is he still alive?'

Cresswell glanced at his wrist-watch. 'I could use a real drink. Pub should be opening soon. What did you say? Is he still alive? Don't know. Shouldn't think so. They said he was pretty far gone when he had his breakdown. Coming for a drink?'

'Sorry. Catching a train to Warwick.'

The railway coach was almost empty. Braden thought, not many people going to Warwick. And why should they? His was the big city's view of the provinces. He'd never been there before himself. Nearest he'd been was to Stratford to the Festival Theatre. With Judy. To see Anthony Sher in *Richard III*. Two, three years ago. Before they'd started living together. Before they'd started, really. Early days. Basic courtship. Flowers and an expensive late supper in The Dirty Duck. Wishing now it had never happened. No, not true! The pain made him think like that. The chronic pain. More like a gnawing ache now. He still needed her, but he was getting used to being without her . . . no, that wasn't true either . . . he was submerging himself in the Calderon case. Remedy for all ills, hard work. Only this one brought him quiet nightmares. He smiled to himself. Witchcraft murder? And people still believing in it, practising it. Only twelve years ago, killing

26

for it at Calderon. Calderon? Strange name for an English village. Calderon.

'Calderon,' he said aloud. 'Calderon . . .' It fitted in with the sound of the wheels on the track.

'I beg your pardon?' This from an elderly man with a long thin face, sitting facing him. Looked like a member of the clergy but wasn't.

'Sorry. Thinking aloud. Falls into the pattern of the train sound.'

The elderly man smiled affably. 'So many things do run through the mind. Should be hypnotic. Though, one journey, I couldn't get to sleep. As if the train was saying . . . oranges and lemons, oranges and lemons. Going through my mind, over and over. And yours was . . .?'

'I'm sorry?'

'Your . . . oranges and lemons? Your phrase?'

'Oh, yes. Place in Warwickshire, Calderon. As you say, over and over.'

'Calderon, indeed.' The old man nodded. 'Heard of it. Read of it. Never been there.'

'What have you read about Calderon?' Braden had determined never to miss an opportunity.

'Ah, yes, well . . . not too much. Not a lot. Come across it here and there. You see, I'm an historian. Was a historian. A university professor, until I retired. Emeritus now. Sounds impressive, means nothing.' His brow furrowed into gorges of lined flesh. 'Calderon . . . yes, mentioned in the Domesday Book.'

'It's as old as that?'

'Oh, older, definitely. Col Edron was its earliest name. I've no idea of its origins. Of course, a lot of these villages in the Cotswolds, and around there, they're almost certainly Saxon. Probably go right back to the Roman occupation. Col Edron . . . It sounds quite biblical. Two villages actually, with a hill behind them. The Edron Hill. As I said, I've never been there. You going there?'

'Maybe. Later. Going to Warwick just now.'

'A nice town. The castle's impressive – fourteenth-century. And two medieval gateways.'

Braden took a deep breath. 'Witchcraft?' he said.

'I beg your pardon?'

'Incidence of witchcraft, in and around the Cotswolds?'

'Oh, certainly, in the Middle Ages all over. In the Cotswolds, certainly. You see, many of these little villages were so isolated. When anything happened, crops failed or there was an outbreak of plague, the church could do nothing. So the people turned back to the old beliefs. Legends, myths, mostly to do with fertility. And, you must remember, these people led narrow, harsh lives. I suppose witchcraft lent a certain spice, eh?'

'But, in modern times, does witchcraft persist?'

The old man's eyes opened wide. 'In modern times? Shouldn't think so. You never know . . . Certainly among certain rather eccentric characters. But mostly city sophisticates. People like Crowley. You've heard of him?'

'Yes.'

'Met him once. Not a very salubrious character. But a city person. As if witchcraft and all that rubbish became a kind of cosmopolitan fad, when I was young.'

'Wasn't there a witchcraft murder in Calderon about twelve years ago?'

The history professor's eyes opened even wider. 'Is that so? Of course, twelve years ago . . . not my period. Never paid much attention to modern history.'

'It was in the newspapers.'

'Oh, I was too busy to bother with newspapers. Nothing but violence and murder. You say, twelve years ago? How very astonishing. Some kind of local aberration, I suppose.'

A local aberration? Was that how murder should be described? A pitchfork through the throat dismissed as a local aberration. And barely remembered twelve years later.

The tannoy in the carriage came alive with a crackling sound.

'The train will arrive in Warwick in five minutes. Passengers leaving the train will please remember to take all their baggage . . .'

The headquarters of Warwick County Constabulary was in a modern redbrick building in the centre of the old city. At the desk, Braden was asked to wait, and some minutes later, a policewoman appeared and escorted him into the bowels of the building. At the top of a staircase, they went through a door marked CID. Behind this was a large outer office at which three young men were working at desks, and beyond this a door led into a small partitioned office. This contained a desk, two chairs and a filing cabinet. As the policewoman departed, a tall thin man rose from behind the desk and stretched out his hand.

'Mister Braden? I'm Drewitt, Do sit down.'

He was dressed in a conservative pin-stripe, the smoothness of the man belied by a slightly creased suit over a white shirt and blue tie. In the voice there was a trace of an accent, possibly rural.

'Good of you to spare the time, Inspector Drewitt,' Braden said, sitting.

A thin smile. 'Our PRO people said I should see you. Important newspaper . . . good for the police image, all that. Said I should give you at least half an hour. What they said. They got a big pull, the PRO people.'

'You mean you wouldn't wanted to have seen me?'

Drewitt sat, an awkward moment, as if his legs were too long. 'Wouldn't say that. Just not used to the national press. Perhaps I'm a little nervous. Tabloid. Sensation. Scandal. Nothing like that here.'

'Of course,' Braden agreed, trying to sound reassuring.

'You here about the bank robbery? Of course, I had a bit of luck there . . .'

'Not about the bank robbery. Much earlier. Twelve years ago.'

Drewitt tried to cross his legs and didn't quite succeed. He shifted uneasily, looking puzzled.

'Twelve years? 'Fraid I won't be much good to you. I was only a constable on the beat twelve years ago.'

'The Calderon murder. You were taken off the beat for that.'

A long silence. Drewitt sat staring at his desk. Then he broke the silence. 'I was still only a constable. It was . . . er, Superintendent Harkness's case.'

'But you worked for him? He asked for you?'

'Yes,'

29

'Why was that?'

'Luck of the draw, I suppose. Because I was there.'

'Because you were born in Calderon?'

The long legs shifted again, as if searching for an invisible purchase. 'In Lesser Calderon. Well, yes, possibly. But I was only seconded to show Harkness around.'

'A good chance for a young copper,' Braden suggested.

Drewitt flushed. 'I suppose so. I didn't think of it at the time.' Which, Braden thought, might indicate a lack of imagination.

'Oh, surely?'

'I did think it might help me get into the CID.'

'And it did.'

'Yes, I suppose so. But you didn't come here to talk about Calderon.'

'As a matter of fact, I did.'

'The case is twelve years old!'

'And unsolved. Killer never found. I've always heard the police never close the file on an unsolved murder. That right?'

'Well, yes, technically. But we haven't the manpower to keep someone on a case for twelve years. Of course, it's still on the books. I suppose it's rather neglected. But then, it was reckoned at the time to be a random killing. The kind almost impossible to solve. If something new ever came up . . .'

'As I said, you were born in Calderon. You'd know it well?'

'I left Calderon when I was a child – eleven, twelve years old. When my father died, my mother left the village and took me with her.'

Drewitt seemed to be sweating. There were beads of perspiration on his upper lip.

'Why did she leave the village?'

'I told you, my father died. There was nothing to keep her there. We . . . we moved away. Braden, what has this to do with your article on the police here?'

'I'm doing a piece on famous unsolved murders. Why? How? Who might have? Is the killer still alive?'

'Oh, I doubt it,' Drewitt said quickly. Very quickly.

'Why do you doubt it?'

'Well, it's twelve years.'

'Not too long. Could easily still be alive.'

'He's never killed again.'

'As far as you know.'

'Now, a random killer would very probably . . .'

Braden's turn to be quick. 'Which really means it may well not be a random killing. If Josh Gideon's death was motivated, then once he was killed, there might be no need to kill again.'

'I'm sure all these things were considered at the time. And it is also possible he did kill again. Another place, somewhere out of our jurisdiction. May have been caught. May be in prison. Would you like some tea?'

'Thank you.'

Drewitt pressed a button on his desk.

Braden went on. 'From what I've read, it didn't seem like a random killing. It seemed . . . local. Mixed up with witchcraft. Old gods. Old credos.'

A young, plain clothes detective came in.

'Sir?'

'Two teas,' Drewitt said. 'Milk and sugar?'

'Milk. No sugar.'

The constable went out, shutting the door behind him.

Drewitt said, 'Witchcraft! A daftness.'

'To us,' Braden seemed to agree. 'But perhaps not to the murderer. Not if the murderer actually believes in witchcraft.'

'Superstition,' Drewitt insisted with simulated irritation. 'Fairy tales, things that go bump in the night. Mr Braden, I'm a busy man . . .' He made a movement as if to rise.

'You've ordered tea. And I was to be given half an hour. I've only had about ten minutes.

A deepening of irritation. 'I told you, I was a constable. I drove Harkness. I stood beside him . . .'

'And listened. You couldn't help hearing.'

'Only some of the time. Harkness was . . . was a loner. Liked to work on his own.' Drewitt gave a small nervous laugh. 'So there'd be no witnesses. That's what he said. No one in sight with rubber-lined pockets for stealing the soup.'

'You remembered that?'

A tap on the door. The young detective brought in two mugs of tea. The mugs were not standard issue. One had a cat design on it. The detective nodded and went out again. Braden reached forward and lifted the mug in front of him.

'Of course, Harkness had cause to be a loner. He nearly got into trouble on a previous case. Assaulting the accused, wasn't that the story?'

Drewitt lifted his mug and took a mouthful of tea. He had a faraway look in his eyes, as if remembering.

'Harkness was a good policeman,' he said, echoing Cresswell. 'When he came up here, he was a good policeman. At the beginning. I suppose he . . . he just didn't know what he was up against.'

Braden looked up from the mug of tea. 'So what was he up against?'

It was as if Drewitt realised at once he had said too much. He tried to change the subject.

'Where are you staying in Warwick?'

'The Woolpack. What was Harkness up against?'

Drewitt stared into space, as if conjuring up the past.

Chapter Four

After a moment, Drewitt, face at once pale, rose awkwardly and went to the window. Outside the day was dying, street lamps coming alight. It was as if he was striving to make a decision.

'I only meant, in some villages like Calderon, the people stick together. Something happens like the death of Gideon and they clam up.' He turned back to face Braden. 'Keep it all inside themselves. That's all I meant.'

'Weren't there any suspects?' Braden asked. 'Anyone who had a grudge against Gideon?'

'We suspected everyone.' The classic detective story reply.

'Oh, come on! There must have been one or two people who had a motive. Gideon couldn't have been an angel.'

'Oh, he wasn't that. He was a bastard!'

Braden was surprised at the vehemence Drewitt put into the word. 'There you are then. One of his enemies killed him. One individual. Okay, so maybe you knew but you couldn't get the evidence. Fair enough. I'm not out to attack the Warwickshire police. Or Harkness, for that matter. But I'd like to know, off the record. We can't afford to accuse someone without evidence. The paper wouldn't like an enormous libel suit. Come on, one name?'

'I know nothing about that!' Again quickly, face expressionless. Resisting decisions.

'But you knew he was a bastard?'

'He had that kind of reputation. That's all I knew.'

'But maybe, later, you suspected someone? Perhaps pulled them in on another charge. That's been known.'

'Nothing!' Drewitt insisted. 'When Harkness left, I was off the case. Back on the beat.' A trace of bitterness there.

'But not for long, Inspector Drewitt. Twelve years from beat constable to detective inspector. Good going.'

'I was lucky. And I worked hard.'

'Must have helped, watching an old hand like Harkness at work.'

'It did. At the beginning. But not later, when he had his breakdown.'

'Tell me about the breakdown.'

Again Drewitt flushed. Embarrassment for an old colleague? Or something else?

'Pressure of work, I suppose. That's what they said.'

'But what did you think?'

'Just that. He . . . he never let up. Later he retired. I heard he retired.'

'The breakdown was because of the case then?'

Drewitt sat down again. Why was the man so edgy.

'I didn't say that. I'm no doctor. Maybe it was the previous case that caused it. The Swanson business. Or maybe he was just . . . ill.'

Another silence, Drewitt sipping his tea, not looking at his visitor. Get him away from personalities, that was the thing, Braden decided.

'Why don't you just tell me about the Calderon case and I won't have to ask any questions. Anything you can remember.'

Drewitt was morose now. 'Ask Harkness. It was his case, not mine. Ask him.'

'I would if I could find him. If he's still alive. Be in his seventies now. Could be dead.'

'He was that type. Out of the force, nothing to live for.'

Braden attempted a smile. 'That brings me back to you.'

'How many times do I have to tell you? I knew nothing. There were others, more senior. Chief Inspector Blakelock, for instance. Before Harkness, and after, when he had his breakdown.'

'Where would I find Blakelock?'

To Drewitt's moroseness was added a bleak look. 'You wouldn't. He retired and died. Who was his sergeant? God, that was Sammy Stevens.' The Warwickshire accent was becoming more pronounced.

'All right, where can I find him?'

'City cemetery. Six years dead too. Car crash. And the Chief Constable at the time, that would be Rollason. Alzheimer's disease. Premature senility. He's in a home. Nothing to be got there.'

'Becoming like the Kennedy assassination, isn't it? All the people who had anything to do with the case ended up in a terminal situation. Except you.'

'I told you, I was a nobody. A standing-around-in-uniform kind of nobody.'

'The sole survivor. Also the one person in the case born in Calderon. There's a thought, Inspector.'

Drewitt focused on Braden. 'What would that be meaning?'

'Haven't the foggiest idea.'

'I told you, my mother took me away from Calderon when I was a kid. I know nothing about that place. Not now, not then. We got out, we came to Warwick.' He rose, decisively now. 'You've had your tea and your half hour, Mr Braden, and I've work to do.'

Braden got to his feet and placed his mug on the table.

'I'll just have to look elsewhere then.'

'It's not that interesting a case.'

'Oh, I disagree. Last witchcraft murder in England. Gets more interesting all the time.'

'You're going out to Calderon?'

'It's a free country, Inspector. It would seem the thing to do. Somebody'll remember something.'

'No, they won't. Not there. They want to forget, there. Don't like raking over cold ashes.'

Braden went to the door of the office and hesitated. 'I suppose it's understandable. On their part. Not on yours. But I expect I'll find others to talk to.'

The idea was there now. Somebody who'd lived in Calderon and got out. If that person was still alive. But Braden knew he must say nothing to Drewitt.

35

'As I said, I'm staying at the Woolpack. Nice hotel. In case you remember anything you might want to tell me. 'Bye, Inspector Drewitt.'

Outside the office he shut the door carefully, aware of the eyes of the three detectives at the desk on him. The walls of the partitioned office were thin. They'd probably heard most of the talk with Drewitt. They looked away from him quickly. He went out, down the stairs, along the corridors, and out into the street. It was dark now, a dark October night. A chill wind was blowing up from the River Avon.

He walked to his hotel in the market place. It was a small, comfortable establishment in a three-storey, early-eighteenth-century building. In the foyer, he asked for a local directory and telephone book and went to his room. He found what he wanted in the telephone book and lay on his bed dozing until it was time for dinner. Only then did he realise he hadn't thought of Judy since getting off the train. And now, thinking of her, he was surprised how little pain he felt.

That night he slept and, if he dreamt, he had no memory of the dream.

A grey, overcast morning. Braden rose early, breakfasted at seven-thirty, and through the hotel porter, arranged the hire of a car. A grey Ford Escort was awaiting him in the hotel car park at nine o'clock.

He drove south, by-passing Stratford-on-Avon, and veered east towards the Cotswolds. Within forty-five minutes of leaving Warwick he was turning off the main road into Lesser Calderon. The two villages were on a loop road which eventually curved back on to the trunk road heading south-east.

Lesser Calderon was drab. There were a few houses, mostly smallish bungalows built in the 30s, and a couple of uninteresting cottages. The road passed a ruined church with a Norman tower and blackened walls, apparently abandoned, the main door shut and boarded up. A number of dull stained-glass windows had been broken and some of the smashed panes were stuffed with cardboard. A notice board hung at an angle, and, apart from the heading 'Church of England', only weather-stained peeling wood was visible. Behind the church

36

was a grey stone building, presumably the vicarage, also with every appearance of being abandoned.

The houses petered out for about two hundred yards, flat fields on either side of the road, and then a signpost, 'Greater Calderon', and Braden drove into the larger of the twin villages.

What had he imagined? Cotswold stone? There were two or three old houses built from the local quarries, and they had the expected medieval air. Beyond the old houses there was a row of council houses, 1950s style. Neat, dull, practical. A woman hanging out washing on a green behind one of the houses; an ordinary-looking woman, thin, hair ill-permed, in a jumper and a brown skirt. Four small children playing on the pavement beside two tricycles. Then, as the road widened into what must be the centre of the village, a row of conventional cottages. Behind them, some bungalows, circa 1930, and yet another row of council houses. The centre of Greater Calderon was uninspired, even depressing, unlike the quainter Cotswold villages. There was a small general store-cum-post-office facing an inn, the more pleasant of the buildings, two storeyed and with a sign proclaiming The Goat and Compasses, the animal itself and a pair of compasses depicted thereon. Below the sign, on the wall, was the inscription 'Free House – Cotswold Ales'. Beside the inn, on the other side of a narrow lane, was another church. Again a Norman tower, a stretch of aging cemetery, and the main building.

Braden brought the Escort to a halt beside the church notice board:

Church of Our Lady in the Wold

RC Church.

Priest: Father Aloysius Duggan,

Address: Boscombe Abbey, Lower Duthwaite

An absentee priest, Braden thought. Lower Duthwaite was fifteen miles away. And yet, behind the church, was yet another residence, an old building in Cotswold stone, the

37

front door shut and barred off by a plank of wood nailed across the entrance. Priests and parsons obviously didn't reside in the Calderons.

He drove on. Passing, on his right, more council houses and a meadow stretching to the foot of a hill some quarter of a mile away. The hill, dotted by shrub and trees, rose gently several hundred feet above the plain. The Edron Hill. And possibly the meadow was the scene of the twelve-year-old murder. Several tall, gnarled trees punctuated the green sward of meadow. Nothing grazed there. Further on, on his left, was farm land, a herd of cows browsing across green stubble. And then he came to a wood, a thick clump of trees bisected by an entrance, an abandoned lodge house and a small, crudely painted sign, 'Calderon Manor – Private Road'. The private road wound into the obscurity of the wood and no house beyond the lodge was visible from the road. It was unkempt, overgrown. If there was a local squire, possibly taxation had taken its toll on the estate. Braden made a mental note to find out.

Then he realised he was through the Calderons, driving back now towards the far end of the loop to rejoin the main road. He drove by a small market garden, a sign advertising potatoes and late plums, and on to the trunk road. That was it, Calderon, Lesser and Greater. Unimpressive, lacking atmosphere, nothing. Not at all what he had expected. He wondered if he should go back, perhaps have a drink at The Goat and Compasses, possibly bring up the old murder. He decided against it. Too soon. And if Drewitt was right, he would learn nothing. If there was anything to learn.

It started to rain. He had to face it. Calderon was a disappointment. And yet . . .

And yet, wasn't there something unusual in its very . . . he searched for the word . . . *ordinariness*? The place was almost too ordinary. Could a place be described as too ordinary?

He stopped and looked back. Greater Calderon was an outline in a haze of thin rain. Ordinary. Except for the Edron Hill dominating the village. Except too for a twelve-year-old murder.

He drove back to Warwick.

The address he had looked up in the telephone book the previous night was on the northern outskirts of the city. In a street of modest bungalows, the house he was looking for was some hundred yards along, fronted by a small neat garden. He parked at the front gate and looked on to a tiny stretch of lawn.

A woman in her early sixties, wrapped in a large coat, was in the garden, pruning an already threadbare hedge. As Braden stepped through the gate, she turned to greet him. Her face was pleasant, the features almost youthful despite a lined, parchment-like skin.

'Hedges,' she said. 'They'll be running wild even when they seem at their worst. Bane of our life, them and greenfly in the summer. The great galloping destroyer, greenfly.'

'So they say,' Braden replied politely. There was the same trace of an accent in the mother as there had been in the son.

'Do they? Thought I'd just said it. Goes to show. Whoever you are, I should warn you, my son is a police inspector and if you've come here pretending to inspect the meter, you'll be in trouble.'

'You're his mother then. I met Inspector Drewitt yesterday. My name is Braden. Eric Braden. I'm a journalist with the *Comet*.'

'You'll be a friend of my son's, then?'

'I know him.'

'That's nice. Of course he doesn't live here. Not now. Lives over the other side of the city. Used to live with me, but he would have a place of his own. I don't know why, not as if he's married. Of course there's still time. You'd better come in and have a cup of tea.'

She escorted him into the bungalow and a pleasant, square living room containing a Co-op three piece suite dominated by a large television set. Braden thought to himself, There should be china ducks on the wall, but there were none. There was, however, a print of an Eastern woman with a green face that he had seen before, and often. He sat on his own for some minutes until she had made the tea and returned from the kitchen carrying a tray with two cups, teapot and accessories, and a plate of plain biscuits. She poured, handed him his cup and saucer, offered him a biscuit and then gave him a penetrating stare.

'You're not from Warwick?'

'London.'

'You've seen my son. Why do you want to see me?'

Braden held his teacup at first, without attempting to drink. It was very hot. He cleared his throat. 'I wanted to ask about Calderon.'

She stared at the surface of the tea in her cup.

'Oh, yes. Calderon. Why there?'

'About the murder,' he went on. 'Twelve years ago. We're doing a series on famous unsolved murders.'

She nodded, still staring into her cup.

'That's why you went to see my son?'

'Yes.'

'Why come to me?'

'Because you lived in Calderon. Your son tells me you both left while he was still a child.'

'That's so.'

'I want to know about Calderon. If this was a witchcraft killing, then I think I should learn about the people of a village who might be involved n witchcraft.'

Mrs Drewitt nodded, the ghost of a smile on her lips. 'I should know everything about Calderon. Lived there for fourteen years. Knew every living soul there. Or used to. Of course, that was before the murder.'

'I wouldn't expect you to know who killed Joshua Gideon . . .'

'Oh, but I do.'

Chapter Five

The reply was so unexpected that Braden, finally essaying a sip of tea, scorched his tongue on the hot liquid.

'You can tell me who killed Gideon?' Rubbing his tongue against the roof of his mouth, he lisped the question.

Mrs Drewitt now looked up at him, a direct stare.

'I can tell you. Josh Gideon was killed by . . . Josh Gideon,' she said.

It would have been too easy, Braden thought. Old murders aren't just solved in twenty-four hours. The apparent revelation irritated him.

'Suicide!' He successfully concealed the sneer in his mind. 'By stabbing himself in the throat with a pitchfork? I don't think so, Mrs Drewitt.'

She was tight-lipped now, irritated by his instant disbelief. 'Did I say suicide?'

'Well, obviously . . .'

'Nothing is obvious, Mr Braden. Not about Calderon. Everything there is under the surface. I said Gideon killed himself. Maybe I should have said, he invited death. By the way he lived. By the way he carried on. They would consider he brought them all into disrepute, in Calderon. They would say that. They could take their own lechery, their own immorality . . . you see, they'd give themselves reasons for all that . . . but they couldn't take *his* immorality. Especially not when he allowed it to be common knowledge. And not just in Calderon, that wouldn't have been important, but in all the surrounding villages. Even as far as here, in Warwick, he was known.'

41

'Immorality? I don't quite understand . . .'

'You couldn't, could you?' Her hands fluttered now, tea-cup down on the table. Hands like butterflies, he suddenly thought. 'You couldn't understand the attitudes in Calderon. Neither could I when I first went to live there. But Gideon, he was Calderon-born. He knowed they not take it from him for all the years. Not unless he was in charge like. Someone would be bound to turn on him. He knowed that . . .'

Like her son, the rural accent had come into her voice. Even more pronounced than her son.

'So he couldn't have been much surprised,' she went on, 'when he was turned upon by whoever. Mebbe one, mebbe more. Whoever, turned on him. And his conceit – oh, he had that too – wouldn't have helped. So it were his own actions led to it, see?'

Braden nodded, uncertainly. 'I think so.'

'That's all you'll be able to do. Can't get into their minds. I could barely do it, after all the years I spent there.'

Another thought came to the journalist. 'Gideon was in his sixties, wasn't he, when he was killed?'

'Late fifties, early sixties, couldn't be sure. He was born old, that one.'

'And yet you're painting a picture of a youngish man. Immoral . . . sexually, I presume you mean?'

'You don't have to be young to be like a dog on heat, do you? He was like a dog on heat. All the time. Isn't a woman in Calderon, he hadn't tried. Some were willing, some not. They say a lot who weren't willing, he took anyway. And in the surrounding villages. Time he died, there were a woman here in Warwick he'd visit too. Oh, he tried me, when I was there . . . and he *was* younger then. But I was strong enough and I could kick. He only tried once.'

'Then the whole motive for the murder could have been sexual jealousy? Or revenge? A betrayed husband?' Braden said.

'No. That was only a part of Gideon, and that they could have forgotten. None o' them were angels in that respect. Might have fought him, but wouldn't have killed him. Not the way he were killed. That were sex too, but mostly the conceit . . . and . . . and the ambition.'

42

'Ambition?'

'Tired of being the dirty wee rascal. Wanted to be king of the castle. Your mouth's open and you're not drinking your tea, Mr Braden.'

He did so. It was cooler now. 'Why did you leave Calderon, Mrs Drewitt?'

'I didn't come from Calderon, y'know. Born in Cheltenham. Was working in Woolworth's there, thirty-six, thirty-seven years ago, when I met Drewitt, not long after the war. He was from Calderon. Started courting me. Eventually we got married. The one condition was I had to live in his cottage in Calderon.'

'What did he do for a living?'

'He was a herdsman, in charge of old Campion's herd of cows. Had a cottage there an' all that. Was better paid than most herdsmen. He said old Campion was a good boss.'

'Campion?'

She smiled. 'That was old Sir Larry. Sir Laurence Campion, Bt., Calderon Manor. Local squire, he called himself. Not one of those fly-by-night knights. Oh, no, he were son of his father. Inherited his title.'

'A baronet?'

'That would be him. 'Course he's dead now. Been dead sixteen years. Daughter inherited. Though I can't say I knew her. Wasn't mixing in society, me and Drewitt. But I went to live in Lesser Calderon. Harold was born there and then, when he was eleven years old, his father died. There was nothing to keep me there. We went back to Cheltenham at first, then came here. I got a good job here, managed a miliner's shop until I retired. And of course Harold went into the police.' She stared into the middle distance, a small, self-satisfied smile on her face.

'Funny,' she went on, 'if we'd stayed in Calderon, Harold would have been a farm labourer. And me, I'd have stayed in that cottage until I died. See, life isn't much at all in a village like that. Mebbe that's why they have to . . . ' Now she stopped suddenly, a look of alarm crossing her face and vanishing instantly.

'More tea?' she said.

'That's why they have to do what, Mrs Drewitt?'

She attempted to pour more tea into his cup, but her hand was trembling and some slopped over into the saucer.

'Oh, I'm sorry.'

Braden persisted. 'What is it they have to do in Calderon, Mrs Drewitt? Is it to do with witchcraft?'

She sat erect now, almost defiant. 'I don't believe in that nonsense.'

'But they believed? In Calderon?'

'An excuse. You ever live in a village like that, sir? Wages was tiny. Couldn't get away. Nothing to do there, except fornication. And when a baby was coming, you made it legal. That was them in Calderon. And the few born there, like Drewitt . . . like my husband . . . if they got away . . . they had to go back.' She frowned, a deep uncertain frown.

Braden waited.

She went on. 'As if they weren't allowed to stay away. As if they were having to come back.'

'You saw this witchcraft cult?'

She shook her head violently. 'I was an outsider. Once, mebbe twice a week, James Drewitt would come back from the byres, clean up, dress up, maybe, and go out again. Leaving me. Only time he ever left me. Said it was a village meeting every week. At the beginning I said, can't I come? He said it was only the men.' Her lips twisted in a tight, humourless smile. 'After a few weeks I found he'd lied. The women went too. The Calderon women. Drewitt and me had a fight about that. Only time he hit me. Then he told me to keep quiet and forget it. For my own good. Eventually I did, because I heard some stories – about incomers who asked questions and then had nasty accidents.'

She fell silent now, staring back into a past Braden reckoned she didn't care to remember.

He broke the silence. 'Why was Gideon killed?'

'He had enemies, I told you.'

'But he *was* one of . . . of them? In this witchcraft business?'

'They all were.' She looked up and into Braden's eyes. 'You want to know about Gideon, why ask me? I was away from there years then. You ask his woman here, in Warwick.'

'His woman?'

'She's still here, living somewhere in Warwick. I see her now and then. Across a street, walking in the road, coming out of a shop. We move past each other. Doesn't know me but I know her. Pretty woman, like I was once. Twelve years ago she was Gideon's woman. One of them. Maybe he was just one of her men. I don't mean that nastily. Can't be mor'n in her early forties now.'

Braden was leaning forward, like an eager kid on his first story. 'You know her name?'

'Jennet Agram. She'll be in the phone book. If she's got a phone.'

Braden stood now. He had another lead. A better one. Best yet, the boy reporter would have said.

'Thank you for the tea, Mrs Drewitt. I'll be going now.'

'Oh, must you? I don't have many visitors. Harold comes when he can. Once a week, usually. But he's so busy. And . . . and I do wish he'd find time to meet a nice girl and get married.'

At the front door, she touched Braden lightly on the arm. 'All that business about witchcraft. They had nothing else to do. No money to do it. It was just an excuse, like a club. With signs and symbols. Black poke hats. Broomsticks and pumpkins. Lot of rubbish. I spent all the time I was there telling myself that.'

'Of course. I do understand,' Braden, aware of being ineffectual.

'Because if there'd been anything else, it would have been pretty unhealthy. No, it was just boredom made them . . .' She stopped suddenly.

'Made them slaughter Joshua Gideon?' Braden said, saw the look on her face, a look of sick horror, and at once wished he hadn't said it.

'Goodbye, Mrs Drewitt.' He walked quickly to the road, against a mist of slanting rain, and climbed into the Escort. When he did finally look back at the bungalow, the front door was already shut. But there was a movement from the curtains in the front room. Was she making sure her visitor had really departed?

*   *   *

45

He had a bar lunch in The Woolpack and then went up to his room. He lay on top of his bed, smoking a cigarette, thinking of Judy. She would be at her office now. She was a production executive in a large advertising agency in the City of London. If she would only phone him, then perhaps there'd be some hope of them getting together again. A large *if*, it would be. And, if she did phone, there'd be no reply. Sure, he could phone her; he'd tried it once, a week after she'd left, only to have the phone slammed down on him. The games people played, he thought. Or was it a game? Why couldn't she understand? So he had got himself involved a couple of times. It had meant nothing. That was the cliché, he knew, but it was still the truth. He wanted only her, and he wanted her back. He'd even asked her to marry him. Big deal, she'd said. And she'd laughed. They'd tried and it hadn't worked. She'd said that. To hell with her then! Why should he care? Yet he did.

He closed his eyes. Forget it. If he could. He was behaving like an adolescent. Stupid. Concentrate on the job. The murder of Joshua Gideon, a character with women, if Mrs Drewitt was to be believed.

The cigarette end burnt his fingers. He half rose and extinguished it in the ashtray beside the bed. There was a knock at the bedroom door.

'Come in.'

Detective Inspector Harold Drewitt came in. Soaking raincoat over the same suit he had worn yesterday.

'Oh, it's you. What do you want?' Braden said, not unpleasantly.

'Who were you expecting?' Why do the police always answer a question with a question?

'No one.'

'You visited my mother?' Another question.

'Why ask if you know?' The mother had to have phoned her son as soon as Braden had left.

'I don't like my mother bothered.'

'I didn't consider I was bothering her. She seemed to enjoy our talk.'

'I told you everything you wanted, didn't I?'

'Did you? I wanted to know what it was like to live in Calderon. You couldn't tell me that. She could.'

46

Scowling, Drewitt took off his damp coat and threw it over a chair.

'She's an old woman,' he said.

'Oh, not really. In her sixties. Not old today. Good memory too. Very clear-headed.'

'I don't want her bothered. She's nothing to do with what you're looking for. She left Calderon long before Gideon was killed.'

'Why are you so concerned, Inspector?'

He didn't answer. He *was* concerned. His hands twisted nervously, beads of sweat were again on his brow. His eyes were moving around the room, looking anywhere but at Braden.

'I drove through Calderon,' Braden went on. 'Before I went to see your mother. There's an inn there. Wonder if it's worth my moving there?'

'You'll learn nothing.'

'You keep telling me.'

Drewitt suddenly focused upon him. 'Stay away from Calderon. Don't want no more trouble . . .'

'What kind of trouble, Inspector?'

Again Drewitt looked away, at the window of the room this time. 'There was one murder, twelve years ago. Don't want another. Don't want that. Not again.'

'Why should there be another murder?'

'If the killer's still at large and you come along, asking damn' fool questions? Don't want to be looking at your body in the morgue.'

'Considerate of you.'

'So keep away!' His voice was rising.

'If I don't go there, I have to talk to people here. Like your mother.'

Drewitt's face was dark now flushed, angry. 'No! You want to have them blaming her if you bring up the whole business again. Stay away from her!'

'I came here to talk to people.'

'Gideon's woman! The one he had here in Warwick. I think she'll still be around. Talk to her. She knows how to look after herself. Agram. Jenny . . . Jennet Agram, that were her.'

47

'Your mother mentioned her,' Braden said, and a thought occurred to him. 'Why is she particularly able to take care of herself?'

Having brought up the name, Drewitt seemed to think he had said enough. 'She is. Ask her yourself. But I don't want no one bothering my mother. Don't want no blame there. Not if anything happens.'

'Like what?'

'Like you ending up in a ditch, dead.'

'Not against a tree with a pitchfork through my throat?'

'You'll not end like that. Not important enough, in their eyes.'

'Thanks for that. In whose eyes?'

Drewitt knew he'd made a mistake, said more than he had meant to say.

'Whoever killed Gideon,' he replied quickly. Hide the mistake, brush it away. He was trying. 'Might just not like someone prying. Not after all these years.'

'That's not an answer,' Braden insisted. 'Why am I not important enough in somebody's eyes?'

Like a small child, the Inspector answered. 'Because. Because you're not involved like Gideon was.'

Take the firm line now. Attack, follow through the gap in the man's defences. 'Drewitt, do you know who killed Gideon?'

'No. At least, I don't know any names. Look, supposing I give you enough for your story, tell you about . . . about what it was like. The way I saw it. Then you leave my mother alone. You write a nice mysterious story, and that's it. What about it?'

'I'll leave your mother alone, sure. As to giving it up, that depends on what you tell me. I can't give blanket guarantees. I may still want to hear other people's stories.'

'For your own sake, it would be better to leave it all alone.'

'I can look after myself. Inspector.'

Drewitt nodded. 'All right. My mother's out of it. I'll tell you what I saw on that case. Tell you what I know.'

Braden gestured to the solitary chair in the bedroom. 'Sit down. I'll order a couple of drinks. Scotch all right?'

48

Drewitt 1976

Chapter Six

Drewitt was on his beat when he was called in to the Calderon murder. A number of constables were needed to assist the Regional Crime Squad. They were transported to the meadow between Greater and Lesser Calderon in a Black Maria. A watery sun struggled between cloud masses and a chill breeze blew down from the Edron Hill. A detective sergeant, Sammy Stevens, smallish for a copper and overweight, greeted them.

'Want you to search this meadow for a start. Fine toothcomb. Looking for anything unusual, different, anything shouldn't be lying around a meadow. In fact, anything short of cowpats you can find, you bring to me. Right! In a line, across the meadow.'

They were kept away from the area around the tree. Screens had been set up and the word was, the body was still there.

'Throat cut, I heard,' Gibbs said. He was next to Drewitt on the line. He was a thin youth with a vivid imagination and a reputation for getting things wrong. 'Ear to ear, what I heard.'

Mason, on the other side of Drewitt, cut in: 'He's got it wrong as usual. Bloke got a pitchfork through his throat.'

'Well, wasn't too far out,' Gibbs insisted.

Drewitt looked back at the villages. Eleven years since he'd been in Lesser Calderon, since he'd lived there. The cottage was just out of sight at the end of the row. Funny, he could and should remember it, eleven years wasn't so long ago, and yet, in his mind, it was like seeing a picture through a haze. A long-gone summer image. He'd gone to school in Greater Calderon, further on and also out of sight. Elementary school . . . when you got older, eleven or twelve, you had to go to the secondary comprehensive in Lower Duthwaite. He never did; that was the summer his father had died, and they went to live in Warwick and he'd gone to secondary school there. The twin villages looked drab and uninteresting today.

'You're suppose to be searching, Drewitt, not standing scratching your arse,' Sergeant Bellows, the uniformed sergeant in charge, called out. 'You heard what Sergeant Stevens said. Look! Now's your big chance to be a detective. Use your bloody eyes.'

Drewitt looked, head down, staring at the grass below him, moving slowly forward. An officer on his right broke ranks and moved to Stevens with a triumphant air. He handed over an empty, dew-sodden packet of Players. Nodding, Stevens put the packet in a cellophane envelope and the constable rejoined the line. Gibbs stood in a cowpat and swore under his breath. He wiped his boots energetically on a patch of thick grass. They moved on.

'You know who reported the murder?' Drewitt asked Mason in a low voice. Might be somebody he'd known in the village years ago. Everybody knew everybody else in Lesser Calderon. And, for that matter, in Greater Calderon too. Not that he could be sure he remembered any of them too well.

'I was in the station when the phone call came through,' Mason replied, also in a low voice. 'Anonymous, I heard. Just a voice on the phone. I came out with the CID. Saw the body. Not nice. Blood all over. Pitchfork shoved in hard, right through his neck. Pinned him to the tree.'

Mason stopped, hesitated, and then with an expression of disgust picked up something from the grass between finger and thumb. It was a used contraceptive, a lump of squashed pink rubber.

'Didn't think they used these any more since the Pill,' he said.

'The Pill ain't got out to these villages yet,' Gibbs explained. 'Not much else has either. Wouldn't surprise me if they were still cannibals in some o' these places. Or at least Druids.'

Mason took the article, reluctantly still, between forefinger and thumb, over to Sergeant Stevens. He considered it momentarily, with some interest, and then refusing to touch it himself, opened another cellophane envelope and permitted Mason to place the contraceptive inside. Mason returned to the line.

After an hour, the meadow would appear to have been covered and Stevens called them back to the Black Maria. Someone had opened a container of hot tea and mugs were duly produced, filled and handed around. Then Stevens called them together again.

'All right, you'll all know we got a murder on our hands. Victim, one Joshua Gideon, farm worker of this godforsaken parish. I want five of you to assist the CID in calling on every house in the village. That is, both Greater and Lesser Calderon. Usual thing, looking for anything suspicious seen or heard by anyone. Probably the murder was committed last night or in the early morning, so that's the time you want to concentrate on.'

He paused, looking around, waiting for his words to take effect.

'Right, five of you.'

Everybody stepped forward. Everybody was keen to work with the Crime Squad. Might lead to greater things, that was the general feeling. Who wanted to be a beat copper all his life when the CID was where the detective work went on? Stevens nodded to the first five men in front of him.

'All right! You five.'

Drewitt, unchosen, pushed his way forward. 'Excuse me, Sergeant . . .'

Stevens glared at him. 'You're excused!'

'I was born in Lesser Calderon.'

Stevens, about to turn away, looked at him with renewed interest.

'That right?'

'Yes, Sarge.'

'Okay.' He beckoned to one of the chosen. 'Let that one in, and you're out.'

The man glared at Drewitt but did as he was told.

'What's your name?' Stevens asked Drewitt.

53

'Drewitt, Sarge. Harold Drewitt.'

'Don't call me "Sarge". Sergeant Stevens to you. DC Hoskins there, he'll tell you what sections of the village you cover. And I want every house, mind, and a report on every house. Right! Get off with you.'

The five chosen constables surrounded Detective Constable Hoskins who allocated parts of the two villages to each man.

'CID'll taken care of the rest,' he said. 'You know what you're on. Anything seen or heard, out of the ordinary, anything known or seen about Joshua Gideon, report to me or Sergeant Stevens.'

Stevens, who was walking back to the screened off area by the tree, turned and shouted to them. 'And, remember, this is no parking offence. This is horrible, bloody murder. So no trying to solve the case on your own, and no trying to arrest the postman 'cause he's cut his finger and is covered in blood. Just report anything like that to me. Me and Chief Inspector Blakelock's the ones who get the handclaps for arresting villainous killers.'

Despite his having been born in Lesser Calderon, Drewitt found himself allocated part of the centre of Greater Calderon. This included The Goat and Compasses, the Catholic church and a number of council houses.

The first council house door was opened by a thin woman with a thin voice. Before he could say anything, she spoke. 'Don't know anything about it. Don't know anything about anything. Don't even know the man who got hisself killed.' And the door was shut in Drewitt's face.

The next council house was opened by a fresh-faced young man about the same age as Drewitt. The face was not only fresh but round, almost moon-shaped, thatched with ill-cut red hair.

'George Numbles, that's me. What do you want to know?'

Drewitt told him he wanted to know as much as possible about the murder of Gideon. Any unusual incidents? He went through the rigmarole of Stevens' instructions.

George Numbles stared at Drewitt. 'Doan't I know yew?'

54

The name had struck a chord with Drewitt although he didn't want to say anything. There'd been a boy called Numbles in his class at the village school.

'Yew're Harry Drewitt, that's who yew are!' Numbles said, his face breaking into a smile. 'Yew came from Lesser Caldy. Up to school wi' me, so yew did. Yew remember me, Georgie Numbles?'

'I remember,' Drewitt said. Remembering Numbles the village baker and his son Georgie. Master Numbles, the baker's son. Like happy bloody families, he thought. A stolid child was now a moon-faced adult.

'You lookin' into seein' who killed Gideon then?' Numbles asked.

'And I'm hoping you might be able to help me, George.' No harm in using the slight advantage of acquaintance. Might lead to something.

'Doan't think I can do that. See, doan't know anythin'. Was in bed asleep all night.'

'You didn't hear anything in the night? You weren't disturbed?'

The face of the man in the moon broke open in a grin that showed a lower front tooth missing. 'Nothin' wakes me in the night. I just jump into the kipper and I'm gone.'

'Did you know anything about Joshua Gideon then?'

'Oh, I knew 'im by sight. Mebbe say "Nice day" to him. He were herdsman for the big house. The manor.' A silence followed.

'That's all you know about him?'

'And he wore a bit of a lad. What they say, innit? Bit of a lad? Yew know.'

Drewitt didn't and asked, 'In what way was he a bit of a lad?'

The moon face flushed. 'Yew know,' Numbles repeated.

'I don't. But I'm hoping you'll tell me.'

'With the ladies, they say.' Almost a suggestion of a lecherous wink. Or was that in Drewitt's mind.

'Who says?' he insisted.

'I dunno. Just . . . everybody, mebbe. People say. Anyway, I don't know nothing else. So I can't help yew, can I? Nothing more to be said, 'cept fancy yew being a policeman.

Call 'em pigs, don't they?' He laughed then, a nervous laugh, almost false. 'Knew yew'd come to a bad end, eh?'

He was about to shut the door of the council house, but Drewitt inserted his boot between lintel and door.

'George – Georgie, that's what we used to call you, wasn't it?

Numbles nodded uncertainly. Drewitt thought, either he's playing the village yokel and knows something . . . The red face could indicate he'd said too much when he mentioned Gideon was 'a bit of a lad. Or else he's a character from 'The Archers', resettled in the Cotswolds.

'Georgie,' he went on, 'joking apart about me being a pig, if I find you know anything and you haven't told me, I'm going to tell the big chief down the road – Chief Inspector Blakelock, that is – and he'll have you behind bars before you can say Joshua Gideon, I promise you.'

The red face altered, became a pasty white.

'Told yew, don't know nothin'. Anyway, if I did I couldn't say anythin'.'

'Why's that Georgie?'

'Why's what?'

'If you knew something, you couldn't say anything? Why?'

Perspiration on his face, George Numbles, wiped his brow.

'Can't say anything'. Yew know. They don't like it if yew say things about 'em.'

'About who?'

'I got to go . . .'

'About who, Georgie?' Was interrogation so easy, or was it only because he was dealing with a simple-minded youth?

'Everybody,' Numbles said. 'All of 'em. Round here. Don't know nothin'. Don't tell you nothin'. Nobody. An' . . . an' I'll bet they don't tell you nothin' neither.'

'Why won't they tell me, Georgie?'

'Because . . . because . . .' Then at once the worry, or was it fear, on his face disappeared. He'd solved his problem. 'Because they don't know nothin', not any of 'em. Yew'll find out. They don't know nothin', so they'll not be tellin' you, will they?'

They stared at each other for a moment. And then Drewitt realised he would get no further with George Numbles.

Village yokel or not, it had penetrated George's mind that he should say no more, and he was determined to stick with that resolution. Drewitt had no option but to allow him to shut the door.

The rest of the council houses tenants reacted in the same way as the first. They knew nothing. They barely knew Joshua Gideon. They had slept all night and heard nothing. Their faces were masks, blank, dull, uncaring or uninterested. Surprisingly, nobody said anything sympathetic. He might have expected at least one expression of horror. What a terrible thing . . . the poor man . . . who would do a thing like that . . .? All the phrases that come to the mouths of innocent bystanders or neighbours of victims, he had heard when assisting the CID on a few occasions in the past. None of them were uttered in Greater Calderon.

He crossed from the council houses to the centre of the village and the church. As he did so he had the feeling eyes were peering at him from behind curtained windows. He looked around but saw nothing. He was not helped by the sun disappearing behind a thick cloud. A greyness descended, a thin drizzle of rain began to fall. And at once it seemed as if the centre of the village became shrouded in a strange, thin mist.

As he reached the middle of the road, from the mist a figure appeared, another young man, dressed in jeans, grey shirt and a checked sports jacket.

'Hello, Drewitt. You remember me?' The accent was there but less pronounced than with Numbles.

Drewitt peered at the speaker. Dark hair fell over a wide brow. Blue eyes staring darkly from a face somehow in shadow. Something familiar there but he could not put a name to the man.

As if he could read Drewitt's mind, the man gave a slight smile and said. 'Hugh. Hughie Caroon. We was at the school together, you and Numbles and me.'

Drewitt remembered the name now: Caroon, a thick-set boy with heavy, sunken eyes. A quiet bully, if memory served, who said little but was not above dragging those who incurred his displeasure around to the rear of the school, to the boys' lavatory where arms were twisted, heads bashed

57

together and, even worse, testicles were squeezed until the victim screamed. All, as Drewitt remembered, without a change of expression on Caroon's face.

The face had changed now though. Apart from being older, thicker, even darker, there was a twist to the lips, a kind of built-in sneer that would not disappear despite Caroon's present attempt at a smile.

'Been seeing old Numbles, eh?' Caroon said with a false affability. 'Saw you at his door. Poor old Numbles. Not quite right, is he? Never has been, not old Numbles.'

'He seemed all right,' Drewitt replied. 'Bit nervous.'

'Oh, he was always that.'

'The uniform does it to some people.'

Caroon grinned crookedly. 'Oh, not to me. Looks very nice to me. Very smart. Yeah. Imagine, little Harry Drewitt now a big policeman. Who'd have thought it? Very . . . impressive. Oh, yeah, I'm impressed.'

'It's a job,' said Drewitt.

'Oh, no, much more than just a job. Me, I got a job. Builder. Got my own business. Not bad at my age. But that's just a job. You now, that's more, much more. Guardian of the law, upholder of the peace. Very impressive.'

'Do you know anything about the murder of Joshua Gideon?' Make use of the encounter, Drewitt told himself. Maybe Caroon wasn't sneering, maybe he was genuine enough.

'Who?' The grin widened.

'Gideon, Joshua.'

'Oh, yeah, nasty business. Don't know nothing about it. Expect you'll find nobody knows nothing about it. Nor wants to know.'

'Did you know Gideon?'

'Not well. No, not at all well. Not a man you'd want to know.'

'Why would that be?'

'Had a bad temper. Bit of a bully, you could say.' The pot, Drewitt thought, shouting that the kettle was black.

'But I didn't really know him. Don't think people did know him. Kept hisself to hisself. Not a bad thing that.' Caroon nodded with assumed geniality then glanced at his wrist-watch. 'Time I was off. Business, y'know. Nice to see you. Fancy you being a copper.'

He made a step to move away, stopped hesitantly, and then turned and looked again into Drewitt's face. And smiled, this time a broad grin showing his teeth. Strong teeth but yellow, stained with tobacco. Or something.

'You won't find out anything, you know. None of you will. But if you happen to come near to finding something, Harry boy, be very, very careful. You don't want to get hurt, do you?'

Drewitt straightened up, assuming an official stance, returning the other's stare. 'Wait a minute, Caroon, is that some kind of a threat to me? Or to the police?'

The grin was steady. 'Lord, no. Just saying, you people dealing with a murderer . . . could be dangerous. Of course, I was forgetting that mebbe you'll be used to such things. Still, wouldn't like nasty things to happen to an old school mate, eh?'

He was off, in a minute a faint outline in the mist. Drewitt turned away, unconvinced by the explanation of what he was still sure was some kind of a threat. He walked towards the church.

Church of Our Lady in the Wold

Holy Apostolic Church of Rome.

Priest: Father Simeon Anselm.

Address: The Old Alms House, Greater Calderon.

The Old Alms House was the building behind the church. It was constructed of dark Cotswold granite. It had been when Drewitt was a boy the residence of the priest, although some time in the Middle Ages it had actually been an alms house for the poor of the parish. Presumably later, probably in the late Victorian era, the priest had become the principal member of the poor locally and the village had given him the alms house to live in.

Before going to the front door of the Alms House, Drewitt entered the church. He'd never been inside Our Lady of the Wold. As a boy he had gone with his mother to the Church of

59

England in Lesser Calderon. For a while anyway. The Episcopalian church had been small, rather desolate, perhaps in line
with the size and attitude of its congregation, also small and
always with an aspect of desolation.

The Catholic church was different. Indeed, this Catholic
church was different from any place of worship Drewitt had
ever been in before.

The first thing that he noticed was that the interior appeared
to have been recently repainted. Everything was in bright,
almost garish colour. Even the vaulted oak beams curving
above his head seemed to have been recently painted or lacquered. Below them, around the walls, the illustrations of the
Stations of the Cross were bright, too bright, and although he
had little knowledge of church decoration, didn't seem quite
right in terms of the Crucifixion story as Drewitt knew it. Not
that he'd had much contact with religion for years. Not that he
was a unbeliever; he was just a young man in a hurry with no
time for eternal values. So he'd once told himself.

He walked down the aisle, footsteps echoing on stone,
towards the altar which actually seemed lit as if by some form of
subtle hidden lighting. Everything stood out clearly, although
again he had a feeling something was wrong.

He coughed loudly, hoping that the priest, Father . . . what
was his name? . . . Anselm, that was it, might be in church and
hear him. Weren't priests always on duty or lurking somewhere
under eaves or arches.

There was no reply to his loud cough.

And then he saw what was wrong at the altar. The large
crucifix with the tormented Christ figure, eight feet in height,
which should have towered above all at the rear of the altar, was
hanging aslant from the wall, as if some attempt had been made
to wrench it from the stone. In gilt and with some gleaming
stones in the halo, the Christ on the Cross hung by one twisted
wire, limply facing the stone floor, the face angled to the side so
that the saintly expression, and the eyes raised heavenward,
were strangely distorted. To Drewitt's eyes, the Saviour's expression at that angle was a cold, contemptuous sneer.

Chapter Seven

The voice seemed to come from directly behind him.

'It really is too bad. The metal pins that held the cross to the wall have rusted and broken, I'm afraid.'

Drewitt turned quickly to find himself staring into space. At the same time the voice seemed to echo through the church so that 'rusted and broken' reverberated from the walls. A feeling of sudden fear gripped him as he turned full-circle, gazing around the building.

The figure came from behind a pillar to the right of the altar. A dark shape at first, slightly bent, vaguely outlined against the light slanting from one of the stained-glass windows. It came into definition as it moved towards Drewitt and into what light there was.

'It must, of course, be attended to.' The voice was slightly high-pitched, with a sing-song quality. The man was dressed in a clerical coat, seemingly black at first but in fact a dark grey. His shoulders were rounded, his back curved. Black trousers and shiny patent leather shoes, like dancing pumps, completed the picture.

Drewitt thought, he looks like a black lizard . . . were there such creatures as black lizards? He moved with a kind of grace, almost feminine in motion and gesture. And then the face came into the light and it was a thin face, that of a man in his forties, with penetrating blue eyes and, below them, a deep line running down each cheek. The hair, also black, was thinning above the forehead and seemed damp, almost matted. Yet there was a seeming benevolence there, a quality of understanding, of kindness even in the expression. The blue eyes moved from the suspended crucifix to Drewitt.

'I am Father Anselm, Constable. You are here on this unfortunate business?'

It occurred to Drewitt that the murder by pitchfork of a man who might have been one of his congregation, certainly a parishioner, deserved more than that 'unfortunate business'.

'The murder of Joshua Gideon, sir,' he said.

'Yes, indeed. Quite shocking. I'm sure no one in Greater or Lesser Calderon could have had anything to do with such a thing.'

'Any reason why you should be so sure, sir?'

Large hands opened, palms towards him in an expression of certainty.

'I know my people,' Father Anselm said.

'Hardly proof, sir.'

'No, no, of course not. And it must be said, who among us can really plumb the depths of the human soul? If, by any chance, this terrible crime was committed by one of my people, then it could only have been caused by some devilish aberration.' A deep frown. 'I can only pray that the perpetrator might show due contrition in the confessional. Although, of course, that would be of no value to you and your superiors. But then, we are on different planes of the same business. I can only represent the justice of God, while you are the emissary of a more mundane justice.'

Long-winded, Drewitt thought. Pedantic and long-winded. An occupational habit.

'But let us not stand here, Constable. It's cold . . . I'm having trouble with the boiler and the heating will not be up to scratch, so to speak, until Sunday. Come across to my home. My housekeeper will give us some tea.'

'I'm afraid I haven't much time, sir.'

'The tea will be ready, I assure you. And you'll wish to ask me . . . whatever you have to ask on such melancholy occasions.'

They left the church by a side door and crossed to the Alms House. Despite its forbidding outer aspect, the interior was more than comfortable. Thickly carpeted with what appeared to be large Persian rugs, furnished with heavy, almost luxurious pieces, the walls decorated with oriental ornaments which even Drewitt could recognise as expensive, the atmosphere was one of opulence. In view of the occupant's profession, all this seemed out of place.

In a large pleasant sitting-room, Father Anselm beckoned the policeman to a seat in a deep armchair. And appeared to read his mind.

'Much too good for a village priest. That's what you're thinking, isn't it, lad?'

'Not my place to . . .'

'Nonsense. You're a detective,' Anselm insisted with a mildly amusing expression. 'You must note everything. The house was furnished by the grace of Miss Campion. The Campion family . . . an old Catholic family, I may say . . . are by way of being the local lords of the manor around here. Alas, the Honourable Miss Margaret Campion is the sole survivor. The furnishings are her gift except for the *chinoiserie* which is my own collection. I was, in my younger days, privileged to spread the word in China and later in the Near East. One picked up unconsidered trifles for a few pence. My little hobby.'

'Very nice,' said Drewitt, feeling the need to say something.

An elderly woman came in, unsummoned, carrying a tray with two cups of tea and a plate of biscuits.

'Mrs Gavel, my housekeeper. Also a mind reader,' Anselm said, nodding his thanks to the woman who at once withdrew. The priest selected a cup and placed it in Drewitt's hands.

'Keep you warm, eh? Now you'll want to know what I know of Joshua Gideon?'

'Well, yes, if you can help us . . .'

'Very little, I'm afraid. However . . .' As he spoke, Anselm wandered the room, teacup and saucer in hand. Quite suddenly he stopped, laid cup and saucer on a small table, and picked up an ornament from a recess in the wall. He held it up, a squat, fat figure of smooth shining metal, grotesque in its ugliness. 'Have you ever seen anything like this? Some artisan's depiction of the god Baal from Sumeria. Strange how the ancients worshipped such ugly manifestations. So unlike our concept of the benevolent deity.'

Drewitt stared at the piece. 'Yes, indeed.'

'I digress,' said the priest. 'Joshua Gideon was into the faith certainly, but was long an apostate. I don't like to say it of a fellow being, but he was not a pleasant man. A lecher and a man of violence, I'm afraid, a great sinner – if one can find a great sinner in such a small rural parish.'

'He'd have enemies then?' Drewitt said quickly.

'He was not universally liked or admired, certainly. But "enemies" . . . too strong a word. He might have been a disruptive influence in our community but I would say most people in Calderon are even-headed, fortunately. Not swayed by example. I would not say I knew of any one person who would kill him. Certainly not in the manner described. I believe there were symbols around the body relating to primitive belief?'

It was the first Drewitt had heard of this. 'I don't know about that.'

'Oh, I heard it said, I heard it said. Witchcraft symbols, so to speak. It would indicate to me the presence . . . perhaps even the perpetration of the deed . . . by Romanys, who often hold such superstitions.'

'We've no word of any gypsies in the district,' said Drewitt truthfully, but noted the thought to be passed on to Sergeant Stevens.

Then, at once, Father Anselm changed tack. 'Don't I know your face?' he said.

'I . . . I'm not a Catholic,' Drewitt replied.

A thin smile from the priest. 'Not all my acquaintances are.'

'I was born in Lesser Calderon.'

'Yes, yes, of course. You'll be Drewitt's son. I knew your father, a hard-working man, died young. And then your mother left Calderon.'

'We went to Warwick.'

'Yes, I heard. And you've become a policeman. Very commendable. How long have you been in the force?'

'Eighteen months, sir.'

The smile again, thin-lipped but not unkindly. 'I do wish I could be of more help, regarding the death of Gideon, but I can tell you no more.'

64

'You heard or saw nothing unusual last night, Father?'

'Indeed, no. But then, I go to bed early and am a sound sleeper. A sign of a clear conscience, I sometimes think. Then I consider I am probably indulging in the sin of pride. I search my conscience for transgressions, find them too, but I still sleep soundly.'

Drewitt rose to his feet stiffly. The dampness outside was getting to him. 'Must get on, sir,' he said.

'Of course, of course. Again, sorry I can't be of more help but I do hope you catch the miscreant.'

Drewitt thought, first time he'd heard a murderer described as a 'miscreant'. He went out into the church yard. The rain had turned into a damp mist that wreathed the tombstones in the tiny cemetery. He stepped on to the road and crossed to the inn.

The Goat and Compasses. Strange name for a pub, and yet there were many of them throughout England. Must mean something . . . possibly to do with Masons, they had compasses in their regalia.

He was standing looking up at the sign when a young girl came out of the front door carrying a mop and a bucket of water. Ignoring Drewitt, she proceeded to scrub down the two stone steps outside the door.

'Goat and Compasses,' Drewitt said aloud, for want of anything else to attract the girl's attention. 'Funny name.'

'The girl looked up, large eyes full of liquidity as if, without reason, she was near to tears.

'It's not funny. It's to do with God,' she said.

'God? How come?'

'It means, "God encompasses".'

'I didn't know that. Funny the things they got up to, naming inns. But . . . er, what's your name?'

'Abbie. Abbie Silver.'

'You live here?' He indicated the inn.

'I work here, and I have work to do now. Got no time to talk.'

Drewitt cleared his throat. 'You have to talk to me. I have to ask you questions. About the murder of Joshua Gideon.'

'I don't know nothing about that.'

'You didn't see or hear anything unusual last night?'

'I'd be asleep.'

'So apparently was everybody in Calderon,' Drewitt said.

'And why should they not be?'

He had no answer. Another figure appeared at the door of the inn. A short, stocky one, with broad shoulders, grizzled hair and a sour expression. Mullion was memorable and Drewitt recognised him at once as the owner of the inn. Even as a kid, he'd known Mullion by sight.

Scowling, he addressed the girl. 'How long does it take you to wash two steps? You'll be all day unless I'm on your tail.'

The girl, face expressionless, said nothing but finished washing the stone steps and, lifting her bucket, went back into the building.

'I remember you,' Drewitt said, this time anticipating his own possible recognition. 'You're Mr Mullion.'

'So I'm Mullion. You'll want to now if I saw anything or know anything about the murder of Gideon? Well, I saw nothing and I know nothing.'

'But . . .'

'And neither would the girl. She's only sixteen, she lives with her aunt, and she'd be fast asleep when Gideon was killed.'

'How do you know when that would be, Mr Mullion?' Drewitt said quickly.

Mullion's head swung round and he glowered at the policeman. 'I don't, but I hear it would be some time last night. Isn't that so?'

Drewitt attempted a smile. In return the innkeeper's glower deepened. 'My father used to know you, Mr Mullion. Alfred Drewitt . . .'

'He died years ago.'

'I'm his son.'

'You would be. You're also a policeman, and I can't help you. And the inn isn't open yet. Except for residents.'

'Are there any?'

'Not this week,' Mullion said. 'And even if you're Drewitt's son, don't be poking your nose in. Otherwise you might get it cut off.' He turned sharply on his heel and stepped back inside the inn, slamming the door behind him.

His section of the village covered, Drewitt reported to Sergeant Stevens who was sitting dourly in the front of the Black Maria, puffing at a pipe. Drewitt told him of the priest's suggestion that the murder might have been committed by gypsies.

'Good idea,' said Stevens. 'And might be very likely – in some people's minds. Whenever anything nasty happens, blame the travelling people. then your own come out clean and sparkling white, and nobody's hurt except some poor Romany who doesn't matter to anyone. Except his own people. And me. Because I don't blame those people for everything. Even if there were any of them within twenty miles of here, which there isn't.'

He climbed down from the van with considerable reluctance. 'My turn now to follow up on all your calls, Drewitt. Me and Blakelock. See, they think they've got rid of the police. Don't realise they've just had the amateurs. Now they get the professionals. You better get into the van. You'll be going back on your beat in Warwick again.'

That was Drewitt's last connection with the Gideon case for the next week. He went back on to his beat in the city and could observe, from a distance, that Chief Inspector Blakelock, Sergeant Stevens and the so-called professionals in the CID were having little success at Calderon.

Some days later word went out that Scotland Yard had been called in, and that some big detective would arrive from London. The next day Drewitt was off his beat and assisting the desk sergeant at police head-quarters when the man came into the station.

Chapter Eight

He stood in front of the desk, legs slightly apart as if having to balance himself; perhaps as if he had a little too much to drink. Which was not so. Indeed, he drank very little. Not then.

'Harkness!' he said loudly. The desk sergeant – it was Bellows doing a stint behind the counter – was occupied catching up on personal reports and didn't even look up. Customers had to wait when sergeants were busy with paperwork.

Harkness was in his late fifties, fifty-nine to be exact, five feet ten or eleven in height, with heavy broad shoulders, alert eyes under heavy eyebrows, and a receding hairline. Not that he could be considered bald or even balding. Greyish-brown hair, clipped short where it sprouted, seemed patchy on his head, a series of random tufts, and attempts to flatten it were never entirely successful. The nose was distinctive, giving the impression of having been broken more than once. Yet it was not a pugilist's nose but rather one that had been expertly repaired, giving an uneven, unstraightened, but not unpleasant aspect. He was dressed in a new, unbattered trench coat, wore a plaid scarf around his neck and carried a definitely battered soft hat (which, Drewitt learned later, he hated wearing).

Now he was staring across at the back of the sergeant who was ignoring him, bending over the pile of reports.

'Harkness,' he barked this time. 'Name of Harkness!'

The sergeant did not even look around.

'Be with you shortly,' he said in a routine monotone. Drewitt made to rise and cross to the counter but a glare from the sergeant restrained him. The desk was Bellows's business. When he was ready.

Harkness glared at the sergeant, lips at once a thin line above the tight jaw. Colour flooded into his face. When he spoke again it wasn't in a loud voice but in a carefully modulated tone as firm as rock.

'I am Superintendent Harkness. I have come over a hundred miles at the invitation of your Chief Constable. I really don't think that, wi' an invitation like that, I should have to wait on the convenience of a bloody sergeant who can't be bothered raising his arse off his seat to do his job!'

Drewitt had never seen Bellows move as fast as he did then. He turned and was at the counter, raising the flap before Drewitt could blink. And as Harkness passed through to the rear of the desk, Bellows, in one large breath, said: 'Yessir. Sorry, sir, didn't-realise-who-you-was-sir-come-right-through-sir.'

A policewoman was called and ushered the Superintendent into the depths of the building. To the Chief Constable's office, to be exact. And Sergeant Bellows avoided Drewitt's eyes for some minutes. They continued with their paperwork. A young, pregnant woman was brought in by a constable and a policewoman and formally charged with shoplifting a tin of corn beef, valued at fifty-eight pence. She at once burst into tears. This created a degree of consternation as Bellows, realising the advanced state of her pregnancy, wanted her taken home before any accidents happened in the charge room.

An hour or so later, another policewoman appeared from the inner corridor.

'Constable Drewitt?'

'That's me!'

'You're wanted. Chief Constable's office. Now.'

A sensation of panic gripped Drewitt. What had he done, what could he have possibly done that would merit . . . was that the right word? . . . shouldn't it be threatened with . . . . the Chief Constable?

70

Bellows glared at him. 'What have you been doing, you shouldn't have been doing?'

Drewitt had no answer.

He went along the corridor and up the stairs, without daring to think of why he had been thus summoned. He'd never spoken to, or even met, the Chief Constable, James Rollason. Almost certainly soon to be Sir James Rollason.

He went through the door marked CHIEF CONSTABLE and found himself in an outer office in front of a desk behind which sat a very attractive policewoman with the rank of sergeant.

'Sergeant,' he said.

She looked up and smiled. 'Constable Drewitt? Go right in.'

He took a deep breath and went in. As if approaching the edge of the world with all the courage he could muster.

It was a large, brightly lit office, the greyness of the day beyond neutralised by strip lighting at full intensity. Behind the desk sat Rollason, in uniform, resembling an aging, tired, field-marshal in dark blue. Sitting in front of the desk were Chief Inspector Blakelock and Superintendent Harkness. Behind them, standing, or rather leaning, against a bookcase – the room was lined with the kind of books that lined rooms but were never read – was Sergeant Stevens.

'Constable Drewitt!' he announced himself, standing stiffly to attention.

'Ah, yes, Drewitt,' Rollason said. 'Stand . . . stand easy . . . at ease, whatever. You know Chief Inspector Blakelock and Sergeant Stevens?'

'Yes, sir.' They were being nice to him! What *was* he here for?

And this is Superintendent Harkness from London.'

Harkness barely glanced around at him. Drewitt said again, 'Yes, sir.'

'Sergeant Stevens tells us you were born in Calderon?'

'Lesser Calderon, sir.' A sense of relief flooded through him. That was why he was here. The local boy from Calderon, the one who might know what went on in that place.

Harkness spoke now, half-turning in his seat to look at Drewitt. 'Want to hear about the place. Kind of people, all that.'

'Yes, sir. But I haven't lived in the place since I was eleven.'

'You'll still know more than anyone else.'

'Yes, sir.'

'Mind you,' said the Chief Constable, 'I have to say, Harkness, that I don't hold much with the witchcraft theory. This is a simple murder, I'm sure, with a simple motive: lust, envy, revenge, whatever you like. The witchcraft nonsense is just that – nonsense. Something to distract us from the facts.'

'I'm not exactly one to believe in mumbo-jumbo myself, sir,' said Harkness, and the Scottish accent was quite pronounced. 'But, whether or not we believe in witchcraft, it may be that Jimmy, our killer, does. Anyway, it's my job to find this Jimmy.'

'Jimmy?' said Blakelock, eyebrows raised.

'A Glasgow expression, Inspector Blakelock. You don't know a character, you call him Jimmy. Until you get his real name.'

Rollason suddenly realised Drewitt was still standing in front of him.

'That'll be all just now, Drewitt. You can go and change into civilian clothes. Consider yourself attached to CID for the time being. And you'll make yourself available to Superintendent Harkness in . . . how long, Harkness?'

'An hour. Downstairs at the desk. Can you drive a car?'

'Yes, sir.'

'Good. Can't be bothered driving. You'll drive me about, unless I have to drive myself. And you'll be telling me about Calderon. See you in an hour.'

As he went towards the door, Drewitt heard Blakelock say, 'We can give you a CID driver . . .'

'No, Drewitt'll do. Oh, don't worry, Inspector, I'll be using your CID. When I'm ready. But, for a start, I want to do a wee bit of rooting around on my own. If you've no objection?'

'Of course he hasn't,' Rollason answered for the Chief Inspector. 'You are in complete charge of this investigation now, Harkness.'

And Drewitt was out of the room, heading for the locker room in the basement and his civilian clothes. Excited, pleased – yes, all of that. He was attached to CID, if only temporarily . . . and he was about to work with Superintendent Harkness of Scotland Yard. Of course he could admit to himself that Harkness, so far, made him nervous. Very nervous. But that would pass. He had the opportunity of a lifetime. Thanks to the dead body found in the meadow in Calderon.

Dressed in sports jacket and flannels, a pullover over a shirt and tie, Drewitt waited at the desk. He was carrying a mackintosh, it was raining outside, and feeling pleased with himself.

Sergeant Bellows glared at him. 'Temporary attachment. Just don't kid yourself it'll be permanent. You know we can't do without you in the uniformed branch, Drewitt.'

He grinned. 'Oh, I know that, Sergeant.'

The glare was unyielding. 'Don't give me no cheek, son. They tell me this Harkness is a right one for having his people jump to it. You'll be glad to get back to us, when this is over. And, by the way, there's been another death at Calderon.'

Drewitt felt cold. 'What!'

'Oh, don't worry, nothing sinister. Car accident. Not in the village anyway. On the main trunk road. Early this morning, bloke tried to cross the road without looking. On his way to work. Stepped right in front of a Leyland truck. Didn't know what hit him. No need to get excited. No suspicious circumstances.'

'Got a name for him, Sergeant?'

'Of course. Might be somebody you know. Got the name here . . . Numbles. George Numbles. Aged twenty-two.'

He looked at Drewitt and saw that his face had gone pale. Bellows frowned. 'You did know him?'

'Yeah. We were at school together.'

'Sorry, son.'

'I didn't know him well. Hadn't seen him since I was a kid. Until the other day. He was one of the blokes I questioned . . .'

Numbles. Poor stupid Numbles. Just the type to walk under a lorry.

The sergeant had said something.

'What was that, Sergeant?'

'Didn't get anything from him, did you? About the murder?'

'No, nothing. There's no chance of anything funny in this?'

'No. The boys on the spot were very particular. Seemingly this Numbles just walked on to the road, hands in his pockets, not looking. Not thinking, obviously. Dreaming. Until the lorry hit him. Just a stupid accident.'

Harkness appeared from the door at the back. This time the light was on his face and Drewitt was able to see him better. Tanned, perhaps weather-beaten, Drewitt thought, his face was like a contour map of the Himalayas: all deep wrinkles, hard ridges; a well-lived in face, seemingly older than his fifty-nine years.

'Ready, Drewitt?'

He told Harkness about the death of Numbles, looking to the sergeant for confirmation which was duly given.

Harkness nursed his jaw for a second with his right hand. 'Tell me about Mr Numbles.'

'Baker's son. A baker himself. Bit simple.'

'When you interviewed him, did he tell you anything?'

'No, sir. Well, not exactly.'

'What exactly?'

Drewitt leaned against the counter, trying to remember.

'He did say Gideon was . . . was a bit of a ladies man.'

'The CID confirmed that. Anything else?'

'He said one thing strange. He said he didn't know anything, but if he did, he couldn't tell me.'

'Now what would he be meaning by that?'

'I asked him,' Drewitt replied. 'He said, "They don't like it if you say things about them." I asked him who *they* were. He seemed to get a bit flustered but he said he only meant everybody in the village. When I asked him why everybody in the village wouldn't like him saying anything, he said it was because they knew nothing.'

Harkness stood for a moment, in thought.

74

'Pity,' he said. 'Pity Mr Numbles had his accident. Sounds like a young man who might just tie himself in a few wee knots.'

'Should I have gone after him? Questioned him more than I did?'

'No, not in those circumstances. You want somebody like that to talk, you bring him in here and scare the breeks off him. That's if he did know anything. Interesting, though, about him being killed accidentally . . .'

Harkness's voice was so matter of fact, Drewitt felt a chill in his spine. After all Numbles had been a human being. Now Harkness was considering him as an interesting – what? – statistic?

Harkness went on, 'Mebbe they cleared away one weak link, whoever they were . . . are.' He looked up at Drewitt then and seemed to sense the coldness in the younger man. He grinned. Without humour. 'You get hardened, Constable.'

'Yes, sir. I suppose so, sir.'

Harkness turned to Sergeant Bellows. 'Will you ask Sergeant Stevens to check the death of this man, Numbles? I want to know if there was any possibility of something other than an accident. Do that, Sergeant.'

'Right away, sir,' said Bellows, and going to the phone, dialled the CID extension.

'Oh, another thing,' Harkness said to Drewitt. 'You weren't at the inquest on Gideon, were you?'

'No, sir. No need.'

'You, Sergeant?'

'Wasn't there, sir, but I read the reports of it.'

'Aye, I have them here. Verdict, murder by person or persons unknown. None of the people from Calderon were called?'

'No, sir,' said Bellows. 'But, you see, none of them knew anything. And whoever reported the body in Mallen's Meadow did it anonymously. Took the call myself that day. All the voice said was, "There's a dead man at Calderon lying on Mallen's Meadow." I said, "Who's that?" and whoever it was hung up. We sent a car out to check, and that's how we discovered Gideon's body.'

75

'The voice on the phone – man or woman?'

'A man, sir. Oh, yes, a man.'

'Young or old?'

'Difficult to say, sir. Kind of a hoarse voice.'

'Or assumed hoarseness?'

'Yes. Yes, it could just have been put on. To disguise the voice.'

'Probably was. Still, in a day or two, I might ask you to go around Calderon, Sergeant. Chat to everybody you can. Might just hear a hoarse voice. Though I doubt it. Get through and make that call to Sergeant Stevens. Meanwhile, Drewitt, you and me'll be off.'

'Yes, sir.'

'Time I had a look at Calderon, Greater and Lesser, eh?'

A car had been laid on, an unmarked police Rover which was standing across the road from police headquarters. Harkness threw the key to Drewitt.

'You drive. I like to be driven. Towards Calderon. Stop about a mile from the place. We'll have some lunch on the way.'

Drewitt slipped the car silently into gear and drove out of Warwick on to the road south. He took the Rover up to fifty-five and settled back gripping the wheel nervously.

'That the fastest you can go?' Harkness said. 'At least get up to sixty-five. I don't want to be on this investigation until my retirement comes through.'

Drewitt did as he was told pressing down the accelerator. His hands were damp with sweat. He knew he mustn't blow this assignment or any chance of joining the CID permanently would be gone. Harkness settled in his seat, hat on the back of his head, and stared at the road.

'Monotonous, driving a car these days,' the Superintendent said, yawning, and then abruptly changed the subject. 'Tell me, lad, why did you become a policeman?'

The question took Drewitt by surprise. It was a question he'd been asked before, but always by people not in the force. Now he was aware that he had to be careful with his answer. Was there an expected response or was he expected to tell the truth? He hesitated.

'Try the truth, lad. Not the answer you think I want.'

'I thought it was a worthwhile job . . .'

'So is digging ditches or being a brain surgeon. But you're neither. Try again.'

'It's . . . it's necessary to have a police force,' Drewitt said. 'And it's not popular. That didn't worry me because I knew . . . I knew it *was* worthwhile.'

'Oh, come on!'

Drewitt took a deep breath. 'I wanted the authority! It was something I'd never had. Being . . . maybe in charge of something. Being given responsibility.'

'Power?' Harkness said.

'No, not power, sir. Authority and responsibility. I don't want to run people's lives, but I want to be able to guide them, help them, maybe.'

'That's fair enough,' said the older man. 'I don't like the guys who want power, who want to push people around. But I like the guidance idea. Aye, it'll do. It's not the best reason, mind, but it's your reason.'

'What was your reason, sir?' Drewitt said.

'No need to ask – I was going to tell you. When I was a kid, I wanted to see how things worked. Used to take watches apart, radios, anything like that. How did it work? Most of the time I never found out, but I was trying. Then later, in the army, a mate of mine was killed. Blown up by a shell. And another mate went adrift, deserted. Killed a couple of people to survive. He was shot. And I thought, two blokes, both dead in different ways, what made them what they were? I didn't have an answer but I started thinking, what are people? What makes them work?'

He drew a packet of cigarettes from his pocket and lit one. 'I'm trying to stop smoking,' he went on, after a brief fit of coughing. 'That's why I'm not offering you one.'

'I don't smoke,' Drewitt said.

'No, you wouldn't. What was I saying? Aye, that's why I joined the police force. To find out what makes people tick. What makes them what they are. Especially at the edge. Joining the police was like opening those watches as a kid. Not that I've ever really found out what people are like. But I did find out what some villains are like.

'Of course, I also couldn't get a job as a psychiatrist. In fact, when I came out the army, I couldn't get a bloody job at all. No qualifications except for killing people, and the money wasn't bad in the force. That was in Glasgow, just after the war.'

He then lapsed into silence until they came upon a Road Chef café.

'Pull in there. We'll have some lunch.'

Over sausage, bacon and chips, Harkness said, 'How far to Calderon?'

'About three miles, Drewitt replied.

'Right. Good bus service on this road?'

'Every two hours.'

'Good. You'll get a bus back. I'm going to drive into the villages on my own. I'll stay there one or two nights. Not as a policeman. Want to sniff around, like. See, unorthodox methods. Great stuff. You can wait here and get a bus back to Warwick. Oh, and pay for the lunch, will you? Claim it on expenses.'

Drewitt coughed on a fragment of crisp bacon. He'd have an hour at least to wait for a bus. And he could just about afford to pay for their meal.

'Only thing I don't like about this is having to drive myself,' Harkness said. 'Still, you have to do what you have to do, don't you? What do you think about the witchcraft angle?'

'Not very much, sir. Of course, there's a lot of superstition in some of those isolated villages. But I think Inspector Blakelock's right to ignore it.'

'Do you now? Well, the rest of today and tomorrow I want you to go through all the local newspapers going back twenty . . . thirty years. Maybe even further. You're looking for any witchcraft stories, or devil worship or ghost stories, around this district. Let's see if anything connected with witches had ever happened around here before. Go up to the university and talk to the anthropology department and the history people. See if they've ever heard of anything like that. Now, finished your lunch? Good! You can see me off.'

Five minutes later he stood outside the café watching Harkness driving off in the Rover towards Greater and Lesser Calderon. On his own. Passing himself off as some kind of commercial traveller. If anyone would believe him.

Chapter Nine

The next morning, Drewitt spent pouring over the clippings from back issues of the *Warwick Gazette and Advertiser*. He was assisted by a Miss Collins, who was in charge of the paper's morgue, a large room in the basement of the building. He had phoned the newspaper the previous evening, and been put on to her. He had told her then what he was looking for.

'I'll do cross-references,' she'd announced in pleasant if efficient tones. 'Witchcraft, devil-worship in the district and the villages of Greater and Lesser Calderon. Also general references to the district. I suggest we go back . . . say, fifty years. The subject will be comparatively rare. See you in the morning.'

A pause and a change of tone. 'You'll find me in the basement.' As if held in some perpetual thrall, and waiting to be rescued.

Miss Collins, when he met her the next morning, proved not unattractive and hardly held in thrall. Dressed in a sensible skirt over which she wore a white sweater, Drewitt could not help but be awed by the prominence of her frontage and the aroma of her perfume. (Opium, from Paris.) She was in her early thirties, perhaps ten years older than Drewitt.

She sat him on an upright chair, in front of a small table. The formica top was stained with rings from the overflow of many, many teacups. Drewitt was left there, waiting, while Miss Collins collected a small bundle of clippings set out the previous evening. She returned carrying them.

'Not a lot, but something,' she announced.

She leant across him and he was conscious of the pressure of her breasts under the sweater against his cheek. She laid the first clipping in front of him. 'You do nothing. I do the work. Just sit and read.'

She blew dust off one of the clippings and he was staring at a page of the newspaper with a date on the corner of the screen: 8 July 1952.

'Don't bother about that,' Miss Collins said. 'It's further on.'

More pages were placed in front of him.

'Look, if you just leave these, I wouldn't take up so much of your time,' he said.

She smiled, almost invitingly. 'It's all right, I'm enjoying it. I rarely get a chance to do anything like this.'

'Here we are,' Miss Collins said enthusiastically. 'Beginning of November.'

Drewitt's relationships with women, he'd told himself, had been limited because he had been too involved in his career. And before that, at school, he had been too involved in school work. He'd resisted the more obvious idea that he was painfully shy . . . why was shyness always considered painful? . . . or perhaps frightened of them. Any thought of involvement brought him out in a cold sweat. As if, he told himself, he could know the theory but never the practice. He was a twenty-two-year-old virgin, and ashamed of the fact. Yet the shame did not overcome the fear. And an assured woman like Miss Collins, slightly older than himself and very aware of her femininity, disturbed him. He had been made aware of her body and was afraid of his awareness.

She was peering over his shoulder. The front page of an edition was in front of him.

In a corner of the front page there was a heading:

CALDERON MAN FOUND UNCONSCIOUS ON HILLSIDE

Joshua Gideon (26) was found unconscious on the Edron Hill above Great Calderon yesterday morning. It was thought he had fallen from the top of the hill injuring his head on rock outcroppings. He was taken to Stratford Memorial Hospital, where his condition is said to be critical.

80

That was all. Gideon had fallen on Edron Hill.

Miss Collins said: 'Isn't that the man who was murdered last week?'

'Yes.'

'I thought that's why you were here.' Her eyes were suddenly shining, 'How fascinating.'

'It's not much of a story,' Drewitt said.

'Oh, that's not all of it. There's more the next day.' She leant over him again and her perfume enveloped him. He coughed. She placed another clipping in front of him. She had a determined look in her eye. She was going to impress this young man come hell, high water, and however many clippings she could find.

CALDERON MAN'S AMAZING RECOVERY

Doctors at Stratford Memorial Hospital are amazed at the speedy recovery of Joshua Gideon, found yesterday morning unconscious on the Edron Hill. (This page yesterday.)

Gideon, thought to be in a coma, became conscious this morning and appeared to be suffering no ill effects from his fall.

It is believed however that Mr Gideon could offer no explanation for his accident, beyond denying to the police that there was any foul play.

'That all?' Drewitt said.

'There's a third story two days later,' said Miss Collins, presenting yet another clipping. And again brushing lightly against his shoulder. There was no reaction.

Another page, this time from the inside of the paper, appeared.

OLD LEGEND OF EDRON HILL RECURS

Strange stories surrounding the Edron Hill above the villages of Greater and Lesser Calderon were revived yesterday when Joshua Gideon (26) was released from Stratford Memorial Hospital. (See story on Monday and Tuesday.)

81

Mr Gideon, who was found unconscious on the Edron Hill, denied he had been attacked, but stated that he had seen the spirit of Herne the Hunter on the hill and this visitation had caused his accident.

Edron Hill has long been the centre of superstition in this part of Warwickshire, and is treated with considerable reverence by the locals. Over hundreds of years manifestations of strange woodland spirits have been recorded.

Professor Edmund Carew, Professor of Anthropology at Warwick University, informed our reporter that there were many legends regarding Herne the Hunter throughout England, although the legend itself is supposed to have originated further south, in Windsor Great Park. The Hunter is purported to be the spirit of a dead huntsman although its origins stretch back to antiquity. It may be, in the Professor's opinion, a manifestation of the Greek God, Pan.

Professor Carew went on to point out that Herne the Hunter takes its place in English mythology alongside that of Puck and possibly the Arthurian cycle.

"Strong beliefs in such myths are still held in many of the outlying villages in the Cotswolds, and indeed throughout England," the Professor said. "And these usually centre around prominences such as the Edron Hill or Glastonbury Tor.

"As regards Mr Gideon's claim," the Professor added, "One would be more interested in estimating the amount of ale he had consumed the evening before the so-called visitation."

At a further interview in his cottage home in Greater Calderon, Mr Gideon, on hearing of the opinion of Professor Carew, refused further comment.

[SEE THE SUNDAY ADVERTISER FOR 'THE HAUNTING OF WARWICKSHIRE' BY PROFESSOR EDMUND CAREW.]

'Unfortunately our files on the old Sunday Advertiser were destroyed,' said Miss Collins. 'So we haven't any record of Professor Carew's article.'

'That's the end of the story then?' Drewitt frowned. 'Who the devil was Herne the Hunter anyway? If he originated at Windsor, what was he doing in Warwickshire?'

'All I know is what it says there,' Miss Collins shrugged. She was close to Drewitt now and he could feel her breath on his cheek and see her lipstick which seemed very dark in the dim light of the basement.

'But it isn't quite the end of the story,' she went on.

'What else'

'Don't know whether or not it's relevant.' She produced another clipping.

'This was a year later almost to the day. In fact, the first of November 1953.'

He blinked at the faded newsprint.

DEATH OF WARWICK UNIVERSITY PROFESSOR.
HEART ATTACK WHILE HILL WALKING

Carew?' Drewitt said.

'Read it,' said Miss Collins.

He read.

PROFESSOR FOUND DEAD ON HILLSIDE

Professor Edmund Carew (68) was found dead on the Edron Hill south of Stratford late last night. It is thought that the Professor had a heart attack while hillwalking, a long-time hobby. The police say there are no suspicious circumstances.

Professor Carew was head of the Department of Anthropology at Warwick University, a post he had held for twenty-two years. He was expected to retire next year. He was the author of numerous works on his subject, including *The Culture of the Ancient Britain*. He was a widower and leaves no family.

'I don't know if it means anything,' said Miss Collins, 'but it is strange. Rather a coincidence, Mister Drewitt.'

'Maybe. Not that I understand it either,' he replied. 'Can I have copies of all these items?'

'I'll get them photostated. Isn't it exciting being part of a murder investigation?'

'It's a job.' He sounded to himself almost ill-mannered, which was not his intention. He meant to sound efficient. 'What else have you got for me?'

Miss Collins produced yet another clipping.

'I don't know if this is anything important. Seven years ago: desecration of a cemetery at Lower Duthwaite. Tombstones overturned, some defaced with graffiti – the usual kind of obscenities.'

She said it in matter-of-fact tones, as if obscenity was an everyday occurrence. Maybe it was, to people in cities. Drewitt had seen enough of that kind of graffiti, scrawled upon walls, crude curses against the world. It always made him shiver; something he could never quite get used to. Yet, as a policeman, he should be accustomed to it after two years in the Force. But even though he had now lived the larger part of his life in Warwick, he could never consider himself city-bred. There was something about people born in cities that made him uncomfortable. As if their morals were looser, their attitudes too loose. Especially the women.

'Shall I give you a copy of that too?' Miss Collins asked.

'Yes, might as well.' Harkness had said he wanted to have anything that might be relevant.

'There's one other one. Easter night, four years ago.'

The final clipping.

FLYING SAUCERS IN THE COTSWOLDS!

Reports of objects and light in the sky have come from a number of villages on the edges of the Cotswold Hills.

A villager in Coombe-in-the-Wold, Mr John Vasson, claimed to have seen a circular object and lights in the sky last night over his cottage. His sighting was confirmed by neighbours. The quaint village, on the eastern side of the Edron Hill, is a popular tourist attraction.

Although there were no other reports in neighbouring villages, a farmer, Edward Molsey, of Appletree Farm, Upper Walcombe, reported seeing strange lights on the Edron Hill late last night.

Mr Molsey told our reporter that he had often seen strange lights on the hill at night, although he did not himself believe in flying saucers.

'Don't believe in any of that nonsense,' Mr Molsey said. 'But I seen them lights and I know what they are. They're lights from devil worshippers holding Black Masses up there on that hill.'

Local police had no comment to make beyond the fact that there were probably gypsies passing the night on the hill. As regards flying saucers, Sergeant Haversham of Lower Duthwaite sub-police station said the so-called 'flying saucer' sightings were almost certainly jet fighters from the RAF base at Glynau, North Wales.

'Anything else on that?' Drewitt asked.

'Nothing. Nobody bothered following it up. Probably didn't think it was worth it,' Miss Collins said. 'Of course, it's not so long ago. Might be somebody on the paper who remembers the story. I could ask around . . .'

'No need.' His voice was tense. He wanted to be away from the girl. Always he had shied away from even the mildest form of intimacy with females. Except, of course, his mother. But in shying away, he found he had a concern, a conscience about why he should do this. He should, he knew, be attracted to some women, it was expected of him; his mother would be delighted to see him, as she put it, finding a nice girl and settling down. Certainly she had said he was young, but she was just as certainly looking for the beginnings of his progress towards a 'nice, comfortable marriage' (her words). It hadn't happened, and Mrs Drewitt had to console herself with the belief that he was a late developer . . . weren't there many young men like that in the world? She turned her mind away from any other explanation. As did Drewitt himself. He told himself his career in the police force came first, anything else a poor second. And, anyway, perhaps he had a low sex drive . . . yes, that was a comforting possibility. Anything else, to Drewitt, was unthinkable.

He pushed the chair back and stood up. Miss Collins picked up the small bundle of clippings.

'If I can help you in any other way, Sergeant . . .' she let the words sink in ' . . . I'd be only too pleased.'

'Thank you, Miss Collins, it's constable. I don't think it'll be necessary.' He tried to smile. It came out as a kind of grimace.

She walked with him from the basement to the steps to the ground floor.

'Do you like the cinema?; she said out of the blue, as they reached the main door of the newspaper office building. 'There's a marvellous new flick at the ABC just now.'

Inwardly Drewitt winced at the word 'flick'. Why can't people use the right words? Film or even movie . . . a little too American, the latter. Slang was so ugly.

She went on, 'A horror film, "Carrie", with Sissy Spacek and Piper Laurie. I do like horror films. As long as I'm not on my own.'

Drewitt had never heard of Sissy Spacek or Piper Laurie . . . such stupid artificial names . . . and, while he did like going to the cinema, he liked serious films like 'Lawrence of Arabia' or 'A Bridge Too Far', men's films, intelligent films. And he preferred to see them on his own, undistracted by female company. On the few occasions he had visited a cinema with a women, he had not enjoyed the film. When he had first joined the force, a WPC had dragged him to see a horror film, 'The Omen', talked through the quieter parts of the film and squealed at the horror parts, grabbing his arm very tightly and generally irritating him.

'Would you like to see it?' Miss Collins said, after an expectant pause that had yielded nothing.

He remembered now to be polite. 'I would, but unfortunately this murder case is taking up all of my time. Goodbye, and thank you again for your help.'

Drewitt had his personal horrors and always exerted strenuous efforts to avoid them.

Chapter Ten

Drewitt had that awe of university premises held by those who have never attended one or even considered the possibility of academic life. He accepted that professors and lecturers must be different . . . men of superior wisdom, perhaps unworldly but certainly erudite. The discipline of anthropology was a mystery to him. The previous night he had looked to the dictionary: 'Anthropology – The science of man in its widest sense.'

Not too helpful. This uncertainty as to the scope of the professor's subject added to his surprise on meeting the holder of the chair. James Leaver was a squat little man in a stained sports jacket, woollen pullover and crumpled flannels. He had an untidy thatch of thinning red hair and a broad Yorkshire accent. Drewitt's afternoon appointment was at Leaver's home, an apartment in a street near the university. The apartment block had been built at the turn of the century and stood between a Chinese take-away and a Pakistani grocer's shop. The living-room was bright but untidy, bookcases lining three walls and books stacked everywhere, on tables, chairs, on a considerable area of the floor space.

'Oh, aye, I knew old Prof. Carew,' he replied to Drewitt's first question. 'One of my own teachers, when I was a student. Like him? You had to like one of the folk who helped give you your early passion for your subject. Specialised in the ancient Britons, maybe a bit to much . . . tended to dwell on that, rather than bring in the broader picture. I mean, meself, I got hooked by Margaret Mead, *Coming of Age in Samoa* an' all

87

that. Some of it discredited now but great stuff. Have a sherry?'

'No thanks, sir.'

'Hate the stuff meself. Kind of expected of the professor to provide sherry though. How about a light ale? More to my peasant tastes.'

They shared a can of light ale.

'So this is about that murder at Calderon?' Leaver said.

'Read about that. Nasty. The things folk do to folk. But what's it to do wi' Carew? Been dead for years.'

Drewitt told him about the newspaper cuttings.

'Oh, aye, that would interest Carew. Old Brit. superstition. Funny that he should die on that hill. The Edron Hill. Still, no suggestion of . . . what do you people call it? . . . foul play?'

'I don't think so. It was so long ago. But it was the link with the victim this time, Joshua Gideon, that seemed of interest.'

'Aye, would do. 'Course, I can't help you about Carew. Think I was abroad at the time. But it's this Gideon business you'll want to know about? Witchcraft murder. Aye, well, suppose they might get around to that.'

'They?'

'The witches.' In a matter-of-fact tone.

'You believe in witches?'

'I believe there are folk arounᴅ who believe in witches. Maybe believe they *are* witches. Oh, aye, there'll be plenty of that goin' on. Plenty of nut-cases,' Leaver said flippantly.

Drewitt was surprised at the quick acceptance of the fact and the flippancy.

'Plenty?' he said.

'Plenty,' Leaver echoed.

'Around Warwick. And . . . and the Cotswolds?'

'And the Malverns and the Mendips . . . and every county in England. Not to mention Scotland and Wales.'

Drewitt expressed his puzzlement. 'I've heard there's always been a few of your nut-cases. But . . . how many are you talking about?'

The Professor's brow furrowed. 'Ah, now, it would be difficult to be precise, lad. Maybe in the entire county, twenty or more covens.'

'What?'

'Oh, aye, at least.'

'Witches?'

'Call themselves that. Thirteen to a coven, that's usual. Of course, you might get some bigger groups. Kind of multiple covens, you might say.'

'All these people are witches?'

Leaver smiled and rubbed his hand over his sparse red hair.

'Now, if you mean they've got . . . what would we call it? . . . supernatural powers, then of course that would be just plain daft. Some of them are people that use witchcraft as an excuse for a little bit of "How's your father". You know what I mean. Sex on the side. Some of it maybe a bit kinky. Y'know? Cavorting. Aye, a bit of a cavort in the woods of a night wi' nothing on. Those ones aren't sinister, though you might call them perverse.'

'What about the sinister ones, Professor Leaver?'

He shrugged and sipped his ale, deliberating.

'Well now, there's always been some funny ones,' he said. 'And I don't mean funny ha-ha. Peculiar, more like. Now in Africa, if you want to take Africa, witch doctors are two-a-penny, and some of them seem to have powers. If you ask me, they do things by auto-suggestion. Tell a man who believes in an African witch doctor that the witch doctor says he's going to die and he usually does. Worries himself to death, you could say. So the locals reckon the witch doctor has magical abilities.'

'Yes, but . . .'

'Same thing goes on in Haiti. Voodoo high priests. Houngans. They use drugs on their people . . .'

'But what we want to know is about this country. Here and now. The sinister ones.'

Leaver shrugged. 'Of course, they may be the biggest con-men of the lot. People like Aleister Crowley who claim to have certain powers. He convinced a lot of people he had them. He almost certainly used hypnosis, called it sexual magic. But here and now . . . I just don't know. If you believe folk have a certain kind of power, it's as if you're giving them that kind of power. And, then again, there are people in the world who just might have some kind of ability not given to

89

the rest of us. Trouble is, lad, mostly my kind of anthropology doesn't deal with the here and now. It deals with the past.'

'The dictionary says anthropology is the science of man in its widest sense. Doesn't that include now?'

This drew a tired smile from Leaver. 'Should do, should do. But we've got a lot to catch up on. So half of us are looking backwards at the past, and the other half, if they're looking at today, are looking at primitive tribes at the end of the world. Oh, I agree we should be looking at social anthropology here and now. In the countryside. In the cities. The lot.' Another shrug. 'Maybe there's just not enough of us.'

Drewitt drained his glass and stood. Reluctantly the Professor came to his feet.

'There are some things you might be interested in,' Leaver said, as if he was enjoying himself and wanted to prolong the conversation. Yet his expression was serious.

Drewitt hesitated. Harkness had said, anything that might be of value.

'Yes, sir?' he said.

'Calderon, and the Edron Hill – lot of history there. Strange things are supposed to have happened on the hill. There was witchcraft in the Middle Ages, and it was documented.'

Leaver crossed to one bookcase wall and, hand outstretched, started searching for a particular volume. Finally he found it, an old leatherbound volume, the binding loose the leather stained. He rifled through it until he found what he was looking for.

'Listen.' He started to read. '"The hill called Edron is widely known as a magical place. It is believed that the Druids held their ceremonies there, at time of equinox. And it was believed also that the hill was enchanted, the world of faerie using it for their own purposes, warning off humans or causing them to disappear or die. Many such disappearances and deaths were recorded."'

He flicked through more pages before starting to read again. '"Before there was the name of Calderon, there was an older village under the Hill of Edron, a village whose origins go back into the darkness of unrecorded time. This was a village of strange and devout rituals to the many gods who

90

haunted the early earth, when man was their new-created creature. Thus it was natural that those who fled from the French king and the betraying Pope should seek out this place and pronounce its name as Calderon. Here too they could carry out their mysteries, in a place accustomed so to; strengthening their own powers with those already strong in the soil of the place they dubbed Calderon.'"

'What does that mean?' Drewitt said as Leaver looked up, eyes gleaming.

'Fascination. The French influence. Almost certainly the Templars. Knights Templar. When the King of France thought they were becoming too cocky, he got permission from the Pope to do them in. Accused 'em of devil worship and blasphemy and all sorts of nasty little habits. A lot of 'em were burnt at the stake, but some escaped to England. Hence Temple Bar in London. Named after the place some of them kipped down. And, from this, some of them settled in Calderon.'

'That's all?'

'Remember the accusations: devil worship and blasphemy. Later in the book, in James I's day, they were looking for witches around England. Somebody reported a coven in Calderon. Nothing much was done at the time.' He went back to the book. 'Aye, here it is here: "A justice was sent to Calderon to investigate charges brought to the notice of the King. But the man never reached Calderon, being found dead in an inn near Coombe from the pestilence; which was considered strange as, at that time there was no other recorded outbreak of the pestilence."'

Leaver stopped, still staring at the book. Drewitt, who was sitting again, taking notes, looked up.

'That it?'

'One more section, just here. "In the time of the Witchfinder General, a visit was paid by that individual to Calderon. There was no outcome of this visit and the Witchfinder General concentrated his activities in the south and the east and never, but that once, came again to Calderon. There were those who, when the man himself fell from high office, said of him that it was in Calderon that he sold his own soul to

91

Lucifer and, from that time on, hunted innocent souls into Hell on behalf of his Master." That's it.'

'What's the book?'

'Oh, it's pretty old. The original was probably written at the end of the eighteenth century. This is a Victorian reprint. Funny title. *Darkness in the English Shires*, author our old friend Anonymous.' Leaver replaced the volume in the bookcase. 'Those are the only references to this part of the world. That was Eddie Carew's book, incidentally. His field, you might say.'

Drewitt shut his notebook and stood for the second time.

'Sure you won't have another beer?' Leaver said.

'No, thank you.'

'If I can be of any more help, lad . . .'

'I'll let Superintendent Harkness know.'

'You do that, you do that. An' good luck with your investigation.'

Night. And darkness. And a gale rattling the roofs of the city of Warwick. Rain slanting down from blackness into blackness.

Drewitt, in his own room (at the time still living with his mother), one up in the semi-detached, thinking about Harkness spending his second night in Calderon. Rather him than . . .

And he turned back to working on the report he would present to Harkness the next day, when the Superintendent came back from Calderon. Funny report. One minute, he felt like laughing . . . load of old rubbish . . . another minute, he felt a cold fascination. Tinged with horror, maybe. He shook his head, as if to rid himself of the horror. Shouldn't be anything like that, in this business. It was a murder case and, if he wanted to get into the CID, he would have to accept the routine of such an investigation. Maybe there would always be horror . . . a slaughtered human being would never be anything but an ugly sight, the proof of the horror that man can mete out to man. Something to which he would have to become accustomed. As Harkness obviously had.

He finished his report, re-read it, making some minor adjustments, and then stared out of his window at the sodium lights of the suburban street. He had forgotten to draw the curtains of his bedroom and now it seemed as if he could not be bothered to rise and do so. There was a kind of comfort in the yellow modernity of the lights, far removed from the suggestions of medieval mysteries of which he had been writing. He then became aware of a dry, sour taste in his mouth, a physical manifestation of the feeling of horror. He must get himself a glass of water.

The telephone rang.

It had been installed in his room when he had finished his police training and joined the Force, so as to avoid disturbing his mother.

It rang again with mechanical persistence.

He stood, crossed the room and lifted the receiver.

'Harold Drewitt here.'

At first there was a sound almost like a sigh, air at the other end of the line, followed by a crackle of atmospheric distortion.

'Drewitt!' he repeated his name.

Then the voice, low, harsh, from the back of the throat.

'Harold?' Familiar, and yet the voice seemed unknown to him.

'This is Harold Drewitt.'

'You've been very busy, Harold. Working for Mr Harkness.'

'Who is that?'

'A friend.' Did he imagine a throaty laugh?

'Who are you and what do you want?'

'Oh, I want many things, Harold. But just now I want to remind you that you were born in Calderon.'

'What the hell is this all about?' He was conscious of his own voice rising in pitch.

'This is what it's about, Harold – hell. Hell and betrayal. You were born among us. That counts for something, whatever you may think. Your father was one of us. That counts too. You'd be surprised how much.'

'I . . . I don't know what you're talking about.' He was aware of a kind of weakness in the uncertainty of his tone.

93

'Keep away from Calderon. Keep away from the investigation of Gideon's death.' The voice was even and unemotional. 'Not that your presence would change anything. But because you were one of us, you should stay away.'

'Is this some kind of a threat?'

'Oh, no. Simply . . . good advice. Because of your father also. You see, Gideon was one who went off on his own. And when he came back, look what happened. Because he tried to interfere. Leave it to Harkness. We can handle him. We need him. Yes, we need him . . .'

'Who is this?'

The line went dead. After a moment he replaced the receiver, feeling cold and puzzled. But mostly cold. He went over to the window and stared into the street. It was pitch black. All the sodium street lights had gone out. All he could see was his own reflection in the glass.

Chapter Eleven

His mother said: 'I don't know anything about what your father did in Calderon!'

She had turned away from him and was staring at the floral design on the living-room curtains, a middle-aged woman, her body held unnaturally tense.

'What did the phone call mean? "He was one of them"? That's what the man told me,' Drewitt said.

'How do I know what a phone call means? Didn't you ask the man?'

'He hung up.'

'Well, then . . .'

'He didn't give his name either.'

'I never did like those kind of phone calls. Where they won't give their name.' Running from the subject.

'Do you know who it was?'

'How am I suppose to know that?'

'Do you?'

Hands twisting with irritation. 'No, of course not!'

He went over and took her arm firmly. As he turned her around to face him, she winced. She was wearing a dress with short sleeves.

'Harold, you're hurting me.'

He let go of her arm and was surprised to see that a bruise, the size, imprint and colouring of a grape, had appeared.

'I remember,' he said. 'I remember my father used to go out alone. Several nights a week. And you didn't like it.'

She was staring at her arm, a wounded expression on her face. 'You hurt me. Look, I'm bruised.'

'Answer me!'

'Of course he went out. He went to the inn. For a drink. He . . . he always liked his sup of ale.'

Drewitt shook his head. 'No. I always knew when he went to the inn. It was the other times. When you barely spoke to him. And . . . and I remember once, you said . . . you said to him something about stopping it. Stopping seeing them . . . whoever "they" were.'

'I don't know what you're talking about.' Said with defiance, but her face was white, bloodless.

'Stopping what, Mother, stopping what?'

'Nothing! What are we talking about?'

He persisted. 'You know. I think you know. For God's sake, this is to do with a murder investigation. You know something . . .'

She went to the fireplace, seeking warmth, and then after a moment turned to face him.

'Why ask your mother? What do I know about that man who was killed? Why don't you go and ask his girl friend? One of them. Lives here in Warwick. Jennet Agram.'

Drewitt had heard the name somewhere. 'How do you know about this . . . this Jennet Agram?'

'Oh, everybody knows about her. People know. Ask anybody.'

He wouldn't forget the name. Jennet? Funny name. To be looked into. Meanwhile, there was his mother.

She went on: 'Anyway, how could I know anything about a murder investigation? This was all years ago. Eleven years since your father was killed. In an accident. What could that have to do with . . . with a murder that happened a week ago?'

'Was my father one of them?'

'One of what?'

He realised that, although she was facing him, her eyes were elsewhere, seeking something they could not find.

He took a deep breath. 'A witches' coven,' he said.

She tried to laugh. Without much success.

'Superstitious nonsense!'

'Was he?'

'It's stupid.'

'Is that why we left Calderon when he died?'

'We left . . . left because there was nothing there for us.'

Then he remembered something. From the past, his past. A picture in the mind from back there. The aroma of a paraffin heater under a stone wall. The figure on the cross staring down. And outside, beyond the coloured saints on the stained-glass windows, the street lights of Warwick, a thin film of snow lining the pavements under the lamp posts. First winter in the city, so different from the village. And now he was in the ill-heated church, candles clashing with the light from unshaded Osram bulbs, casting strangely distorted shadows on flagstones. Only the minister and his mother and himself. And another – yes, old Uncle George who was to be his godfather but didn't last long as he died three months later.

'You had me baptised in the church here at the age of twelve. Why?'

'You . . . you hadn't ever been baptised. I . . . I wanted you to be. It was something we'd just never got around to before.'

'Never got around to? Or was it because my father objected? Didn't want me baptised.'

She was irritable now. 'I don't know whether he did or he didn't. It just . . . hadn't been done. I wanted it done. That's why.'

She held out her arm, staring at the bruise which was deepening to a dark purple.

'It's all right,' he said. 'Just a bruise. I'm sorry. But you have to realise . . .'

'What have I to realise?' Still not looking at him, preoccupied with her arm.

'A man was murdered in Calderon. It could be linked with the past. You have to answer me. Do you know anything about witchcraft cults in the village?'

She said nothing, but shook her head violently, as if to dissipate anything she might know.

'Was my father one of them?' he said yet again.

At once she looked tired, exhausted, weary, all the words for a kind of surrender.

'I never believed in it,' she said. 'I never could understand how he believed in it. I told him, I never believed in it. Lot of nonsense. But he wouldn't listen. And . . . and at first I thought it was like a club. Or like the Masons. Something like that. But in the end, I knew it wasn't.'

She was pacing in front of the fireplace now, her brow furrowed as she seemed to be trying to remember. Yet, he thought, eleven years wasn't so long. It shouldn't be so difficult.

She went on: 'He said once it was like a religion. Called it something else, not witchcraft. I remember because I said to him, "How can you believe in all that silliness?" Like pumpkins and old women on broomsticks. What witchcraft meant to me.'

She was silent for a moment now, as if uncertain as to whether or not she should go on; whether it was sensible to go on.

'Yes?' he said expectantly.

'That's when he said it was like a religion. Only . . . only more so. That's what he said. *More so*. Something about having . . . power. I laughed at that. He was a farm labourer. What kind of power was that? I asked him. He got angry then. Said I didn't understand. I said, "Then tell me, make me understand. Take me with you. Or else leave them." I gave him an ultimatum then: take me or leave Calderon, leave these people.' She stopped pacing and faced her son. 'He went very pale then. I remember being surprised that someone could go so pale, so quickly. And . . . and he said he wanted out but he didn't think they would let him go. I said that was silly, it was a free country . . . all that. He promised me then we would go. He would tell them . . . at the next . . . next meeting, he would tell them.'

She drew herself erect, holding her body rigid. He realised then she was trying to stop herself from shivering, and was not quite able to do so. Both her hands shook.

'I think he did,' she said. 'The only thing was . . . three days later he had his . . . his accident. And he was dead.'

Before nine o'clock the next morning Drewitt went to the office assigned to Harkness. It wasn't a big office, but to compensate for its size, it had been scrubbed out and refurnished. There was a large desk behind which stood a comfortable high-backed swivel chair; in front of the desk, two other upright chairs, a filing cabinet and a small side table, on which were glasses and a jug of fresh water. The room had a large window with venetian blinds, open, and a view of the police car-park one storey below.

As Drewitt entered, a policewoman was placing several large files on the desk.

Drewitt knew her, a slim, smart women in her early thirties, blonde hair pinned up, and only a suggestion of lipstick on her lips.

'Hello, Harry. You working with him?'

'For now.'

She nodded. 'He phoned. He's coming in some time this morning. God knows where he is.'

'I know.'

'Big deal. In his confidence, are you? Anyway, he wants everything ready. Forensic and autopsy reports, photographs, scene of crime officer's report, and all the interview reports. Also sandwiches laid on for lunch, beef or ham but not cheese, and a pot of coffee. A real wait-on hand and foot merchant, this one! And I'm to be his secretary. Next thing he'll want my knickers down.'

'I wouldn't do too much wishful thinking,' Drewitt said. 'He's a good copper.'

'So they say. They also say he's brute of a man. I knew a WPC in London worked with him. Seemed to enjoy using rough stuff to get what he wanted. And, if he didn't, he blew his top – and anybody else's within shouting range!'

She arranged the bulky files on one side of the desk. 'That's it then,' she said. 'Done all he wanted. Can't blow up on me now. Thing I don't understand is, he gets here day before yesterday, and he wastes two days before getting down to all this.'

Drewitt said smugly: 'I think you'll find he's already had a quick look at that lot. Now he'll do his homework properly. But I wouldn't think he'll have wasted his two days.'

'She went to the door and grinned. He didn't like her when she grinned. She said: 'I know what you're on. Bucking for permanent CID, eh? You'll be lucky!'

She shut the door noisily behind her, leaving him staring at the files on the desk. He took his own report, now in a plain file, from under his arm and placed it beside the others. It seemed thin in comparison. He had written his name and the word 'Calderon' neatly on the cover.

He was tempted to sit down and start going through the files. After all, he was working on the case. Why should he not study these files? Except that, with his luck, Harkness would walk through the door and find him sitting there, reading. At the least it would be embarrassing. No, not something he should do. He contented himself with standing at the side of the desk and flicking over the top file. It was the 'scene of crime' photographs.

The top one was a long shot showing the body sitting under the tree. That was exactly what it looked like: a man sitting under a tree. Drewitt had to look closely to see the handle of the pitchfork. And the man's chest was dark. The next photograph, taken at a much closer range, showed the darkness to be blood. From the throat downwards, shirt and jacket were soaked in blood down to the waist. Then various shots from various angles. And then a close-up, showing the head and the throat and the trunk of the tree behind. So close that he could see the rough, dark texture of the bark. And the prong of the fork entering the throat just above the adam's apple.

But it was the face that caught his eye. Of course the mouth was open . . . it would be as Gideon choked and struggled to breathe . . . the tongue could just be seen, protruding, and a gout of partially congealed blood surrounded it and spilt over on to the chin. A thin trickle of blood ran from one nostril. Above the nose, the eyes stared straight ahead. Drewitt would have expected them to be wide open in horror but this was not so. The eye stared straight ahead, expressionless, almost serene in their sightless gaze.

A memory came to mind. A sense of *déjà-vu*. An old memory.

His father, driving the tractor across a field. It had struck a boulder, so he'd been told, and his father had been thrown off. And then the tractor had tipped over on to its side and his father's body. Crushing, almost severing the body at the waist. His father had lived for some minutes and should have been in agony. But, it seemed, there had been little pain. The man lay staring at the sky, and in his eyes there was the same serene look as in those of Joshua Gideon. The eleven-year-old Harold had been there. He ran in a panic across the field when the tractor tipped and then went over.

He remembered.

Staring down at his father. The blood was crimson on the grass and on his father's lips. And finally, after some minutes, his father had died. Unable to speak but with his eyes open.

The same look.

Drewitt shut the file, suddenly feeling hot, phlegm rising at the back of his throat. He went to the window and looked down at the car-park, breathing heavily. He stood for some minutes, allowing his stomach to settle and his temperature to return to normal.

He waited.

Somewhere, a clock chimed half-past nine.

He's coming from Calderon, Drewitt thought. Probably won't leave until after breakfast. So he won't be here until after ten. Maybe even later. Why should he wait around here for an hour or so? He went out and down to the canteen. He hadn't had breakfast, not that he felt like eating, but he drank two mugs of tea, sitting alone at a corner table. Then he was joined by Gibbs and Mason, off night beat and red-eyed.

Some people get lucky, working plain clothes,' said Gibbs.

'He's jealous,' Mason grinned. 'So am I?'

'I hear Harkness came and went. Off back home for a break before he even started.' Another of Gibb's legends.

'Not quite,' Drewitt replied.

'Aw, come on. Left you in charge, eh?'

'You live in a world of your own, Gibbs.'

'And I wish he'd keep it to himself,' said Mason, yawning.

Gibbs scowled. 'If it wasn't for me, you wouldn't know what's going on.'

'If it wasn't for you, I wouldn't care.'

101

Drewitt left them still squabbling and went up to Harkness's office. He knocked.

'Come!'

Harkness was back. He sat behind the desk, dark lines under his eyes, a mug of coffee in his hand. He looked tired. Detective-Sergeant Stevens was standing at the side of the desk. Harkness looked up at Drewitt.

'I'll get to you,' he said, and turned back to Stevens. 'I want the incident wagon back in Calderon. Six DCs and maybe a couple of uniforms. And yourself. We go through everything again, from the start.'

Stevens said: 'We did a pretty thorough job last week. All the statements are there and . . .'

Harkness cut in incisively: 'And you found nothing. All right, I'm not getting at you or Chief Inspector Blakelock, but I'm in charge now and we have to crack this one.'

'Excuse me, sir, but we have one lead. The gypsies were only a few miles south . . .'

Harkness's glare silenced him. 'Gypsies. Travelling people. Whenever you've no lead, blame the travelling people. The nearest of them were in camp ten miles away.'

'I suppose they could have come over to Calderon . . .'

'Why? Motive? Let's go to Calderon and stick a pitchfork in somebody? And put wee corn dolls around the body, for fun? I know travelling people. They don't go looking for more trouble than they've got. There's nothing to connect them. Also, everybody in both the Calderons has gone dead stum! Why? Because they know one of their people did it, that's why. So we start looking for that character. And for his tie-up with . . . witchcraft.'

'All right, sir, you're probably right about the gypsies. But don't you think this witchcraft business is a lot of nonsense?' said Stevens. 'Maybe to confuse us. I mean, nobody believes in witchcraft today.'

Harkness kept glaring at him. 'You don't believe in witchcraft Stevens. I don't believe in witchcraft. But it doesn't matter a tuppenny toss, Sergeant, whether or not *we* believe. What matters if the character who stuck that pitchfork into Gideon's throat, *he* believed! Now, get everything organised. We're going into Calderon again this afternoon.'

Eyes averted, Stevens went out.

Harkness turned to Drewitt.

'My report's on your desk, sir.'

'I've read it. Good. Worthwhile. Background stuff. Interesting about Professor Carew's death. Have to check that one. Also confirms they believe in the old witchcraft business. Important. As I said to Stevens . . . *they* believe, that's what counts. And this Agram woman . . .'

'You want I should go and see her, sir?'

'No, think I'll do that myself.'

Drewitt had not mentioned the anonymous phone call he'd received the previous night. He did so now. Harkness frowned.

'Does it worry you, lad?'

'No, not really.' He couldn't conceal the hesitancy in his voice.

'Well, it worries me. They know you in that place. In Calderon. And they know where you and your mother live. I don't like that. I think it's time you went back on the beat.'

'But, sir. I do know Calderon.'

'And I'm getting to know it. After two nights.' He stared straight ahead and, it seemed to Drewitt, he shivered. Then he seemed to pull himself together with some kind of effort.

'Aye, you've been useful but you're off the case now. Oh, don't worry, I'll put in a good report for you. But I don't want the liability of worrying about one of my own men being got at. Thanks, lad.'

Drewitt hesitated. 'I would like to go on.'

'I wouldn't like you to. So that's it! Better get your uniform on and report to the duty sergeant. 'Bye.'

It was as quick as that. One minute he was on the case, the next he wasn't.

That was Constable Drewitt's experience of the Calderon murder case.

Braden 1988

Chapter Twelve

They'd finished half a bottle of Scotch, sitting facing each other in Braden's room. Drewitt had of course done most of the talking, his voice growing hoarse and small droplets of perspiration gathering on his brow.

He'd told his story, Braden reckoned, as truthfully as he could. All the events. Excluding, in the main, his own feelings and emotions. These Braden could only guess at. Though draining the last dregs of whisky from his tumbler, he believed those guesses would be valid.

There was something feminine in Drewitt's manner, a precision, a neatness of gesture, an uncertainty, not usual in a police inspector. Also, he moved with a lightness surprising in so tall a man. He'd lived with his mother until he'd reached the rank of sergeant and then determinedly had moved into his own apartment. And come out of the closet? As far as a police officer could come out of the closet. Which wouldn't be very far. And everything, of necessity, with the utmost discretion. None of this had been said, of course, but it was there to be seen by the perceptive. And Braden had always considered himself perceptive. Not that all this mattered. It had no obvious link with the twelve-year-old murder.

'Could I have a glass of water?' Drewitt said. He'd finished his whisky. 'Too much alcohol seems to lead to a kind of dehydration .'

Braden brought him a glass of water which he drained. When he had finished, he looked wearily across at the journalist.

107

'I've told you everything I know. I hope you'll not bother my mother again?'

'I'm sure I won't. And you've been a great help,' Braden replied.

'I don't see how. I was taken off the case. And . . . and a few weeks later Harkness had his breakdown, and he was off the case. Oh, Blakelock tried to carry on, but there were no real leads. The case died.'

Braden forced a grin. 'I suppose I wouldn't be writing this article if it hadn't.'

Drewitt didn't return the grin. His face assumed, if anything, a mournful look. 'It's all so long ago. I sometimes think, what does it matter? And then I remember something else Harkness said, that last day.'

'What was that?'

Drewitt rubbed his left hand over his eyes, trying to remember. 'He . . . he asked me what I thought the law was. I told him, the rules for running society. He said, maybe, but it's something else too. A mouth, a great maw, always wide open to consume the breakers of the law. And our job was to feed that mouth. It was always hungry for felons, lawbreakers . . . sometimes even innocents who accidentally got in the way. And he said, that was just their hard luck. That's why, once a man has been convicted, it's so difficult to get him out of prison, even when you find it's certain he's innocent. It's just his bad luck, and if he does manage to prove he's innocent and gets out, we pay him money to stop him howling.'

'Cynical way of looking at it,' Braden said.

'That was Harkness. Better, he said, that ten innocent men go to jail than one villain goes free.'

'He should have been the Chief Constable of Manchester! Or some other big city. They get away with saying things like that.'

'Anyway, what does it matter? He's gone now.'

'Harkness is dead then?'

'He was very ill just after. I'm supposing he is dead. Something happened to him in Calderon . . .'

'What happened to him?'

'Oh, his strength was just . . . just sapped. Drained away. You know, they found him sitting at his desk, weeping. Complete nervous breakdown. Of course the other business before Calderon . . . the Swanson business . . . that couldn't have helped.'

Drewitt stood up and looked at his watch. 'Better go. Just as well I'm off duty, I'm pissed as a newt. Got enough for your story now then?'

'Some of it. Need more.' Deliberately casual.

Drewitt, swaying slightly at the door, said: 'Not many more places to go. Could look up that old stuff I found at the university. Leaver is still Professor there.'

'I'll bear that in mind. Of course, there is somebody else I could talk to . . .'

'Who would that be?'

'Jennet Agram.'

He'd found the address in the phone book. After Drewitt had departed, he ordered a pot of black coffee. He drank two cups and, settling on the bed, slept for two hours. It was late afternoon when he drove to the address in the book.

Darkness was falling but the street was still alive with children. Running, shouting, playing out their games, they ignored the few passing cars, recklessly risking life, limb and the nerves of the drivers. It was a council estate, good of its kind, with green spaces between the houses. Each contained four separate flats of four or five small rooms. The estate had the usual drawbacks: an amount of sprayed graffiti on bare walls – youths' gang symbols, exhortations to impossible sexual activities, and personal messages and name calling; an amount of refuse on the streets, though not in excess; and some unkempt small lawns between others that were minor miracles of the art of the amateur gardener. Not too far away, on the horizon, stood a gasometer.

The door was at the side of a house halfway along the street. Which meant she occupied the upper floor. There was a neat plastic sign under the doorbell: 'Agram'.

No initial, no indication of whether or not there was a Mr whatever. He rang the bell.

There was a heavy thumping sound, footsteps on wooden stairs. The door opened and a small female child stared up at Braden. Perhaps not so much stared as glared. Ten or eleven years of age, with very blonde hair, she was neatly dressed in a skirt and woollen pullover.

· Braden said: 'Hello.'

The child did not respond to him but, steadily gazing on him, called, 'It's a man, Mum!'

'Coming!' A woman's voice from above. Then more footsteps on the stairs, and Jennet Agram faced him.

'Yes?' she said, not unpleasantly.

He explained he was from the *Comet*. She was in shadow, but he could make out she was a tall, well-built woman.

'The *Comet*?' she said. 'Oh, I never read it. I don't take out subscriptions to papers, nor do I have anything to advertise in them. However, if I have been chosen as the winner in some competition with a large financial reward, I'll be glad to accept the winnings gracefully.'

She had a sense of humour, he decided and was pleased. So far no one he'd interviewed had a sense of humour.

'I'm afraid you haven't won any competition,' he said. 'Actually, I wonder if I could talk to you?'

'You are talking to me.' She spoke in quiet, almost cultured tones, with only a bare suggestion of an accent, and that suggestion more of Somerset than Warwickshire.

'My name is Braden. Eric Braden. I'm writing an article on the Calderon murder,' he said. 'I believe you knew the victim, and was hoping you might talk about it to me.'

She showed no sign of surprise. 'That was twelve years ago. Hardly news today.'

'It's for a series on unsolved murders.'

'I don't think I want to be involved in sensational journalism,' she said.

'I hope it won't be particularly sensational,' Braden persisted. 'Although it could become that if I discovered the identity of the murderer.'

'Indeed it could,' she said. 'You would undoubtedly be hailed as the new Sherlock Holmes. Well, I suppose you're only doing your job. You'd better come up.'

110

She turned to the child. 'Go and see if Isobel's in, and ask her mother if you can stay there and play for a while.'

Pleased, the child nodded and ran around to the front of the building.

'Pretty girl,' said Braden. 'Yours?'

'One and only,' she said, and indicated that he should follow her up the stairs. Halfway up, she stopped.

'I suppose I should ask you for identification. What do they tell you on television? Never let a strange man into your house?'

At the top of the stairs, a solitary electric bulb hung from the ceiling. Braden presented his Press pass to her. She gave it a cursory glance.

'Come into the living room,' she said, opening a door on her right.

Braden said: 'I won't be disturbing your husband?' And at once felt he shouldn't have said it.

'I'm not married,' she replied, and ushered him into a small square room.

It was untidy. A pram stood beside a sofa, a doll on one of the two armchairs, an uneven pile of magazines on a table beside a 14" television set. There was no fireplace, but two storage heaters and an electric fire, which was on. A shelf where a mantlepiece might have been, held some snapshots, framed and unframed, and various souvenirs. Not the usual kind of souvenirs. There were two African masks in dark wood, slit eyes gazing vacuously into the room; an odd kind of primitive doll, also possibly African . . . or perhaps Asian (a fertility doll?); a small, ornate Indian elephant; and a strange wooden wheel with spokes and protruberances.

The woman saw this his gaze was on the round object.

'It's a Buddhist prayer wheel,' she explained. 'I like it. Would you take tea or coffee?'

The taste of black coffee was still in his mouth.

'Tea would be fine.'

'You don't mind a mug?'

'No.'

She went out, returning some minutes later, carrying two mugs of tea and balancing on one a plate of biscuits. He took a mug, accepted a biscuit and sat on one of the armchairs, facing her. And now, for the first time, he could study Jennet Agram, while she offered him small talk about his job on the paper and the type of articles he wrote. At that point, while he studied her, they seemed to avoid talking of Calderon and the reason for his visit.

She was in her early forties, a big woman, not fat but big-boned, large-breasted, with wide shoulders. She was dressed in a kind of caftan but this was pulled in at the waist by a thick, ornate belt which showed some of her figure, emphasising she still had a waistline, and one of which she had no reason to be ashamed. Her hair was dark and tied back into an approximation of a loose pony tail. But it was her face that was her most striking feature.

Braden had covered beauty contests, interviewed female actresses and so-called beauties but, for all her size and air of carelessness, Jennet Agram's face was one of the most beautiful he had ever seen. Never mind she was in her forties, forget the crow's feet creeping around the eyes, the face was, in its own way, perfect. High cheekbones created a slight slant to the startlingly green eyes. The mouth was full and Braden told himself, sensual to say the least. The skin was fresh, pale except around the cheekbones where there was a healthy flush, a tinge of pink. The green eyes, too, were frank and intelligent.

'You'll have interviewed Inspector Drewitt,' she said suddenly.

'Yes. Well, I suppose he's one of the few surviving police-men who was on the Calderon case.'

'One of them. He doesn't approve of me. Not that he would say anything to you. Very careful about slander, Harold Drewitt would be. But of course he considers me a . . . a professional lady. Yes, that's how he would put it. A profes-sional lady. Not that it matters, but he'd be wrong.'

'What exactly are you, Miss Agram?' Braden heard himself say, and was vaguely surprised at a kind of insolence in the question.

She did not, however, appear to resent it. 'What am I?' she replied pensively. 'I suppose, a mother . . . unmarried, but I don't mind that. I prefer it. Quite common nowadays, isn't it?

112

Oh, but I'm other things too. Before you ask your questions, shall I surprise you?'

'Please.' He felt pleasantly relaxed.

'It's a small vanity of mine. And I suppose you'll want to know about me anyway.'

And Braden found, to his surprise, that he *did* want to know about her.

'I'm a country girl, from outside Wells. Somerset. My father was a farm labourer, like Josh Gideon. Perhaps, therein lay the attraction. But I was a clever country girl. Went on to grammar school. That was not expected of me.'

Braden gave what he thought was an encouraging smile. The grammar school seductress, he thought.

'I was, of course expected to marry a local . . . preferably a farmer. My father thought that would be a step up in the world. I disappointed him.'

'By not marrying a farmer?'

'By not even putting myself in the market place. I went from school to London University.'

He must have shown his surprise now, and openly. She gave a broad smile revealing large, white teeth.

'You . . . you graduated from London University?'

'Yes, I read Ethics and Moral Philosophy. Graduated with first class honours. I like telling it. People are always surprised. At me, living here, I suppose.'

'I can understand that. Why aren't you . . .'

'Doing something better? Depends on what you consider better. After London, I went to Oxford to do a Ph.D. But by that time I was getting restless. I never finished the Ph.D. I took advantage of certain bursaries and went off around the world. Oh, not studying, just living. And observing. but that's my little bit of vanity satisfied. You want to know about Gideon . . .'

Oh, certainly, he wanted to know about Gideon, but not yet. He wanted to know more about Jennet Agram. There might well be another story here. He said so, but momentarily he felt awkward.

'I suppose I wanted to learn about certain things that were not on the academic curricula,' she said.

'Like what?'

'I stayed in Haiti for a time. Wanted to know about voodoo. Not the little displays put on for tourists. The real voodoo. I studied for some months with a houngan. That's a voodoo witch doctor.'

'Yes, I know,' he said with a certain smug satisfaction. She wasn't going to have it all her own way, he told himself.

'Of course, it's nothing to do with the witchcraft business at Calderon.' She hesitated then. 'At least, no more than any form of witchcraft has to do with any other form.'

'You're interested in witchcraft?'

'If you mean, did I kill Gideon, no. But interested . . . well, we'll come to that, shall we? Where was I? Haiti. Yes. It was a sad, cruel island. That was during Papa Doc's reign. I grew tired of that. Moved on. Went to America, north and south. Ended up in Brazil. Have you ever heard of macumba, Mr Braden?'

'I'm afraid not.'

'Macumba. Damballah. All forms of voodoo. Fascinating. After Brazil, I crossed the Pacific to Japan. Couldn't get into China at that time, so I went to India. Nepal. Where the prayer wheel came from. I liked Nepal. I was there for over a year.'

'Doing what?'

'Studying Buddhism. In a lamasery.'

'A kind of Shangri-la?'

She was amused. 'Not in the least! It was cold, cramped, and rather dirty. But it was worthwhile. Eventually I came home and settled here. I can't really remember why I picked Warwick. Yes, I can. This was my aunt's council house and she was ailing. I came to nurse her. Anyway, I didn't want to go back to Wells. My mother was dead and I never really got on with my father. He was disappointed because I didn't marry that farmer, I suppose. Eventually my aunt died and they let me take over this house. It was all I needed.'

She sat now with a small smile on her face, waiting for him to speak.

'After all this round-the-world travel, you were content to settle here?'

'One can read and study anywhere. As long as the library facilities are available.'

114

'You are still studying?'

'I *am* still studying.'

Braden was still puzzled. 'Why particularly these . . . these esoteric studies, Miss Agram?'

'Because I am perhaps what you are looking for, to explain something of this murder case, Mr Braden. Not that I can be sure who killed Josh, but I'm the second best person to come to. The first would be Superintendent Harkness. But I'm certainly the second.'

'Because you knew Gideon?'

'That might be of help, but not so much. The real reason is, I'm a witch, Mr Braden.'

Chapter Thirteen

For a brief moment Braden thought he'd misheard her. Then she smiled again and he knew he hadn't. He tried to dismiss her statement lightly.

'It's a term thrown about easily.'

'Oh, but it's perfectly true,' she insisted, the smile still there.

'You . . . you believe in that kind of . . . superstition?'

'Believe it? Know it! Know all about it.' The green eyes were fixed on him. 'What's the expression? "Things I was taught at my mother's knee"? Such a good way of putting it. Oh, it has other names today: sympathetic magic, homeopathic medicine. I rather like being called a witch.'

She hesitated then, a mild frown on her face, and said quietly: 'A white witch, of course. That's important.'

'There are other kinds?' Braden said, and realised how naïve that must sound.

There was no smile on her face now. 'Others? Oh, yes, there are others. But you really want to know about Gideon, don't you?'

Braden nodded. 'Anything you can tell me.'

There was a sad smile on her face now. 'Poor Josh. Not a choice piece of work, but he was a powerful man. A man of power, you might say.'

'You loved him?' The moment the question was asked, Braden realised the answer was important to him. As if he might be jealous of the answer and of a man twelve years dead. He thought, How very stupid. Why should I feel so? He'd barely known the woman for twenty minutes. And then

117

he looked across at her – eight, perhaps ten years older than he was, and yet she could stir in him emotions that he did not want to analyse; emotions that made him forget his own recent problems; made him forget Judy; perhaps made him forget why he was here, sitting in this box-like room in this dowdy council house, alone and in thrall to this woman. Stupid. Stupid and ridiculous, and yet it was so.

'Loved Gideon?' Jennet Agram replied with a throaty laugh. 'No, no, I didn't love Gideon. Only one man in my life I ever really loved. It wasn't Gideon. With Gideon, it was the power attracted me. I suppose. Oh, I *was* attracted. And I was a free woman. The child, she wasn't born then, so I was even freer'n I am now. A free woman, Mr Braden. Not a professional one like Drewitt thinks. Never that. If I liked a man, then, if there was no harm, I pleased myself, I did. And if they brought me presents in those days, fine. If they didn't, also fine. Long as I liked them. And if they liked me, and there was no harm, no grieving wife at home, salting the soot of the fireplace with her tears . . .'

The more she talked, the stronger the Somerset accent, the more of the farm girl appeared and the honours graduate faded. And then came back.

'Of course, I was no Emma Bovary. Wouldn't marry. So I had the reputation of being the local *femme fatale* . . . or, to be less polite, one of the district bicycles. Still have it. And me well over forty. Flattering, eh?'

'As it should be,' Braden heard himself say.

'Then I should be living in a penthouse, in London, Paris, New York. Hardly a council house in Warwick, East. But I'm getting away from Gideon, aren't I? Poor Josh! For all his power and ambition . . . and he had those in plenty . . . he couldn't see further than his own narrow horizon. He was a country man with power and could have been . . . oh, big in a city, maybe even in another country. But his ambition wouldn't let him see his way out of Calderon. It was why he was killed, Mr Braden, because he wanted Calderon for himself.'

'What does that mean, wanted Calderon for himself?'

'He wanted the control. The others had it. You asked about other than white witches. They're there in Calderon, you see.

118

The followers of the left hand path. The old differences. Good. Evil. With Gideon, because I admired the power, I tried to wean him away from the left hand. I told him so much he could do, away from Calderon. On the right. A power for good. But always he would go back to Calderon . . . You know why, Mr Braden?'

'Tell me.'

'Because it's deep there, in Calderon. A deep evil. And old. God alone knows how old. I could feel that, the few times I went there. Frightened me – oh, yes. The age of it. Back, so far back, before history, back to the beginnings of man. Something planted deep there . . .' She fell silent, staring at the blank television screen, almost as if she'd hypnotised herself.

Braden found himself held by all she was saying. With anyone else, he might have listened politely, telling himself he was listening to nonsense . . . even if on a grand scale. But not with Jennet Agram. She believed and she conveyed her belief. She carried him along with her.

Then, at once, she shook her head, as if to waken herself, and turned back to Braden.

'Not a nice place, Calderon,' she said, her tone now deliberately light. 'But Gideon would have it was the place he wanted to . . . to what? Conquer? Control? Win? I told him he didn't have a hope in hell, and that was the place he was at. But he was also a male chauvinist pig.' The laugh again, deep-throated. 'Wouldn't listen to me. The mere woman! Wouldn't listen to anybody. Had to try, have his day, make his onslaught. Had to be slaughtered.'

She stopped for a second and then said bleakly: 'Well, he was. And they drove a pitchfork through his throat.'

Braden took a deep breath. Now *the* question. 'Who are they?'

She turned to face him and it was as if her face had been erased. Oh, the features were still there, but barely so. Dim. Fading. And obscure. Expressionless, emotionless. A voice chanted a reply.

'Adonai and all the others would now . . . Tifareth, Yesod, Geburah the basilisk, Malkut, Kether and the rest. But the regions are different, those of Baal and Beelzebub, himself,

119

Lord of the flies . . . there in that swamp that is Calderon so many may linger. For it is one of the entrances to the other region . . .'

Her features cleared and he could see her eyes were shut. As if again she was in a trance and not in control. He moved to lean forward and grab her shoulders then hesitated. Was it dangerous for her if he did so? Was it some kind of epileptic fit where one must guide but not attempt to force the victim?

And then her eyes opened and she said, 'Don't concern yourself, Mr Braden. Sometimes one is vulnerable to attack. But it doesn't matter, if one has the strength and knowledge to combat it. As I have.'

'Those in . . . in Calderon?'

'Whoever they are,' she replied, 'and I couldn't tell you who, they are simply there.'

'And they killed Gideon?'

'And they killed him. Because he threatened to take over from them. There! If I can't give you names, I can give you cause. Reason.'

She sat up erect then. 'Would you like some more tea? Another biscuit?' So casual now. As if she'd been discussing the respective merits of two supermarkets. Or perhaps, considering her academic achievements, the relative abilities of two lecturers. That brought another question to him.

'With your degree . . . why don't you finish your PhD? You could easily get an academic post.'

'Oh, yes?' She lifted the teapot and, leaning over, refilled his tea-cup. 'Can you see it? Ethics, moral philosophy and witchcraft. I'd be dismissed as a madwoman. A heretic. Plato and Montague Summers? Aristotle and the alchemists? I might get by with a little homeopathic medicine, provided I don't clash with the GPs, but for the rest, it wouldn't work. I'd be a terrible embarrassment to the dons of Lady Margaret Hall.'

'Then . . . then why did you do it? Why go? Why take your degree?'

'Because I had to learn as much as I could. Of their philosophies, of my own . . . of all that was within me. I'm still learning.'

'But how do you live?'

120

The deep laugh again. 'You're concerned for me, Mr Braden? How good of you. How do I live? There are certain allowances. For the child . . .'

'From the father?'

'Oh, goodness, no! He doesn't even know she exists. Nor will he. Unless . . .' she hesitated. 'Unless it would be good for him. But I don't think it would. No, I meant the child allowance. And I do a little tutoring. My daughter and I don't need much to live on. Also . . . sometimes . . . I *help* people. Not for money.'

'How?'

'How do you think? I have certain talents. I can cure a migraine, heal a diseased wound, give some ease and comfort when it is there to be given.'

'You mean, witchcraft?'

Coolly now, with firmness, 'Certain remedies. Some taught to me by my mother. She was a great woman. No education, no university degrees, no knowledge of philosophy – she would have thought Heraclitus was some kind of disease of the elbow. Yet she might have agreed with him that reality is transitory, and that every object is a harmony of opposite tensions. She lived almost all her life in a cottage outside Wells, yet she was a healer known to everyone in Somerset.'

'And you tell fortunes?' The moment he said it, Braden regretted it.

She showed no sign of anger. 'I don't tell fortunes. And if I could, I wouldn't. Not for anything.' She gave a small shrug. 'Sometimes I give advice. As I see it. Sometimes it helps, sometimes it doesn't.'

She refilled her own cup now, in silence, then looked up at Braden. 'You want me to demonstrate something to you? Prove I'm a witch. What should I do? Levitate to the ceiling? A little telekinesis perhaps? Move an object without touching it? Bend a spoon? Is that what great power is reduced to in the twentieth century? Bending cutlery? Give you a love philtre to make your Judy come back to you? Isn't that what witches are supposed to be able to do?'

She took a mouthful of tea and then a deep breath.

'No! I will do nothing. I am what I am. That's all. You can believe or not. Your privilege. And I will think no less of you for your disbelief.'

Then they were silent. He drained his teacup, thinking. Something was there, at the back of his mind, just out of reach, and it was worrying him. He tried to grasp the thought and it moved away. Elusive. Or an illusion.

He broke the silence: 'There's nothing more you can tell me about Calderon, and the murder?'

'No, I'm sorry. I probably haven't helped you, except in telling you why he was killed. Even that may not be satisfactory. Never mind, I'm sure you will write an intelligent article. Even for the *Comet*.'

He acknowledged the compliment. 'Thanks for that at least. And for your time.'

He rose, finding himself reluctant to go, but with no excuse to stay longer.'

She rose too and showed him from the room. In the small hall, he found another question.

'Is there anyone else connected with the case I should talk to?'

Her face again became solemn. 'I don't know whether I should suggest it or not. He . . . he may still be a sick man. Very probably. Not easy for him to remember. If he can remember . . .'

'Who would that be?'

'Harkness, of course.'

The four walls of the hall seemed, for a fraction of a second, to turn around on themselves.

'He's still alive?'

'Oh, yes, he's alive. In a way. Went back home to Glasgow. He has a daughter there . . . she must be about my age. She looks after him.'

'You have his address?'

'Somewhere. Of course, I haven't seen him since . . . since the case. Twelve years ago. Nor have I contacted him. But for some reason, I kept his address.'

'Could I have it?'

She didn't reply but went into another room, the bedroom, he presumed, and came out a few minutes later and handed him a slip of paper.

'I've written it down for you.'

'I'm very grateful, Miss Agram.'

'Yes. Well, promise me, if you come back to Warwick, you'll come and see me.'

It would be an easy promise to keep. He wanted to see her again, although he wouldn't have been able to explain why. Perhaps some lurking personal fantasy.

'Tell Mr Harkness I was asking for him. And then come and tell me how he is. I had . . . a great respect for him.'

'Yes, of course I will.'

They shook hands quite formally. Or was it as the French do – a greeting and a farewell. One up for the French.

It was only when he was driving back to his hotel that he realised what it was that had worried him, back in Jennet Agram's living room. A tiny thing, but it was her demonstration of some kind of power, despite her seeming refusal to do so.

What was it she'd said? He tried to remember the exact words.

'. . . *give you a love philtre to make your Judy come back to you* . . .'

He had never spoken of Judy, never mentioned her name, said nothing about their separation. Yet Jennet Agram knew.

He found his hands were shaking and forced himself to grip the steering wheel tightly.

Chapter Fourteen

Four o'clock in the morning. He awoke, heart pounding, pyjama top damp with cold sweat. He pulled himself up out of sleep, fearful that the dream might be real. And then he lay back, staring at the ceiling trying to remember the fast dissolving nightmare.

Jennet Agram had been there, large and dominating, face appearing and disappearing, changing to that of Judy, but so much more than Judy . . . that part he hadn't minded . . . he had been about to make love to the Jennet/Judy figure who was lying on her back, semi-nude, waiting for him. Then, before he could reach the recumbent body, other shapes surrounded her, forcing him away, tugging and dragging at the woman. They were faceless yet he knew them for what they were. The denizens of Calderon. Unreal. Shadow bodies, with no faces. And turning away from the woman, they grasped him and were pulling him towards . . . towards a tree in a meadow. Then somehow Drewitt was there, standing staring down at him, and shaking his head.

'Another pitchfork murder. We'll never solve it.'

The pitchfork was through Braden's throat yet somehow he was still alive.

And the dream went on, deeper and deeper into horror and into sleep. He could no longer remember what had happened, except for the struggle up to wakefulness. He stared at the ceiling, patterned by the reflection of street lights through the crack in the curtain. The patterns formed faces and figures. Looking at them one way, there was an old man gazing at the centre light. Another way, a woman's body, an erotic shape, ample and naked.

Jennet Agram.

The woman had achieved a firm hold on his imagination. Even invading his dreams. But then the whole business was invading his dreams. A twelve-year-old murder clouded and distorted by superstition. Even Jennet believed in witches, believed she was a white witch. Underlying all her education, her worldliness, primitive concepts inherited from her childhood were still strong. A strangeness.

Time to think about something else, in case he fell back into the dream. He had to admit he was afraid of falling back into the dream. Think about the coming day. About meeting Harkness. He would drive to Glasgow after breakfast, arrive mid-afternoon, and present himself unannounced at the address Jennet had given him. Better not to phone and ask to see the man. Too easy to put him off, refuse an interview, get rid of him. With the excuse that the old man was too sick to see him. Better just to arrive.

He'd phoned the paper on his return from the interview with Jennet Agram, and spoken to Jordan.

'You're going to Glasgow!'

'Glasgow. Scotland. On the Clyde. You've heard of it?'

'Very funny. What the hell are you going to Glasgow for?' Jordan, typically irascible.

'To interview Harkness.'

'Who the hell's Harkness?'

'The Scotland Yard man who was on the case.'

'Oh! That Harkness. Thought he was dead.'

'So did I. But he's not. He's alive and living in Glasgow.'

'He must be mad. Look, this series is taking up too much of your time. Wish to hell you'd never thought up the idea in the first place!'

'I didn't. You did.'

Jordan coughed at the end of the line. 'That's neither here nor there. Anyway, it *was* a good idea. But the time it's taking, you could write a book. All right, go to bloody Glasgow. Dig up this Harkness character. But get it over quickly and get the thing written. To hell with a series. That

126

would take you to kingdom come to do. Just the one article. And then you can get on with something else.'

Braden's heart sank. What new concept had the editor's infertile brain come up with?'

'What would that be?' he said.

'How should I know? Wait! Yes, there is something. Fertility pills and the incidence of multiple births. That's always news. Call it . . . "Baby Pills for Big Families". Paper could offer a thousand quid to the first family to have octuplets. No, wait, ten grand. Hardly likely to happen. Another angle: what happens when the Chinese get hold of fertility pills. The earth would be swamped. Over population. Good angle. Makes the paper seem intelligent . . .'

He was going on and on. Braden thought, That's my one laugh for the day. Jordan in full flood became almost surrealistic. And Braden wanted his dinner.

He cut in. 'Bye, Mr Jordan. See you after the baby boom.'

He'd hung up then and gone to have his dinner. At least he'd been spared one horror later. Jordan hadn't intruded on his nightmare.

He breakfasted at seven-thirty, packed and paid his bill, warning the receptionist that he might be back in a day or so.

The Ford Escort was in the car park at the rear of the hotel. While he was loading his luggage in the boot, he noticed the flat tyre. At the front, on the driver's side. He swore under his breath, surveying the tyre with dismay. 'All things doth conspire,' he thought.

'Nasty one, that!' A nasal voice from behind him.

He turned to face a tall, thin man in his thirties, face pitted with blemishes and hollows, as if the skin had been ravaged by smallpox. Despite the seeming tones of sympathy, the man's lips were twisted into a smile that held all the elements of a sneer.

'I wonder how it happened?' Braden said, suddenly certain that damage had been inflicted upon the tyre.

'A nail, mebbe. A slow puncture. Hold you up, do it?'

'Where's the nearest garage?'

'That'll be Holbrook's. Not far. Show you, if you like. You gonna drive with it like that?'

127

Accepting the offer of guidance, Braden drove the car slowly, the man sitting in the passenger seat.

'You're lucky.' he said. 'That happen on the road at seventy miles an hour, you'd be dead. Could happen too.'

'I suppose it could always happen. If one is unlucky.'

'Surely. 'Course, there's luck and luck. An' if you don't concentrate, it could happen again. Hired car, is it?'

How the hell did he know that? 'Yes, it is.'

'Never know with hired cars.'

Braden drove the car, bumping and leaning to one side, into the forecourt of a large garage.

'That drive won't have done the tyre much good, eh?' the stranger said.

'Thank you for your time. The garage'll handle it now?'

The man climbed from the car but seemed reluctant to go. A mechanic brought a large jack out and started to raise the car.

'Can you tell me what caused the puncture?' Braden said.

'Do my best, sir, when I find it,' the mechanic replied. 'There's a waiting room over there. Got a coffee making machine too.'

He indicated a small hut. Braden made his way to the hut, surprised to find the stranger was following him.

'Could do with a coffee,' the man said.

'Isn't this keeping you from your . . . work?'

'I got the morning free.'

With a hint of acidity: 'How nice for you. In that case, let me buy you a coffee. A small thanks for directing me here.'

'Very nice of you, I'm sure, mister.'

Inside the hut Braden inserted the requisite coins into the coffee machine, and carried two plastic cups of coffee across to a small bench where the man was esconced.

'There you are, Mr . . . I didn't catch your name.'

'Didn't throw it. Caroon. Hugh Caroon.' Said with an awkward smile.

'Mr Caroon.'

He'd heard the name the day before, from Drewitt. Caroon. From Calderon. Now he was sure the flat tyre was no accident. Yet he determined to say nothing. Caroon would

128

not necessarily be aware that Drewitt had mentioned his name. Let the man talk, that was the thing to be done.

'You here on business?' Caroon said.

'You could say. I'm a journalist.'

'Ah! Reporter, like?'

'Something like.'

The mechanic came into the hut. 'You'll need a new tyre. 'Fraid that one's had it.'

'Yes all right. You can do it right away?'

'No problem. Cost you for the new tyre.'

'Of course. You'll take a credit card? What caused the puncture.'

The mechanic rubbed his cheek. 'Dunno. Wasn't no nail, can tell you that. Ruddy great hole gouged into the rubber. Looks like vandals to me. Be about five minutes more.'

'Fine. Thanks.'

The mechanic went. Braden turned to Caroon who had finished coffee and risen from the bench.

'Vandals,' Braden said.

'Lot of them about,' said Caroon. 'Nasty. Hear they got ways of doing it so the tyre don't go down until you're away and drivin' fast. Like I said, it goes at seventy on them motorways, you're in trouble. Mebbe dead.'

'You have a distinctly morbid streak, Mr Caroon.'

'Newspaper reporter, you tell me,' Caroon said.

Braden ignored the non sequitur. 'Of course, you were just passing and noticed the flat tyre?'

'They say you reporters are always poking your noses into things don't concern you.'

Braden thought, Now it's coming. The threat. Menaces. Whatever. Don't be led into it. Don't even look at him. Pretend you're not listening.

'Lucky you were passing, Caroon. Of course, the hotel would have helped.'

'Even things that happened years ago – always bringing them up again. Getting people all excited about things should be long forgotten.'

'Still, you probably saved me time, showing me the way to the garage.'

'Another tyre could just blow on the motorway. That is, if you go on asking them questions.'

Now Braden turned and looked into the ravaged face of the man. 'Smallpox, was it, did that to your face?'

Caroon coloured self-consciously.

'Or the life you lead?' Braden went on. 'Like Dorian Gray. Without his portrait in the attic.'

'You don't ought to be saying things like that, mister. Like you're asking for more trouble. Bigger trouble. Like burning up on the motorway.'

'I take that as a threat. And puncturing my tyre as an act of vandalism. Shall I call the police now?'

There was no phone in the hut, but he'd seen a phone in the garage office across the forecourt.

'You can't prove anythin'!' Caroon said, on the defensive.

'Maybe not. But maybe the police'll find you have record. Your type always does have a record. Petty larceny, petty theft, petty acts of vandalism . . . always some offence with the word "petty" before it. You've got dirty hands too, Caroon. Get like that when you slashed the tyre?'

Caroon stared at his hands. It had been a guess on Braden's part. A lucky guess. The hands were smeared with dirt.

'I'll be back,' said Braden, and went out. He walked across the forecourt to the office. There was a pay-phone on the office wall, and a tattered phone book. He found the number of police headquarters. As he was dialling, he could see the hut. Caroon came out, and stood staring across at him. He was connected with police headquarters.

'Inspector Drewitt, please. My name is Braden.'

He waited, and looked again across at the hut. There was no sign of Caroon.

'Drewitt here.'

'You mentioned somebody you knew in Calderon, yesterday. Name of Caroon.'

'That was twelve years ago.'

'I'll bet he has a police record.'

'What's this all about, Braden?'

Braden told him. About the tyre. And the threats. And the fact that he was leaving. For the time being.

'Can you prove he slashed your tyre?' Drewitt asked.

130

'No, but I don't like being threatened. And why am I being threatened? They don't like me digging up the Calderon business, I suppose.'

'What can I do? I can pull him in, but I can't charge him with anything.'

'You can frighten him.'

A long pause.

'Yes, I can do that.'

'You should try it. I'll see you next time I'm in Warwick. That'll be soon.'

'Where are you going now, Braden?'

'Visiting. Some distance away. See you.'

He replaced the receiver. The mechanic appeared behind him.

'Car's ready.'

'Do me one more job – check all the tyres. I've a long drive ahead of me.'

He should, he reckoned, have reached Glasgow in six hours. It took him eight. He stopped four times at motorway cafes, to drink black coffee. It was as if he was suffering from lack of sleep. He assumed it was that, and the dream the night before, and the monotony of the motorway. The tyres gave him no more trouble but it was nearly six o'clock in the evening when he drove into Glasgow. Darkness was falling. It was another hour before he found the address Jennet Agram had scrawled on the piece of paper.

Tassie Street was on the south side of the city, a narrow street in a district called Shawlands. Solid four-storey red brick tenements were perched on the beginnings of a small hill. Two rooms, hall, kitchen and bathroom would have been a house agent's description. The one he was looking for was on the top floor and, after parking the car at the kerb and climbing innumerable stairs, he was breathless as he stood in front of the door to the apartment. The name-plate read, 'Graham/Harkness'. Gulping air greedily, he determined to cut down on his smoking, and rang the doorbell.

The woman who answered was in her forties, tired eyes, a tired face, and tired, mouse-coloured hair curving under the chin, a once permanent wave revealing its impermanence. This time, he presented his Press card.

'A journalist,' she said, reading the card. There was only a very mild Glasgow accent.

'My name is Braden. Eric Braden.'

'I see that from you card. Well, you'll not be wanting to see me, so it must be my father you'll want.'

'You're Miss Harkness?'

'I was Mrs Graham, but that was a time ago. Miss Harkness'll do. What do you want to see my father for?'

'I'm doing a series on old murder cases,' he said. Why mention Calderon? Not at this stage.

'There's no point,' Miss Harkness replied. 'My father doesn't talk about his work.'

'I was hoping he might talk to me.'

'Why? You so different from anybody else?'

'It's a serious article I'm doing. History, if you like. Unsolved cases. I think he might enjoy talking . . .'

'Unsolved cases. That'll be the Calderon business. He'll not talk about that.'

'Perhaps you'd ask him?'

She scowled. It was a tired scowl. 'You don't understand, mister. He doesn't talk because I'm not sure he even remembers.'

A voice called from behind her. An old voice.

'Who is it, Lizzie?'

Before she could reply, Braden said very loudly: 'A Miss Jennet Agram gave me the address.'

The voice came back, even louder. 'Who the hell is it, Lizzie?'

Reluctantly she replied, 'A man from a newspaper.'

'From London,' Braden added, even louder. As if the distance might impress the voice: 'Want to interview you, Mr Harkness.'

'Nothing to bother about, Father!' Lizzie Harkness called angrily. And then her voice dropped and it seemed as if she was gritting her teeth to control her anger. 'I don't want him upset, Mr Braden, I don't want him upset.'

'I've no intention of . . .'

She cut in on him. 'I do not want Calderon brought up! Not at all. So I must ask you to leave.'

'Don't you think your father is old enough to make up his own mind?' Braden insisted.

'What do you know about the state of my father's mind? That's the trouble. He *is* too old. In his mind.'

The voice came again from the depths of the apartment. 'Did he say Jennet Agram? Let the man come in, Lizzie. Tell him . . . tell him . . . come in . . .'

'That damn' Calderon business nearly took his mind away from him!' she hissed. '*Did* take his mind away for a long time!'

'Show the man in, Lizzie!'

She wasn't strong enough to fight Braden and the voice from within. She gave in gracelessly.

'All right, all right, go in. I can't fight him, not any more. But, if you upset him, you're out. Even if I have to call the fuckin' police.'

The sudden obscenity startled Braden. Lizzie Harkness didn't look the type to swear. Unless, perhaps, *in extremis*. Which the father's insistent voice must have brought on.

'I've no wish to upset him, Miss Harkness,' he said, as she stepped aside. He went in.

A dim hall, the walls, once cream, now almost grey. A carpet and an old-fashioned hatstand, the only pieces of furniture. He was led across this minor wasteland and into what obviously was a kitchen/sitting room. The room was dominated by an even older fashioned black-leaded kitchen range. A kitchen table, three kitchen chairs and, in a corner, under a solitary window, a gas-cooker, a refrigerator and a kitchen sink. A mantelpiece with two small, framed snapshots and a clock. At the right side of the range was a small table on which stood a large television set, operational and in use. On the screen, a snooker game was in progress. Facing the television set and with one side to the fire was a tall, highbacked chair. From the rear of the chair all Braden could see was a hand on the arm rest. It was thin, the skin yellow and parchment-like, ridged with blue veins, and dotted with liver-spots.

Lizzie Harkness stood at the door as Braden went in, and circled around to get a view of the old man. In front of the fire now, he found himself staring into the face of Detective Superintendent Jack Harkness, CID, retired; formerly star of Scotland Yard's murder squad, terror of East End gangsters, indeed of all law-breakers.

Chapter Fifteen

He would be seventy-one, but he appeared much older; he might have been well into his eighties. His face was pale, once heavy features now lean and criss-crossed with a multitude of line, punctuated by brown blotches. There was on one side a slight movement, a nervous tic. The eyes, deep-set under thinning white eyebrows, were pale, each iris with only a trace of blue, on the lower lids, a suggestion of rheum. A face lived in, Braden determined, used, and now out of use. Waiting, if he was conscious of waiting, for oblivion.

The old man addressed his daughter. 'That's him? The newspaperman from London?'

'Aye, that's him.'

'Name's Braden, Mr Harkness. Eric Braden.'

'Superintendent Harkness. Retired. If these army pips-queaks can hang on to their rank, why no' me, eh? Sit down. Bring the man something, Lizzie.'

The daughter, sullenly and with some effort, turned to Braden. 'Would you take some tea?'

'Aw, that's great,' said Harkness with sarcasm dripping from his voice. 'Comes all the way from London, and you offer him a wee cup of tea. Pour out two drams, for God's sake.'

'You're not to drink spirits!'

'Well, give him a big one and I'll sit here and breathe the fumes in.'

'Tea'll be fine,' Braden said. There was a need here for conciliation.

'Away and bring two cups of tea, and a dram as well. For him, for him!'

You can say please,' said the woman. 'I'm your daughter, not your skivvy.'

'Please then. Pretty please.' And then to Braden, 'I'd be better off wi' a skivvy.'

'Then why don't you get one and I'll get on with my life?' So saying Lizzie Harkness turned on her heel and went out, shutting the door loudly behind her.

'Says she's my daughter, so she does,' Harkness laughed harshly. 'But if you ask me, there was a mistake all those years ago at the bloody hospital. Though, thinking about it, she's her mother's image. Maybe she was playing around. The mother, I mean. I was lucky enough to get away from that, many years ago. Well, sit down where I can see you.'

Braden lifted a chair and sat facing the old man.

'So what do you want?'

Braden essayed a smile. 'I'm doing a series on unsolved murder cases.'

'Aye, well, most of mine were solved.'

'Not the Calderon witchcraft murder.'

The old man swayed in his seat. His eyes strayed to the television set.

'You like watching snooker, mister? On the telly. See me, I watch it all the time.'

'About Calderon . . .?'

'Should have been a snooker player, me. Aye. Should have . . . taken it up. When I was young. Should have taken it up . . .'

Braden, being polite: 'They certainly earn big money today.'

A mildly irate reaction. 'Only people earn big money are crooks and politicians. See!'

Harkness rubbed his chin. Stubble under his hand. He frowned.

'Would have been good. A champion. Potting those balls into those pockets. Did I ever tell you, Archie, I once met the great Joe Davis?' A look across at Braden. 'You're not Archie. Where the hell is Archie?'

'My name's Braden, Mr Harkness. From the newspaper. The *Comet*.'

Irritation now. 'Know who you are! Doing a series on unsolved murders. It's just that I thought you were Archie. Friend of mine. Best friend. I think he's dead, but sometimes I think he's here, visiting me.

'Do you believe the dead come back, mister?' This was added in matter-of-fact tones.

'I haven't seen any sign of it.' Braden was being affable now.

'Not an answer. Anyway, I don't think they come back. But . . . but maybe some things do. What are you wanting here?'

Braden tried a new tack. 'I was in Warwick, Mr Harkness, getting material for my article on the Calderon murder. Jennet Agram sent her love.'

His head came round quickly. 'Jennet!'

'She sent her love.'

His gaze was fixed on Braden, unwavering, steady for the first time. 'Aye, Jennet,' he said.

'Interesting woman.'

'Aye, she would be. She was a lot younger than me. Unsolved murders, you say?'

'Particularly Calderon.'

The thin lips became thinner. 'Who said Calderon was unsolved?'

The question took Braden by surprise. 'The . . . the records. No one was ever arrested.'

'Doesn't mean it was unsolved because nobody was arrested. And records, what do they know? Records can be changed. By the people on the edge. After the event, you might say. Maybe that's how the powers that be want it: unsolved. Cosier that way. More comfortable for all concerned, see?'

'In what way, Superintendent?'

A pause then he said: 'Television. All phoney. Keeps you from thinking . . .'

Braden thought, Maybe he's had a stroke. The tic on the cheek, the wandering eyes, could well be the result of a stroke. Or approaching senility. Could be something else too. Some defect in his make-up making him what he was. Or did

137

what he was induce the defect? The chicken or the egg syndrome. Certainly something was missing. He was now one of life's walking wounded. Scars inflicted during the investigation at Calderon? Or some place else, some earlier case? A man who could beat up suspects, wasn't that what he was supposed to have done to Ronnie Swanson? And how many others? Oh, yes, policemen were known to beat up on suspected characters now and then. Especially those who hit out at them. But senior police officers, handling important suspects, knew better. Should know better. Yet Braden could sense, in this old man, there had once been a quality of careless ruthlessness. It was documented over the years, in the papers he'd seen. Not in so many words, but between the lines. Harkness – not above violence; not above dissembling. Harkness, who would never achieve his wish to be Chief Constable because of his erratic record. Caused by the defect of birth, upbringing, environment or occupation. Whatever.

Harkness said: 'Don't think it doesn't happen – suppressing evidence. Not hearing what they don't want to hear. Same thing in reverse when they bring to trial those poor sods who haven't committed any crime. And they still get convicted! I never had anything to do with that. But don't think it doesn't happen. Characters go to prison, innocent as bloody lambs, because the powers that be find it convenient. A cover to hide the truth. See, the truth's not always beautiful or required. Might destroy too many folk in high places.'

He paused, considering the martyrdom of the innocent. Then he peered across at Braden. 'What were you wantin' to know?'

'You know who killed Gideon?'

'Ach, I didn't say I *knew* who killed Gideon. I didn't say that.'

'You said it wasn't an unsolved case.'

'I never had an unsolved case. Oh, maybe there was no conviction in some cases, but I always knew what it was all about . . . always. Even when the bloody mighty were protecting themselves by fixing some poor sod up, I knew, all right.'

'Was it like that on the Calderon case?'

138

'No, no, that was something else. That was the Bascomb case. Years ago. Bascomb was a bloody MP and all. Got off, clean as a whistle. But I knew he was bent as a corkscrew.' He giggled. 'Clean as a whistle, bent as a corkscrew . . . I like that. You mind the Bascomb case?'

Braden had a vague memory. An MP, a junior government minister, a hit and run accident, a dead child, and the minister picked up later with a dented fender on the front of his car and whisky on his breath. Bascomb had been cleared, took up his seat again but, with the grime of an unsolved homicide case still clinging to him, was not adopted after the next election, and faded into the oblivion of forgotten junior ministers.

'Aye,' said Harkness, 'the truth's a bastard for some folk. And when you know it, it drains you. That and other things, they leave your soul dehydrated.'

'You had a breakdown at the end of the Calderon case. Drewitt told me.'

'Drewitt? Oh, aye, Drewitt. A beat man. Constable. Came from that place, Calderon. Why I used him. But I let him off the hook when he started to get threats. I think they were too close to him.' He did not define who *they* were but it was still a moment of clarity. Perhaps a rare moment, perhaps not. Braden pressed on, using Drewitt as a peg.

'He's an Inspector now.'

'That so? Played his cards right, climbed a couple of steps on the greasy pole, eh? He was the type. Make a neat, obedient Chief Constable, that one will. Funny, though.'

'What's funny?'

'In the Bible, they talk about men speaking in tongues. Big con trick, that book. Men don't speak in tongues, they speak in clichés. Greasy pole, bent as a corkscrew . . . all clichés. Like brown boots. Or Inspector Drewitt. The cliché police inspector. All's well that ends well. Which is true. Clichés are all true, see?'

Braden didn't, but said nothing.

'Death,' Harkness went on, 'the final cliché. Under a tree. With a pitchfork. Gideon's end. Why not? Good a way as any. Except it's illegal.'

The door opened and his daughter came in carrying a tray.

'Your tea,' she said.

'Put it down. He can pour,' Harkness growled.

'I'll pour,' Lizzie said.

'Nobody asked you.'

'Nobody ever asks me anything,' she grumbled, setting down the tray on a side table. She started to pour three cups of tea.

'Why three cups?' Harkness said.

'I'm having a cup,' she replied.

'We're talking.'

'So talk!'

'Private conversation,' Harkness mumbled. 'She's never heard of such a thing. Always wants to know what's going on. Never hear any good of herself that way. Cow! Ever since her husband walked out, been like that. Frustrated. Nobody to fuck her. And she's got a black temper, like me. What were we on about, mister?'

'Calderon.' Braden said, sure he must sound weary now.

Harkness laughed. It was a harsh sound, without humour, and ended in a paroxysm of coughing. 'Harkness's last case,' he gasped. 'Why that one? There were others, y'know. Here in Glasgow. You know what they say? "Glasgow's miles better." It's true. Better at bloody murder! I mind, New Year's Day, twenty-five years ago. Murdered kids, two of them, laid out side by side and mutilated. There's stinkin' evil for you.'

'He's not come to hear your horror stories,' said Lizzie Harkness.

'What else has he come for?' Harkness turned on her indignantly. 'What else is there in the whole stinkin' cesspit of a world.'

He said it with such vehemence that Braden shivered. Lizzie, placing a cup of tea in his hand, was aware of the shiver.

'Except for my first arrest, it was all horror,' Harkness went on. 'That first arrest . . . just before Christmas, all those years back. Me on my beat, and a day so cold the brass monkeys were getting embarrassed. Called into Marks and Sparks food department. In there, it was too hot wi' the central heating. Old girl had fainted. Eighty if she was a day. Three woollen sweaters an' a heavy coat on. And a woolly cap pulled down

140

to her ears. Took her into the manager's office to bring her round, being very nice to her. Thought the heat inside had been too much after the cold outside. Until they took off her woolly bunnet – and found under it, on the top of her head, a frozen chicken. She fainted because of the chicken she'd nicked. Me, I said they should let her off, and they did. We were laughing for weeks. She had a record for shop-lifting going back forty years.'

He laughed now and took his cup of tea from his daughter without a word of thanks.

'Did I tell you about Ronnie Swanson? Made the Kray brothers look like fairies. Which one of them was. Swanson was an animal. Sadistic bastard. I put him away and got hell for it, because I hit him a few times. For what he did, he should be been killed, slowly.'

'Would have made you just like him,' Lizzie said bitterly. 'Maybe you were.'

'You know nothing, girl!'

So many families were bound by affection, but how many were equally strongly bound by hatred? thought Braden. And now the daughter was getting restless.

'Tell him what you know about Calderon and let him go.'

'I'll tell what I have to tell him when you leave us alone.'

She glared at him yet again, seemed about to say something, then rose, teacup and saucer in hand, and went out of the room, slamming the door behind her.

Harkness laughed. 'One of the Harpies. You've heard of the Harpies? Sent from hell to plague us. Oh, aye, from hell, that one. But then, I was at the entrance to hell most of my life. Especially in Calderon. Like in Italy. A place called Lake Avernus. Dante said it was one of the entrances to hell. Calderon was another.'

'Tell me about it,' Braden said quietly.

Harkness stared at him. 'I forget things.'

'Tell me what you remember.'

Harkness told him.

Harkness 1976

Chapter Sixteen

Certainly he was twelve years younger then, and didn't look his age. Although he did have the same quick, sharp temper – as he'd shown when he'd first walked into the headquarters building in Warwick and the duty sergeant had at first ignored him. Until he had barked his name and rank, and been ushered into the presence of the Chief Constable.

He'd read the reports of the local investigation quickly, skimming over details. Time enough to acquaint himself with the *minutiae* of the crime scene. And then he'd ordered Constable Drewitt to drive him towards Calderon. He'd left Drewitt standing, open-mouthed, outside the Road Chef, and driven himself in the direction of the two villages.

He'd made up his mind the key to the murder was in the Calderons. The witchcraft business made it local. Anywhere other than a country village, he might have believed it was a red herring, some ornate embroidery concealing the true motivation. In his experience the motivation for most murders was very ordinary. Avarice or jealousy. either expressed in a sudden rage and a striking out in anger, or else the outcome of a long nursed hatred nurtured to a premeditated crime. This one was the latter. All the signs of premeditation were there; the symbols of witchcraft, the body ensconced against the tree, the pitchfork to hand.

All this determined he would go into Calderon at first alone. And not as the investigating police officer but under an alias. That way he would absorb some of the atmosphere of the villages, perhaps hear confidences that otherwise would not be made to a policeman. Village crimes resulted in a closing of ranks among the inhabitants. That was something he understood. No one wants to disturb the equilibrium of the small community; no one wants to betray their neighbour. After all, long after the murder investigation, these people had to go on living in their village. And, if there was some superstitious link through a pagan belief in witchcraft, the silence of those involved would be so much stronger. Years before Harkness had investigated the slaying of a Mason by one of his fellows. A loud silence had permeated the investigation. No matter how serious the crime, one did not betray one's comrades. He rated the witchcraft angle as no higher than that.

He drove for some seven miles before being assured he had missed the turn-off on the main road. He drove back, saw the Road Chef café and knew he had again passed the side road. It was as if the village did not want to be found. Again he reversed the car and drove very slowly. He finally saw the opening to his left and the road sign, almost obscured by an overgrown hedge.

He turned off the main road and drove into Lesser Calderon. On his right, the Episcopalian church, like religion throughout the country falling into a neglected decay. A few rows of cottages and behind them a line of council houses, and then he steered the car around a hundred yard curve, meadow on either side, and into Greater Calderon. More council houses, more cottages, and into what passed for the village green. The inn, The Goat and Compasses' was on one side of the green; another church, the Roman variety, on the other.

Parking the car outside, Harkness took his overnight case from the back seat and stepped towards the inn. As bold as a Glasgow whore in Blytheswood Square on a hot Saturday, he told himself. Assuming, too, another character, that of the commercial on a new territory. A name change, he thought unnecessary. Outside London and Glasgow, Harkness meant nothing.

The inn was an old building, parts of it, he reckoned, sixteenth- or early-seventeenth-century. He stopped automatically under a heavy dark beam over the entrance and noted the sign, 'R.J. MULLION, LICENSEE'. The foyer was low-ceilinged and led to a reception counter, and to the left a door

146

to the public bar. To the right was what appeared to be a small restaurant.

Behind the counter was a squat but broad man, mine host behind his own small altar. Underfoot the wooden floorboards creaked. At the side and slightly behind reception was a narrow staircase leading upwards.

Mine host, presumably R.J. Mullion looked up as Harkness came to the counter.

'What can I do for you, sir?' said, not impolitely, but hardly welcoming.

'A room, mebbe. With bath,' Harkness said.

'No private baths, I'm afraid.' The reply indicating that Mullion was not disappointed at asserting the lack of amenities.

'But you'll have baths somewhere?' Harkness persisted.

'Oh, yes. Five rooms, one bathroom at the end of the corridor.'

'That'll be fine. You have a room?'

Almost grudgingly: 'We have a room. For how long?'

'Two nights should be enough.'

'Enough? For what, can I ask?' Insolence took the place of the grudging tone.

'Business,' Harkness said. 'Commercial. I'm selling a new range of products.'

'Eighteen pound a night, bed and breakfast. We can give you an evening meal at four pound.'

'That'll do.'

Mullion produced from under the counter a battered ledger.

'If you'll be signing the register, sir . . .'

An old-fashioned pen with nib was handed to Harkness. There was an inkpot on the counter. He signed, the nib irritating him with its scratching sound.

'Thank you, Mr . . .' Mullion spun the ledger round and read the name '. . . Harkness. What kind of product would you be selling, sir? Might be able to point you in the right direction for a bit of business.'

'Give me a few tips, eh? Always welcome.'

'Not that there's many outlets in Greater Calderon. Or Lesser Calderon, for that matter.'

147

'There's always a call for my products,' said Harkness with assumed confidence. He'd used this ruse before and carried a small case of specimen products he'd had made up by his sergeant at Scotland Yard. 'Aye, so there is, Mr . . .?'

'Mullion.'

'Landlord?'

'Owner and proprietor. Free house. As I said, five rooms. Also bar snacks and real ale. What exactly are you trying to sell?'

Harkness knew the routine by heart. 'Consider, Mr Mullion, what is always with us? What surrounds us? Accumulates every minute of the day? Even in the fresh country air of these two hamlets?'

'You'll be telling me,' Mullion replied dourly.

'Dirt, Mr Mullion! Dust, filth, ordure. And I bring methods of combatting dirt. Of bringing it to light and sweeping it away. I'm selling the latest in cleansing materials,'

'Uh-huh. Door to door? Like them brush salesmen?'

'Any method of spreading the good word and selling the product, but mostly retail outlets.'

'That'll be the village grocery shop,' said Mullion. 'You'll not sell much there.'

'Ah, but you don't know . . .'

'Oh, I know all right, I own the shop. And I'm fully stocked with that kind of thing. You'll be wasting two nights, staying here.'

'Oh, I don't think so. Thought I'd use your inn as a base. Cover the surrounding villages. And you must let me show you what we have to offer, Mr Mullion.'

'Well, you'll know you own business, but I'll have no time to waste on something I don't need. Still, you'll want to see your room.'

He leaned forward and pressed a bell-push at the side of the counter. 'The girl'll show you up.'

She appeared from somewhere beyond the reception counter; a small, thin girl, straggling hair and deep-sunken eyes, with the look of an anorexic. Sixteen or seventeen, Harkness estimated, and, from the blank expression on her face, possibly simple.

148

She came around the innkeeper and lifted Harkness's suitcase. He made a motion to dissuade her, indicating he would carry the case himself, but she ignored this and limped towards the stairs. The limp was not caused by carrying the case. It as as if she had a deformed hip. Harkness nodded to Mullion and followed her up the narrow staircase.

The room, on the first floor, was low-ceilinged, two heavy oak beams straddling the part of the ceiling above the bed. At the end of the bed, the ceiling sloped downwards to a small window and, to look out of the window, Harkness would have to duck his head down. The bed was large, a great wooden headboard dominating. On the walls were framed cases containing specimens of butterflies and moths, each neatly pinned to cardboard, and behind glass. Below each specimen was its Latin name neatly printed in fading, yellowing ink. Unusual, thought Harkness, but not uninteresting. Especially if you were keen on butterflies. Which he wasn't.

The girl deposited the case at the foot of the bed. She'd led him to the room in silence, and he wondered whether or not she might be a mute.

He decided to find out. 'Nice room,' he said. 'The Hilton it may not be but it's quaint. Hotel busy? Other guests?'

'Nobody else,' the girl said. At least she wasn't a mute. Nor was she exactly sociable. She made for the door, without even waiting for a tip.

'I'm the only one?' Harkness said quickly. 'Of course, I heard you had some trouble here a week ago.'

The girls' brow furrowed. 'No trouble, sir,' she said.

'I thought I read in the papers somebody was murdered here?'

'I never read the papers, sir.' Her face bland and dull.

Harkness shrugged. 'Ah, well, doesn't matter. Maybe I was mistaken. Some other village, eh? Your name's Abbie?'

'Yes, sir.' She was standing at the door of the room now, as if waiting for dismissal.

'Anything to do round here in the evenings?' he asked.

'What would you be wanting to do, sir?'

'Oh, I don't know. A cinema, mebbe?'

'Used to be picture shows in the village hall. Not now. Have to go all the way to Stratford for that.'

'But you have a village hall?'

'It's closed.'

'No village dances? Saturday hops?'

'No, sir.'

'Must be something to do.' He stopped and moved to the window, peering out. On to the churchyard.

'There's the television. Downstairs, sir, in the bar.'

Harkness sighed. 'There's always and only the television. At Armageddon, there'll be television. There's light across the road. The hall next to the churchyard.'

'Church hall,' said the girl. 'Our Lady in the Wold. That's the church. Hall's next to it.'

'So you've two churches? I saw one in Lesser Calderon.'

'Episcopalian,' said the girl, and showed the first sign of feeling; a curling of the lip into a sneer. 'English Church. We'm Romans. Nobbudy . . . or few . . . are English.' And then, for some reason, the sneer vanished and she giggled.

'At least you have a priest and a minister handy,' said Harkness. 'You attend church regularly, Abbie?'

'Most everybody does, sir. Most everybody goes to Our Lady.'

'Most everybody? Doesn't happen throughout the rest of the country. Most everybody there is in bed or on the golf course on Sunday. Calderon must be a very religious place.'

The girl looked puzzled. He was talking of another world. Harkness had timed his next question carefully.

'Did Joshua Gideon go to church like most everybody?'

Only her eyes registered. She blinked. A distant shutting of the eyes.

'Don't know any Josh Gideon living in Calderon,' she said.

'Surely he drank here? No place else in the two villages to have a drink.'

Another blink. 'Don't know everybody drinks here. Didn't know Gideon.'

'Come on, it's a small village. All right, two small villages.'

'Didn't know him,' she insisted. 'Cept maybe by sight.'

'So you knew the victim by sight. Interesting. Did he go to Our Lady like the rest of you?'

'Used to. But then Father Anselm forbade him to come.'

'Father Anselm?'

'The priest, sir. Father Anselm. He's a good man, Father Anselm.' She seemed to like the priest's name, rolling it around her tongue.

'Father Anselm,' Harkness found himself repeating the name. 'You say he forbade Gideon the church? That's unusual. I thought the church was open to saint and sinner alike?'

'Dunno,' said Abbie. 'Maybe he did something. Or said something. You know, you can go to hell for saying some things'

Harkness laughed. 'You mean swearing. Using bad language. I don't think the punishment is that strict.'

She shook her head. 'Not swearing. Not talking like swearing. For saying some other things. That's what I'm saying.'

'Was that why Gideon wasn't allowed in the church? For swearing? Blasphemy?'

'Not just that, sir.'

'Anyway, I thought you didn't even know the man.'

'Because they told us not to know him.'

'Who told you?'

'My uncle. Mullion. And . . . and another.'

'Who?'

'Father Anselm. Told us all. Keep away from the man. So, see I didn't know him but you can't help seeing with your eyes.'

'How long ago was this?'

'Year, Two years. I got to go. I got to be getting back to my duties, sir.'

Harkness chose to ignore her plea to leave. 'Why was he ostracised . . . why were you told to stay away from him?'

'He was bad with girls, sir.'

That was logical. The village ram would be singled out by the priest, the girls would be warned. Still, there was something that made Harkness uneasy. As if the girl, Abbie, was holding something back.

'He was bad with girls?' Harkness echoed the girl.

'More'n that,' Abbie said.

'What more?'

'Father Anselm said he was one of them.'

'One of who?'

'Then. He was one of them demons. You know, demons from hell itself.'

151

Chapter Seventeen

Demons. Or daemons – the antique spelling. Much more sinister, Harkness thought, smiling.

He was sitting at the window. The girl had gone, taking her daemons and a pound tip with her. He was again looking down at the churchyard and cemetery. A mist had risen, only a few feet high, but swirling and twisting around the bases of the tombstones. One of the stone crosses stood at an angle, like the set of an old Universal horror film, circa the early thirties. Any moment now, Frankenstein's monster would appear, lurching among the graves, Karloff in heavy make-up . . . he'd read it took about four hours to put on . . . looking for his bride to be, the as yet uncreated Elsa Lanchester, herself to appear looking like an Egyptian mummy. Below the cemetery became even more shrouded. A case of nature imitating art.

He came away from the window. Despite the mist it was time he explored the village. With a comforting thought: there'd been no council houses in the background of the Frankenstein movies. He put on his rain coat and went downstairs.

There was no one behind the reception counter. But, as he went to the front door, Mullion called out from the bar.

'Going out, Mister Harkness?'

'Thought I'd take a walk.'

'Mist come up. They say the Calderons is built on what was once a marsh. That's where the mists come from. You'd be warmer in here with a glass in your hand.'

'Wee bit early for me. I think I'll just take some air.'

'You'll not be wanting me to have a look at your samples them?'

Framed in the door, Harkness frowned to himself. One moment the man wasn't interested, the next he wanted to see the samples. Or did he want to stop Harkness wandering around the village?

'Thought you weren't interested?'

Mullion came to the door of the bar. 'No harm in looking.'

'I was going to make an appointment.'

The innkeeper shrugged. 'What about now?'

'What about tomorrow morning? Had a long drive . . . want to be in good selling form.'

'Where were you driving from?'

'I wrote it in your register.'

'I didn't look.' Mullion was lying.

'London. How about after breakfast tomorrow?'

'What?'

'For me to try and sell you on our stuff.'

'Oh. Yes, well, if I've got time,' Mullion, grudgingly.

Harkness stepped into the street and walked quickly away through the ground-clinging mist, leaving his car parked outside the inn. He would go on foot and see the village in close-up. He walked south towards Lesser Calderon, the beginnings of the Calderons. Start at the beginning and move forward to the conclusion; only way, in every investigation. He had complete certainty that there would be the required conclusion, no matter what occurred on the way.

He remembered things that he had encountered on the way through other cases. Always he tried to avoid thinking about cases in the past. They were over and done, solved, finished. Malefactors were dead or in prison. A good word, malefactors. Producers of evil. But the evil was always recurring in memory. The slaughtered children in the Glasgow tenement, walls awash with blood. The wife, bisected by the husband, the two parts left in the bath. Two entire families gunned to death in their sleep by the psychopath who simply giggled when the police arrested him. And so many other cases, stretching back down the years. Yet still, in all their reality, returning to him in clear, stark memory.

154

The meadows on either side of the road between the two villages now. The mist still there, like grey cotton wool, knee-high on the gorse and scrub-land. A marsh, Mullion had said, like fen-land where there should be no fen-land. Once, and still perhaps, an unhealthy place.

The Norman tower of the English church rose up ahead of him. Lesser Calderon was the smaller village, an annex, an afterthought. As if some people had wanted to be separated from Greater Calderon, cut off from the main village. First he came to the council houses: dull, uninteresting, practical units for living, boxes in which people could be placed, docketed and left to their own devices – whatever those devices might be. Then he came to the cottages. Not particularly pictur-esque, simply late-nineteenth-century cottages, bricks and cement, aging and crumbling. No oak beams from three- and four-masted ships here, as in Greater Calderon. Artisan's dwellings, that's what they'd be called.

He came to the church and another cemetery. Here, the tombstones were broken and crumbling. Some had fallen over, flat lumps of scarred stone, inscriptions long since obscured by moss and the ravages of weather. Grass was overgrown, uncut, entwined and clogged with weeds; the building itself in a state of decay. A crack on one wall had been crudely shored up. At least one of the stained-glass windows was broken.

The door leading to the vestry was ajar. As Harkness pushed it open, it creaked noisily. He entered, walking over a wooden floor, his footsteps heavy and echoing, a hollow sound. The vestry was untidy and cluttered. A spade and a hoe were propped against the walls; a bag of cement, half-open, appeared to have been dumped in a corner where it had solidified. A noticeboard hung crookedly from one wall. The church notices were yellowing and tattered, some years out of date. Harkness was stepping towards the door to the church itself when it opened and a woman appeared.

'Can I help you?' she said.

She was in her thirties, not unattractive, with a pleasant open face, country-tanned and freckled. There was a sugges-tion of light pink lipstick. Rather "county" in dress, Harkness thought. Whatever that meant. Sensible shoes, a warm skirt and wool sweater, quite expensive, under a coat, mackintosh-type but stylish in cut. A shapeless hat with a brim. Might have had the odd fly for fishing pinned to it, but didn't. The only decoration was a broach, half seen under the coat, and a single string of pearls around the throat.

'I was walking, taking a stroll,' Harkness explained lamely. 'Thought I'd come in.'

'The church is always open,' she said. 'They are supposed to be, aren't they?'

'The minister around?' he said as casually as possible.

'You mean the vicar?' One-upmanship. They don't call them "ministers" in England.

'Aye, I suppose I do. See, I'm a Scot, from way back. Always called the minister in Scotland.'

'Ah, yes, so I believe. Mr Haydock – the vicar . . . isn't too well. A little under the weather.'

Harkness looked about him. 'Like his church, eh? Wee bit ramshackled, you could say. High Church fallen low.'

'It needs work,' she admitted grudgingly.

He stepped past her into the back of the main church – And into a puddle of water.

'Roof leaks too! You'll be . . .?'

'Margaret Campion.'

'And who is Margaret Campion?'

She seemed amused at the interrogation. 'I live at Calderon House. The big house. And you are?'

'Harkness. Jack Harkness. I'm a commercial traveller. Looking at old churches is a kind of hobby. You live at Calderon House, you'll be the laird's wife. Leastways, that's what we call them in Scotland.'

'I would never have guessed,' she said with heavy irony. 'Here we might say "Lady of the Manor". No lord. I'm unmarried.'

'I'm unmarried myself now. I was married once. Didn't like it too much.'

'You preferred old churches?'

He returned her smile. He liked the irony. It matched his own sarcasm, which only came out when he was roused. 'Well, old churches put you in perspective, like. Especially the tombstones – intimations of mortality. The atmosphere gives you time to think. You'll be one of his congregation?'

'As a matter of fact, no. I belong to the other lot in Greater Calderon. But I like to look in on . . . on my people, when they're not too well.'

'A charitable visit?'

'Let's say a neighbourly one. You're not staying in the village?'

'Oh, aye, I am,' Harkness replied smugly. 'Couple of nights. Thought I might use The Goat and Compasses as a base. For my business calls, you understand.'

'I thought it might be out of morbid curiosity. We had a murder here just over a week ago.'

'Yeah, read about it. Maybe a bit of curiosity at that.'

'Interested in churches *and* murders, eh?' Her smile seemed fixed. Could get monotonous. She glanced at her wristwatch. 'Well, I hope you enjoy your stay. I have to be going. If you go through the door at the side of the altar and knock, you'll find the vicar. He should be able to tell you all about the church . . . if he's up to it. As I said, he's not well. I wouldn't stay long.'

'I'll mind that.'

'And I wouldn't talk too much about your other hobby. The murder has upset Mr Haydock.'

'Upset a lot of people,' he said as she turned to move away. 'Girl at the inn wouldn't talk about it. Pretended it hadn't happened. Kind of ostrich mentality, that. Put your head under ground and see nothing.'

She shrugged. 'What do you expect? Like most people who live in small villages, they're close. Tight-lipped. Keep themselves to themselves. Mind their own business.'

'I've always counted murder as everybody's business. It's a social evil – or rather, antisocial. The ultimate act, Miss Campion. The most extreme thing man can do to man.'

'You can't blame them really,' she went on, ignoring his comment. 'It's a small community. Crime is rare for them. A thing like that brings all of them under suspicion. They don't like strangers who ask questions. Why should they? 'Never mind, Mr Harkness. If you get too many icy shoulders, come

157

up to Calderon Hall. I'll give you a cup of tea or something stronger, and an ear to listen, a voice to tell you what I know.'

'And a shoulder to cry on?'

'Perhaps. If you need one. Have a nice day, Mr Harkness.'

She went off among the tombstones to the road. The mist covered her feet and ankles. It gave him the impression she was floating above the ground rather than walking. An optical illusion. Still, she had a trim figure, floating or walking. And a pretty face. He thought some time he might take up her offer of tea and sympathy.

He turned and walked down the centre aisle of the church. On either side, the pews were dusty, some of them chipped and broken. Even the figure on the cross above the altar looked unwashed. Was it deliberate? Christ, the poor carpenter on the crucifix, dying in grime and amid derision. It was a viewpoint. He walked to the heavy wooden door at the side of the altar and knocked.

The reply was faint. 'Come in.'

Harkness went in.

He was sitting in a chair beside an ancient, roll-top desk. Or rather slumped, elbows on the desk, head down. An old man, but not as old as he seemed. Sixty-five passing for eighty, Harkness reckoned. Sparse white hair was combed across a shining scalp. His long thin hands trembled as if in the grip of Parkinson's Disease. The skin was so thinly layered across the tight drawn cheeks that Harkness imagined he could see the bone beneath. The man looked up as Harkness entered. His eyes were yellow where they should be white, the iris of each a light brown, the pupil a needlepoint, the whole rimmed with red, as if he had been weeping.

'Mister Haydock?' Harkness said.

'Yes, I am he. Who are you?'

'A . . . a traveller.' Harkness found himself oddly hesitant. 'Just . . . passing through. In need of information and maybe some spiritual advice.'

A hand waved vaguely in the air, a gesture of futility. 'I don't give spiritual advice. Not any more.'

Harkness was surprised, at the admission of defeat and also at the hopelessness of the tone. There was only one way to treat someone in that state: firmness, even indignation.

158

'You're a minister aren't you? A vicar? Priest of the Church of England? Appointed to attend to the spiritual needs of your parish, and those who're just passing by?'

'Not now. Not any longer.' Haydock made an attempt to straighten up but it only resulted in the shaking in the hands increasing. 'It's over. There is no church here now. A church is its congregation and I have none to speak of. The roof is sagging, the pews are broken. There's mould and mildew on the altar. There's mould and mildew on the priest. And look at the Christ on the cross above the altar. No eyes. Blind and broken.'

Harkness tried a kind of mild jocularity. 'Needs a bit of paint and a carpenter.'

The old man's eyes filled with tears. 'The carpenter is dead.'

'Come on, maybe a wee bit of advertising is needed. Come and join us. Trumpets in the market place . . .'

'And a priest who has ceased to believe in God? What were those slogans in the seventies? God is dead! Yes, I believe that. God is dead, and the people cry for other things.'

'Not dead. Maybe just eased aside. Elbowed out of the way. But he can come back,' Harkness said, and was surprised to hear himself say it. He'd never been a believer. His closest approach to faith had been a kind of open-minded agnosticism in his teens.

'Not that I've ever been sure, myself,' he went on, feeling the need here for honesty. 'But I've always been open to received information. Like I'm open to draughts. As if I might catch religion like you catch a cold.'

Haydock was staring at him, probably not hearing, with a penetrating stare. 'Who are you?' he said. 'One of them come to make sure I'm truly lost?'

'I'm not one of them, whoever they are. That I'm not.'

'You would say that. You would have to say that . . .'

'Right enough. But I do occasionally tell the truth.'

Haydock shuddered. 'Oh, I know what the truth is. Whoever you are doesn't matter, because I know . . . God has gone. But nature abhors a vacuum, so they are going to fill that vacuum. I believe them too.'

He stood, bringing his hand to his mouth, and gnawed at his lower lip until a speck of blood appeared on his chin.

And then, quite suddenly, he started to giggle, like a child with the knowledge of some secret childish joke he was delighted by.

'They're going to do it, you know. They can do it. They can put Lucifer in place of God. Raise him from Hell and put him on the empty throne. Crown him . . . oh, that'll be a coronation, I know it will. I know they can . . .'

He swayed and his whole body started to shudder as if in the grip of an epileptic fit. He would have fallen on to the hard wood of the floor had Harkness not stepped forward to catch him. Then, as the policeman gripped the thin arms through the clerical grey of the old man's suit it was as if an electric shock passed through his entire body and he was forced to jump back, letting the old man slide to the floor.

Chapter Eighteen

They were in the vicarage.

Harkness had helped the old man from the church and over to the building on the other side of the cemetery. It was as ramshackled as the church. Undusted, festooned with cobwebs, the living room was drab and dull, half-empty bookcases around the walls and, at the same time, books stacked in piles on the floor, on chairs and on the large refectory table. The bedroom door was open, showing an unmade bed. The kitchen wherein Harkness went to make tea for himself and Haydock was dim and equally drab; unwashed dishes in the sink, a half-empty bottle of milk and a mildewed loaf on the table. Harkness managed to find two mugs, wash them and, from a box of teabags, made tea for both of them. When he returned to the living room, Haydock was sitting up in a high-backed chair at the table, having regained a degree of composure.

'You're a cynical man,' Haydock said.

'Why do you say that?' He placed a mug on the table in front of the vicar.

'You say you occasionally tell the truth . . .'

'Not cynical, practical. Who can afford to tell the truth all the time?'

The old man shrugged. 'In my calling, one has to try.'

'Even when you're accusing people of raising the devil? Oh, I presume you meant that metaphorically.' Harkness paused. 'Didn't you?'

The old man's hands were shaking again. 'You'll have to excuse the state of the vicarage. I have a woman who comes in

161

to clean for me twice a week, but this week she appears to be ill.'

Harkness ignored the change of subject. 'What's happening in Calderon?'

'Happening?'

'What are they doing to you, Mr Haydock?'

'Not important, what they're doing to me?'

'Then you can tell me.'

Haydock blinked, as if trying to focus on some object in the middle distance.

'It's as if they were sucking me dry,' he said. 'Taking from me all the goodness and mercy they can find. Draining faith away . . . and not only faith but sins as well. Mine. Theirs. It's all one. As if they can use them – each sin – for their own purposes. Weaknesses are sought out. They seek out every weakness. A wilderness of sin. An empty vessel. You see, I know all the biblical clichés! Empty vessels, eye of the needle, turn the other cheek, whores of Babylon . . . Cliché! Meaningless. Nothing left.'

The words came out in a nervous flood of sound, some running together, others broken and indistinct. To Harkness, it was almost meaningless, fragmented sense only. But he had to use what he could.

'Is this what they did to Joshua Gideon? Sucked him dry and then performed the terminal cliché? "And did murder him." The legal cliché.'

Yet again the expression of fear appeared upon Haydock's face. 'I know nothing about that!'

There was another change of subject. 'You know, the Calderons are unhealthy places. Built in a hollow under that damned hill! A swamp at one time. Damp throughout the year. Plagued with flies in the summer. And . . . and other flying inspects. It's very unhealthy.'

'Especially for Gideon! But he wasn't killed by flying insects.'

'Swatted, like a disease-ridden fly,' Haydock said vaguely. 'A judgement for all the sins of the flesh indulged in. "The lecher and adulterer shall perish."'

162

'At the hands of someone wielding a pitchfork? Someone who surrounded the body with fertility dolls and runic symbols?'

Haydock made an effort to pull himself together. This time he managed to focus on Harkness. 'Again, who are you? Why are you so interested in Gideon's death?'

Harkness forced himself to smile. 'Who am I? Nobody. Or mebbe a wee Daniel come to judge. Mebbe just a reader of the more sensational press. Saw the headlines. "Witchcraft in Warwickshire", "Murder Under the Old Oak Tree". Or was it an ash tree? Isn't there something symbolic about the ash tree? "Satan worshippers dancing nude under the full moon". Bound to attract sensation seekers like me. If you know nothing about the killing, who would be knowing?'

'You must not ask questions like that. Things happen here to those who ask questions. Or answer them. Like poor George Numbles. A motor accident, they said.'

'Wasn't it?'

'Oh, yes. But, you see, he was a talker. So there was a real motor accident. Or . . . or you could end up as I have. Empty. Never sleeping, and never awake. In a kind of limbo. Haunted by libidinous dreams. Nightmares that might, or might not, be real. Words that come from my mouth and yet never quite say what I mean them to say.'

'Or else end up like Gideon?'

'Gideon was something else. God forgive me, he may have deserved to die. Who would know? Perhaps the woman in Warwick.' He paused, nurturing the thought of the woman in Warwick. One of his libidinous dreams, thought Harkness.

'The woman in Warwick?' he pressed.

'Agram. Jennet Agram. They say she's a witch. Of course I didn't believe in witches . . . didn't, not then . . .'

'Could she have killed Gideon?'

Haydock's forehead creased. A puzzled look came over his face. 'No, no, that wouldn't be right. No. I would not wish it to be her. But she would know if it was a deserved death.' A glance at Harkness. 'Can death be deserved? Perhaps I deserve to die. Or else to live. Which would be God's greater punishment?'

163

'Isn't it immaterial, since you've decided He may no longer exist?'

'He who sins in the mind is as guilty as if he had sinned in the flesh.'

'And what was your sin, old man?'

Haydock's head dropped. 'Could you absolve me? Or would you be like them, here, twisting and turning the thought in my mind until . . . until I don't know whether or not it is real. So many years ago, was there the thought or the action?'

'And what was the thought, Mr Haydock?'

Irrationally, it seemed to Harkness, the old man became angry. '"The corruption of the innocent", they called it that. One of the greater sins. The corruption of a child. How dare they? I am a priest! I am permitted to administer the sacraments. I would never . . .'

As quickly as it had arisen, the anger subsided, and was replaced by a tearful whining tone.

'I was in a position of trust. I couldn't . . . wouldn't . . . have abused that position. Such a beautiful child . . . but I did nothing. I'm sure I did nothing. How did they find out? That's what I could never understand. It was . . . it was only in the mind. I *think* it was only in the mind. And . . . and I loved the child. No, I didn't! But they took the sin from my brain and . . . and twisted it for their own purposes.'

Harkness looked down at the old man, hollow cheeks streaked with tears, hands trembling, eyes wandering in some past world, some half-forgotten action or emotion. He'd heard confessions like this often; long delayed, pouring out in a flood of guilt and self-pity. Old sins came back to haunt and torment. Where they were real, Harkness had little sympathy.

'Could be worse,' he said coldly. 'You could have been put inside. And when it's a kid involved, the other lags take you apart. And the screws stand by and watch.'

Haydock looked up at him. 'I told you, it was only in the mind. I think it was only in the mind . . .'

'I hope it was, for your sake now. For the child's then,' said Harkness. 'Time I was going . . .'

'No, please, stay and talk, Mr . . .'

164

'Harkness. Nothing more to be got here. I'm going.'

'If you go, I have to sleep . . .'

'But you told me you can't sleep.'

'I pretend, Mr Harkness, I pretend. I can delude them sometimes. Other times, they come in waking dreams. So much worse than nightmares . . . so much worse! Please stay.'

'Sorry.' He wanted to be away now, far from this shell of a man. Harkness could never understand how anyone could get like Haydock: sick of a self-imposed sickness. Or the result of conscience at some past iniquity.

Haydock rallied. He forced himself to sit erect with an effort. As Harkness went out of the vicarage, he heard the priest's voice echoing behind him.

'Goodbye, Mr Harkness, whoever you are . . .'

The afternoon was dying when he came out of the vicarage. Twilight threatened; a damp, still mist-ridden twilight. He walked briskly back to Greater Calderon, a false briskness, a deliberate forcing of the pace. Away from Haydock, a dead church, a dying priest.

It was almost dark when he reached The Goat and Compasses. He hesitated outside the inn, suddenly weary, considering whether or not he should give up for the day. A short first day, he decided, too short. And too much to be done. He looked towards the other church: Church of Our Lady in the Wold, Holy Apostolic Church of Rome. As he stood staring at the building, three figures came out of the inn.

'Hey, you!' The first of the three was speaking. In his twenties, a sallow-faced, thick-set young man.

'You speaking to me?' Harkness said.

'Who else is there?'

'Your two friends? Or perhaps you're talking to yourself.'

'Man's got a big mouth. Could make it even bigger. Like with a swollen lip.'

Harkness remembered all that Drewitt had told him of his questioning of the villagers.

'Now I just bet your name is Caroon.'

The young man was non-plussed. 'How do you know my name?'

165

There was a temptation to say it had already figured in police files as a possible suspect. But then, at this point he was J. Harkness, travelling salesman, and not a senior police officer.

'Heard it around,' he said quickly. 'Somebody mentioned the village bully.'

Caroon flushed. 'Who you been talkin' to?'

'A number of people.'

Caroon glanced at his two companions who seemed in the dim light to be smirking at him. He had to reassert the authority.

'What are you doing here in our village?'

'Not that it's your business, but what's why I'm here – business.'

'He'll be the commercial traveller,' said one of the other youths.

'Sure,' Caroon said. 'An' I've heard all kinds of dirty jokes about them. Commercial travelling, huh! Coming here looking for whores, that's what commercial travellers are like. No whores here, mister. Wasting your time. Suggest you get in your motor and fuck off out of here.'

'I'll bear your advice in mind.' Harkness was cool and polite, and irritating to Caroon.

'I think you should do more than that! Hey, boys, I think we should show him the way out of town.' He looked around. 'That your car?'

'That's my car.'

'That's a nasty dent you've got on the door. Can you not see it? It's just there.'

He went over to the Rover and kicked the side of the door with considerable force. A dent appeared.

'Can you see it now?'

'I can see it. And I don't like it.'

'Could be you instead of the car.' He came back and stood in front of Harkness. 'Come on boys, let's have a bit of fun.'

His two companions moved uncertainly up on either side of him, not as daring as Caroon but not daring to let him down.

'We don't like you commercials. We don't even like strangers in our village. So we're going to do you a favour. Discourage you from staying. Encourage you to go.'

166

Harkness thought how often he had seen this before: violence for the sake of violence. Motiveless, unless you counted sadism as a motive. And always the victim was outnumbered. The question was, how would Caroon start the violence. With fists? With a weapon? He looked at Caroon's hands. Despite his hands the light above the door revealed the cause of the glitter. Rings. Large, heavy, cheap rings. As effective as a knuckleduster. Worn for two purposes: vanity, and as a weapon. The second more important than the first. But he wouldn't just strike out directly, that would be too dangerous for Caroon's kind. There would be something else, a feint, a seemingly innocent move. Harkness knew the techniques too well.

Then Caroon's face broke into a seemingly amiable grin. 'Aw, hell, we're just kiddin', mister. Aren't we just kiddin', boys? Sure we're just kiddin' . . .'

He stepped to the side and put out one arm, as if to embrace Harkness. The arm moved lazily, without apparent deliberation, and his other arm hung loosely at his side. This was the feint. The outstretched arm suddenly moved fast to encircle Harkness's neck. And the other arm came up, fist clenched, rings gleaming.

It was all very fast now. Harkness side-stepped, ducking low, beneath the embracing arm. His clenched right hand punched out and upwards at Caroon's crotch. Caroon folded, like a book closing, mouth open, the first sound being a gasp as the blow forced him to expel air.

The other two youths began to move forward, not to counter-act Harkness's blow, but belatedly to back up their leader.

Harkness followed up his initial blow by standing now and, left-handedly, punched the bowed Caroon on the mouth, a fast upper-cut. Before it connected Caroon expressed the pain of the first blow by screaming. The scream was suppressed by the second blow which uprooted three teeth and forced them back into his throat. The scream became a gurgle. Before the second of the three youths could reach Harkness he had followed the punch through by side-chopping Caroon's head, throwing himself sideways to collide with the second youth. Both Caroon and the youth fell with considerable force on to the surface of the road.

Harkness was left to face the remaining assailant. The youth hesitated, not quite sure of what he was seeing. The policeman struck him twice on each cheek with his open hand. The youth staggered back and Harkness delivered a final blow, a straightforward punch in the face which flattened the youth's nose, causing blood at once to squirt over Harkness's fist and the youth's mouth and chin.

Harkness stood back, surveying the small battlefield, waiting. Was it over, or did Caroon and his friends have more courage than he had estimated?

Of course it wasn't courage but something else. The blade of a knife in Caroon's right hand, flashing in the light from the inn. Caroon rose, blood on his mouth, pain in his eyes. But now, as if a mechanised corps were attacking infantry, he had his steel advantage. The blade.

Harkness judged the distance, and his approach. The knife didn't faze him, he'd dealt with too many over the years. He was simply assessing his methods. One way, Caroon would end up with a broken wrist or arm. The other, he'd be at least unconscious for some time, bruised but with unbroken bones. The former, Harkness decided. Might discourage him permanently from threatening with a blade.

Caroon circled him, knife weaving in the air.

And then came the voice, high-pitched but incisive, speaking with authority.

'Put it away, Caroon! That's enough. Otherwise the man will break your arm, possibly your neck, and I may even help him!'

Chapter Nineteen

The effect on Caroon was electric. He dropped the knife and straightened up, suddenly looking sheepish.

'Just kidding around, sir. Just kidding around.'

'Well, stop it, and go away.'

Harkness turned to face the speaker. Black hair and a black suit, relieved only by the spot of white at the throat, the clerical collar. A Roman collar. Of medium height, the man had a slight stoop and an ingratiating smile. This must be Father Anselm.

The figure confirmed it by introducing himself, hand outstretched.

The policeman grasped the extended hand and found it firm but cold.

'Harkness,' he said. 'Just visiting . . .'

'And not too impressed by your welcome,' said Anselm, nodding in the direction of the retreating youths. 'I am ashamed. They are of my congregation, when they are so minded. Rarely enough, with those ones. But one has to keep trying.'

'Rather you than me.'

'The sickness of modern youth. Delinquency stemming from envy of those more fortunate than themselves. And frustration caused by lack of opportunity . . .'

'I've heard it said.'

'You will not judge us by them?'

'I won't,' Harkness reassured him. Might judge the whole village by the death of Joshua Gideon, though.

'Of course, one had heard there was a traveller in our midst. Villages, you know. Word travels by bush telegraph. As you will gather, I am the priest of this parish. Catholic priest. We also have an Episcopalian priest . . .'

'I've met him.'

'Indeed!' A look of concern came over Anselm's face. 'How is Mr Haydock? Such a dear man, and so unfortunate . . .'

'How so?' Harkness asked, trying to sound as casual as possible.

'His health is not good. And such a small congregation – it must be most discouraging. But then, my people are in the majority in this district. A historical accident. When did you meet Mr Haydock?' The question was slipped in.

'I . . . I visited his church,' Harkness replied. 'A hobby of mine, churches. 'Fraid I'm not religious but the architecture fascinates me. And the atmosphere . . .'

Anselm beamed expansively. 'Then you must see Our Lady of The Wold, my church. Oh, doesn't that sound arrogant? The sin of pride. Our church. You're not a Catholic?'

'Not anything, unless you can count being a supporter of Glasgow Rangers. Which in Glasgow is tantamount to being a Protestant. In fact, I was brought up a Wee Free. The Free Church of Scotland. But I'm sorry, Father, I couldn't live even with that. Of course the word "free" is a misnomer. Its followers are the least free of any religion I know. But I would like to see your church, if you don't object to a half-agnostic, half-atheist?'

'No need for apology, Mr Harkness. Your beliefs are your own affair. Though I might consider you an empty vessel waiting to be filled. Come, let me show you.'

The vestry was bright, the walls appearing to have been recently painted white. Beyond the vestry, it was as Drewitt had said: garish, somehow too bright, as if the paint on everything had a luminous quality. The brown wood of the pews seemed newly lacquered, the finish so light as to be almost red in the light of the electric lights which Anselm had switched on.

170

'We're rather proud of our Stations of the Cross,' he said, indicating the frieze of pictures high on the walls.

Harkness had perfect vision, and he'd been in churches before, seen the Stations of the Cross many times. But, and again Drewitt was right, they weren't like this. It wasn't simply the garishness of the paint; there was something else, in the paintings themselves. Even from below he could see the faces of the figures. There was the Christ-figure, burdened by the weight of the cross, and surrounded and . . . followed by the people of Jerusalem as he staggered towards Calvary. But it was the faces of the people that caught his eye.

They seemed to be laughing, crudely mocking the Christ. Daemonic faces were there, gloating, baiting, giggling. And more. The Christ-figure was crudely depicted, almost obscene in stance and position. It was not quite definable, but there nonetheless.

'Of course, we're aware that some of the painting is . . . different,' said the priest. 'Unusual, one might say. But then, these young, modern artists . . . they have their own approach.'

'Colourful,' Harkness murmured.

'But alive, Mr Harkness.'

'Who is the artist?'

'One of our locals. A talented man but he will go his own way.'

'Not quite the colours of religion.'

'But more like the colours of life, perhaps,' Anselm said. 'Religion is so often drab, dull and dreary. Isn't that so? Especially where you come from.'

'Aye, well, the Church of Scotland and the Wee Frees aren't into ornamentation. No graven images, like. I think it was John Knox who insisted the walls of St Giles Cathedral in Edinburgh be whitewashed. Still and all, you do have a healthy congregation?'

'Most of the people of the two Calderons worship here regularly.'

'Luckier than Mr Haydock.'

'A Catholic district. As I said, a historical accident. Such a pleasant man too, Haydock. Allows himself to get so depressed about it. Not his fault. The conditions that prevail.'

171

Anselm led the way towards the altar. The Christ-figure behind and above the altar was in position. If, as Drewitt had stated, it had once been detached from the wall, repairs had now been effected. Yet the crucified figure too seemed newly repainted and as garish as the rest of the church. Raw colours, overly realistic flesh tones, and the scarlet of blood, bright beneath the crown of thorns and on the side where the spear had penetrated. The expression on the face too was wrong. The mouth was open revealing the teeth, the whole macabre impression being of a wolfish grin. As if the figure was taking a masochistic pleasure in his own torture.

And, amazingly, Anselm could not see this. Or preferred not to see it. Or even, in his own ignorance, attributed it to modern art. Yet to Harkness, a man without religion, it seemed a kind of blasphemy.

He decided to change the subject as casually as he could.

'Was the man who was murdered one of your congregation?'

There was no particular reaction from Anselm. 'Joshua Gideon? he said. 'Why do you ask?'

'Read about it in the papers. Always a bit of a fascination, reading about murder.'

'Indeed?' Cool. Very cool.

'Suppose it's a kind of terminal act,' Harkness went on, as if a curiosity seeker, a reader of the more sensational press. 'I mean, you can't help being interested. Something that always happens to other people. Never to yourself or your own family.'

'We do feel like that here. Not that Gideon had any family. He had been a member of my flock. Rather an unsuitable member. Latterly an apostate. A rebel. An arrogant, immoral rebel,'

'That kind would make enemies?'

'As you say. His moral lapses did not encourage friendship. The man was a lecher. A womaniser. Oh, I know it's uncharitable to speak ill of the dead, but I'm afraid it's the truth. And I fear he incurred the wrath of some . . . deranged husband, possibly. And not necessarily from Calderon. His activities ranged around the county. There were even women in Warwick. Oh, I tried, on occasion, to reason with him. Pointed out the sin of venery was destructive at once to himself and to so many others.'

Anselm paused, gave a deep sigh, and shook his head regretfully. 'You know, he laughed at me. And yet it was as if I was foreseeing the tragedy. And now I can only feel a deep sorrow for the murderer. Driven, I'm sure, to such a terrible act.'

'I heard the murderer surrounded the body with artifacts connected to witchcraft. Of course, I thought that might be a bit of newspaper sensationalism . . .'

'Sadly, it is true, I believe. Not that it surprises me. In this part of the world some – many – of the old superstitions linger. No matter how much one tries to discourage that kind of thing.'

'A kind of blasphemy?' Harkness said.

'In general, a kind of childish hangover from the old days. The grandmothers in so many rural families nurturing what one can only call rustic legends, passing on to the youngers like faery tales. It's harmless.'

'Hardly, in Gideon's case!'

'No, no, of course not. As you say, the thing carried to extremes is blasphemous. But there are vestiges of the older religion, still traces of it around.'

'What religion would that be?' Harkness was deliberately naïve.

'Pagan beliefs. Fertility rites linked to old gods. Cruel beliefs, dealing in human sacrifice and so on. Possibly linked to the Roman Gods brought over when the Romans were conquerors, or even further back – to the Druidical religions. Of course, I'm hardly an expert. Certainly not since my student days. Dear me, you must have read the popular press avidly, Mr Harkness.'

'Suppose it's another hobby of mine, like old churches, murders and reading about them. I read a book recently that said Jack the Ripper was mebbe a Royal personage. Now there's a chilling thought.'

Anselm shook his head again. 'I've never understood the preoccupation of the lay mind with homicide.'

Harkness shrugged apologetically at his own seemingly gruesome interest. 'As I said, easy enough to understand: the

173

terminal act. Steal a man's treasure, he can always get it back. But steal a man's life, there's no returning it.'

'And what of his soul?' Anselm said.

Harkness laughed. 'Oh, that's more in your line than mine, Father. Never gone much on the idea of souls. Can't feel 'em or see 'em. No direct proof of their existence. No fingerprints, for example.'

'You sound like a policeman, Mr Harkness,' Anselm responded, and then changed the subject. It seemed that subjects were easily changed in Greater Calderon.

'Now do look over there. Under the largest of our stained glass windows.'

Harkness followed the priest across the front of the altar and into what seemed like a smaller chapel. But there was no altar here, only an ancient stone tomb on top of which was carved the life-sized figure of a medieval knight at rest, hunting dog at his feet.

'A perfect example of a fourteenth-century sarcophagus,' said Anselm. 'The knight of legend and romance at his final rest.'

Harkness strolled around the bulk of the tomb. The stone was in an almost perfect state of preservation. He commented on this.

'Ah, yes,' said the priest, 'it has been carefully looked after for seven hundred years, by my predecessors and by the people of the village. You see, this is the tomb of Gerard de Champion. He was one of Calderon's earliest, and possibly greatest, benefactors. I suppose, the first Lord of the Manor . . .'

At the side of the tomb, Harkness, suddenly realised he was sweating profusely. The small side chapel was much warmer than the main church. Uncomfortably warm.

'Any relation to the lady who resides at the Manor today?' he asked, loosening his raincoat.

'Miss Campion is a direct descendant. Somewhere along the years the "H" in the name was dropped. A kind of anglicisation. Gerard de Champion was, of course, a French knight,'

'One of the Normans, eh?' Harkness eased a finger under his collar which had become damp with sweat.

174

'No, no, not Norman. I believe he came from the south of France, Provence or thereabouts. Came to this country perhaps as a political refugee . . . they had them in those days too. According to the little we know, he settled at first in London, at Temple Bar, and then chose, or was granted, suzerainty over Greater and Lesser Calderon and lands around the villages for some distance.'

The heat was now overpowering. Harkness felt himself swaying, and touched the tomb to steady himself.

'Are you all right, Mr Harkness?' said the priest with some concern. 'You've gone quite pale.'

'I think I need some air.'

'Of course I'm used to it, but it is rather warm in this part of the building. My predecessor said it was something to do with the old marshes around Calderon. As if heat from some underground swamp had found an outlet under the foundations here. A little improbable, I've always thought. But come, sir, over to my house and we'll have a cup of tea. Or something stronger if you prefer it?'

'I'm awash wi' tea,' Harkness replied politely, the instant image of an emaciated, dehydrating commercial traveller in mind. 'Perhaps another time? I think some air and a return to the inn would be the best thing.'

The bar of the inn was beginning to get busy as he came in. A momentary silence descended as he entered and was duly surveyed by the locals. Having noted his arrival, they then resumed their talk, ignoring him. He went over to the bar and faced Mullion who was serving. But the landlord made him wait some moments while he poured and served several pints of ale before addressing his one lodger.

'You'll be wanting your evenin' meal then?'

'I think just some sandwiches and a pint of beer in my room.'

'As you like. You're lookin' a bit under the weather.'

'I'm all right. Been looking around the village.'

The landlord raised an eyebrow. 'Oh, yes? Find what you were lookin' for?'

'I wasn't looking for anything. Just getting my bearings, you could say. Be out to work tomorrow.'

'Well, you can miss me out,' Mullion said, leaning on the bar. 'Been checkin' over my stock on the shop. Don't need any of your stuff. So you could be movin' on tomorrow.'

Harkness forced a tired smile. 'Anxious to be rid of me?'

'I didn't say that.'

'Well, then, I'll still be using Greater Calderon as my base. You'll send the beer and sandwiches to my room?'

'Directly.'

'I'll say goodnight.'

The room seemed smaller this time. He thought, probably the electric light and the sloping roof made it seem so. It was however deathly cold, a contrast to the church. An ancient gasfire stood in the corner against what had once been the chimney. The clay mantles of the fire were cracked and broken but the gas still came on and provided a measure of heat.

Ten minutes later the girl, Abbie, arrived carrying a tray on which there were three large chicken sandwiches and a pint mug of ale. She placed it on the small table beside the bed and made to leave.

'A minute, Abbie,' he said.

She stopped halfway to the door, a nervous look on her face.

'Sir?'

'Mr Mullion doesn't seem to like having guests at his inn.'

'We just don't get many, sir.'

'You'd think he'd be pleased to have customers.'

She shrugged, disinterested. 'Can't say, sir. Will there be anything else?'

'You could give me a morning call. Say, seven-thirty? What time's breakfast?'

'Suppose it'll be when you're ready for it, sir. You want it in your room?'

'No, I'll be down for it. About eight.'

'I'll tell Mr Mullion. Oh, an' I put a hot water bottle in your bed. Gets cold here some nights.'

'Thank you, Abbie.'

'You're welcome, sir.'

She went, closing the door quietly behind her. He ate two of the sandwiches and, draining the mug of beer, donned his

176

pyjamas and climbed into the bed. He felt exhausted, unusually since it was barely eight-thirty and normally he was never an early bedder. Somehow, too, his time in the village seemed to have passed at speed. It was as if some hours had dropped away, gone missing.

He switched off the bed light. He was in darkness except for a faint light coming around the edges of the curtained window. He lay, waiting for sleep. And then a thought came to him. The room, and sleep, were waiting for him. He felt chilled now and his feet searched for the hot water bottle. He found it, not the usual rubber affair but an old fashioned stone pig. Very hot. He brought it up to within an inch of the small of his back, and gratefully felt the warmth permeate his pyjamas.

He fell asleep easily now. After all, sleep was waiting for him.

And so, he found, were the dreams.

Chapter Twenty

Dreaming.

Going back into the past. His past. A dream of things that were, and in sleep come back again.

So many years ago. How many years ago? Not that time matters. The room and the events will be with him always; maybe the room and the events were there already, before they happened, a kind of foresight, a dread, a fear that this, and so many other events, were bound to happen by nature of his profession . . . either chosen or forced upon him by the circumstances of his life.

The living room, if it could be so called, is barely furnished. A television set and two battered chairs. A second hand folding table, green-baize on top, the baize discoloured and stained. A tin cup and a mug on it, the dregs of some liquid later identified as cheap wine in both, and a tin lid used as an ash-tray and filled to overflowing with ash and cigarette ends. A grate that has seen no fire in years and is stuffed with paper and other pieces of rubbish.

Harkness spends little time in that room just now. A cursory glance and then through into the other room, the so-called bedroom. It lacks a bed. It has two mattresses on the floor. Both are large and one has two sheets and some blankets on it. On the other are the bodies. Two children, a boy and a girl. The boy about six, the girl perhaps four years old. Both are naked or would be seen to be so if it were not they seemed to be dressed in scarlet rags. The rags, on closer inspection, are bloodstained, the stains spread extensively over various parts of the two bodies. The injuries are horrific.

179

Apart from the bodies, the mattress is soaked in blood and there are splashes of scarlet turning to brown on the walls behind the mattress. Harkness tells himself that on a brief examination but does not care to study them too closely at this point. Later he will read the details of the injuries in the medical report and, even then, try to put those details out of his mind, an attempt which proves impossible.

He feels nauseous on viewing the bodies and will feel equally nauseous later, reading the medical report.

A detective constable, kneeling by the bodies, looks up. Harkness doesn't know the man. He says: 'Detective Sergeant Harkness, Murder Squad.'

'D.C. Macdonald,' the man replies. 'From Partick. Woman next door found the front door open. Inquisitive old bird. Came in and found them. Had hysterics and phoned us. Then she had hysterics again. She's still having them next door.'

'Wouldn't you?' Harkness says. 'Whose kids?'

As he asks the question he turns away, quickly, and goes back into the other room. Macdonald follows him.

'Woman called Graeme. Lives here with her man.'

'Husband?'

'Fancy man. Husband lives in the next street. On his own. We've sent for him but he'll be at his work.'

'Which is?'

'Works for Glasgow Corporation Cleansing Department. Seems he's a straight type. But the wife left him for this character, name of Mahoney. Pronounced "Maney". Kevin Mahoney. A nut-case.'

Harkness is conscious of looking surprised. 'You've been busy, MacDonald.'

'Got it all from the woman who found them, Mrs Gogarty. One of those types knows everything that goes on in the district.'

'If only there were more of them, it would make our job a bit easier. If what she says is accurate . . .'

'Been confirmed by the man in the flat below.'

'And this Mahoney, what does he do for a living?' Harkness asks, gazing around the room. The wallpaper is ancient and peeling.

'On the buroo, they tell me.'

'Social security, Macdonald. Always be accurate.'

'And wife beating apparently. But not his own wife – not that he has one of his own. Mrs Gogarty tells us he waded into Mrs Graeme regularly, and the two kids. Once . . . twice a week. Like other couples have sex. Only his foreplay seems to have been black eyes and bloody noses first.'

'You have an interesting way of putting it.'

'Well, it makes you wonder,' Macdonald says. 'Why the hell a woman would leave a seemingly hard working type to live with somebody like Mahoney?'

'The ways of human nature are pretty odd.'

'Maybe she liked being beaten up. They tell me some women do . . .'

'And have we any idea where this masochistic female and her sadistic lover are now?'

'Man downstairs saw them going out in a hurry, a time ago. Maybe three hours before the bodies were found. I've been onto C.R. about Mahoney and alerted all stations about keeping an eye open for them.'

'You'll obviously make chief constable yet, Macdonald. Have you found the murder weapon?'

Macdonald flushes. 'Been a bit busy getting the whole story, Sergeant.'

Harkness walks over to the grate and, bending down, takes out a handkerchief. With infinite care, he lifts something between finger and thumb, wrapped in the handkerchief. It is a knife, possibly the type used by butchers. The blade is encrusted with blood.

'This,' he said, 'might be what you are looking for?'

Macdonald's mouth opens, expressing suitable astonishment. 'How the hell did you see that, Sarge?'

Harkness enjoys the small moment. 'Because I looked. Have been looking, ever since I came in. You would have found it – eventually.'

The knife is carefully transferred to a cellophane envelope. And at that moment Superintendent Ogilvy, head of the city's murder squad, arrives accompanied by a well-dressed man in his forties, one of Glasgow's procurator-fiscals.

181

The bodies are again viewed, Macdonald's account is again rendered and . . .

. . . the scene changes as it can only do in memory or in dreams.

Kevin Mahoney. Arrested at Glasgow's Central Station trying to board the London train. He had dumped the woman after beating her up and taking what money she had. He is guilty as hell. Blood on his clothes. Ogilvy has handed over his interrogation to Harkness. Now, Mahoney sits in the interrogation room and, for hours, blames the woman.

'Wasnae me. She cut them. Her kids. Aye, her.'

Two interrogators work on him, with Harkness watching. He accuses the woman over and over again. Finally Harkness takes over.

'She didn't kill her own kids, Mahoney.'

'Aye, she did!'

'Your fingerprints are on the knife.'

'Mebbe I touched it. Mebbe.'

There is something that gets to Harkness. Reaches out, surrounds him. He tries, as he questions the man, to define this. An aura – if one believes in auras, it could be so described – of evil. The presence of evil. Can such a thing be sensed? Can such a thing even be tangible?

Then, after many hours, Mahoney cracks. 'Aw right! Aw right, I did the little bastards! Aye screamin' and bawlin'. Open mouths, wantin' something . . . wantin', wantin'! Till I wanted to shut them up, an' I did! An' I liked it. Only wish I'd done the bint as well.'

Harkness is expressionless. He listens, apparently without emotion. Inside he feels sick. As if the evil the man exudes is seeping into him.

Later still, they find Mahoney has killed before. Another child. Twenty-two stab wounds. And possibly two women.

Another interrogation. 'See, it's easy,' he says, boasting now. 'Kids. Tarts. Nae problem. Askin' for it.'

The psychiatrist, after examining him, pronounces: 'A psychopathic personality.'

Harkness says: 'To me, he's an evil bastard.'

'No such thing, Sergeant. That's a moral concept. The man is sick.'

'And he's still an evil bastard.'

On remand, awaiting trial, Mahoney is beaten up by his fellow prisoners. Harkness is pleased. Shouldn't be, but is.

Mahoney in the dock at the High Court overlooking the grey River Clyde. A Victorian building. A Victorian judge. He is found guilty and sentenced to life imprisonment. God, Harkness thinks, he could be back on the streets in ten years. If he survives the attentions of his fellow prisoners. They don't take kindly to child killers. Harkness hopes he won't survive . . .

. . . an earlier time. Also in Glasgow. As a beat constable. Harkness is watching as a man is assaulted and kicked as he lies on the ground. The assailant is a large man. Harkness stops him.

'You know the man you attacked?'

'Never seen him before in ma life.'

'Then why . . .?'

'Because I enjoyed it, like. Aye, I did. See him, the wee bastard, I enjoyed it . . .'

His wife, Alice Jean Harkness, *née* Murdoch.

'You're never here! You weren't when your daughter was born. You weren't at her christening. It's a wonder you managed to get to your wedding!'

The usual complaint from a policeman's wife, so he tells himself. And tells her.

'It's the job . . .'

'Others manage to be home more often than you do!'

'I'm doing my job! You knew when you married me . . .'

It's a half-truth. He could be home more often than he is. Jack Harkness, the dedicated crime fighter, is sometimes too tired to go home, he tells himself. Or is it that he prefers not to go home? Home becomes a ritual. Not going home is easier.

And there are other diversions.

The woman is a prostitute. At times she walks the pavement just off Blytheswood Square. But not so much now. Not since they've been trying to get the girls off the streets. She has a room in the Cowcaddens. And a telephone. One of the first Glasgow call girls.

He likes her. She is honest and uncomplicated and she has a good body. To get lost in. Sex is simple, the act and variations on the act. And she likes him to get violent. Their sex is rough, brutal. She never complains. After all, he may be useful, a sergeant in the CID. Still, he insists, if she's in trouble, leave him out of it. He pays her but knows, professionally, he is taking a chance. But then, he's not the first policeman to get it off with a whore. And won't be the last.

It becomes easier when his wife leaves him and takes their daughter with her.

He is able to see the woman more often now. And he likes the brutality of their coupling.

London. Years later. Years after he transferred to London. (What happened to the whore? He can't remember.)

He arrests Ronnie Swanson after a six months investigation and finally faces his antagonist in an interview room.

'Think you've got me then, Harkness?'

'Oh, I've got you Ronnie. By the short and curlies. Murder, robbery, intimidation, conspiracy, money with menaces . . . oh, aye, it's a long list. And the evidence . . .'

'You're dreaming, policeman.'

'You'll get life, with a minimum of twenty-five years. Like locking you up and burying the key. You'll be nearly . . . what? . . . seventy when they let you out.'

'You think? You'll be dead, Harkness. You're dead already. The walking dead. The boys'll get you, carve you up like a joint of beef.'

'The boys are tripping over themselves to see you go down, Ronnie. They're falling apart. Confessing to everything. A little more pressure and somebody'll shop you for the Jack the Ripper killings. Hell, if we hadnae got Crippen, we'd have you for doin' in his wife.'

'You're quite a comedian. There'll always be someone left out there – someone who does what I tell them. If they can't get to you, well, I've heard you've a daughter up in Scotland. Not a kid . . . we wouldn't touch a kid . . . but a grown woman. That's nice. I mean, that makes it easy. I go down, I send word and your girl's in trouble.'

'You bastard!'

'Well, I mean, a grown woman . . . might just enjoy what the boys'll do. Might. Might not. Won't enjoy the bit afterwards. See, they may just get to mark her. She's pretty now. Who knows what she'll be like after?'

Harkness takes a step forward. The detective inspector – Roberts, it was, Jimmy Roberts – standing behind him moves too.

'Wait a minute, sir . . .'

'Get out of here, Roberts.'

'He can't touch your daughter. We can make sure of that.'

'Whether he can or he can't, it's enough he's thinking about it. Now, get out, that's an order! And shut the door.'

Roberts hesitates.

'I said, get out!'

Roberts goes. Harkness is alone with Ronnie Swanson. No windows in the room. The door is shut.

Time passing. Dream time. He's hitting Swanson. On the body and then, what the hell, on the face. Swanson's on the floor, moaning. Afraid.

'No! No more! You mad bastard, you'll kill me . . .'

'Like Hanson. And Terry Marvin. Took a time to kill him, didn't you? Nailed him to the floor by his balls. Up till then you'd only done it through the knee caps. But a poor little sod like Marvin . . . you had to try a new trick or two, before you killed him. Or did he just give up and die? Like you're going to do.'

'No . . . no, wasn't me . . .'

'Aye, it was.'

Using the boot now. Swanson screams.

'It was, wasn't it?'

'Yes, yes, it bloody well was . . .'

'We'll have you sign that one. A confession. Just to sew everything up.'

'I'll sign, I'll sign!'

Later, he was signing a statement.

'Under fucking duress, that statement. I want to see my brief. I want him to see what you done to me . . .'

Then there is another session in a cell. The two of them alone.

185

'Heh, Harkness, you enjoyed it, right? You enjoyed putting the boot in. You'd enjoy killing me, wouldn't you, Superintendent?'

'I will kill you.'

'But not because I'm a villain, Harkness. Not because of what I done. I'll tell you why – because you're like me, Harkness. Two sides of a bent penny. You're doing it to me because you enjoy doing it. That's why you got me, y'know. Because you know how I think. There's no fuckin' difference between us.'

Then, out of context, 'Whatever happened to that whore of yours in Glasgow?'

Was that Swanson's voice or his own?

'Whatever happened to that whore in Glasgow?'

They come and pull him away from Swanson two minutes later. There is Roberts and the duty sergeant and two constables. Swanson is nearly unconscious after this, the second beating.

Later Harkness is brought up before the Commander and suspended from all duties, pending investigation. There is no investigation. They have to cover it up because he's a hero. The man who broke Swanson's reign of terror in the East End. Also it can never be admitted that a senior officer used violence. What does the judge say at the Old Bailey?

'To believe these unproved and therefore unfounded allegations made against an officer with an unblemished record would be to cast doubts on the honour of the entire police establishment . . . not a case against an over-enthusiastic and inexperienced young constable . . . but an allegation besmirching the officer who so carefully and painstakingly built up a case against the accused. And who is the accused? A man of unsavoury reputation now standing convicted of a horrendous catalogue of capital crimes. Superintendent Harkness leaves this court with his reputation still unsullied and has the gratitude of this court and the entire country for removing this social menace from our midst.'

But Harkness does not leave the court until he hears the sentence. Swanson is given life imprisonment with a recommendation that he serve at least thirty years.

Lying in bed later. Funny, lying in bed, dreaming you're lying in bed. And drenched in sweat.

Swanson saying it. Over and over. Someone saying it. Inside Harkness's head.

'. . . you're doing it to me because you enjoy doing it . . . no fucking difference between us . . . you enjoy doing it . . . no difference between us . . . whatever happened to that whore . . . whatever . . .?'

Fighting now, forcing himself up from sleep, have to get out of the dream, have to get out . . .

Harkness comes awake.

Chapter Twenty-One

Awake, he felt exhausted. Drained. Hadn't somebody else said that? Haydock, the Church of England minister, yes, he'd said it. Wearily, Harkness climbed from the bed and moved over to a mirror above the hand basin. A drawn face stared at him. A face older than its years. The result of a bad night, a bad nightmare. It was reflected, too, in the butterfly specimen cases around the walls. Ten, twenty, thirty drawn faces.

He looked at his watch. It was midday. He'd overslept, and that despite the request he'd put to Abbie to wake him at seven-thirty. He'd slept for fifteen and a half hours. Why the hell hadn't the girl wakened him?

He washed, shaved and, dressing quickly, went downstairs. The girl was in the small dining room area, sweeping the floor with a brush.

'Why didn't you wake me?' he said.

She frowned. 'I did wake you!'

'I never heard you.'

'Half-past seven sharp, I knocked on your door. And you called out to me: "Right!" That's what you called out. Then you never appeared for breakfast so I thought, "Changed his mind, he has." That's what I thought. Told Mr Mullion too, I did. He told me just to be leavin' you. You'd had your call, so best just to be leavin' you. Which I done.'

He stared at the girl for a moment and she stared back steadily. Could he have come half-awake and called out? It was not something he usually did. Usually, once awake, he stayed awake. Still, it was always possible. He'd travelled

189

from London on an early train, been on the go for a long day. So he'd overslept.

'Sorry. Must have overslept,' he said.

'You want something to eat?' she asked. 'Breakfast's over but I can get you some bacon and eggs.'

'Could you make it a cup of coffee and a bacon roll?'

Ten minutes later he ate his roll and drank his coffee in the empty bar. Mullion looked in, nodded to him, and went out without saying anything.

It was nearly two o'clock when he started out, driving the Rover through Lower Calderon and on to the main road. Once out of the two villages, he felt he could drop the guise of commercial traveller. He drove to the nearest village, Down-ingham, and there called at the local inn, asking to see the landlord.

A small globular man with a globular stomach appeared and, showing his police warrant, Harkness asked him if he knew anything about the murder of Joshua Gideon in Calderon.

'Only what I read in the papers,' the globular man said.

'But you probably know some of the people in Calderon? Anything you say is in confidence. Also I'd appreciate it if you would say nothing to anyone from Calderon about this call on you.'

'Don't know nothing about Calderon people. Not many of them come here. After all, we're eight miles from them.'

'No friends, relatives, acquaintances?'

'Not me. Not any I know of.'

'I heard Gideon was quite a ladies man. Anybody here he may have visited?'

'Told you, don't know 'bout that. Best ask them in Calderon.'

'Oh, I will, I will. But I just thought, since this is the nearest village . . .'

'Thought wrong. Keep themselves to themselves, they do.'

A pause. Harkness looked around. A pleasant country inn. More so than The Goat and Compasses in Calderon. He took a deep breath. The next question he put into one word.

'Witchcraft?'

'What's that?'

'I hear there are still people around here believe in witchcraft.'

'Not in Downingham, there aren't. Whatever you heard.'

'But in Calderon?'

'You ask 'em. They want to play around with that rubbish, let 'em. But not here. Too busy here, earning a livin', we are.'

Murder, it seemed to the globular man, was something that happened to other people, in other places. Not in Downingham. Harkness sipped a pint and left.

The village was bigger than the two Calderons together. It seemed older too. The houses in the centre of Downingham looked ancient, were built of heavy dark stone and were probably eighteenth-century. There were, around the town, some pleasant bungalows, circa the thirties, and several blocks of semi-detached council houses. There was also a police station. Dowingham was big enough to have its own, one-man sub-station, the incumbent living on the premises.

The sole constable, uniformed, was drinking a mug of tea when Harkness entered and showed his credentials.

'Harrod, sir, Constable Reggie Harrod. Anything I can do, sir?' He was an old hand, in his fifties, face browned by sun and weather.

'Since this is the nearest village to Calderon, I thought I might pick up some gossip about the place and the murder,' Harkness said.

'Not here, you won't sir,' said Harrod. 'Not in any of the villages around here. See, the folk in Calderon keep themselves to themselves. So the folk here, they just do the same. Of course, when the body was discovered, Warwick phoned me. Being as how I'm the local man.'

'And you went up to Calderon?'

'Right away, sir. First officer on the spot. See, I went up to make sure it weren't no practical joke . . .'

'You get practical jokes like that?'

'No, sir. Trouble is, we don't get no crime from Calderon. That's why I wanted to make sure it wasn't no joke. Then, 'course, when I got there and saw the body, I phoned back to Warwick right away. And they brought the murder squad up. That was my only job. Once they arrived, I came back here.'

'You've no idea who phoned from Calderon?'

'Warwick said it was an anonymous call. And, when I got to Calderon, there was the body. And nobody else around.'

'You go to Calderon a lot?'

'No, sir. I drive up . . . mebbe once, twice a week . . . just drive through . . . see everything's all right. Sometimes have a pint with Mr Mullion at the pub. And away. I got a big enough territory to cover, you might say. 'Course, if they sent for me . . . if there were a crime took place, I'd be straight up there.'

'That happens now and then?'

'Never sir. Not in my eight years here. Law abiding, I'd say. Until now. Until the murder.'

'Did you know Gideon?'

'I seen him, sir a couple of times, in the pub there. Never spoke to him. But you couldn't miss him. Big fellow.'

'And do you know anybody else in the Calderons? Apart from Mullion?'

'I've met Miss Campion a couple of times. Not officially. Just to pass the time of day when I was through. She'd say, "No problems, Constable?" And I'll say, "No problems, Miss." The ministers too they'll say "Good morning". That'll be all. Oh, and while I was waiting for the squad, the morning I found the body, I spoke to Mullion and a couple of the people who lived nearest.'

He paused for a moment, scratched his neck where his shirt collar seemed too tight, and said, 'Would you like some tea, sir?'

'No, thank you. Did Mullion, and the others you spoke to say anything?'

'No, sir. Didn't know nothing. Were all very quiet. Surprised me a bit.'

'How so?'

'Well, I been on a murder enquiry before I came here. In Warwick, ten, fifteen year ago. I was put to questioning the neighbours then. Got the usual reactions. You know the kind of thing: "Saw him only yesterday . . . he can't be murdered." Or: "I knowed he'd come to a bad end. You want to talk to that bloke he were always arguing with at the end of the street." All the gossip, like you find surrounding a

192

murder. Didn't get none of that in Calderon. Nobody knew nothing or said nothing. Nobody seemed even surprised. Funny, that.'

'And what about all the stories you hear around the countryside about witchcraft?'

Harrod laughed. 'Oh, that! You hear stories 'bout that all over this part of the world. But I never seen anything. Reckon it's some daft kids or an excuse for a bit of "hows-your-father" in the woods. The rest is old wives' tales. Oh, and there were a spot of vandalism over at Lower Duthwaite a few years back. Messin' around in the graveyard. Paintin' slogans on tombstones and that. But I reckon it was teenagers havin' a nasty kind of lark.'

'What kind of slogans?'

'Dirty, obscene. Swear words. And slogans. One, I remember, saying, "God is Dead". And on one gravestone, "Move over and make room, Charlie". Charlie Penrose's stone. He were a Methodist lay preacher, died twenty year ago.'

Harkness drove back to Greater Calderon. He was surprised to find it was nearly five o'clock and getting dark, as if time passed quicker here than anywhere else. His visit to Calderon incognito had been a failure. None of the people he'd met would talk. They wouldn't even talk to people in the neighbouring villages. Calderon was its own place, its own island. Isolated by itself and its occupants. Only one way to handle it now: bring back the murder wagon and the full power and authority of the police. It had failed before, sure, but then he hadn't been in charge. The Warwick police hadn't the experience. These people had to be frightened into talking; into telling all their stories, all the rumours, all the whispering that surrounded murder. Out of those rumours and whispers came the leads that would open up the case and lead to an arrest. That was his experience in the past. It usually produced results. He'd hoped, by coming in as an unofficial stranger, he'd hear at least gossip. But not in Calderon. They were tight as clams, he should have known that. One more night, he'd spend, and drink in the bar of The Goat and Compasses and listen. Not that now he expected to hear anything. But tomorrow he'd be back. In charge. With authority. Then he would see and hear.

He dined that evening in the dining room of the inn. Alone, served by Abbie, Mullion looking in once to see if everything was to his satisfaction. Boiled mutton, cabbage and chipped potatoes. It was tasteless, but he said nothing.

The public bar was half-full. The middle-aged citizens, surprisingly no women in sight, stood around the bar. The younger inhabitants of Greater Calderon were around the inevitable battered dartboard. Three old men sat at a corner table playing dominoes. The bar was typical . . . almost too typical, Harkness thought . . . of the English village pub. How it should be, how it was expected to be. On his entry there was the usual momentary hush and then the gabble of conversation recommenced. A number of the older men nodded at Harkness, not in an unfriendly fashion, but the nods could hardly be called affable. Among the youths around the dartboard, he noticed the familiar bruised face of Caroon. But the youth seemed to be deliberately avoiding his eyes.

'What'll you be having, Mr Harkness?' said Mullion behind the bar, with what might pass for a smile.

'A dram. Scotch.'

The whisky appeared in front of him. He downed it with one gulp and ordered another. The man next to him turned with a mild look of astonishment.

'Like your whisky, do you, sir?'

'My native drink,' Harkness replied, surprised at one of the locals talking to him.

'You from Scotland?'

'Originally.'

'Ah, well . . .' said the man, and seemed lost for any further comment.

'You'll have one with me?' Harkness said.

'Beer drinker myself, sir. And I have a pint here, thank you kindly.'

He turned away. End of socialising, Harkness thought.

It was. He was now ignored, the foreigner in their midst. Could hardly believe one of them had even bothered to talk to him. Or was that the token acknowledgement? Once rendered, no need to be repeated.

He sipped the second whisky slowly, savouring the taste, and the heat at the back of his throat. And listened.

There were fragments of conversation.

'. . . two heifers . . . good beasts . . . well worth the price . . .'

'. . . hate that chemical stuff . . . give me good old fashioned shit any day . . .'

'. . . more market gardeners around here went bust last year than in the last ten year. Thanks to the bloody Minister of bloody Agriculture . . .'

'. . . wouldn't know a raspberry from a lump of cow dung, that one wouldn't . . .'

Harkness thought, they'll be on to the fatstock prices any minute. Or was that what the heifers were about?

Time passing.

The kids at the dartboard, loud, now as the competition increased. Harsh laughter about something. He edged closer.

'. . . open her legs for anyone . . .'

'. . . no anyone. Everyone . . .'

'. . . say Gideon started her off . . .'

'. . . shut up about him!'

The door of the bar opened. Another hush descended, faces turning.

Father Anselm entered.

'Good evening, gentlemen. Hello, George. Harry. Ah, Mr Mullion . . .' He was at the bar now. The silence was unbroken. 'A small sherry, I think.'

As Harkness stood, whisky glass in hand, he became aware of something. Everyone in the room, with the exception of Mullion who was pouring the sherry, was looking from Anselm to him and back. Still in silence. Harkness to Anselm. Anselm to Harkness. Even the darts players had stopped playing. The three old men who were playing dominoes had stopped, immobile, and seemed at that moment frozen in time. They alone were not staring at him or Anselm but were sitting staring in front of them now perhaps awaiting some signal to move again.

Then Anselm looked over at Harkness and spoke. 'Good evening, Mr Harkness.'

The greeting was the magical signal. 'Open Sesame!' At once the domino players carried on with their game and again everybody resumed talking.

'. . . two heifers . . . good beasts . . . well worth the price . . .'

'. . . hate that chemical stuff . . .'

'. . . wouldn't know a raspberry from . . .'

No, that couldn't be. As if they were saying the same things he had heard moments before, a long echo of themselves.

'. . . open her legs for . . .'

'. . . everyone . . .'

As if time had been rewound. An instant replay. Ridiculous . . . unless they were playing games with him.

'And have you had a good day, Mr Harkness?' Father Anselm was at his side now, sherry glass in hand, talking once more. In the strong light from above the bar, his face was pallid. More than pallid . . . white, and smooth, the skin unlined where it should be lined. A trick of the light, Harkness presumed.

'Not very good, business wise,' he replied. 'But it'll get better.'

'You're not leaving tomorrow then?'

'Oh, yes, I'm going. But I'll be back. Yes, I'll be back.'

'Persistent, eh? Ah, well, one of the assets of good salesmanship. You'll let me buy you a drink?'

'I'll have a last scotch, thank you. Before I go to bed.'

'And a last sherry for me, Mr Mullion,' said Anselm. His eyes seemed to sparkle good-naturedly. He seemed so much a contented man, more even, a man who was enjoying life. Certainly a contrast to Haydock, sitting in his decaying church and decayed hopes.

The drinks arrived.

'To you, Father.' Harkness raised his glass.

'To all of us here, Mr Harkness.'

They drank. It seemed to Harkness that, although engaged in their own conversations, the villagers in the bar were watching them out of the corners of their eyes. Covert glances when they were supposedly listening to their companions . . . sidelong looks when they thought they were unobserved.

'Pay no attention,' Anselm said, as if reading Harkness's mind. 'Curiosity. Because they can find nothing themselves to say to you, they are curious about what I might be saying. Country people, Mr Harkness. A new face spells alien to them. So few visitors, you might be a man from Mars. To them a big city like London, or your own Glasgow, is as remote as Mars.'

'They don't get around much then?'

'That surprised me too when I first came here. So few leave Calderon, even on a visit. Oh, now and then they go into Warwick or Stratford, but I don't think they like it. Too busy, too many strange faces, too much rushing. That man Gideon . . . the one who was killed . . . now he was one of few that liked going to the cities. But then his reasons were hardly commendable. For the others, everything is so much easier here. They work, mostly on the land; they know their neighbours and socialise with them here. And the rest of the world, they see on the television.'

'Not a very existing existence.'

'But secure. Workwise, you might say. Each has his job . . . farmer, market gardener or employee of one or the other. And we have the butcher, baker and candlestick maker – that's Mr Mullion, one of the few entrepreneurs. But then, no society can afford to be without at least one entrepreneur. You have a burst pipe, your roof leaks, you need an electrician . . . you find Mullion will provide. Do you know, the only housepainter in the two villages works for Mullion?'

'At least you have full employment here.' Harkness drained the last of his whisky.

'Exactly. If they had to go out into the outside world, they'd be lost. Add to Mrs Thatcher's so many million unemployed. So they stay. For spiritual guidance they have myself. And if any misfortune strikes, Miss Campion at the manor proves only too often she is a benevolent lady squire . . . or, if you like, a good fairy.'

'So it's all sewn up,' Harkness said, feeling suddenly very tired, his head heavy. Three scotches were having their effect. Not that three should have. Usually he could hold more than that. Still and all, he told himself, he'd had an unsettled night. Now why was that? Oh, yes, the long nightmare. Tonight he would sleep, and soon.

'Not quite Utopia, of course. Not from my point of view. A certain amount of inbreeding is inevitable. And immorality.

197

Oh, I'm not going to preach to you. But, out of working hours, time can hang heavily, and that breeds a certain laxity in sexual matters. The man who was killed, Gideon, was a prime example. And we're not entirely removed from the scourge of unemployment. Farming being what it is, we have our share of seasonal unemployment. We even have two, no, three incorrigibles who just won't work. At least one of them will be in here tonight.'

Anselm looked around the room, as if seeking the incorrigible one. He was unsuccessful.

'Heaven knows where they get the money to come in here,' he went on, 'Far less, survive.'

'There's always the Social Security,' Harkness suggested, and found himself slurring the last two words.

'Ah, yes, thank the Lord for the Social Security. Are you all right, Mr Harkness?'

Harkness found the room seemed to be tilting slightly. He shook his head, and it righted itself immediately.

'A bit tired, I think. Sleeping in a strange bed too.'

'Yes, indeed. A strange bed. Well, I'm off anyway. You take yourself to your strange bed. You'll have grown accustomed to it after the first night.'

Father Anselm was right. Or appeared to be. Fifteen minutes later Harkness was in his room. He drew the curtains, had a quick wash, undressed, donned his pyjamas and climbed into bed. He noted before putting out the bedlight that it was five minutes to eleven. Sleep came almost at once. Deep, dreamless.

Something woke him, it seemed hours later. A tapping sound at the window. The branch of a tree against the glass. And another noise, an unidentifiable wisp of sound under the tapping. He switched on the light and looked at his watch on the bedside table. To his surprise it was only five minutes past eleven. He had been asleep for no longer than ten minutes.

He listened but since he'd switched on the light, the sounds had gone.

He switched the light off again.

And then it started.

Chapter Twenty-Two

The tapping on the window began again. The branch of a tree, disturbed by a night breeze, had to be brushing against the glass. And the other sound, whispering in the air, it too was back. Harkness lay, eyes open, staring into the darkness. No light, not even a trace filtering around the edges of the curtains. He felt ice-cold then, a chill that, despite the two blankets on the bed, permeated through to the bone.

Then something brushed against his cheek. With his right hand he flicked it, and felt something flutter against his fingers.

He reached out for the bedlight switch. There was something again, this time on the back of his hand. He pressed the switch.

The light came on. Not the usual flood of light, but a dull, yellow glow which barely illuminated the room and cast long shadows on walls and ceiling. The ceiling seemed to be moving with small fainter dancing shadows. He threw back the bedclothes and rose. Something brushed his neck. And again his cheek. The air in front of him now appeared to be a mass of movement. The tapping sound on the window increased. Something touched his forehead and fluttered against his right eye, settling on his cheek.

Then he saw that the room was alive with butterflies and moths! Swooping and diving, their wings fluttered in the dim, yellow light. The bed light was even duller in intensity now. He peered at it. The shade was covered in moths, one upon the other, each struggling to get closer to the light. Something settled on the back of his hand. He stared at it, amazed at the

199

mottled colour of the wings. A moth settled beside the butterfly and a sudden feeling of revulsion came over Harkness. It was as if they were feeding off his flesh. He brushed them both away with one hand only to have them flutter and swoop again on his skin.

He turned away towards the bed. The counterpane was a mass of movement. Moth upon butterfly upon moth. His revulsion increased. He looked around the walls of the room. The specimen cases were still there, unbroken, the subdued light reflecting on the glass. But where the corpses of butterfly and moth had been, each neatly pinned to white board, there was nothing but the board.

It wasn't possible, he told himself. He stood in the centre of the room, blinking, and shook his head. Surely it was some kind of optical illusion.

A moth settled on his forehead above his left eye. Another almost on top of the first. And another. They were on his hands too now. Both hands. On his neck above the pyjama top. Not on the pyjamas, they were not landing on his pyjamas but only on the exposed skin. He swayed, feeling nauseous. He tried to brush them from his head, but to no avail. They rose and settled again, wings brushing the air. There was no pain but only the sensation of things crawling on flesh. Fluttering things. *Lepidoptera*. The word came back to him from schooldays. One hundred thousand different species. Living on nectar and the juices of plants; not on human flesh. Never on human flesh. He knew it and yet was unconvinced. And dead and pinned to cardboard, they could not come to life.

Scale-covered wings were before his eyes. Still they were settling on him. One on his right eye-lid now. And another. His hands brushed his face and he flayed the air, trying to dislodge the swarm. That's what they were like, a swarm of bees. But moths and butterflies didn't swarm. Not normal for them to do so.

They were in his hair now . . . he could feel them. He could feel them crawling under his pyjamas. He gave a low moan and staggered in the direction of the door of the room, shuddering as he moved. Hardly able to see now for the wings, the flying bodies in the air.

200

He reached the door, hands outstretched, feeling the wood of the panelling. So little light now. His right hand searching for the door handle, his left flaying again at his face.

He found the handle and tried to turn it. It wouldn't turn. His hand felt as if it was covered in light moth's wings. He pulled at the handle. Nothing. Had to be . . . hadn't locked the door . . . try again . . . legs feeling weak . . . about to buckle under him . . . stupid . . . no weight and yet being sucked down . . . both hands away from the door now . . . across his face . . . some dislodged and then back on to his face . . . crawling . . . probing . . . fluttering . . .

Now he was beating on the door, hands battering on the wooden panels. And shouting, not words but sounds, groans, moaning to himself. Small bodies on his lips, trying to get into his open mouth. He was starting to choke.

The door was opened from the outside.

Light! From the hall, from the bedlight behind him. The sensation on his skin gone.

He blinked and found himself facing Mullion. The landlord was standing in the corridor, a puzzled expression on his face, staring.

'You all right?'

'Wha' . . . what was it?' Surprised to find he could speak.

'You were hammering on the door. Could hear you from downstairs.'

'Couldn't . . . couldn't get the door open.'

The landlord gave him a quizzical look.

'Opened all right. Just turned the knob.' Mullion stepped into the room and, closing the door, tried the door handle from the inside. He opened the door with ease. 'There you are. No problem.'

'Moths . . .' Harkness said. And, turning, looked around the room. It was as it should be. The clean counterpane on the bed, blankets and sheets thrown aside where he had risen. The bedlight shone clearly through the room, its shade a pristine white.

'You had a bit to drink tonight, Mr Harkness.'

'Moths,' he said again. 'And butterflies. In the room.'

'Bit late in the year for them,' Mullion said, looking around. 'Get them in the summer, sure. Built on a swamp,

201

they used to say, and that attracted them. Maybe more than some places. Of course, you always get 'em in the country. Must have been an odd late survivor. You allergic to moths or somethin'? Or is it a touch of the old DTs?'

'No. But . . .'

'Knew a fellow had a touch of them. Right here in the village. Kept seeing things, like dragons and monsters and witches on broomsticks riding across the moon. Ended up, they took him away, for a nice long rest. Never did come back.'

'They were all over the room. They were . . .'

'Sure they are. All neatly pinned, in their little specimen cases. Hobby of me dad's, collecting things. Moths, butterflies, stamps, coins. Couldn't stop collecting. A kind of nervous habit. And money too. He collected that all right. I was grateful for that, though. But I know what's the matter with you – all them specimens.'

'No! I wasn't dreaming!' Harkness insisted, straightening up now. He was damp with perspiration and trying to get a grip on himself. Superintendent Harkness, senior police officer in charge, never flustered, always able to hold his liquor . . . but this. It was crazy, daft, but not a dream. Couldn't be a dream. Yet here he was, a fifty-nine-year-old man, behaving like a small boy.

'Them,' said Mullion, pointing. 'On the walls. You been dreaming about them.'

Mullion was right. He had to be right. Another dream, like last night.

'Yes, of course, Mr Mullion. I must have been dreaming. Unaccustomed surroundings, strange bed. I'm . . . I'm sorry to have disturbed you?'

For the first time since Harkness had met him, the landlord essayed a grin. It came out crookedly and without humour.

'That's all right. Just as well there was no one else staying here. Would have wakened them all. Just as well there's only me and the girl. You'll be off tomorrow them?'

'I'll be off. After breakfast.'

'Stratford should be your next stop. You'll do better there. Big turnover. Tourist trade. Very hygienic place, Stratford. All the American tourists.'

'Oh, I told you I might come back here again soon,' Harkness said. Himself again. Baiting the landlord. 'Never like to move on without a . . . a sale. It's like a challenge.'

The grin vanished. 'We get busy around Christmas. Lot of the farms come in for the holidays. Might not have room for you.'

'Oh, it might well be before Christmas. You never know. Anyway, I'll see you at breakfast, eh?'

'At breakfast.' Mullion nodded and went out into the corridor.

'Oh, and Mr Mullion, you'll be sure I get an early call for breakfast this morning?'

'I'll wake you myself.'

Harkness closed the bedroom door, and then, on impulse, opened it. To make sure. It opened easily. And closed easily. He turned and looked around the room yet again. Everything as it should be. The rumpled bed, the white sheets, the white counterpane, the light by the beside, its shade clear. The curtains drawn across the window. No sound except for a distant night breeze outside. No tapping of branches outside the window. The breeze must have changed direction.

He went over and, opening the blinds, stared out into the night. One street lamp across the road outside the church, solitary, forming a circular pool of light on the kerb, reaching to the front of the hotel. His car was parked down there. There was no other light. Away from the street lamp, only the thick, velvet blackness of the countryside.

There was no tree in front of the hotel.

No tree or branch that could tap against his window.

Part of the dream. It had to be part of the dream. Like the moths. And the panic.

He drew the curtain across the window and went back to the bed. He climbed in between the sheets still warm from his body before . . . before what? The panic, the dream.

He lay, listening.

No sound. Even the breeze had faded away. He reached out and switched off the bedlight, still listening. The noises had come only in the darkness. But now there was nothing but the sound of his own breathing. A sense of relief flooded over him. The fear had been with him that once again in the darkness . . . no, that was stupid. It was a nightmare.

He switched the light on. Rising, he found a cigarette packet in his jacket pocket and his lighter. He lit a cigarette, placed the lighter and packet on the table by the bed light, found an ashtray and put it by the cigarette packet. Then he lay on the bed smoking, staring at the ceiling. No moving shadows now. A thin crack running across one corner. And the centre bulb, unshaded. In his panic he'd never thought about putting on the centre light. Then, why should he? In a dream, one never thought of the obvious.

He inhaled, savouring the tobacco.

And felt something brush against his hand.

The edge of the sheet, he told himself. Then looked down at his hand.

It lay, half on the sheet, half on the side of his hand. The wings were spread out so that it was about an inch in length. Brown with panelled wings.

It was dead.

His hand shaking, he lifted it and stared down at the corpse. One dead moth. Long dead. The pin was still through the centre of the body between the forewings and hindwings, a trace of dusty fluff upon it.

Harkness looked across to the wall and the nearest specimen case. It was unopened, the glass unbroken. There should have been five moths pinned to the cardboard, two on each side and one in the centre.

The moth that had been in the centre was missing.

Then he knew there had been no nightmare.

Chapter Twenty-three

As a young man, Harkness had had an image of himself as a CID officer. The trench-coated senior detective, he would approach the scene of crime with an outward appearance of cool self-confidence, survey the situation unemotionally, note any relevant clues and, after a patient but firm interrogation of those concerned, arrest the guilty party.

It had never been like that. At most murder scenes in the home – and ninety percent of murders took place in the home or family circle – he found that he and other investigators were faced with a hysterical or semi-hysterical assassin, remorse bleeding from him as profusely as the tears on his face, the inevitable confession babbled with an incoherence that allowed an advocate to deny its content at a later date. There would follow a flood of excuses for the enormity of the crime. 'He drove me to it!' 'She just went on and on until I hit her!' And so on.

In the other murders, the random killings in the street, the sex crimes whose only motivation was perverted lust, there were few opportunities for the cool young detective Harkness imagined himself to be. Many were never solved, and those that the police succeeded in were brought to a successful conclusion either by luck of hard, meticulous, slogging police work of the dullest kind. A hundred, two hundred people were questioned over months; small, seemingly inconsequential fragments of information were put together, and sometimes, somehow, a case was made against the perpetrator. And sometimes no one was ever charged.

Burglars, the older professionals, caught in the act, would simply grin awkwardly, shrug, and accept their ill fortune. There was one with a sense of humour who, on being apprehended in front of a safe in a district branch of the Bank of Scotland at midnight, looked around in amazement and asked the inimitable question, 'How did I get here?'

Violence, of course, came with the young amateurs who would offer resistance, and on such occasions the young Detective Constable Harkness found his imagined coolness deserting him. He would return violence with violence and think little of it; or the process he was undergoing of being hardened, tempered into an individual he would, in his youth, never have recognised.

Now, looking at himself in the mirror the morning after his nightmare visitation, he could see no traces of that cool young policeman. A tired man stared bleakly back at him from the glass; eyes in the process of ageing towards death, the flesh around them dark from lack of sleep; skin yellowing, drawn and ridged with deep lines; hair, thinning at the temples, greying to white where it had once been full and dark brown.

After Mullion's departure, he had lain awake for some hours, perhaps fearful of sleep and, in sleep, the dream of feather-like wings in the air. Of course, it had to be a dream, he told himself. Of course there was the dead moth on the edge of the pillow . . . what could that prove? Something irrational, illogical, impossible. Yet it had been there. Dead, impaled, but out of its specimen case which was unopened, the glass unbroken. Not to be thought on, not now, perhaps not even later. Eventually, with the faint rays of the dawn filtering around the curtains, he had fallen into a doze, a fitful surface sleep which brought little rest.

It seemed he had dozed for no time at all before he was awakened by the knock on the door. It was seven-thirty. He washed, shaved and dressed with unaccustomed weariness. Alone in the tiny dining room, he was served by a silent Abbie. There was no sign of Mullion until he went to the reception desk to pay his bill. The landlord made no reference to the incidents of the previous night but merely presented an already prepared bill.

It was another grey morning as he drove out of Greater Calderon. He stopped the Rover between the two villages and looked back. The mist was again on the fields. Around the council houses, despite the obvious dampness, washing hung out on the small greens. The entire village looked depressingly ordinary. And, the thought occured to him, its very existence seemed pointless. It was not built on the banks of a river or stream, as so many early settlements had been, providing a reason for their founding. It was not a central point to an area where the inhabitants of several villages and farms might congregate. Beyond being under a hill, there was no geographical feature which might have encouraged the creation of a settlement. Certainly, in the past, the manor house had been built. But in a not particularly pleasing spot. The countryside below the hill was flat and uninteresting. There was no vista of beauty or range to encourage the building of the house. He made a mental note that on his official return he would take up the Campion woman's offer of tea and visit the manor. In his guise as a commercial man there had seemed little reason for visiting on this trip.

He started the car again, driving through Lesser Calderon. Even less reason for its existence. Apart from the council houses, here there was a look of decay. As if the place should have been abandoned long ago. And in its desolation, even more depressing than the larger village.

He drove on.

He reached police headquarters in Warwick an hour later. He went directly to the office prepared for him. Drewitt's report was on his desk. He read it quickly and then, lifting the telephone, asked for Sergeant Stevens. He was connected at once.

'My office, now, Sergeant.'

Stevens appeared a few minutes later.

'Sir?'

'I want the incident wagon back in Greater Calderon this afternoon. Yourself, five of your best detective constables and two uniformed men to man the wagon. We behave as if we're starting the investigation from scratch.'

'Yes, sir, but we'll be going over ground already covered,' said Stevens.

'Yes, we will. But there is a difference.'

'Sir?'

'I'll be there. And questioning will be done, not by inexperienced uniformed constables but by trained detectives. Under my supervision. And yours, Sergeant.'

The sergeant nodded, pleased. At least he was being given his due.

'You want Drewitt with us? As he was born there?'

'He's been useful,' Harkness replied, 'and he's been doing some work for me. But I don't think I'll want him with us now. I'll see him before I go.'

He lifted the phone. 'I want two mugs of coffee. And then there's one visit I have to make in Warwick . . . to Miss Jennet Agram.'

'Don't know her.'

'You should, Sergeant. I found out about her. So did Drewitt. She has to be interviewed.'

'You want me to . . .?'

'I think I'd like to meet the woman myself. Gideon's lady friend in Warwick. Could be very informative. You see, Stevens, there are areas you have missed.'

Stevens reddened. 'Yes, sir.'

There was a knock on the door.

'Come,' said Harkness.

Drewitt came in.

'I'll get to you,' Harkness said, and turned to Stevens. 'Right, get the wagon back to Calderon . . .'

Drewitt waited while he issued orders to the detective sergeant. Finally Stevens left and Harkness turned to Drewitt.

'I've read your report. Good. Worthwhile. Background stuff.' He went on with a degree of praise for the young constable. He believed in praise, when deserved. And then he told Drewitt he was off the case.

'They know you in that place. And know where you and your mother live. I don't like that. I think it's time you went back on the beat . . . You've been very useful.'

'I would like to go on, sir.'

'And I wouldn't like you to, so that's it. Better get your uniform on and report to the duty sergeant. 'Bye.'

Thus he dismissed Drewitt from the case. And then left to meet Jennet Agram.

She greeted him at the door of her council house. She was in her early thirties, a big-boned woman with the face of an angel. So Harkness thought the moment she opened the door. She was dressed in a full skirt and what was known as a peasant-type blouse, low in the front revealing considerable cleavage, the tops of her ample breasts like half moons.

He introduced himself. 'My name is Superintendent Harkness. I'm acting for the Warwickshire County Police . . .'

'I've been expecting you,' she said. 'Come in.'

The living room was clean but untidy. It seemed cluttered with books and ornaments and jars. The walls were covered with paintings, the work of various local artists, none famous but all of interest. She removed some papers from an aged armchair and beckoned for him to sit.

'You'll be here about the death of Josh Gideon,' she said. 'May I call you Mister Harkness? I dislike official designations . . . rather dehumanising . . . and you have enough authority within yourself not to need the ranking title.'

He acquiesced, amused at the compliment.

'Would you like some tea or coffee, Mr Harkness?'

'Thank you, no. About Gideon . . .'

'Yes. About Gideon.'

'You knew him well?'

She sat facing him. Her skirt made a rustling sound as she did so. 'I suppose I could say that.'

'You'll appreciate I have to be rather personal in such a serious enquiry? It has been said that you and Gideon were . . . more than good friends?'

'You mean, was I his mistress? Yes, it's true I was. Some time ago.'

The directness of the answer fascinated him as did the face of the woman. The angel face. A strong face but beautiful and with great serenity. Her long-fingered hands rested on her lap, not nervously but naturally and at ease.

'But not recently?' Harkness said.

'Not recently.'

'There was a reason for this? A quarrel? A disagreement?'

'I decided to end that side of our relationship. I told him and he accepted it. Grudgingly, I might say, but with no great argument.'

'Why did you end the relationship, Miss Agram? Again, I'm sorry I have to ask such questions . . .'

She shook her head calmly. 'No, that's perfectly all right. The reason was that Gideon had changed. Or perhaps he wasn't quite the person I thought he was.'

'What kind of person was he?'

She hesitated and then replied: 'It's not easy to explain. Gideon had become a . . . a greedy man. A man with a greed for power. Not power from within himself, he always had that, but power over others. He wanted to dominate people. I was not prepared to be dominated.'

'What do you mean, a man of power?'

She gave a slight smile and moved in her chair, rustling the skirt again.

'You may find my judgements different from those of other people. A man of power . . . You are a man of power, Mr Harkness. Oh, I don't mean your rank or position in the police force. I mean, within yourself. A man with greater depths of personality than is normal. And able to utilise such depths to . . . to achieve whatever you might want in life.'

Again he thought, compliments. Is she playing a game with me? Flattery, cleverly used, to avoid truths?

She seemed to read his mind. 'Oh, I'm not flattering you, Mr Harkness. I have an ability to see simple truths rather clearly. You've probably heard I'm called a witch? It's true. I have myself certain abilities which other people call witch-craft. "Country lore", the more enlightened might call them.'

Harkness coughed to cover a certain feeling of embarrassment.

She smiled broadly. 'The Shakespearian designation of country matters is not intended. Though, I would say in all modesty, it could be.'

And she laughed, a light pleasant sound. Almost certainly, he was aware, at the expression of embarrassment on his face.

210

'Gideon was found dead surrounded by certain symbols of witchcraft,' he said.

'Yes, he was,' she replied evenly, the smile gone from her face. 'So I heard. I can only say that had nothing to do with me. Those were symbols of a craft I do not practise. Gideon himself did, but I am what is called a white witch, Mr Harkness. A follower, if you like, of the right hand path. A white witch is one whose knowledge and practice is directed towards constructive ends. Towards, if you like, the good. White magic. The reason that I broke off a relationship with Joshua Gideon was that he had begun to practise black magic.'

Harkness stared at her, feeling uneasy, a chill deep in his spine.

'Where were you on the night he was killed?' he asked quietly, not wishing to sound as if he was making an accusation.

'I was here. I had some visitors that evening. People who needed help with small matters. The mother of a little boy who had whooping cough. A young woman whose sex life with her husband was . . . not satisfactory. I gave advice, and help. A herbal nostrum for the little boy. Oh, yes, Mr Harkness, I practise a kind of medicine. You'd call it quackery. I call it herbal. I don't clash with medical practitioners, but the little boy doesn't have whooping cough now. The last of my visitors left about eleven-thirty. So I suppose I could have reached Greater Calderon, killed Gideon and returned here for the morning. Only I didn't. I went to bed and slept until seven-thirty. However, I slept alone. So I can't prove I was here,'

He believed her. He couldn't say why, but he did. He was annoyed at himself for doing so. He didn't like taking anything on trust in a murder case, but Jennet Agram was not an ordinary suspect.

'Have you any idea who killed Gideon? Did he give you any hint that he was threatened?'

'He gave me no hint. Although I knew he was . . . living dangerously. Anyone who indulges in black magic does that. Makes enemies.'

'What enemies?'

'Those other practitioners. There are quite a few in this country. As to who might have killed him . . . Josh made enemies easily. His determination to attain power over others made this inevitable. He was, in pursuit of his aim, a ruthless man. As you are, in pursuit of perhaps more worthy causes.'

'I've been told he was a womaniser.'

She smiled again. 'Oh, yes, he was that. And would have made enemies there too. If he wanted a woman, he would be ruthless again in pursuit. He also used certain abilities . . . have you ever heard of Aleister Crowley, Mr Harkness?'

'I've heard of him.'

'Gideon had the same ability. Crowley had the reputation of being able to seduce women with a look. I think it was a slight exaggeration but I do believe he used hypnotic abilities. As did Gideon. And of course he made enemies of husbands and lovers.'

'You could give me names?'

'No. I didn't ask or know. You could look among the women of Calderon although, under the circumstances, I don't think you'll get many admissions of adultery. His death will have relieved them of that.'

'He . . . he used this hypnosis on you?'

The laugh again. 'Oh, no. When I first knew him, I was attracted. He was an attractive man. Determined to use his power, his ability to . . . to progress in his life, better himself. But at no one else's expense. Then, later, he became callous. He had no concern but to achieve his aims. Over the bodies of others. That's when our affair ended.'

'And you stopped seeing him?'

'No, I still saw him. He came here occasionally. The last time about ten days before his death. I . . . I think he hoped we would come together again. But I had made my decision. I would talk to him, perhaps even try and dissuade him from the way he was going, but our relationship had ended.'

'He told you what he was trying to achieve?'

She shook her head. 'Not in detail. Never mentioning names. But I believe he was engaged in a struggle for control.'

'Control. Of what?'

212

'A group of people. A coven, if you like. People who followed the same path as he did. Experimenting in . . . things that should not be touched.'

Harkness thought, She really believes in all this. He was surprised. Perhaps disappointed. That a woman who was so attractive should believe in myth, legend. In nonsense.

Again she seemed to read his mind. 'You don't believe, do you, Mr Harkness? I suppose it is to be expected. You have always lived in cities. There's rarely time any more in cities to believe in such things. But in the country, the old beliefs are deep-rooted. Where the magic of modern technology has no meaning; where the distractions of modern society are absent; where life is ridden with poverty, people find other things to occupy their minds, their dreams and fantasies. Some of these things are very real.'

He nodded stiffly. 'I have heard the lecture but don't necessarily accept the premise.'

She leaned forward then, her expression serious. 'You *are* very like Gideon, you know. The power is there. And the rashness. And the ruthlessness. You've gone too far on occasion, Harkness. Never mind that your motives were right. You went too far with the man Swanson. You nearly lost the case, and you damaged yourself badly!'

Chapter Twenty-Four

'What the hell do you know about Swanson?' he said.

She shrugged. 'A man you had to arrest.'

'You got that from the newspapers.' He felt a sense of unease. The newspapers had not mentioned the accusation that he had assaulted Swanson. The judge had dismissed any such suggestion. There had been no reference to it in his summing-up, and indeed he had congratulated Harkness on his handling of the case.

'I rarely read the newspapers,' the woman said.

'They didn't print anything about . . . about what happened to Swanson.'

She looked at her finger-tips. She had long unpainted nails. 'Sometimes I know things. Call me psychic. I don't think I can help you any further, Mr Harkness.'

'You timing's good, Miss Agram. Pick the right moment, drop in the phoney fortune-telling bit . . .'

She rose, her face flushing.

'It is time you left.'

'I'm conducting a murder investigation – I leave when I'm ready. Just now I'm after hard facts. What have you given me? Gideon was a stud. Fair enough, I've heard that. Then you go on to a bit about a witches' coven. There's a lot of it about in this case. But a human hand drove that pitchfork into Gideon's throat, no magic about that. Maybe you want me to believe in magic and witchcraft? Keep me from looking elsewhere. In the right direction maybe. A jealous lady loses her boy friend. Or another boy friend decides to put Gideon out of the picture?'

'There is no jealous boy friend, Mr Harkness. Not that I expect you to believe me. Not yet. As for witchcraft, it isn't important whether or not you believe in it. It's the others who believe. Magic? That's something else.'

He was sneering now. 'Or nothing else.'

'Nothing that is dreamt of in your philosophy, Mr Harkness. You *are* like Gideon, you know, intolerant. But more so. He at least admitted . . . other possibilities.'

'I allow for all possibilities, but not fairy tales or bits of hocus-pocus thrown in to impress me.' He rose now, facing her. It was the first time he noticed she was almost as tall as he was. 'I'll be back, Miss Agram, with more questions. I hope you'll have more answers. And practical ones.'

He went to the door of the room.

She said: 'About moths and butterflies?'

He stopped, feeling ice cold. He took a deep breath and forced himself to sound casual. 'You read minds? Tune into dreams?'

'Was it a dream? Or something they created for you? A beginning, Mr Harkness.'

'It was a dream!'

'Was the dead moth on the pillow a dream?'

He forced a sour grin. 'Or maybe you were there. Maybe you know Mullion.'

'I've heard of him. But I've never met him and I wasn't there.'

'As I said, I'll be back.'

'Yes, you will.'

He switched the car heater on and drove to Calderon, thinking about Jennet Agram and all he'd heard. A clever, tricky woman. It had to be a trick, her appearing to know so much about him. He wouldn't be fooled. He didn't believe in magic, black or white. But there just might be something in mind-reading. What did they call it? Extra-sensory perception. People did believe in that. But people believed in what they wanted to believe in. It was true, too, when she'd said it didn't matter whether or not he believed in witchcraft. If the people who killed Gideon believed in it, that would be motive enough.

216

His unease continued, emanating from all she'd said about Gideon. As if he and the dead man had anything in common! Yet Swanson had said something like that too. They were alike, that's what he had said. Swanson had been a violent, vicious crook. Superintendent Jack Harkness had spent his life fighting such people. Sure, there were times violence had to be met with violence. Didn't mean he enjoyed it. He never enjoyed it Damn them, never! Not unless he was faced with people like Swanson, Like . . . what was his name . . . Mahoney. Who'd killed those kids at New Year, all those years ago. Kevin Mahoney. They'd tried to say Mahoney was insane. He wasn't. Mahoney had known exactly what he was doing. But he'd had his moment with Mahoney, alone in a cell. He hadn't enjoyed it though. It was anger, rage, all the things like that. Not enjoyment. Not really enjoyment. Forget it. Think on something else. On who killed Gideon . . .

When he arrived in Greater Calderon, the incident van was outside The Goat and Compasses. He parked outside the inn and went at once into the van. Stevens was already there with the six detective constables and two uniformed men.

Harkness wasted no time.

'In case you don't know who I am, Harkness is the name,' he informed them. 'Sit down and relax. It'll be the only chance you'll get.'

They did so, awkwardly. Stevens took up a position at Harkness's side.

'You two uniformed men will be in here most of the time. You'll take phone calls and gather reports from the CID men. These reports will be read by you, copies made and fed into the files at Warwick via the computers you have in front of you. They will also be checked for any cross-references, information from different sources which ties together and provides possible corroboration. Every report will be submitted to me.'

He turned to the detectives. 'You will divide the two villages into sections. You'll work in pairs and take your own section. You will question everybody in that section. Everybody – man, woman and child. You will ask them where they were on the night Gideon was murdered. You will try and find from family or friends corroboration for each alibi. Family corroboration you will, however, treat with a degree of suspicion, since husbands, wives, relatives do tend to back up each other. You will ask if they knew Gideon, what they knew about him, his affairs, his work, anything . . .'

He took a deep breath. One of the older of the detectives was frowning.

'Something worrying you, Constable?'

'We did this before, sir. You'll have all our reports.'

'You'll do it again. And even more thoroughly than before.' He turned briefly to the uniformed men. 'You two'll check the new reports of interviews with the old ones. See if they differ. If they do, it'll be brought to my attention. We'll want to know why they differ.'

He turned back to the CID men. 'The reason you may be going over ground you've already covered is because I'm in charge, and I'm trained to notice things other people may have missed. Which is why I am a detective superintendent. You will, in other words, find out everything these people know about Gideon: his murder, his reputation, his friends and his enemies. I want verbatim reports which is why you'll work in pairs. I want to know everything that's said, and how it is said. Understand?'

'Sir?' It was a fresh-faced young detective.

'Yes?'

'A lot of these country people, they keep things to themselves. Don't like to talk to strangers. And particularly the police.'

'You're a trained CID man, aren't you? You know the interrogation technique?'

'Yes, sir.' The tone of the reply was doubtful.

'Then use your training! If possible, gain their confidence. Damn it, a murderer is loose. He could strike again. If anyone refuses to talk, you can always charge them with obstructing the police in the pursuit of their enquiries.'

It was Sergeant Stevens who broke in now. 'Is that legal, sir? I mean, people are entitled not to talk to the police.'

'If they're charged with a crime, yes. They're also entitled to solicitors. Anyone who adopts that attitude is suspect right away. Look, I'll take responsibility for any threats you have to make.' He paused, his thoughts back on the same tack as

218

during his drive to the village. 'Short of violence. But make these people talk. No matter how many weeks, months, whatever, we are going to question everyone in the two Calderons. And surrounding districts. And when we're finished, if we still haven't a murderer under arrest, we'll start all over again. Understood?'

There was a chorus of assent. They all understood.

He went on: 'You'll be working here until all hours at night. So you can tell wives, children and sweethearts you'll see them when you see them. If ever. I'll be staying in the village. The van here will be manned at night by two night shift officers. You'll arrange that, Sergeant Stevens?'

'Yes, sir.'

'You'll be taken back to Warwick some time every night in the mobile van. You will be picked up at six in the morning in Warwick and brought out here to carry on with your work. Interrogations will not be rushed. Take your time, learn all you can. If you strike lucky, believe you have come in contact with our man, you will allay any suspicions in the suspect and report to me. If you get a confession, bring the confessor back to me without further questioning. Anything worries you or you find suspicious, report back to me. I'll be here or in the inn there. Or out doing my own questioning. I can be contacted by your pocket radio. Any further questions?'

There were none.

'Right, Sergeant Stevens will give you your sectors of the village. Exclude the manor house for the time being – I'll take that one on. You'll be here, Stevens, co-ordinating everything with the uniformed men. And hold yourself available to accompany me. Get on with it. I shall be registering at the inn.'

He went into The Goat and Compasses, feeling smug. He could tell himself this was where he was at his best, organising the routine of a murder investigation. No nonsense about extra-sensory perception or witchcraft. The hard slog to which he was accustomed was beginning and, with his belief in himself and a certain ruthless quality he would admit to, he was confident he would find the killer of Joshua Gideon.

Behind the reception desk, Mullion was waiting.

'You're back.'

'I told you I would be.'

Mullion's mouth twisted into a sneer. 'As a policeman this time.'

'And from now on.'

'Didn't fool anybody last time. Asking too many questions.'

'I've a lot more to ask, Mr Mullion. Like where were you when Gideon was killed?'

'I'd be right here, wouldn't I? In my own place, minding my own business.'

'That so? What would you have been doing?'

'That time, I'd have closed up. Be doing my books for the day. Counting bar takings and the like.'

'What time would that be?'

'Midnight. Mebbe between midnight and half-past one.'

Harkness came back quickly now. 'You'd know that was when Gideon was killed then?'

Mullion's face turned the colour of his bed-linen, white with crumpled edges.

'I heard it . . . read it somewhere. It would be in the newspapers.'

Harkness shook his head slowly. 'Never was in the papers. Never was told by the police. Not even at the inquest. Just "the night of" . . . no time was given.'

'I just thought . . .'

'Or knew? Maybe you were there, Mister Mullion. Out in the field, in the dark, waiting. For Gideon.'

'Why . . . why should I want to kill Gideon?'

'You tell me. You didn't like him, did you?'

'Nobody liked him. He wasn't a likeable man. Doesn't mean I killed him. Try that on somebody else. It might fit better.'

Harkness smiled. 'Fits you well enough. But who do you suggest?'

Mullion didn't reply.

Harkness said: 'I want a room.'

'No vacancies!'

'Come on, Mullion, you know there's nobody staying here.'

'I don't have to have you here.'

220

'And I might have to charge you with obstructing a police investigation. That might be useful. Have you where I want you . . . when I want you. We could go over again how you knew when Gideon was killed. If, of course, that's when he was killed.'

'You can't charge me for not giving you a room.'

'We can always find something to charge you with. We're good at that. When necessary.'

Mullion's resistance was crumbling. After a moment it fell away. He pushed the registration book across the counter to Harkness.

'You have to register. It's the law.'

'I know the law, Mullion.'

'You'll not be wanting your old room.'

The smile was fixed on Harkness's face now. 'Why shouldn't I?'

'I just thought . . .'

'That I might get nightmares again? Let's find out, shall we? The butterfly room. Good name for it. Apposite. I'll want a meal about seven and then I'll be in my room reading reports. You can take the bag out of my car and carry it up.'

Mullion nodded. 'I'll get Abbie to . . .'

'No. You, Mullion. It's heavy. Not for a young kid. You carry it.'

He went outside and climbed into the incident van. Stevens was sitting drinking a second cup of coffee with the two uniformed men. When Harkness came in, he jumped to his feet, and was followed at once by the uniforms.

'Relax,' Harkness said. 'All we can do until the lads bring in their first reports is to wait. And you and me, Sergeant Stevens, can go through the reports of Blakelock's initial investigation – until we know them by heart, and can spot any inconsistencies.

'Yes, sir.' With forced enthusiasm.

'Never mind. Tomorrow, you and me'll go up to the manor for tea and biscuits with the lady. You'll like that better, Sergeant.'

They worked their way through the reports of Blakelock's investigation, Harkness making notes in a large note-book.

221

'Incidentally,' he said to Stevens. 'I want you to feed all the names I'm noting into your computer at HQ, and into the National Police Computer. I want to know if any of these people have records of any offences, criminal or civil. Especially Caroon. Oh, and check with the ecclesiastical authorities about the vicar, Mr Haydock. And with the Catholic hierarchy about Father Anselm.'

'You don't think the priests have anything to do with this?' said Stevens, surprised.

'I don't think anything, I simply want to know. Do it tomorrow morning. I shan't expect you back here until noon.'

Stevens nodded bleakly.

At ten minutes to seven, the detectives started bringing in their first reports.

'Anything worth my hearing?' Harkness asked.

'Bit of blaming other people,' said the senior of the detectives. 'I think we all found that. At least it's different from the last time. Then, they wouldn't say anything. Now it's all: "Look at Mr So-and-So." Or, "This woman was carrying on with Gideon, and so was that one. Where were the husbands?" Looks as if we're going to get a lot of that. It's all in the reports.'

'Good,' said Harkness, inserting them into a newly opened file. 'I'll be reading all these tonight. Nothing else?'

'That's it, sir.'

'One thing,' said another detective, a tall man with receding hair and a wide forehead. 'We was to see the vicar, Mister Haydock. But the woman who comes in to keep house for him wouldn't let us see him. Said he was ill. Couldn't see nobody?'

'All right, he'll see me tomorrow. Pack it in for the night, lads. Carry on as you've been doing in the morning.'

He took his evening meal alone, the only diner in the small room. Abbie served him, taking his order and saying nothing. Her silence made him wonder if she was nervous, but she gave no sign of being so.

He started reading the various reports while he ate. They differed from those produced by Blakelock's men. In these early reports, nobody had admitted to knowing anything. They had been asleep, they'd heard nothing, they knew nothing. But these first reports from his men were different.

222

'Didn't really know Gideon, except by sight. Told the kids to keep away from him. He was a violent man . . . always picking fights.'

'Ask that Megan Haslett. She knew him. She saw a lot of him. She'd know something.' This, from a woman called Annie Gayford.

'Jason Matthews' wife, she could tell you about Josh Gideon.'

'Enemies? Be better asking if he had any friends.'

'Annie Gayford, she knew him. Well. Better than her man knew.' This from Megan Haslett. The two ladies were obviously not on friendly terms.

He'd been through about half the reports by the time he'd finished his coffee. It seemed now the villagers were turning on each other, viciously. But it was creating a confusion of motives. Perhaps intentionally so. And no one had a good word to say about Gideon. There were even a few new suggestions as to what he got up to.

'Sure we were keepin' the youngsters from him. Not safe around the children, he wasn't?' The double negative added to the confusion but the general implication was there.

At eight-thirty he picked up the file of reports and went out of the dining-room. There was no one behind the reception desk and no sound. He looked into the bar. It was empty. Last night it had been packed with the male citizenry of Greater Calderon. Tonight, no one.

'You've killed my business.' Mullion had appeared silently behind him.

'My heart bleeds,' Harkness replied. 'In my home town, when there was a murder, the pubs were full of folk talking about it.'

'That was a big town. This is a village. They don't like being under suspicion. They don't like you staying here now they know you're a policeman.'

'I'm going to bed early tonight, Mullion. I lost some sleep last night so I've got some catching up to do. If I can. So you can spread the word . . . they can drink without being bothered by me. After all, what else can you do in a wee village like this? Watch television, fornicate or drink. Maybe spice it

223

up with a bit of witchcraft nonsense to give yourselves the excuse for an orgy . . . or a murder, eh? Good night!'

He went up to his room and went in. The butterflies and moths were still in their glass cases on the walls. There was still a blank space where the moth he'd found on his bed should have been.

The room was cold and silent. Waiting.

Chapter Twenty-five

The room's been waiting. But it's not going to happen tonight. I've been around the room, staring at the butterflies and moths. In their glass cases. Unable to get out. Pinned to cardboard. Dead. Dead moths under glass. Can't get out. Can't fly. Even if I dream it. Tonight I'll not be dreaming that dream or hearing tappings at the window. Looked into the mirror in the room before I climbed into bed and saw just my face, scars and all. Tired, yes, sure. But ready and able to work in the morning.

Witchcraft! I should laugh, will laugh. In their minds, that's all. In Jennet Agram's mind. Pity about Agram. An attractive woman. But not above suspicion. None of them, above suspicion.

Don't think about it now. Don't think about anything except sleep. God, I'm tired. Too tired to do anything else. Too tired to care if the butterflies were to come back, which they won't.

Dead men.

Part of my mind on dead men. On death. Seen it too often. Down among the dead men, Gideon and all the others through the years. More than most. Like a ruddy undertaker.

Too tired to think. Yet can't switch my mind off. Unless I sleep. God, let it come.

They say Gideon was evil. They didn't know Kevin Mahoney, child murderer. No, not Mahoney, dreamt too often about Mahoney. Always, just at the edge of sleep. Think on something else. Jennet Agram. Again. Big-breasted, broad-shouldered, stupid ideas but humour in her eyes . . . of course, she'll not be liking me. Few people . . . can be expected . . . to like investigating police officers. Few people like pigs. Few people . . . few . . . can . . . be . . . expected . . . to like . . . Jack Harkness.

Nearly went just then. Closer to sleep, closer my God to thee . . . that was a ship sinking . . . so the story goes.

Getting warm now. In a warm pit of sheets and blankets. Time to sleep . . .

Who am I? Me. The character of the man. Not likeable. Not on a murder case. Or any police business for that matter. Broke up my marriage. No, that was me. All on my ownsome. Should never have got married . . . all the time ago . . . when . . . when was it? . . . can't even remember her face . . . can see the girl today . . . my daughter . . . but can't even mind my wife . . . no face any more . . . Try, for God's sake try . . . you can mind all the other faces . . . not hers . . . no, that's the Agram woman . . . and the others . . . the whore in Piccadilly . . . and her sister was another . . . in the dark . . . into the dark. Now . . . into the dark . . .

. . . a sound in the dark. Loud, black, thumping sound . . .

He forced himself up from the depths of sleep. From the sound. Yet it followed him to wakefulness. He reached out and switched on the bedlight.

Someone was banging on the door. No dream now.

'Mister Harkness! Mister Harkness!' Abbie's voice.

'Aye . . . wha' . . . what is it?'

'Telephone, Mr Harkness. Woman says it's important.'

What woman?

He swung his legs from the bed and into the chill of the room, and stood, reaching for the dressing gown on the chair across from the bed.

'Coming!' he called, the warmth of sleep draining from him. Better be important, he thought. Can't think what woman would phone him? His daughter? Lizzie hadn't been in touch for years. If it was some stupid policewoman in Warwick, she'd hear the voice of Glasgow in the raw. He glanced at his watch. God Almighty, it was one forty-five in the morning.

226

The only telephone was downstairs on the reception desk, the receiver off the hook.

Lifting it, he said, 'Harkness here! What is it?'

A woman's voice. 'I'm sorry to bother you. Superintendent. This is Margaret Campion. We met the other day . . . before you were a policeman.' There was fleeting humour in the voice.

'Aye, I remember . . . at the church in Lesser Calderon. Sorry about the wee deception but I was . . . even then . . . really a police officer. On duty. Er, what can I do for you?'

The humour vanished from the voice. 'I'm sorry to phone you in the middle of the night, but it really is serious. The Reverend Mr Haydock was taken ill early this evening. The woman who cleans the vicarage called me and I went down to see him. He wasn't looking too well, so I decided to bring him up to the manor house. He became worse so I called my doctor in Stratford.'

'Stratford?'

'There isn't a doctor in Calderon, Superintendent. Anyway, my doctor came . . . he's with Mr Haydock now.'

'Any idea what's the matter with him?'

'Heart attack, Doctor Sanders tells me. But the reason I'm phoning is, Mr Haydock is asking to see you.'

'Me? He'll not be thinking I'm still a commercial traveller.'

'You don't know villages, Mr Harkness. Do I call you Mister or Superintendent? Anyway, he knows who you are and he's asking to see you. In a highly excited state.'

'Can I come right up?'

'Of course. You know the way?'

'The side road beyond the two villages?'

'That's the one. Quarter of a mile through the trees and you'll see the manor.'

'Be there in fifteen minutes. And as for what you call me, Miss Campion – Jack Harkness'll do.'

He dressed hurriedly, in crushed shirt and creased suit, and was out of the inn in ten minutes. He put his head around the door of the incident van. One constable was asleep in a corner, the other smoking a cigarette and reading the sports page of a newspaper. The newspaper went down and the cigarette was crushed out as the man snapped to his feet.

227

'Sir!'

'Congratulations. You're awake. I've been called up to the manor house. You can kick your mate there in the crotch and send him on patrol around the village. You're supposed to take turns in doing just that. I won't be long so you'd both better be alert and on duty when I get back.'

'Yes, sir!'

Harkness drove into the blackness beyond Greater and Lesser Calderon, his headlights bisecting the night, turning hedges into great twisting barriers, trees into misty giants. He almost missed the side road to the manor and had to reverse to turn from the main road.

He went through yet another blackness of trees, the tarmac gone beneath him, and then he was driving over rutted gravel. Finally the gravel widened out in the headlights and he saw the front of the manor. It was a modest country house, an oblong Georgian shape but with large high windows and little other exterior embellishments.

Parking the car beside a Range Rover and a large Silver Jaguar with a sticker 'Doctor on Call,' he rang the doorbell.

A plump woman wrapped in a dressing gown and various scarves opened the door.

'Superintendent Harkness,' he said. 'Miss Campion is expecting me.'

'Oh, yes, come in, sir. I'm Mrs Chalmers, the housekeeper. What a night we've had.' She shook her head sadly, apple cheeks wobbling.

Despite the seeming modesty of the exterior, the manor's hall was large. A wide staircase led up to a landing above. There was little furniture: two chairs against a panelled wall, a number of paintings on the walls (ancestors, Harkness learned later, of the Campion family), and on the floor a huge Persian carpet took up the centre of the polished surrounds. Below the staircase, defiantly staring at the world, stood a seven foot tall stuffed black bear. Not a young, recently stuffed bear, no masterpiece of the taxidermist's art, as shown by the holes in the fur and the emergence of padding from the holes.

'I'll take your coat, Superintendent,' said Mrs Chalmers. 'Miss Campion'll be down directly.'

He stood barely a minute before he heard her voice from the landing above. 'Come up, Mr Harkness!'

She was wearing a warm towelling dressing-gown over a barely visible nightdress. Her hair was in disarray and she looked tired. He climbed the stairs to the landing.

'I'm sorry to have dragged you out in the middle of the night,' she said, running her hand through her hair.

'No, that's all right. How is he?'

The reply came from behind her, at the door of one of the bedrooms. 'Not good, I'm afraid. He's had two heart attacks.'

Margaret Campion turned. 'Oh, Superintendent, this is Doctor Rex Sanders. Superintendent Harkness.'

Sanders was in his forties, a towering figure at least six feet three in height, dark hair like polished leather above a broad forehead and aquiline nose. Despite the hour, he was immaculately dressed in a pin-striped suit, white shirt and dark blue tie. The air of the perfect professional, Harkness thought.

'Good evening,' said Sanders. 'I'm afraid you won't have very long with Haydock. I phoned Stratford for an ambulance. He needs hospitalisation – if it's not too late.'

'As bad as that?'

'Worse. He may not last out. The second attack was pretty massive. If you want to see him, try not to get him excited. And . . . it'll only be for a few minutes.'

Margaret Campion led Harkness to the bedroom door. At the door, Harkness paused and turned to Sanders.

'Any idea what caused the heart attack?'

Sanders shrugged. 'I'm not his regular physician. He might well have had a history of heart trouble, angina, or he could have been under pressure. Miss Campion tells me there's been something like that.'

'He's had his problems.'

Harkness went into the bedroom. It was a spacious, comfortable room with a large comfortable double bed. The Reverend Mr Haydock lay in the centre of the bed, head on two pillows, face pallid, lips tinged with purple. His eyes were shut and his breathing laboured. Harkness sat on the edge of the bed.

'Mr Haydock?'

The old man stirred, eyelids fluttering.

229

'It's Superintendent Harkness. Can you hear me?'

The lips moved. 'Commercial traveller turns out to be . . . to be a policeman.'

'That's me. Sorry about the deception, sir.'

'All . . . all deception . . . yes, all deception . . .'

'What would that include, Mr Haydock?'

'Them . . . all of them. You have to stop them . . . have to stop him . . .'

'And who would that be?'

Haydock's face contorted in pain.

'Who have I got to stop, Mr Haydock?'

The old man moved in the bed, slowly and painfully, muttering indistinctly: 'Crowley tried it . . . nearly drove him mad . . . now they know how to . . .'

'Who are they?'

A bubble of saliva appeared at the corner of Haydock's mouth. His lips twitched as if to dislodge the bubble.

'The deceiver . . . he boasts of it . . . without fear . . . I . . . I said, I don't believe . . . he laughed. Just laughed at me.'

'Can you tell me who he is?'

Haydock's body seemed to become rigid. '"Ye . . . ye shall know them . . . by their appearance . . . and . . . and . . ."'

'Yes?'

'I . . . I face the fires of hell. They start to burn. They have . . . consigned me to the fire. Already I feel the burning in my body.'

'You've had a small heart attack.' Harkness found the lie easy.

'And, Harkness, when they . . . they raise him up . . . when they do that . . .'

'Yes?'

'*You* shall be the vessel.'

Then a silence. Finally the old man's body shuddered and an expression of agony came over his face. Harkness leaned forward.

'Who is *he*?' Harkness repeated unable to keep the urgency from his voice.

'I think that's enough, Superintendent,' said Sanders from behind.

230

The doctor thrust Harkness to one side and took his place on the bed, taking up the old man's wrist in his hand and feeling for the pulse.

'How is he?' Harkness said, and realised he had little feeling for Haydock but only for the questions the old man could answer.

'Very weak. The heart's going.' Sanders glanced at his watch. 'If he can hold out until we get him to the cardiac unit at Stratford, he might have a chance. I'm afraid I'll have to ask you to wait outside.'

'I've got more questions,' Harkness said.

'I don't think he's got any more answers, Superintendent. Please, go.'

Harkness went out of the room. Margaret Campion was waiting on the landing.

'How is he?' she asked.

'Not good, I'm afraid.'

'You must be tired yourself, Mr Harkness. Can I offer you something. Tea? Coffee? Or something stronger. Perhaps a brandy?'

'I could use a brandy.'

'Come down to the living room.'

They went downstairs and into a room off the hall. The housekeeper was putting coal on a great open fire. The room was large, high-ceilinged, and with two long high windows, heavily curtained. Two of the walls were lined with books from floor to ceiling. There was an old but comfortable leather sofa and two matching armchairs, both well worn. At the side of the fire was a large television set. It was a lived-in room, Harkness thought, untidy but with the remnants of a decaying elegance.

Opposite the television set was an ornate, lacquered Chinese cabinet scored and marked with signs of considerable antiquity. It was to this that Margaret Campion went. From its interior she produced two glasses and a decanter of golden liquid and poured out two large drinks.

'That business of passing yourself off as a commercial traveller – wasn't it little unorthodox?' she said, handing him one of the glasses.

231

'I've got that kind of reputation. Just a wee fishing expedition to see how the land lay. Not very successful.'

She smiled. 'The people of Calderon are rather clannish. My own family has been here six hundred years and more, and sometimes I think we're still treated as incomers.'

'There's places in Scotland like that, but you have to teach them about the police. That we're here for everyone's good. Anyway, I don't think Jack Harkness, commercial traveller, fooled anybody.' He raised his glass and gave her the old Gaelic toast. '*Slainte!*'

'Cheers!'

He became aware, as she answered his toast, of her perfume. Subtle, aromatic, different. More eastern than western. India or China, perhaps. Certainly not Paris. Which surprised him. She was so upper middle-class English. Should be Chanel Number 5, or one of the newer ones, Opium or Poison. But it wasn't. And it wasn't just the perfume that caught his attention now. There was something else. She was different from the woman he'd met in the church at Lesser Calderon. There, she'd been the typical young country woman in sweater, skirt and sensible shoes. But now he could sense there was more to her. Something in the way she moved, a languorous quality, an easy suggestion of sensuousness.

The door opened and the doctor came in.

'I'm sorry, he's gone,' he said, his face set in an expression of earnest compassion. Harkness could not rid himself of the thought that the expression was well-used and easily assumed.

Margaret Campion said: 'Oh, God!' but quietly and with feeling.

'I did my best but . . .' Sanders shrugged. 'Three heart attacks in a row, and the last two were massive. Even if we'd got him to Stratford, I doubt if the cardiac unit could have saved him.'

'In view of the circumstances, there'd better be a post-mortem,' Harkness said.

Sanders nodded. 'If you think so. Although I don't think they'll find anything else.'

'I'm sure they won't. But in the middle of a murder case . . .'

Sanders glanced towards Margaret. 'When the ambulance arrives, I'll have them take the body to Stratford and notify the coroner. That'll save Miss Campion any more bother.'

'I'd be obliged, doctor,' Harkness said, and took a gulp of brandy.

'Will you have a drink, doctor?' Margaret asked, but Sanders shook his head.

'With the police here and me about to drive back to Stratford? I think not.'

From outside there came a distant sound of a clanging bell.

'The ambulance,' Margaret said.

Sanders looked puzzled. 'It's too soon. Unless he was doing a hundred miles an hour.'

He went over to the window and drew the heavy curtain aside.

'Not the ambulance. That's the fire brigade. God, look at the sky!'

Harkness and Margaret came up to the window behind him.

'The wood's on fire.' Harkness peered out at the red hue against the black sky.

'No!' said Margaret Campion. 'That's not the wood. That's further away. That's in Calderon!'

Chapter Twenty-Six

The fire was in Lesser Calderon. It was the church, Haydock's church. As the man died, so his church burned. What was it he'd said? Harkness asked himself.

'They have consigned me to the fire.'

It was as if the dying man had known.

They had driven from the manor, Margaret Campion in Harkness's car. The doctor, feeling he might be needed at the site of the fire, had followed in his Jaguar, having left instructions for the ambulance to collect Haydock's body.

When they arrived, Sanders was not needed. The rear of the church had been ablaze and was still smouldering. It appeared the fire had been somehow started in the empty building, and first had been noticed by a long-distance lorry driver on the main road. This man had at once alerted the nearby villagers who had called for the nearest fire-brigade which was at Downingham. While this brigade was on its way, the villagers had brought out from a nearby shed an old but well-maintained machine manned by volunteers. And the volunteers had turned out and worked with a will, hosing down the flames with considerable efficiency. By the time Harkness and Margaret Campion reached the building, the Downingham brigade had taken over and the blaze was under control. The villagers now seemed to have fallen back to become spectators, heavy coats and jackets covering night attire.

Harkness made his way across the snake-like battery of hoses to the Downingham Fire-Master, and presented his credentials.

'Any idea what started it?' he said to the officer.

'Bit early for that, sir. Have to have a look around when it cools down. Main thing is, it's under control and we should have it out shortly.'

Harkness nodded. 'I want your report as soon as possible, and I want an expert's opinion. You'll phone Warwick tomorrow and have an arson officer to inspect the place with you. Right?'

The Fire-Master looked dubious. 'If we can find out. These things can start with a cigarette end thrown in the wrong place . . .'

'Apart from the fact that people don't usually smoke in church, I want to know. I'm conducting a murder investigation here, and this may well be related.'

'What about the vicar?'

'The vicar had a heart attack earlier this evening. He died in the manor house over a mile away. We're hardly likely to learn anything there. How much damage has been done?'

'Rear of the church badly damaged. Rear wall's collapsed. Whatever caused it, it started at the back of the church. As far as we can see, somewhere around the altar.'

'Isn't it mostly stone?'

'The altar's a wooden table . . . or was. The church is pretty old and shored up by wooden beams. They went up, the stone-work collapsed. And everything flammable went. We can go in the front now and I can show you.'

They walked towards the front door of the church, two figures under the scrutiny of the small crowd that had inevitably gathered. Apart from the volunteer firemen this consisted of villagers in dressing gowns over pyjamas, duffel coats, heavy rubber boots grabbed and quickly donned. Even here a fire brings out the sightseers, Harkness told himself, and wondered whether it was the fascination of flames in the sky or the morbid excitement of being close to the possible death of some luckless soul.

At the portico of the building it might have been difficult to realise there had been a fire. Apart from trails of smoke in the air and the harsh smell of burnt wood, there was no sign here of a conflagration. The door into the vestry was open and they went in. Again only the smoke and the smell. They went through the vestry with its tattered notices, begrimed not only by smoke but by age. Inside the church, the smoke was thicker, but now drifting down to the stone floor and thinning into a kind of mist.

The rear of the church had gone. The altar, the pulpit, the large crucifix, the decorations behind the altar, were now burried or burnt under a pile of rubble. The rear wall of the church had collapsed inwards. The stained-glass windows had cracked and broken in the heat, leaving headless saints, wingless angels, cherubim, some without bodies, some lacking limbs, all seemingly unconcerned, going about their heavenly affairs. Through the gaps, the blackness of the night sky could be seen, giving a patchwork effect to the glass, and in some cases, it appeared as if one was looking at a negative image. The empty pews, still intact, faced the rubble and the night beyond, the serried rows giving the impression of having, in one short evening, been turned into something resembling the stalls in an open-air cinema.

Harkness did not linger. He came out followed by the Fire Master and rejoined Margaret Campion.

'Poor Haydock,' she said. 'His life and his work gone in one night.'

He stared at her. She seemed genuinely near to tears. Yet she had received the news of Haydock's death with less compassion than she was now exhibiting. Perhaps the destruction of the church served to underline the death of its servant.

Sanders, who was standing behind her, said, 'I'm not needed here. Better get back to Stratford.'

'I'll want the autopsy report as soon as possible,' Harkness said.

'You'll have it.'

They watched the Jaguar driving towards the main road. He's getting out of this place, Harkness thought, and envied the doctor. So easy to drive away from a murder case, from two dark villages, and fires and frowns and sidelong looks and frightened silences. And deep within, Harkness had to acknowledge the growing, uneasy fear. Of what? Not of murder, of what men could do to men; he'd never feared that. Too accustomed to it. Never really feared his own death.

Been too near to it. So what was there to fear? Butterflies and moths and other nightmares in dreams? Nonsense! Failure, perhaps? No, he didn't like failure, didn't really consider it, but if it happened, then he could accept it. With ill grace. God knows, his record was too good. Perhaps it was time for a failure. But not yet. Not in this place.

He stared at the untouched façade of the church for a moment and then said, 'Better drive you home, Miss Campion. You've had quite a night. And I have to be up and working in a few hours.'

They drove back to the manor in silence, each lost in their own thoughts. At the door, she got out of the car and turned to him.

'It's late,' she said. 'Or rather, early in the morning. You could stay until breakfast. We have plenty of room and it would save you the trip back to the inn.'

Was it his imagination or was there more in her invitation than a demonstration of practical kindness? A suggestion of something else, another kind of invitation in the twist of the lips and the look in the eyes? Or was he imagining a lasciviousness that wasn't there?

'Better get back to the inn,' he replied. 'Only a couple of hours until my men arrive from Warwick and we get down to the day's work.'

She smiled. 'Of course. I understand.'

He had been imagining things. The rejection had been taken in the same matter-of-fact manner as the invitation was made. He'd been celibate too long, he could tell himself, alone too long. Months since he'd had a woman. Back in London before the Swanson case, it had been. And then with a certain professional lady of his acquaintance. There was a kind of friendship between them, an acceptance of his need on her part, and on his, a knowledge that his protection could be valuable in the sexual jungle of commercial sex in London. It had been a discreet liaison, his protection also an insurance against the possibility of blackmail. After all, he was a single man, long divorced.

'You'll come to dinner soon?' Margaret Campion said. 'I'll invite somebody with a knowledge of the village. Might help your investigation.'

'Be good of you.' An almost grudging acceptance. Was he resenting the 'somebody' with the knowledge of the village?

'The sooner this business is cleared up the better,' she went on. 'I don't know what's happened to Calderon. Used to be just a pair of pleasant little villages. Now, there's murder, and fire and death. It has to stop. Please, Superintendent, you have to make it stop.'

A sudden, strained desperation in her voice.

'Do my best, Miss Campion. Meanwhile you try and get some sleep. I'll see you again soon.'

She went in, her face pale and bleak.

Back at the inn, the two constables were drinking tea in the incident van. One of them was dishevelled, face, hands and uniform besmirched with soot and grime. He'd been at the fire.

'See anything out of the ordinary, Constable?' Harkness asked.

'Can't say I did, sir. When I got there the alarm had been raised. Saw you arrive just behind me. The usual spectators had turned out and the local volunteers were trying to put out the fire.'

Harkness nodded. No more than he expected. 'You'll be relieved in a couple of hours,' he told them. 'Let's hope it'll be a peaceful couple of hours.'

The interior of the hotel was in darkness. If Mullion had been astir because of the fire, he was still out or had long retired to his bed. There was no sign of Abbie.

In his room, the bed light glinted on the specimen cases. Everything was as it should be. Harkness stripped to shirt and trousers, and lay on top of the bed. Two hours and he would be up again and working. Like old times. Twenty hours a day on a murder investigation. No sleep and little need of it. He was younger then. And hardened, tempered like metal to accept horror. To look on blood on pavements without emotion. A world of sticky scarlet dying to a dull brown. The gutted children in the tenement had exhausted his ability to be sickened. Later, there had been the old woman behind the counter of the sub-post-office. Shot-gunned by a youth with a need for money, no conscience and less imagination. He had pressed the trigger, blown off the top of her head and stolen two pounds, eleven shillings. That was in the days before decimalisation. And when he had been arrested the youth had wept, not for the old woman but for himself. That was the trouble with that kind of animal. No imagination and an excuse of self pity. Perhaps that was the origin and the meaning of evil.

Harkness slept . . .

. . . dreaming of Margaret Campion. Or was it Margaret Campion? A woman in the dream – taking her clothes off, baring her breast for him, embracing his mouth, open, tongue raping his mouth . . .

. . . and then the routine excitement of movement and caress, hand cupping the breast, mouth on the nipple.

Margaret Campion's face changing to Jennet Agram's, moving against him. And he, burying his face deep in her body, kissing, licking . . . then, above him, the face changing again to his one-time wife's . . . to the woman in London . . . what was her name? . . . to so many women. A bedroom in a bungalow . . . on the floor in front of a fireplace in a tenement . . . against the wall in an alley in Glasgow – a knee-trembler, they called it. So many names over the years, so many bodies moving under him . . . all struggling towards him, as he struggled towards them . . . and then he entered, thrusting forward, forcing entry . . . concerned only now with his own need . . . moving in and out and in . . . all the violence of consenting rape . . . the two bodies coming together . . . all awareness of anything but the now and the need and the climax . . . as if they were rolling over and over and deeper and deeper . . .

He came awake.

Sweating. Excited. And erect.

Oh, Christ, he didn't need this.

He rose, staggering over to the washhand basin. And drenching his face in ice-cold water. Felt it trickling down his chest.

He washed and shaved and dressed. And tried to put the dream and its eroticism from his mind.

The night of the fire was over.

Chapter Twenty-Seven

The next week was spent in what was, to Harkness, the routine investigation of a murder. Like the naming of names, came the questioning of suspects. And now the silence had gone and the villagers talked to the police, enumerating the various clashes between Joshua Gideon with his fellow villagers. Of course, no one admitted anything. Everyone accused someone else.

Caroon had a fight with Gideon in the bar of The Goat and Compasses, two weeks before Gideon's death. This was reported by one, Peter Hayward, a farm worker.

Caroon confirmed, 'Sure we had an argument. More a kind of argy-bargy. Gideon was always sounding off that he knew everything. We all got kind of fed up with it.'

'What specifically was the argument about?'

'Can't call that to mind. Warn't a fight, just words.'

This was confirmed by Mullion and others present.

'They just had words. Go back over the years, everybody had words with Gideon.'

He was a man who invited words. So, all right, where was Caroon when Gideon was killed?

'Abed, like everybody else.'

'Except Gideon and those who killed him.'

'That'd be right enough.'

'Nobody around to confirm you were in bed that night?'

'My mother saw me goin' to bed.'

'Your father?'

A broad grin, teeth bared. 'Never knew him. Hasn't been around for years.'

Caroon was like everyone else. In bed, asleep, unaware. Married men gave alibis for their wives, wives gave alibis for their husbands.

Reports of Gideon's sexual affairs came in. Always accusations by one woman against another. And denied by the other. The denials were backed up by indignant husbands.

With one exception.

The woman, it was said, had been caught *in flagrante* by husband and his friend. Harkness visited her while her husband was out working. He was the village flesher (there was a word to conjure with, Harkness thought) and butcher with a tiny shop behind The Goat and Compasses.

Her name was Marnay and she was a small woman with black hair drawn back into a bun. She was in her early thirties and despite the severity of her hairstyle and lack of make-up, she had a good face, even a pretty one. Her figure too was good if slightly top heavy. Under a dress and jumper was an ample and interestingly well-shaped bosom (described by one of the local males as, "A good pair of tits.")

She lived in one of the council houses, and Harkness interviewed her in a small but spotless sitting room.

'You knew Joshua Gideon?'

She said: 'You been listening to gossip.'

'I am investigating Gideon's murder. I have to listen to everything. I assure you, however, that I am not interested in personal morality.'

'Just in gossip, eh?'

'You did know Gideon?'

'I know most everybody in Calderon.'

'Your husband had an altercation with him?'

'If you mean Michael punched him, yes, he did that. Trouble is, Gideon hit him back an' Gideon were bigger than Michael. So Michael got a bloody nose, and serves him right.'

Harkness coughed, avoiding the woman's defiant gaze, and found himself staring at her breasts. He looked over her shoulder.

'This fight was to do with Gideon . . . er, paying undue attention to you?'

242

'You know what it were about. I were in bed with Gideon. He were givin' me something Michael's barely able to give. He were fuckin' me and I enjoyed it.'

Her directness startled Harkness. At least there was no dissimulation here.

'Didn't mean I liked him, but he knew how to give a woman what she needed. An' there's plenty here could tell you that. Still, I knew it would be nothin' regular, just Gideon playing his games, and me thinking what harm could he be doing.'

'Your husband was angry?'

'Man doesn't like horns bein' put on him. But he got over it. Had to, or else all he could do was throw me out. Michael Marnay isn't up to that.'

'Might he be up to . . . getting his own back?'

'You mean, did he kill Gideon? He's not man enough to. Besides that, the night Gideon were killed he were in bed wi' me. Swear to it in court, I would.'

Michael Marnay confirmed his wife's statement.

'Sure I hit him, I'd a killed him then, given half a chance. An' swung cheerfully for it.'

'They abolished the death penalty,' Harkness said dryly.

'But I didn't kill him later. Wasn't worth it. Bloody great pig of a man.' Marnay gave a smug and unpleasant grin. 'She'd not tell you I beat her up too, did she? Later, I did. Wouldn't show herself for a week, the cow. All she is, a bloody cow with great udders. Good for fuckin' and that's about all. An' she'll tell you I was in bed with her the night Gideon was done.'

'She told me.'

Harkness thought, There's motive but little else. And Marnay wasn't the only one with that kind of motive. He was just one that caught his wife out. Harkness could be sure there were others among the women of the two villages who had enjoyed the favours and attention of Joshua Gideon. And always, for the night of the murder, the couples would alibi each other.

Later he was interviewing Father Anselm at the Alms House.

'I too have no alibi, Superintendent. After supper that night, the woman who keeps house for me went off . . . she

243

doesn't sleep in . . . and I read for a time and went off to bed. That, of course, is the trouble in small villages. People go quietly to their beds of a night. After Mullion has shut his bar.'

'And nobody's going to admit they were abroad that night, eh?' said Harkness.

'Unlike life in the cities where people are about until all hours, life is quieter here. And neighbours don't live quite so close to each other. Occasionally one might pass down the street at a late hour and see lights in windows. But one knows who lives there, and one doesn't bother to look in. In other words, we don't look at what our neighbours are up to, because they'll be up to very little.' The priest's thin face twisted into a reluctant smile.

'So husbands alibi wives and vice-versa. All automatically.'

'If they were lying, would you ever know?'

'As you say, Father.'

'Of course I'd be loath to admit this crime was committed by any one of my flock.'

'For all that they make noises now, they're a tight-mouthed people.'

The priest nodded his agreement. 'The villages are isolated, Superintendent. Isolation breeds a taciturn attitude. Yet they are talking to you now.'

'And saying little.'

'Perhaps because they've little to say. You're a foreigner to them, an intruder from a world which pays little attention to them. Why should they pay attention to it?'

He left the priest's house and returned to the incident van, to receive the coroner's report on the death of Haydock. He read this, feet stretched out in front of him, back against the side of the van.

'. . . massive coronary occlusion . . . death by natural causes . . .'

Of no relevance to the murder. Except in what the old man had said before he had died. If that were relevant.

And there was the report of the fire officer on the burning of the church.

244

There is no evidence of what actually caused the conflagration. Obviously it could have been a discarded
cigarette end or some such accidental cause.

There is nothing to support a presumption of arson;
no traces of gasoline or any combustible material deliberately placed. The fire seems to have originated beside
the altar. And, although it would be a distinct oddity, the
lack of evidence of origin might indicate a rare example
of spontaneous combustion, possibly induced by marsh
gas seeping through from the foundations. It must be
emphasised however, that this can be nothing more than
a theory . . .

Harkness stared for some time at the report. Nothing there of
value. The history of the investigation so far. Nothing of
value, nothing pertinent. He felt irritation rising within him, a
feeling triggered by the stronger emotion of frustration. The
old saying came to mind: When one door closes, another
slams in your face. The true history of the murder investigation at Greater Calderon. In any other case, by this time there
should be some sort of breakthrough. Excluding random
killing, there was usually some palpable clue, something that
indicated a little light at the end of the tunnel. But not here,
not now.

And there was something else which was creating a growing
annoyance. His frustration was mixed with a growing feeling
of claustrophobia, as if the two villages were a tiny world in
which he was enclosed; to which he was exiled. The drab
council houses and the older buildings, considered by some
though not by Harkness to be picturesque, were equally drab
and oppressive to him, as were the lives of those who inhabited them. Drab and narrow. And narrowing all the time. Oh,
these people talked, they discussed the weather, the local
gossip, who was fornicating with who; and under all their talk,
ran a barely concealed thread of violence. Not necessarily the
kind of violence that led to murder. Simply a casual approach
to brutality. Young Caroon was a prime example in this
respect. Anyone who disagreed with him might be threatened
with a bashing, a kicking . . . no Queensbury rules there . . .
and this attitude was reflected in all the others.

'Allgood loses another of my sheep and he'll find himself without any teeth!'

'Like to get that bastard alone one dark night and he'll be goin' home holdin' in his broken ribs. Owed me that fiver for over three months, he has!'

'She warn't happy 'bout marryin' him an' he knew it. So, first night, he spread-eagles her on the bed. Ties her hands and feet to each corner, so's she's lying there like a great Maltese Cross. Still with her clothes on. Then he cuts open all the front of her clothes, so's she's naked in front. Then he rapes her . . . if you can be said to rape your wife . . . making use of every aperture in her body. That's how he puts it. Leaves her tied like that for three days, havin' her whenever he feels like it. Goes off to work at the bottle factory in between. By the time he's finished, she's a good obedient wife. Said, in the end, she liked it, so she did!'

'They say, when Georgie Numbles was hit by that lorry, there was nothing left of his face. Nothing you could call a face.' This said with a kind of relish, in the bar of The Goat and Compasses by a middle-aged man who should have known better.

'Tied the husband up with the clothes-line in the kitchen. Then hauled him up to the roof and had his wife wi' him hanging there, watchin'.'

An ugly people, Harkness thought, never read a book beyond the hymn-book in the church, never thought about the human condition unless there was violence or sex involved; a people who would have no concern about the act of murder committed in their midst. Yet there wasn't a shard of evidence against any one of them.

Since the night of the butterflies, as Harkness called it to himself, the night of the nightmare, he told himself, he'd slept well enough. Occasionally his own thoughts had kept him awake for some time, as he ran over the day's reports in his head. Looking for something, a speck of light, a relevant statement, a solitary clue he might have missed. There was nothing.

A sound behind him. Someone on the steps up to the van. He straightened up, consigning the Fire Officer's report to the pile on the desk at the side of the van.

Margaret Campion came in.

'I've been expecting you to come to me. To . . . grill me. Is that the correct expression?'

He rose to his feet. 'Only in American movies,' he replied. 'In this country, we call it a few routine questions. Unless you're guilty, in which case we call it helping us with our enquiries.'

'I felt left out, so I came to you. And to invite you to dinner next Saturday, if you can come.'

'I'd like to. Unless anything untoward arises.'

'Has anything arisen so far? Or shouldn't I ask?'

'You shouldn't,' he said, 'but I'll tell you. So far we are faced with the blankest of blank walls. Do sit down. But carefully.'

She sat on the edge of one of the official issue folding chairs.

'Of course the blank wall doesn't surprise me. As I've said, they're a close-mouthed people.'

Harkness rubbed his chin. 'I wouldn't say that. They talk nineteen to the dozen. Accuse each other. But wi'out evidence. So far there's no evidence of anything. Apart from the corpse.'

'It's a form of being close-mouthed. Talking too much and saying nothing. Perhaps, after all, Gideon was killed by an outsider.'

'It might be a way out for me. But I don't believe it.'

There was a non-pregnant pause. An awkwardness.

Then she said: 'Aren't you going to ask me where I was the night of the murder?'

He obliged. 'Where were you the night of the murder?'

'In bed. Asleep.'

'Same as everybody else.'

'No witnesses. I sleep alone, mostly.'

'You never married?' It was, he was at once aware, an irrelevant question.

'Never met anyone I wanted to marry. Oh, I'm quite normal, Superintendent. No virgin I. Except in Calderon, where I have to be respectable. But there have been a few . . . relationships in London. Nothing permanent. Just to keep me healthy.'

'You're very honest.'

'No, I'm not. I say what I want to say. And honesty can be tactical.'

'If you're campaigning.'

'I might be. Any other questions? Relating to your investigation, of course?'

'Josh Gideon? You knew him?'

'We all knew him. Me? Not in the biblical sense. He had a certain animal charm, but I appreciate a degree of finesse. I suppose, in the end, I'm a snob. I knew he wreaked havoc among the local women. But he'd been doing that for years, without being murdered.'

'You've no idea why he might have been murdered?'

'None at all.'

'You've seen or heard nothing that might be relevant?'

'Not that I'm aware of. But then, that means nothing. There can be . . . how can I put it? . . . underlying currents of emotion in places like this. They can run strong, possibly strong enough to drive someone to murder. But I'm afraid I know nothing of them.'

'That's all you can tell me?'

'"Fraid so. Perhaps, when you come to dinner and we talk, something might come out that I don't even realise is important.' She rose. 'If there's nothing else?'

'Nothing.'

'Saturday then. Seven-thirty.' She gave a mischievous smile. 'I've asked Father Anselm as well. But he won't stay late.'

She went down the steps into the road and walked quickly away, as if she didn't want to be seen coming from the incident van. He watched her go, aware of unspoken invitations underlying the spoken ones. Or was it his imagination? She seemed to be attracted. He could only admit to himself that he too was attracted. Not a good thing in the middle of a murder enquiry. But it had still been a long time since he'd had a woman. He'd begun to think he was getting past it.

Sergeant Stevens and a number of the detectives appeared outside the van. They'd been asking questions at the outlying farms. The interrogations in the two villages were almost complete. They would be coming to write up the results of their interrogations. He decided to leave them to it. He would go through the few reports in the morning. It was nearly time for dinner.

He exchanged a few words with the arrivals. Nothing in the new interrogations seemed important. He left them writing reports and waiting for their transport back to Warwick, and went into The Goat and Compasses, to await dinner and later to sleep.

He wasn't aware then that there would be little sleep for him that night.

of the contents of the vial. That does not matter. As long as one of us believes, and I certainly do. Though God knows why. Yet, without that belief, I am nothing.

Keep the vial by you. In time, it may be of help. It is all I can leave anyone in this world. Why you, you will ask?

Because you are the one in greatest danger of eternal damnation.

Sincerely,
Arthur Haydock.

Harkness sat gazing down at the sheet of paper. The epistle according to Arthur Haydock, late vicar of this parish. It was dated the morning of his death. Or rather of the day he had been taken ill. He had died in the small hours of the next morning. Perhaps trying to say something of what he had said in the note.

What the hell did it mean?

Was it simply the scribblings of a man who could see his own death and was clutching at the one solid article of his failing faith that he possessed?

Harkness put the note in his pocket. And, replacing the vial in the cigar cylinder, he replaced the top and put it too in his pocket. Some kind of evidence, he supposed, although of what, and what its meaning might be, he had no idea. Why did Haydock state he, Harkness, was in danger of damnation? Harkness did not believe in damnation. Nor in the efficacy of holy water. He did believe that Haydock had had a presentiment of his own imminent death. But then, the man was weak and sickly. He had died from natural causes. His heart had given out, valves or blood vessels had burst. There was no mystery about his death.

And yet . . .

And yet he had claimed the causes were not natural. A heart attack induced by fear. That was always a possibility, but not provable. The old Scots verdict on the accused: not proven. Never could be proven.

Harkness washed in cold water, too impatient to wait for the hot water to flow through the pipes. Perhaps to induce an alertness he did not feel. At the same time he filed his questions about the note and the vial of water at the back of his mind. To be thought upon later, at another time, when the answers might fall into place. That was the usual pattern in a normal criminal investigation. Which this was definitely not.

He dined alone in the claustrophobic narrowness of the small dining room. With the sound of conversation coming from the bar across the corridor. Knowing that, when he entered, there would be the momentary hush, then the rise again of small talk. And it would be small talk. As if care was being taken to avoid mention of the reason for his presence. As it had been each evening he had been there.

Tonight he determined to give the bar a miss. He finished a dinner of cold mutton, salad and underdone potatoes, thinking that each night the meal worsened. To encourage and speed his eventual departure perhaps? He lessened the tastelessness of the meal with a bottle of Chablis, a pleasing discovery from the small cellar of the inn, and went back up to his room.

Although tired, he started to go over the various reports of his detectives on their interviews with the villagers. For a third time, he read carefully through them, looking for something – a remark, a mistake, a hint of a clue – that might provide a lead. There was again that growing sense of desperation in him. Usually, by this time, there was some clue, some sign that might lead him forward. But not here, not among these reports. Of course it was possible the detectives had missed something; if not in the words, perhaps in the intonations of those interrogated. Intonations did not appear on paper. He had asked the CID men to include as a footnote any impression they had received from those interviewed as to attitudes. There had been few footnotes and none of them had gone beyond noting the natural nervousness of many of those interviewed. And Harkness knew even the most innocent of people revealed such nervousness on being questioned by the police. As if the minor sins of everyday life might rise up and be used against them. Conscience of triviality makes cowards of us all, he thought.

Finally he put aside the reports and, undressing, climbed into bed. Around him the specimen cases reflected the glare of the bedlight. The moths and butterflies were unmoving in their skewered death. That dream, he was sure, would not recur. He took off his wrist-watch. It was eleven minutes to midnight. He placed it on the bedside table and switched off the bedlight.

He fell asleep almost at once. A deep dreamless sleep.

For a time.

An awareness that he was not alone came to him, drew him up to consciousness, not without a struggle. He was unwilling to waken, loath to desert the comforting depths. And when he did awaken, it was to darkness. Groggily he stretched out an arm, hand searching for the bedside lamp. He found the switch and flooded the room with light. Lifting his watch, he peered at the dial. Fifteen minutes to one. He had slept barely an hour. He turned to stare towards the foot of the bed.

She is there, facing him. Naked. Standing erect, gazing down, an image in some erotic dream. But it is no dream. A half smile on her face, she leans forward, small but firm breasts hanging over the front of the bed, a thin line of down visible, stretching from the navel to the thick bush between her thighs. The skin is milk white even in the yellow light from the lamp, the pubic hair black against it. No blacker than the hair on her head which cascades down and over her bare shoulders. Her eyes are wide and staring as if she is in some kind of waking dream of her own, a sleepwalker unaware of where she was.

He uttered her name, not loudly but with the hope that, if she was asleep, he might gently wake her.

'Abbie!'

She shook her head. Her hair swirled around her shoulders. She was awake and in the gesture indicated a kind of lascivious pleasure at being so, and in front of him.

'Harkness,' she said.

It was his turn to shake his head, to bring himself to full wakefulness.

'What are you doing here?' he asked in a whisper, suddenly fearful of being found with the girl like this in his room.

She smiled, a bold, careless smile. 'Why do you whisper? No one can hear us. Only Mullion is in the inn and he'll be fast asleep and far from this room.'

'What do you want?'

255

'You know.'

He struggled to a sitting position. The front of his pyjama jacket was open, his chest bare.

She came round the bed now and to his left side. He could see the slight swelling of her belly and a glistening sheen on her skin, the dampness of sweat. Still she smiled.

'You want me, mister, you want me, don't you? Long time since you've had a woman, far less a young girl. Why I'm here. Because you have a need of me.'

He shook his head again, with violent emphasis.

'Out of here,' he said. 'You shouldn't be here!'

'Most natural thing in the world, me bein' here. Most natural.' She reached out and caressed his chest. He pushed her hand away.

'Don't be stupid, girl!'

'What's stupid. I come because I want to come. Because I know you want to fuck me. An' I want for you to fuck me. I want for you to be inside me, on top of me, riding me. Like you want to.'

He thought, This is deliberately planned. To intimidate, to trap. With a girl young enough to be his grand-daughter.

The thought should revolt him, evoke a kind of disgust bred of the remnants of his Scots Presbyterian upbringing. In the past he'd arrested and even beaten up men, jailed them for having carnal knowledge of girls not much younger than Abbie. Yet he couldn't deny the physical stirring of desire, rising within him. And without.

Undismayed by being pushed away, she again caressed his chest and then, with a sudden movement, threw back the bedclothes and was groping and grasping him with an experienced hand that belied her age.

'See!' she said. 'Knew you wanted me. An' you do. You're just ready to ram that into me, aren't you? Be better too than them young boys around here. Hardly knowing what to do with it, and then, when they do it's all over before its started.'

With both hands he forced himself to grab her wrists and thrust her away from him. He was aware of her right breast touching his cheek; the sense of excitement taking him over and the need to suppress it, rid himself of her body and of the desire it had wrought.

256

'Get the hell out of here!' he shouted, throwing her back across the room. He was out of bed now, standing facing her, pyjamas in some disarray.

She was still laughing.

'You're funny, mister. Is it the violence that excites you? I've had some like that before.'

'Get out!'

'But you don't want me to go!'

She was close to him again, pressing her body against his. He could smell the musky odour of her cheap perfume.

'You like me bein' here,' she went on. 'An' you want me. Why fight it? You're gettin' on mister. Won't be too many more opportunities like this. Don't tell me you've never had a young girl before . . .'

So many years ago. Back in his past, away down deep in memory . . . as a beat policeman . . . she'd been on the street in Glasgow . . . off Blytheswood Square . . . he'd picked her up for soliciting, but never charged her. Instead she made him an offer and he'd taken her up on it . . . in a narrow lane off the square . . . a knee-trembler, they called it . . . and afterwards she told him, laughing, that she was only fifteen. In all his career he'd never taken money, never taken a bribe . . . but there'd been the kid in the lane off Blytheswood Square . . . he'd never really forgotten . . .

'Come on, Mr Harkness,' she was saying. 'What harm can it do? You want me and I'm here to be had.'

He took her by the shoulders now and forced her away towards the door. She tried to squirm back but he held her away with one hand and slapped her on the face hard with the other.

'Who told you to come here?'

She didn't reply but put her hand to her face. A look of puzzled reproach came into her eyes. He slapped her again. The smile vanished.

'Don't,' she said faintly.

'Who sent you?'

No . . . nobody. I . . . I just knew . . .'

'You knew they wanted you to come?'

She nodded, bewildered now.

He let go of her shoulder. 'Get out!' Knowing he was forcing himself to say it. Knowing he was still tempted.

'If . . . if I go . . . it'll be . . . worse.'

'What does that mean? More nightmares with moths?'

Her eyes were dark now, black-rimmed, almost fearful.

'Worse. It only gets worse. Until . . . until they be needing you.'

He opened the door, and gripping her shoulder, propelled her into the dark corridor.

'Worse,' she repeated.

He shut the door and turned the key in the lock. He was rid of her.

And then the thought came to him: What did she mean? 'Until they be needing you.'

Haydock, dying, had said something too.

'You shall be the vessel . . .'

Chapter Twenty-Nine

Harkness went back to bed, but he could not sleep. He was certain the girl had been sent to his room. To blackmail him? For what reason? And by whom? He'd uncovered so little in his investigation. So many words had been uttered in all the statements and, in the end, so little had been said. So little had happened. A dying Church of England priest had warned him of danger to himself. A youth, Caroon, had threatened him. For no other reason than youths of that age threatened the police to assert their arrogance, their hatred of authority. He'd had a nightmare about moths and butterflies. He'd seen a church burn down, with no sign of the cause of the conflagration. And he was no nearer to knowing the identity of the killer of Joshua Gideon than he had been on that first day he had arrived in Calderon.

He looked up, suddenly aware of the room. Shrouded in shadows cast by the bed lamp. Deep shadows. Growing deeper. And blacker. A greater contrast between light and dark. Everything in the light sharp-edged yet somehow diminishing. As if the darkness was taking over. Or was it that the darkness too was getting smaller, the entire room was shrinking?

He shook his head violently, to keep himself awake. If he wasn't already asleep. Wasn't even now starting to dream, to fall into yet another nightmare.

He stared at the walls and the specimen cases. They were as before. The glass reflected the light. The moths were motionless, impaled by their pins. Dead. Motionless.

Silence filled the room.

For a time.

There is a sound.

A slithering scratching sound. On the wall to his left. No, not on the wall but behind the wall. He stares in the direction of the sound and, momentarily his eyes blur. He bring his right hand up to his forehead and massages his brow. His eyes clear.

Another sound. A deeper throbbing sound behind the wall. Harkness frowns. No dream, this. Old water pipes behind the wall. The sound grows louder.

'If . . . if I go . . . it'll be worse . . .'

The girl had said that.

'It only gets worse . . .'

The sound increases.

Something is beating on the other side of the wall. Thudding against lathe and plaster and wood.

He can see the wall clearly now.

It shakes as each blow resounds around the room. He looks at the ceiling. The beam that straps across the wall, even the beam is shaking.

He tells himself he must be asleep and passing again through a nightmare. He stares down at his hands above the bed covers. Clenches and unclenches his fists.

'I'm awake!' Speaking aloud, above the sound of the blows.

The wall shakes even more now. Something is trying to break through.

Something trying to get into the room.

No dream. He knows he *is* awake.

The plaster cracks in front of his eyes – a long, deep, running crack from cornice down to floor. Flakes of plaster break off and drift in the air.

The sound reverberates through his head. He is shuddering now, spasms running through his body, and with each spasm he feels pain. It is as if every pore in his flesh is open and needles are being pressed into each one. He throws aside the bed clothes and lies on top of the bed, twisting and writhing.

The crack on the wall deepens, and through it flows a viscous, red fluid. The wall bleeds.

260

With each blow, the blood flows, oozes out, and drips down over the wallpaper.

He remembers: two dead children all those years ago, in a room that looked like a slaughterhouse. Their blood, and all the blood he has ever seen. Enough to fill the room and drown him in blood. The blood of all the victims he has seen, all the bodies he has viewed down the years. Not as human beings but simply as the corpses of victims. Without humanity.

'Not my fault!'

He hears the scream. His own scream.

Not just the wall on his left now but all four walls, being pounded from the other side. Sound is filling the room, louder and louder, beating on his eardrums. Filling his head.

Another crack appears above the door, from ceiling to lintel.

He shuts his eyes.

'It must stop!'

He can shut out the sight but not the sound. Beside the blows to the wall, there is a tearing sound – the wallpaper tearing, ripping under the force of each blow.

Something is trying to break into the room, bleeding with the very effort.

He opens his eyes again to see blood above the door, still oozing down over the wood and varnish, staining it a bright scarlet.

This is insane, without reality or logic. This should not be happening.

'God in heaven, in whom I have no belief, help me!'

It goes on. The sound filling the room, cramming into every brain cell in his head.

The walls streaked with blood.

He tells himself, they were human, all those victims. They bled real blood, from veins and torn flesh. He is not responsible. Never was. His job was to find the perpetrator. Nothing more . . .

. . . more . . . more . . . more . . .

. . . reverberating . . . pounding . . .

The walls are moving now. Bulging. Taking shapes. Pressing out there and there. Form and shape. The shapes of the things behind the walls. Those things that bleed and pound.

261

Shapes without shape, forms without form. Trying to break through, struggling to get into the room.

He knows, if they get into the room, he is finished, destroyed, dead or insane. Knows that with complete certainty. And can do nothing to prevent them breaking through.

More shapes. Coming and going. Hard-edged, sharp, pointed, twisting and struggling.

Is this what Haydock endured? Is this what drove him to his death, terrified him into his heart attacks?

Could his God not have prevented it?

If he could believe in Haydock's God . . .

Yet it had not saved the priest.

'God help me!'

He shuts his eyes and addresses Haydock's God.

Silence.

He opens his eyes again.

It is over.

Yet the walls are not as they were before. There are cracks where there had been unbroken surfaces, and the left-hand wall is stained, not scarlet now, but a dull brown, the colour of dried blood. The door is marked with it. There are newly made cracks on the other walls.

No sound now. Silence over all.

Harkness lay on top of the bed, his body drenched in perspiration. At least there was no longer pain.

For which relief, much thanks, he told himself.

Yet he had not imagined it. It was no nightmare. The signs of what had been were still around him.

He looked at his watch on the bedside table. It was seven-thirty in the morning. Daylight was beginning to filter round the edges of the curtains. The night was over. What had seemed to pass in minutes had taken hours.

Half an hour later he was sitting drinking coffee in the dining room, served by Abbie who behaved as if the night before had never happened. She spoke only when spoken to, and then in monosyllables. She was careful to avoid his eyes. For this he was grateful. He was thinking of all that had taken place after she had left his room, and found his hands

262

trembling, his mouth dry, and his mind in a kind of terrified chaos.

What had happened? What had caused it to happen? Cause and effect, the basis of all logical detective work; Harkness's answer to everything.

Except a room that screamed, and walls that bled.

Occurrences utterly beyond his comprehension.

Abbie returned, carrying the usual tray of bacon and eggs. He refused this and went out to the incident van. Sergeant Stevens had arrived and was briefing the squad of detectives on interviewing the occupants of various outlying farms. And, at once, it seemed to Harkness like a last desperate resort. They would learn no more from these people than they had already learned from the villagers. The answer to the murder of Joshua Gideon would not be there, he was sure. It was here in the Calderons, and there was no rational explanation.

But there was someone who might be able to explain it or at least allow him to begin to understand what had happened here, what was still happening.

'You'll take charge here,' he told Stevens. 'Until I get back.'

'Where can I contact you, sir, if anything comes up?'

'I'm not sure. I'll be in touch with you, if I feel it's necessary.'

He drove fast away from the villages. Only when he was on the main road, driving north, did he feel the sense of oppression lifted from him. It seemed as if he'd been living with the weight of that oppression over him since he had arrived in Calderon. He was only aware of it now that he had left the two villages.

Three-quarters of an hour later he was in the outskirts of Warwick. He avoided the centre of the town, heading for the council estate and the street with the gasworks in view at one end.

She opened the door so quickly she might have been waiting behind it for him to ring the bell.

'I was expecting you,' Jennet Agram greeted him.

'You said that the last time I was here. Anyway, I told you I'd be back.'

'Yes, you did. Come in. You'll take some tea.'

'Yes, I will, this time.'

She was dressed as before, in a loose blouse and long skirt. He sat on the sofa in silence as she made the tea and brought it on a battered tin tray, a motif of rose petals just discernible on the surface.

'You don't mind drinking from mugs?' she asked.

'I didn't know there was any other way.'

'Milk and sugar?'

'Both, thank you.'

The hot tea seemed infinitely more pleasant than the coffee an hour before. He relaxed.

'You've more questions?' she said.

'In a way. Different questions. Not so much about the murder of Gideon this time, although that'll still be the aim of the exercise.'

'Ask me, then.'

He coughed, feeling a vague sense of the ridiculous.

'In your own time,' she said with a small smile.

He took a gulp of tea, and feeling in his pockets, finally brought out a crushed packet of cigarettes. He offered it to her.

'I've given them up,' she responded. 'Bad for you.'

'I know. But maybe it's the lesser of the two evils. The opiate eases the problems.'

'Tell me about the problems.'

He told her. Starting with the night of the moths and butterflies, and then everything else: the questioning, the return to the villages, the death of Haydock and the burning of his church, the vial of water Haydock had sent to him. He told her about the night before, the visit of Abbie and all that had happened after her visit. Jennet Agram listened in silence. When he had finished, he felt exhausted, drained of energy, as if he had endured it all for a second time.

There was a short silence. Then she said: 'You've had a time.'

'I . . . I think I have.' He felt his voice breaking; he was a child again and close to tears.

'It's interesting,' she said guardedly.

'That's all you can say?'

'No, you misunderstand. All through this, you have had memories . . .'

'Memories?'

'Of past cases, past crimes you've worked on. That's so?'

Dead and mutilated children on New Year's Eve. There's memories for you.

'Yes, I suppose it is.'

'Past horrors?'

The murderers of children?

'Yes. But . . . there are always some things you can't forget. Things that are always with you.'

She poured him another mug of tea. 'Yes, but your memories are particularly bad.'

A dead prostitute, her breasts cut off, throat slashed, head almost severed from her body. On Hampstead Heath, was it as long as fifteen years ago? More like yesterday.

'The nature of the job.'

Walls have never cracked and blood had never poured from the cracks before.

'But haven't these memories recurred more often in this case?' Jennet Agram asked.

'I . . . I suppose they have. I don't know why.'

'No, you don't. But it could be important.'

He was astonished. 'Important? Killings perpetrated by maniacs and perverts. They *were* important to be at the time but they're over. I don't find it important to remember them. I usually find things like that best forgotten. To go on functioning, I have to put things like that away.'

'Hide them in the subconscious? Yes, it would be the only way. Except that during this investigation, they return.'

'All right, they return. Mebbe this business is so . . . nightmarish it brings them back.'

'And maybe that is the intention,' she said.

'I don't understand that. Anyway, my memories aren't the problem. I want . . . I have to know what the hell is happening to me in that place. Am I cracking up, going off my head, or just having bad dreams? Fucking nightmares that seem so bloody real I don't know whether or not I'm awake or asleep.'

He gulped air and howled: 'What in God's name is happening to me?'

265

The question hung between them. Harkness, his hands trembling, sat back in the sofa, feeling weak and exhausted. Jennet stared directly at him and it was she who spoke first.

'They're getting at you.'

'Who? Who are getting at me?'

'The people you're looking for. The people who killed Gideon.'

'People? In the plural? More than one?'

'Almost certainly more than one. There's a great deal of power here.'

'You mean . . . they created these nightmares?'

'Yes, I mean that.'

'How?' As he asked the question he realised at once he was rejecting the premise. 'How can they create my dream of being attacked by flying insects? Or hear a room scream and see the walls bleed?'

'You still think they're merely nightmares?'

'For God's sake, what else?'

'And the room this morning? The walls cracked and stained?'

'Part of the dream? Or else some natural cause. A structural fault. Maybe that even caused the dream? It could be that, couldn't it?'

The sensation of clutching at straws. An act of desperation.

Jennet Agram shook her head. 'No! Not that. Not nightmares. The girl coming to the room was real. You even understood she'd been sent. That served its purpose, even though you didn't succumb. They found a need in you, Harkness. One weakness to be exploited further. Then came the physical attack. The room bleeds and screams. Another attack, like the moths. Each time they weaken you further.'

'But why? To prevent me from finding out who killed Gideon?'

'Oh, no, much more than that. They want you now, Harkness. Body and soul, they want you.'

'That's daft! Insane. For what reason would they be wanting me . . . whatever than means?'

'Perhaps because of all your memories. You see, you've experienced much more of pure evil than most people. By

266

nature of your profession. I would think they want to use that.'

'Use it as what?'

'There is a power in pure evil. The experience of it, I believe, could be turned to strengthening that power.'

Harkness stared at her in amazement. 'You expect me to believe that?'

'Not yet, Superintendent. But, you see, it doesn't matter what you believe. It's enough that *they* believe it.'

She hesitated now, as if reluctant to go on. And then decided to do so. 'And because they believe it with a strength that you lack, that puts you in danger.'

'What strength do I lack? I believe in the law. I believe in justice. In a clean, decent society. I'm a senior ranking law officer with all the power of rank and authority . . .'

'But you don't believe in the power of good and evil. And, if you don't believe it, you are as nothing. You don't believe it even though it has been used against you. Even though you've seen it, you dismiss it as illusion, nightmare or waking dreams. And if you go on dismissing it, you will allow these people to use you and destroy you. Unless you realise what is happening, they will destroy you, Harkness.

'How can they?'

'Oh, they can. And not just your body, Harkness. I'm talking about your immortal soul.'

Chapter Thirty

They talked. The sceptic Jack Harkness against the believer Jennet Agram. The sceptic was a disturbed man, almost frightened, and there were few things that could frighten him. But Jennet Agram had the ability to call up in his mind in chilling and realistic detail everything that had happened to him in Calderon. When they talked of the fire in the church, it was as if he could smell the smoke, see again the flames. When they talked of the previous night, he experienced again the sounds in the room, the bulging, cracking walls, the blood that seeped from them.

It was the same when he discussed his past career. She could take him back in memory, and more than memory, to the room containing the bodies of the two murdered children. He could smell again the sickly sweet odour of blood and death. And, in the end, it was too much.

For the first time in his life, Harkness broke down. He found himself trembling, weeping, feeling suddenly alone, isolated, and finally admitting his fears to this strange young woman. He found himself wanting sympathy. He received a kind of strength from her.

It was a long day. He lost track of time. Eventually, he remembered, she learned he hadn't eaten, and made him a meal. Afterwards, and he was never sure how it came about, he found himself reaching out towards her and he was in her arms. There was, he could acknowledge later, a build up within him of sexual tension. The veiled invitation he imagined he had received from Margaret Campion (was it nothing but his imagination?), the direct and provocative appearance

269

of Abbie in his room, all this and his long celibacy undoubt-edly played its part. He could never be sure whether he had been seduced or was the seducer.

It started in the living room and moved into the bedroom. On her bed, he stripped her slowly, lingering over her breasts, which were large and firm. It occurred to him that he was behaving like a youth having his first sexual experience. He caressed and kissed the large aureoles, cupped them in his hands, and all the time, she uttered small moaning sounds. As he undressed her, so she undressed him. And then, body against body, they moved together with a perfect understand-ing of each other's needs. She used her mouth in ways he'd never experienced and, when he finally entered her, uttered a sudden cry of animal pleasure.

She made love with a wild quality, a strangely wise aban-don. As if nothing was calculated, but everything directed with deliberation towards their mutual pleasure. She moaned when it seemed to Harkness he wanted her to moan. She cried out, 'Ride me!' which he found served to increase his excite-ment. They came together simultaneously.

And lay afterwards, side by side, in what was to Harkness an awed silence.

After a while they talked again. He could never remember quite what they talked about. It was his impression that they told each other about their lives up until that time. Not, Harkness recalled, his professional life, but details of his youth and later his marriage. She talked of her country childhood and later her time as a young girl at university and after. They slept a little and then, some time in the night, they made love again. This time it was calmer, with less sound and fury, but gently, each with infinite consideration for the other.

When he woke it was morning. He was alone in bed but the house was small and he could hear her in the kitchen. She made bacon and eggs and coffee and Harkness found he was ravenously hungry. They ate in the kitchen, and after break-fast sat, facing each other across the small table.

He said, awkwardly: 'First time I've ever made love to a woman who might be a material witness.'

270

She laughed. 'I've never been called that before! But I can't be a witness. I was never near Calderon.'

'No, but you knew Gideon. Were involved with him. Mebbe character witness would be a better description. Still, it's a first time. And not strictly ethical.'

'Or moral? Depends on your morality, Superintendent.'

'God, after last night call me Jack . . . or Harkness. But no' Superintendent.'

'If you like. Harkness, I think. Jack seems too . . . too young.'

'I'll not thank you for that.'

A pause. She poured him a second cup of coffee.

'Why not ethical?' she asked.

'Officers should not have personal attachments with those involved in their investigation.'

'I didn't kill Josh Gideon.'

'No, I don't think you did. But you were . . . involved with him.' Harkness didn't like the thought.

As before, she seemed to be able to read his mind.

'It was a long time ago, that part of my involvement with Gideon. Before I knew what he was really like. When I knew, it stopped. That part of it.'

'What was he really like then?'

'Back to work, Harkness. I told you, he was a man who wanted power. Was greedy for power. The wrong kind. The wrong path.'

He drained his coffee cup. 'Ach, I find all this . . . well, it's barely credible.'

'The walls of the room cracked. They dripped blood. You've seen it.'

'I've seen it. Don't like it, or understand it, or want to understand it.'

'Then don't go back to Calderon.'

'I have to. It's my job.'

She frowned. 'You're out of your depth.'

'Aye, but I can swim.'

'They want you to go back, Harkness. They want to use you.'

'They can try. They'll not succeed.'

271

She took the cups from the table and went to the sink. She had her back to him.

'Can you be sure of that?'

'Look, whatever they do, I don't believe in . . . in the supernatural. What they've done is mebbe a kind of hypnosis. They've put things in my mind. All right! Now I know they can do that, it doesn't mean I believe in their . . . their magic. It's my job to find out who they are and apprehend them for the murder of Joshua Gideon. Now that's a fact, the murder. A pitchfork through the throat, an' somebody put it there. Person or persons unknown so far. But I'll know them in time and I'll arrest them.'

'Or they'll destroy you.' She said it flatly, controlling any emotion she might be feeling.

'They can try. It's been tried before. I'm still here.'

She swung round angrily to face him.

'Last night meant something to me, you know! It wasn't just a one-night thing.'

'And to me, Jennet,' he insisted, and realised he was calling her by her name for the first time.

'Then I'm telling you not to go back . . .'

'And I've told you, I have to. What would you want me to do? Say, "Sorry, Chief Constable, but they've frightened me off." And he'd say, "Who are they?" And I'm supposed to reply, "Boogie men, ghosts and ghoulies and things that go bump in the night."'

He stopped then, thinking to himself there *were* things that went bump in the night.

'Tell him it's hopeless. That you'll never be able to find out who killed Gideon.'

'Oh, aye, after barely a week's work? I'm no wantin' to draw my pension just yet.'

'You may be drawing it sooner than you think.'

He stood up. 'Look, I've got to get back. I've men waiting out there to report to me. You never know – one of them might just bring me something that takes me through to the end.'

'At least say you won't stay the night out there. Come back at night to Warwick. You can . . . you can stay here, if you

272

want. Any night. Every night.' A quality of desperation had come into her voice.

'No, Jennet, out there is where the action is. And I want to try something else. I'm ready for them now. Mebbe, thanks to you, I'll be understanding better what's happening to me. Have an idea of how it's done.' He laughed. 'Even if I don't fully understand what's going on.'

'It's not as easy as that,' she said.

'Nothing's ever as easy as we think. Or as difficult. Comes the time, we usually find we can get through anything.'

He went out and salvaged his coat from where he'd left it, in the sitting room. She followed him.

'I want you back here,' she insisted.

'I'll be back,' he replied. 'Last night meant something to me too. But I'll be back when it's over. Not before. It has to be over first.'

'Ethics?' Her voice was tinged with scorn.

'Aye, I suppose so. But when it's over there'll be no ethical reason not to come back here. And a hell of a lot of reasons why I'd like to.'

His coat on, he turned to face her. She was staring at him, a frightened expression on her face.

'If you go back there, if you spend the night there, you won't be back,' she said.

'Another bit of prophecy? Second sight or whatever?'

'Yes, if you like. Do you know what date this is, Harkness?'

He was vague. 'End of October. Beginning of November.'

'Tonight is the thirty-first of October.'

'Aye. Well . . .'

'All Hallows Eve. Hallowe'en.'

'Oh, come on,' he said. 'What does that mean? I turn into a pumpkin? Look into a mirror and see the Wicked Queen?'

She gave a slight shrug. 'It was a pagan festival. When the souls of the dead were thought to revisit their homes.'

'Maybe Gideon'll turn up and tell me who killed him.'

'It's one of *their* nights, Harkness. It's to do with power being released. A time when their kind of power can be strongest.'

273

'Hallowe'en's for the kids, Jennet. I'm not playing kid's games. As the lady said of ducking for apples: There but for the change of one letter is the story of my life. I'll see you.'

'No, I don't think you will.'

'I'll do my best to prove you wrong, girl.' He went to the front door of the house. 'Last night was something in my life.'

Outside, he looked back before climbing into his car. He was sure she'd be at the window. He was wrong.

He drove out of Warwick and on to the road to the Calderons. Outside the city a pale sun was struggling to break through the mist. The mist was winning. the deserted huts of small market gardening establishments passed by, bleak little edifices enduring a kind of death until the spring came to bring them back to life. There were, however, outside some of them rotund orange pumpkins for sale. It was indeed Hallowe'en.

By the time Harkness reached Greater Calderon and the police incident van, the mist had taken over and the entire village was shroud in a damp veil.

Sergeant Stevens was on duty with one uniformed man.

'We were thinking of sending out search parties, sir. Thought you'd got lost,' he said, an eyebrow raised, awaiting an explanation he was not to get.

'I'm back now,' Harkness replied. 'Reports?'

'Everything here on the desk, sir. I'm afraid, nothing of any help.'

'The DCs out?'

'Questioning the farmers beyond the hill today. After that, we'll have seen everything that lives in a ten mile radius. And then, what, sir?'

'We have a meeting tomorrow. I want personal impressions, anything they might not have included in their reports. And then we'll consider the next move. Meanwhile I'll read these reports in the hotel.'

'More comfortable, sir,' said by Stevens, not without a trace of envy.

Harkness felt a twinge of conscience for the previous night. 'Have your lunch in the hotel, Sergeant. And the constable. Tell them to put it on my bill.'

274

Stevens cheered up. 'Thank you, sir. Very good of you. Oh, one other thing, Sir . . . Miss Campion phoned this morning, wondering if you'd be free for dinner tonight at the manor.'

Again the thought, what did she want of him? He couldn't forget the feeling he'd had when she'd suggested he should stay the night after the fire. Probably his imagination.

Stevens added, 'She said she'd invited Father Anselm.'

It dispelled any suspicions he might have had of her motives for inviting him.

'Do me a favour, Sergeant, ring her and tell her I accept her kind invitation. Might be useful to get more of her views on the villages, and the priest's. Meanwhile I'm going to get my head down with these reports.'

He went into the inn. Mullion, behind the desk, nodded to him.

'See you spent the night out. And you've had trouble in your room,' the innkeeper said.

'Yes, cracks in the wall and some strange colouring. What would cause that, Mr Mullion?' All this said with his face expressionless. 'Just woke yesterday morning to find the walls like that.'

Mullion's expression matched his own. 'To do with subsidence, sir. Had it before. And that staining, sir, they say it's a kind of dampness comes up from the old swamps. I'll have to get the builders in. You want me to move you to another room? You could go into the room next door. Be warmer, you might say.'

'Why not? A gas fire there, is there?'

'Oh, yes, sir. Same as the other room.'

'Fine. I'll go up just now. I've work to do and I'll need a bit of heat. You'll move my luggage in?'

'Do it myself, Mr Harkness.'

He was suddenly so obliging, quite a change. But why?

In his new room, Harkness switched on the gas fire and spread his reports out on the small dressing table. Before he started to go through them, he leant back in the chair and thought about Hallowe'en. Did Jennet Agram really believe there was something special about the night? What was it she'd said? Something about power. *They* increased their power on All Hallows Eve. He dismissed the thought. Leave it to Jennet to believe in such things.

Anyway he was going to a Hallowe'en dinner that night. Deliberately held on this night of all nights?

Chapter Thirty-One

He bathed and shaved and put on a clean shirt, and then sat reading the reports. There was nothing there that was new; no leads or suggestions of leads. The people of Greater and Lesser Calderon and its environs proclaimed over and over again their ignorance of the identity of Gideon's killer.

Under the reports was a paper stamped 'Criminal Records Office.' It had been forwarded from that office through Warwick Police Headquarters to Harkness following a request he had made when he had first arrived in Warwick. It was a list of all the citizens of the two villages who had police records. It was a short list. A few minor parking offences, a case of shop-lifting brought against a local housewife (fined ten pounds and bound over), and a case of assault brought against one Hugh Caroon, who while under the influence of alcohol had attacked an American tourist in Stratford High Street. He had been fined fifty pounds. A note indicated the charge might have been the more serious one of attempted robbery but this could not be proved.

Par for the course, Harkness thought. That would be Caroon. But was he capable of murder? Harkness considered it doubtful. The man was a bully, certainly, and a coward. Cowardice would seem to rule out premeditated murder by Caroon. Unless . . .

. . . unless he was not acting alone. There was a possibility. One of several.

Jennet Agram always spoke of *them*.

And with the killing and the symbols around the body, all carefully arranged, there was some evidence of the crime having been committed by a small number of persons acting together. How many? Impossible to say. Twelve?

Twelve is the number of a coven.

So what does that mean?

He was about to throw the CRO report on the carpet when he noticed there was yet another sheet of paper, a small addendum: Father (first name unknown) Anselm.

'While compiling these reports the name of the village priest was included. No known criminal record . . .'

That was to be expected, Harkness told himself. Village priests might be difficult but rarely exhibited criminal tendencies.

He read on: 'But an investigation into Catholic records indicates that there is no Father Anselm in charge of a parish in this country at this time. Have we got his name or his denomination wrong?'

Harkness pondered the addendum. It presented an interesting question. Who was Father Anselm, and why was he not included in the register of parish priests in the United Kingdom? One way of settling the question was to ask Anselm, face him with it tonight and watch him squirm. But could it relate to the murder? Harkness put the addendum in his pocket and relaxed.

As far as he could. Which wasn't very far. He could feel the tension rising within him again. He had been under a strain since he had come to Calderon, and it was still so despite last night when there had been a certain easing within him because of Jennet Agram. And there was something he'd forgotten about last night. Something he hadn't done for years . . . not since he was a child. He'd forgotten and now he remembered. Lying beside Jennet in the small hours, he'd wept against her bare shoulders. It had been a kind of release, an escape from the years when he should have wept . . . perhaps for the dead, perhaps for the living. But it annoyed him, that memory. Scots policemen in their fifty-ninth year don't cry like children.

He dozed until it was time to go to the manor for dinner. He walked. It would allow him to drink without having to drive later. It was just under a mile. Darkness had fallen. There was a trace of mist just above ground level.

There was also an ominous feeling as if something was going to happen.

Out of Greater Calderon, he came to the road leading up to the manor, through the trees into a deep blackness. A city copper, he told himself, was unused to the absence of light, the complete darkness of the countryside. Velvet darkness – wasn't that the phrase in popular fiction. Not that it *was* velvet, more like cold damp cotton dyed black.

Then there were the footsteps behind him.

It seemed to become colder. He turned. Father Anselm loomed through the darkness.

'Ah, Superintendent, I thought it would be you. We are headed for the same destination, I believe.'

And this, thought Harkness, will give me the opportunity to ask some pertinent questions. They moved forward over gravel, unseen at their feet.

'Are you making progress?' Anselm asked.

'Possibly. We are looking into the backgrounds of the villagers.'

'I should think that would be very dull.'

'Not entirely. For instance, Father Anselm, your name is not listed among those of parish priests of the Catholic faith. Isn't that unusual?'

The priest laughed. 'It must seem so. I hadn't thought.'

'Perhaps you might think about it now, before we get to the manor? I wouldn't want to spoil Miss Campion's dinner.'

'Of course, of course,' said Father Anselm in jovial tones. 'You wish an explanation?'

'I would like one.'

Father Anselm cleared his throat. 'You will perhaps know of the dispute between the Vatican and Archbishop Lefebvre and his followers?'

Harkness had some recollection of something read in the newspapers.

Anselm went on: 'When the Vatican insisted the Mass be celebrated no longer in Latin – that is, the Tridentine Mass – but in the language of the country . . . in English, here . . . a number of us did not find this to our liking. It seemed to us that it detracted from the great mystery of the Mass.'

279

'You mean, the people who didn't understand Latin would accept that it was all a mystery?'

Again the priest laughed. 'Not exactly. But the Latin Mass, you might say, contained the actual words of St Peter. The original sound, the beauty of the language . . . a kind of authenticity.'

'Wouldn't it have been even more authentic in Hebrew?' Harkness said.

The laugh again, becoming slightly strained in the darkness.

'Or Aramaic. A point, sir, a definite point. The Mass in the language of Christ. There would be a thing. But did Christ preach in Hebrew or Aramaic? Aramaic, I think. And not many of us are familiar with that. Anyway, we wished to retain the Latin Mass. Rome demanded otherwise. Bishops were recalled to Rome. Priests were relieved of their charges. I was one of those priests.'

'You disobeyed?'

'I disobeyed my bishop at the request of my parishioners. When I told them I was ordered to practise the Eucharist in English or give up my charge here, they objected. They wanted the Latin Mass. They wanted me to remain here. I had, I know, taken an oath of obedience, but my conscience was clear. I determined to stay.'

'And your superiors did nothing?'

'They sent another priest. No one took communion or went to the confessional. I had asked the people here at least to give the poor man a hearing but they wouldn't. He went away, I stayed. Oh, I have not been defrocked but I should not be here, and officially the church is closed, for the time being. I continue to celebrate the Mass in Latin, I continue to preach – until they remove me. But I am no longer officially a parish priest. Hence the omission of my name from your list.'

'So what will happen?'

'That is up to the bishop. I have been reprimanded. I have been ordered away. The bishop suggested a period of retreat and meditation in a monastery. I have not taken up his suggestion.'

'And if you continue to disobey?'

They were nearing the manor house now. Lights broke the darkness ahead of them.

'The bishop may enforce my removal in some more energetic manner. I shall have to then go. But until that time I stay. If I maintain my disobedience I could be defrocked, although that would be an extreme act. And there is another even more extreme . . .'

'That would be?'

'Excommunication, though I doubt if they'd cast my immortal soul into the pit. Oh, doubtless I shall have to go some time. But not yet . . . not yet.'

He straightened up as they reached the door of the house.

'Does that satisfy you, Superintendent?'

'I suppose it does.'

'Then, since my time here is limited, I propose to enjoy my dinner tonight. It might well be my last.'

They went in.

The dinner was served by Mrs Chalmers, the housekeeper, on a long refectory table. The dining room was large and impressive. An ancient tapestry depicting medieval knights in what looked like combat covered one wall. The other three walls were covered in oak panelling, several coats of arms set high upon it.

'The coat of arms of my family,' Margaret Campion explained. 'In a direct line from Gerard de Champion. The others are those of his companions who came from France with him.'

'They had to leave in a hurry,' Father Anselm said, 'They had displeased the King of France.'

The three of them were dining at one end of the long table, with Margaret Campion at the head. The first course was pheasant soup. This was followed by *sole meunière*, and then slightly underdone roast beef. Chablis was followed by red Bordeaux. Father Anselm, however, drank only water.

'Not that I don't like wine,' he explained, 'but this is a small penance. I swore I would not drink wine until I was officially reinstated as parish priest. I explained to the Superintendent my present *contretemps* with my superiors, Margaret.'

She smiled and Harkness was again aware that she was an attractive woman.

'One of our other problems, Mister Harkness. Apart from the murder. I suppose to you it must seem insignificant, but not to us here. We consider our beliefs of some importance. I wonder if you can understand our concern for Father Anselm's dilemma?'

'I think I can,' Harkness replied. 'Not so much from my own experience but we've some awareness of religion and the problems it brings in Scotland.'

'Like my family,' Margaret Campion said. 'You see the tapestry? The story of Sir Gerard's departure from France. He was a Templar.'

'The order,' Anselm explained, 'was formed to protect travellers to the Holy Land.'

'That was at the beginning,' Margaret went on quietly. 'Unfortunately, they became rather a wealthy order of knights.'

'That was unfortunate?' Harkness couldn't help the irony in his tone.

'For the Templars, yes. They achieved great prominence in France. My ancestor was one of the highest ranking. With wealth came power. Philip IV of France felt threatened by them. He denounced them as worshippers of the Devil . . .'

'A political move,' Anselm interposed. 'Political parties don't resort even to those accusations nowadays.'

Margaret Campion went on, 'They were proscribed, massacred, burnt at the stake . . . the full medieval panoply of horrors. Some escaped, however, including my ancestor. They fled to England, settled in what is now called the Temple in London. Sir Gerard was a kind of pastoral philosopher . . . he bought this estate and spent the rest of his days here.'

'Cruel times,' Anselm said. 'Also difficult to separate the good men from the bad. You have it much easier today, Harkness. The villains are more obvious.'

'When you can find them,' he said.

'You're no nearer to finding your murderer?' asked Margaret.

'Depends,' Harkness replied. 'We don't know his identity yet. We think there may be more than one person involved.'

'Surely not? Father Anselm and I would be saddened, if that were so. I suppose we both look on the people of the

Calderons as our own people. Our own charges, if you like. I know they're difficult, perhaps strange to an outsider, but they are *our* people.'

'Then you'll have to make up your mind you've got some sick ones among them.'

The subject was changed. Margaret Campion asked Harkness about some of his previous cases.

'Must be an exciting life,' she said.

'Mostly a hard slog, with a bit of luck thrown in. Also pretty harrowing. See, it's in the nature of the serious crimes such as murder to be unpleasant, horrific even. The evil that men do . . .'

'You believe in abstract evil, Harkness?' the priest asked.

'I believe in concrete evil, Father. The evil in the way many people are killed by their fellow men. But abstract evil . . . I don't know what that is.'

'Perhaps the thing that drives men to carry out such acts?' said Anselm.

'Mostly a lack of imagination, Father. They can inflict pain and death without being able to comprehend what they are doing to another human being. As if, whatever they do, they do to inanimate objects. They can't comprehend the pain of others. Their own objectives, mebbe their own pain, but not that of others. See, no imagination!'

'I've always thought it might be to do with power,' Anselm said. 'The desire to have power over others. The power of life and death. Sometimes, sadly, I think power is the great driving force. Not self-preservation or sex . . . as the psychologists would have it . . . or love as the church would preach but a desire for power over others. You know Joshua Gideon was like that.'

'I've gathered he wasn't a very pleasant character.'

'One should look for goodness in everyone. But with Gideon it was difficult. He so wanted to dominate. Perhaps to take over from . . . his betters.'

'And who would they be, Father?'

There was a silence. Anselm looked down at his coffee cup. Margaret Campion broke the silence.

'He certainly tried to tell me how to run the estate,' she said.

'He tried to interfere in everything,' Anselm added, still preoccupied.

'To take power from those who already had power?' Harkness put it in the form of a question.

'I should imagine, if there was . . . power, he would certainly have tried.' The priest took up his coffee cup and sipped, thin lips puckered.

'I think there *is* power and because he tried to take it, he was killed,' Harkness said.

'My dear, sir, I might agree with you if I could see any evidence of this so-called power in Greater or Lesser Calderon.'

Harkness suddenly realised he was enjoying himself. As if he was probing at the priest, even at his hostess, although it would seem the conversation was lost on her.

He went on: 'I'm not sure if I actually believe in it, but some would call it a kind of psychic power. No, I'm saying it wrong – I didn't believe it when I first came here, but I think I do now?'

'Psychic power?' said Margaret Campion. 'You mean, like in spiritualism?'

'Something like that,' Harkness said. 'See, I've a reputation as a hard-nosed policeman, but since I've been here, I've seen some strange-like things.'

'What kind of things?' Anselm said.

'Things moving without anyone moving them. Disturbances, you might call them. On the other hand, you could say I imagined or dreamt them. But, since I've never before dreamt such things, it might seem as if someone was putting them in my mind.'

'The church would consider such things dangerous, Mr Harkness. Yes, dangerous. To be avoided.'

Was the priest warning him? The thin lips of the man were damp and there seemed to be beads of perspiration on his brow.

'Is it warm in here tonight, Margaret,' he said. 'Or am I about to get influenza.'

'It is warm, Father,' their hostess replied. 'It was so cold outside, I put the heating up. Too far, I think. Shall we go into the sitting-room?'

They left the dining-room and with the change of venue came another change in conversation. Margaret Campion talked of the problems of managing a small estate. Harkness was urged to tell some of his lighter experiences as a police-man. After a while, he looked at his watch. It was quarter to eleven.

'Time I went back to the inn. I have an early start.'

'You could stay here, Mr Harkness,' said Margaret Campion. 'I have so much room and you'd be much more comfortable.'

Harkness searched for something in her voice, some additional invitation, as he had felt on the previous occasion she had invited him. There was nothing. But then, the priest was present.

'I sometimes think Mullion is not the most genial of hosts,' Anselm added. 'I should take up Margaret's invitation. Much more comfortable. And perhaps less . . . vulnerable.'

'To what, Father?'

'To those nightmares you were talking of.'

'You forget, I have a police incident van outside the inn. It's manned twenty-four hours a day. They have to know where I am all the time.'

'You could phone them,' Margaret said.

'I like to be close to them. But thank you for the invitation all the same. Perhaps when my investigation is finished . . .'

They took their leave some moments later, the priest and the policeman, and walked together into the darkness, saying little until they reached the village green where Harkness went one way and Anselm, the other.

'A pleasant evening,' said the priest.

'Aye, very pleasant. You're not superstitious, Father?'

'Only in so far as the humanists would call my religion superstitious. Why do you ask?'

'This is All Hallows Eve, isn't it?'

'Indeed it is. Do you know, I'd forgotten?' said Anselm. Somehow Harkness felt he was lying. He had not forgotten.

They said their goodnights and Harkness walked towards the inn, feeling uneasy. As if something was about to happen.

A

Chapter Thirty-Two

He'd been asleep, a deep dreamless sleep, and then he was awake. He came up from sleep with a start, to instant nervous alertness, tense, expectant. The bed linen was in disarray.

He reached out and switched on the bedside light, staring at once around the room. The light cast deep shadows on the walls, the shapes of the one armchair in the room, an upright chair, the foot of the bed. There were no specimen cases on the walls of this room; only two prints, one of Anne Hathaway's cottage at Stratford, the other, Poussin's '*Et in Arcadia Ego*', with its shepherds beside a tomb. There were no cracks on these walls, only shadows.

Harkness waited. For what, he did not know. There were words for what he might expect. 'A psychic attack', whatever that was. Another attack by moths? It seemed like an old Hollywood movie: 'Attack of the Killer Moths'? 'Invasion of the Giant Crabs'? Or 'Night of the Demon'? That might be even more appropriate.

But what had wakened him? Something . . . a sound barely heard.

He listened, as one listens alone in a house, imagining every creak to be the noise of an intruder.

At first, nothing. The deafening sound of silence.

And then . . .

. . . distant, barely audible, a kind of chanting. Plainsong, but faint and so far away.

He was sitting up in bed now. The sound was coming from outside, from somewhere beyond the inn.

Harkness rose and going over to the window, pulled back the curtains and stared out.

Into greyness. A thick grey mist, swirling and twisting and pressing itself against the window pane; a mist that obscured everything beyond the glass.

He could hear the singing now. It was still far away but coming closer. He could not understand the words . . . it was like listening to Latin from a great distance.

Harkness felt his eyes start to water from the strain of staring into a grey nothingness, the imagined pin-points of light dancing before his eyes. He stepped back from the window, shaking his head to clear away the last vestiges of sleep, and peered out again.

The pin-points of light were not his imagination. Needle points, he could see them now through the fog, moving, almost dancing. Fire-flies? No, not fireflies. Lights in a row shining through the mist. Moving towards the inn.

The chanting was louder now. Nearer. Plainsong, medieval church music, questions and responses in Latin. Harkness stared in nervous fascination as the lights came closer.

And then they were passing under the window and he could see the lights were candles held in the hands of shadowy, shrouded grey figures. They were indistinct, moving as they did through the thick mist. As they passed under his window they seemed to be dressed in grey monk's habits and cowls. Each figure held a candle in the left hand like a scene from some medieval pageant, or the movie equivalent thereof. Why was reality so like imagination; so close to the equivalent fictions? In pairs, they moved by the inn, the lower parts of their bodies disappearing into the ground mist so that it appeared they were not walking but floating over the ground.

They moved in the direction of the church.

Was this some kind of local religious festival held in the depths of the night? An unlikely proposition, Harkness told himself. But what else should it be?

Below him, beyond the window, they floated on, a long line of paired figures. The animals went in two by two. There must be over a hundred of them coming out of the mistness, disappearing into the greyness by the church. Still they chanted as they moved.

Then it occurred to Harkness that he should be able to see the police incident van from where he stood. He should be able to see the lights of the van's interior. He peered down again.

Nothing. No spill of electric light broke the night, only the moving figures and the chanting. And now the end of the row of moving figures was below him; the candle-holding procession was disappearing, and the chanting receding.

Harkness dressed quickly in shirt and trousers, a thick polo-necked sweater under his jacket. Reaching into his case, he dug under the clothes, fingers searching for and finding the cool, slightly oily butt of the Smith and Wesson automatic. He'd been authorised to carry it for years yet rarely did so. Tonight he felt the need of it, the reassurance of grey metal. If asked, he could not have explained why, on this night of all nights. It was just so.

Outside the corridor was in darkness. At the end was the light switch that would illuminate the narrow stairway. He pressed the switch down. Nothing happened. Either the bulb in the light above the stairs had gone, or the lights were switched off at the mains.

He moved carefully down the stairs. The desk and foyer of the inn were in darkness, the only illumination a lighter grey coming from the windows.

Harkness opened the door and stepped into nothingness. Two steps and a look behind him and he could no longer see the inn.

He moved in the direction he judged the incident van should be. After a few steps he tripped and barked his shins against the metal steps leading to the van. It was in darkness. With infinite care he climbed the steps and went into the van. With his right hand he felt for the light switch and found it. It was at the "on" position, yet the van was dark.

He stood, listening.

There was the sound of a man breathing heavily. Harkness groped his way along the right side of the van and felt for a built-in drawer which should contain a number of heavy duty torches. After a moment, he found the drawer and took out a torch.

The beam, cutting through the darkness, showed one of the constables . . . Goston that was the man's name . . . slumped into his chair. He seemed to be asleep yet his mouth and eyes were open. Harkness stepped forward and shook him by the shoulder. There was no reaction. The man slept on. If, indeed, he was asleep. It seemed more like a coma. Harkness felt for his pulse. It was normal. Goston was in a deep sleep, and no amount of shaking would wake the man. It was possible he had been drugged. There was no sign of the other constable who should have been on duty.

Faintly Harkness could hear again the sound of chanting from the direction of the church.

Torch in hand, he climbed down from the van and stared into the swirling mist. It was a strange kind of vapour, warm and dry when it should be damp and cold. There was a chemical odour in the air that he couldn't quite place. Harkness turned in the direction of the church but could see nothing. He switched on the torch. It had no effect. It was as if the mist flattened and diffused the beam. He switched it off and moved forward slowly, towards the sound, towards the church. After some stumbling steps on tarmac, there was grass under his feet. He could be standing now at the edge of the churchyard.

Then, all at once, he felt ill, gripped by nausea. He stumbled, feeling completely disorientated. He turned, a three hundred and sixty degree turn, trying to get his bearings and his balance. It seemed he was in the centre of a vortex of warm greyness, floating in a grey limbo.

Then the man appeared. A tall figure, taller than Harkness, coming not so much out of the mist but as if he was formed from it. A grey man, hair falling over his brow in disarray, eyes wide, staring at Harkness, yet staring past him. The face, Harkness thought, was familiar. He knew this man, yet he didn't know him.

'You heard the chanting?' Harkness said in a low tone.

The man nodded. He was dressed in what had once been a white shirt and trousers. But the shirt had dark stains around the collar.

'Where did they go?'

The man looked towards the church and spoke. His voice was a hoarse whisper.

'There,' he said, 'to Anselm's church. They want you to follow.'

Harkness grinned without humour. 'Oh, I'd follow, if I could see where I was going.'

'I'll take you there,' said the man. He turned in the direction of the church. As he did so, Harkness saw again the stains on the shirt and it seemed to him that they were still damp.

They moved forward.

Harkness said: 'I know you. Have I questioned you?'

'No.'

'One of the CID men then?'

'No. No one.'

'Are you from Greater Calderon?'

'I was.'

Then what seemed like a blinding light filled Harkness's vision. Dazzled, he blinked and rubbed at his eyes, and realised the light was in the entrance to the church, and no brighter than usual.

Beyond the light, they were in the church. No blinding light here, but a dim flickering illumination from a solitary candle at the far end of the church by the side of the altar.

The sound of plainsong was nearer again and yet there was no one in the church. Rows of empty pews and shadowed alcoves, the altar still garish even in the dim light.

'The singing's coming from . . . from below now,' Harkness said, surprised to find he was whispering. He turned, addressing his companion who was standing in the shadow of a pillar. Even in shadow the face was familiar.

'I *have* seen you before, haven't I?'

The man did not reply to his question but said softly, 'We have to go on.' And stepping from out of the shadow of the pillar, he led the way down the centre aisle towards the altar. Harkness followed.

He could hear his own footsteps echoing against the walls of the building. His own footsteps . . . not those of the man in front of him.

Some kind of distortion of sound, he decided. Yet it disturbed him. He should, he thought, feel cold. Everything about the church should be cold. Yet he found himself sweating, could feel the warm dampness on his brow.

The man had now reached the altar and was standing beside the solitary candle.

'Where the hell are we going?' Harkness said loudly. No more whispering. His companion seemed almost deaf to whispers.

The man turned and stared at him, a blank expressionless look. In the light of the candle, for the first time, Harkness could see his face clearly.

The policeman felt a chill on the back of his neck. The stains below the neck of the shirt were blood red, and he knew where he'd seen the man's face before.

On a photograph in a file. The photograph of a man with a pitchfork through his throat. A dead man.

He had been led into the church by Josh Gideon.

Chapter Thirty-Three

In the dim light, the walls seemed to shake in silence and settle again. Mist swirled around the interior of the church, and as quickly thinned out. Harkness found himself swaying and was forced to steady himself by gripping the wooden back of one of the pews. Under his hand the wood felt damp and slimy.

Somewhere, it seemed inside his head, he heard someone laugh. A harsh, grating sound.

And then the voice, a familiar voice. 'I should not laugh but your confusion is so obvious. You must know, nothing is what it seems, Harkness.'

The figure in front of him had changed. A phrase came to mind from some long forgotten book: a shapechanger.

'You see what we want you to see, Superintendent.'

Anselm stood in front of him where he had imagined the figure of Gideon, the priest in a black robe with his pastoral cross on his breast. But somehow different. Wrong.

At first he couldn't make out what was wrong, an item disturbing the eye, out of kilter. Then he saw it. The cross was upside down. Not a cross, a crucifix. The body of Christ upside down.

'I . . . I was following you?' Harkness said.

'You didn't have to follow me, Harkness. We would have come for you.'

'But it wasn't you . . .'

'As I said, you see what we want you to see. Like moths and butterflies and dead men.' The priest, if indeed he was a priest, was smiling affably. 'A game to prepare you. You

293

know, you were a bonus for us. After we killed Gideon, we didn't expect such a bonus.'

'You killed Gideon?' Harkness muttered hoarsely.

'We all did. The villagers of Calderon. The Believers. Surely you realised that?'

'I was beginning to.'

'And then you came and we read of your career. Fascinating. Such experiences of pure evil . . . so necessary for us.'

What was the man talking about? Harkness shook his head, as if to clear it; as if the mist around him was also inside his head.

'I don't understand,' he said.

'We need you, my friend. We need all your experiences. Tonight especially we need them. Through all the years there are only a few nights such as this. Not just *Walpurgis Nacht*, but a time that is permitted to us only a very few times over the centuries. A time when we take the place of the Old Knights Templar and are permitted to raise up their Lord and Master.'

The man was talking nonsense, Harkness told himself. The kind of dangerous nonsense that had resulted in the death of Gideon. And Anselm was now confessing to his participation in the man's murder. With the others, if he was to be believed. Which presented a fine legal point. How do you arrest an entire village for murder? Were there exceptions? Had the children participated? Of course it came under 'conspiracy to murder'; that would be the way. A massive conspiracy.

Anselm seemed to read his mind. 'Gideon tried to get above himself. He had to be dealt with. No one will ever be convicted of his murder, believe me, Superintendent. The power we raise tonight will protect us, and make use of you.'

'Killing me will do you no good,' Harkness replied, calmer now, telling himself the man was only able to create an illusion. It was a form of hypnotism that could be contained.

'You kill a police officer,' he went on, 'you'll have every policeman in the country around your ears.'

'My dear man, we have no intention of *killing* you. Oh, no, that will not be necessary. We simply want to draw from you the wealth of experience you have. We want to use the evil you have seen, the horrors you have known . . .'

294

'You're off your head Anselm.'

'It must seem so to you.'

Damn the man's imperturbability. He was too cool, lacking the element of panic he should have when facing the law.

'But you really want to see what happens here in Calderon tonight,' Anselm went on. 'And we want to show you. Because now you are necessary to us.'

'I'm necessary to you? How the hell am I necessary to you?'

The priest, if he was indeed a priest, smiled. A cold crooked smile, it seemed to the policeman.

'You are part of our ceremonies. But come now, you wanted to follow us. You *have* to follow, all the way.'

Harkness stood, unmoving. 'I don't have to do anything, Anselm. Except caution you and place you under arrest.'

'How very proper and correct. But surely you have curiosity, Harkness? Surely you want to see what goes on at the darker edges of our world? The others will be there, should you want to arrest and caution them.'

The priest moved to an archway beyond the altar and now Harkness moved after him, telling himself the man was right. If the others were there, they had to be cautioned. Telling himself that and yet knowing he should not follow the priest. Not that he was afraid. There was no fear in him. Simply the impulse to follow. Forced upon him . . . no, not that. A kind of curiosity . . .

Beyond the archway, a staircase at the side leading downwards. A stone staircase, twisting around and around as it went down and down, dimly lit by lanterns hanging from the walls at every twist and turn, leading to the catacombs of the church. He went down, following the priest over well-worn slabs of stone. He recalled a print in an old book he'd once seen as a youth in Scotland: a figure leading another figure downwards, Dante being led into the circles of hell.

The stairway, Harkness thought, should be cold and damp; the village had been built on a swamp, centuries ago. Yet it was not so. Heat was coming upwards. The stone blocks that made up the walls of the stairway were covered with a yellowish dust – sulphur or some other chemical – and webbed with the weavings of many spiders.

Again Anselm seemed to read his thoughts.

295

'We're below the catacombs now, Harkness. Going much deeper.'

Still they went down.

Harkness noticed that every now and then one of the stone blocks on the wall was embossed with figures and shapes.

'Built by the Templars when they first came here,' Anselm said, still descending. 'Some of these are the coats of arms of the great Templar families. Others are the symbols of their worship. The Kabbalistic signs of Baphomet who was their principal demon. And others. It was here they learned to go further, to achieve greater power which they passed on to us. Until, tonight we are able to go even further towards our Masters.'

The man was mad, Harkness decided. He'd gone beyond the rational into insane fantasies dredged up from some imagined past. Probably inspired the killing of Gideon himself.

Still they descended, then came to the foot of the stairway.

Harkness found himself looking into an enormous cavern, or so it seemed. Yet he felt appearance was outdistancing reality. He felt it falling away from him, like a serpent shedding its skin. Distortions were appearing in the fabric of his perception.

The cavern seemed to be circular. A raised area ran round the walls, torches burning there providing illumination. On this area they stood, policeman and dubious priest. Around them were most of the villagers: over a hundred figures, men and women, in monkish grey cowls, faces visible. They were familiar to Harkness, villagers he had interrogated in the last days. They ignoring him now, faces averted, staring expectantly.

Some five or six feet below them was the floor of the cavern. Circular lines ran towards the centre like the spokes of a wheel. The hub was a smaller circular shape, a round steel circle, like some metal cover over what might have been the entrance to a well. The surface of this disc was etched with Kabbalistic symbols, strange twisted shapes, obscure, ancient, almost illegible letters and cyphers. Staring, Harkness reckoned the steel circle was about seven feet in diameter.

Around it, breaking through the spokes of the wheel, was yet another symbol.

'The pentagram,' Anselm was at his ear, reading his mind again or merely following his eyeline. 'To keep us safe. To hold in what might arise from the pit.'

Harkness turned to the pale thin face beside him. 'Pit?' he said, sounding at once obtuse and aware of being so.

'Beneath the metal cover,' Anselm explained. 'The reason the Templars settled here. One of the entrances to . . .' The thin shoulders shrugged.

'You're daft! An old well . . . something like that'

'Waterless? Generating heat?'

'Volcanic then,' Harkness insisted. 'From the smell of sulphur, certainly volcanic. A blowhole still active from some ancient volcanic activity.'

'At Lake Avernus near Naples, Virgil found one of the ancient entrances to the Lower Regions. A way to Hades. But you'll see for yourself, Harkness. They're waiting for us down at the entrance.'

From the shadows around the metal cover came the figures. Cowled like the rest of the villagers, but the cowls of a different shade, black instead of brown. Eleven figures around what Anselm called the pit.

He followed Anselm then, uncertain as to why; as if impelled to do so. They descended steps carved from the rock, old and eroded by time and the feet of others who had gone before. They descended to the floor of the cavern. Anselm moved forward through the circle created by the eleven figures, eleven older members of the village community. There was Mullion, among them, eyes fixed on the metallic circle. None of them paid any attention to Harkness.

Anselm turned and faced him, a twisted humourless smile on his face. 'Twelve of us, Harkness, and yourself.'

'I make the magic thirteen, do I?' said the police officer, wondering at the kind of gullibility that could hold so many people in a kind of thrall.

'Oh, no, Superintendent, not you. You are here for quite a different purpose. You see, you are, although you may not realise it, a repository of evil.'

'What the hell are you talking about?'

'Your career. Your life. All you've seen and experienced. All the horrors of that life. There, inside you. To be brought out. To feed . . . *he who is coming.*'

Harkness stared fixedly at the man, remembering madness as he'd seen it in the past: open, obsessional, terrifying in its derangement.

'You really are crazy.' Such an inadequate statement, without effect on the man.

'They said Aleister Crowley raised up the god Pan in a room in Paris,' Anselm went on, 'he and one other. The next morning, his companion was dead and Crowley half mad.'

'Fairy tales for sick minds.'

'You'd like to think so, but it was true. His mistake was he lacked the power to control. Here, we will have the full coven of thirteen and a hundred minds behind us, willing us to success without disaster. Willing us the power we'll be granted when we succeed.'

'What kind of power can you hope to have through Hallowe'en games and daft rituals?'

'The power to control others. The power to forge the future. A power that Templars sought for hundreds of years. The power of the Lord of Light himself.'

Harkness thought, the man's delirious. Out of control. Ruled by an obsession he has somehow transferred to the hundred faces looking down. A beguiled, stupid, vicious little community, perverted over the years by Anselm and his predecessors. It had to be stopped, he told himself, had to be stopped now.

He swung around, staring upwards at the cowled figures of the villagers.

'All of you, listen to me! This lunatic has fooled you, driven you to an act of murder. If you stop now, then something can be done. Anselm, as ringleader, is under arrest. While you all bear some degree of culpability, his influence will be taken into account. Now, I want you to disperse, go to your homes and await further calls from the authorities. Statements will be taken and some charges will be made but . . . I cannot . . . can't see . . . mass arrests . . .'

He faltered and finally stopped speaking, aware that no one was listening to him; that their eyes had lifted and were

298

staring over his head. Sounds were coming from them, a kind of low chanting, the words, indeed the language, obscure and unintelligible.

He spun around on his heels.

Behind him from the darkness had come another figure. Tall, towering over the eleven others, wearing a cloak studded with jewels moulded into strange shapes, a larger cowl covering the face, features masked in darkness.

The villagers above seemed to bow as their chanting grew louder. The twelve figures around Harkness bowed. Even Anselm's head dropped.

The thirteenth member of the coven. The leader.

Unrecognisable. Someone else, Harkness thought. Someone new. The one who bore the ultimate responsibility.

He stepped forward.

'No!' One word from the new arrival.

And Harkness stopped as if coming against an invisible barrier. Unable to move. Bound by invisible elements, and a barrier he couldn't see. Finding himself unable to speak. Unable to take his eyes from the figure in front of him.

Then the figure gestured, an authoritative movement of the hands, permission granted. Two of the thirteen moved back into shadow. After a moment, with a loud metallic sound, the seemingly solid metal circle appeared to split across its centre and the two halves began to slide aside – slowly, infinitely slowly. The two figures came back from the darkness and took up their positions again, all of them just outside the line of the pentagram.

As the metal circle parted and opened as if controlled by an unseen mechanism, a great ray of light shot up from the depths of the pit, a ray surrounded by a whirling miasma of smoke or steam, twisting and turning in the air. The sudden glare illuminated the entire cavern with a dazzling brightness so intense as momentarily to blind all of those assembled there.

Chapter Thirty-Four

After a moment, despite the intensity of the light, Harkness could see again. He still found himself unable to move but his eyes had become quickly accustomed to the light. And he was aware that the figure wearing the jewel-studded cloak was staring at him. Although he could not distinguish the other features of the face, he could see the eyes, dark and penetrating, as if gazing deep into his soul.

Drawing something from within him.

Memories. Events experienced. Events he had long forgotten – or would have wished to forget. The past being drawn from him, all the evil and vileness he had seen in his long career.

There were the murdered children again, and other bodies, hanging, twisted and mutilated. And with the image, sounds he could never have heard but could only imagine. The screams of the children as an insane hand killed them. Eviscerated bodies in a cold room, the walls covered in blood, as if veins and arteries had spouted fountains of red.

Another image from further back when he had been a young constable: the body of an old man, a down-and-out, curled up in a Glasgow alley. Blackened and contorted in a shape no living body could have achieved. Petrol had been thrown on him by two youths who had then set him alight. In the police station, they laughed at their exploit . . .

A woman, gang raped and beaten until she had nearly died. The body, naked, lying in a black court, thrown on to a pile of rubbish. Unable to speak. Eyes moving fearfully, on the edge of madness . . .

Other images, memories being drawn from him as if to feed some appetite for evil, for horror. Now a child starved to death . . . now, a man slashed to death with cut-throat razors . . . the small man, himself a villain, nailed by his kneecaps to the floor of a room: one of Swanson's victims. Another found floating in the Thames, in the water over a week, brought out like some bloated, obscene caricature of humanity. Yet another, a young prostitute, screaming in agony, having had acid thrown – no, not thrown – dripped on to her face.

And others, so many others.

Finally, Harkness alone with Mahoney, the man who had killed the children. And later, so many years later, alone with Swanson. Harkness hitting out, beating both men, wanting to mutilate and kill. The infection of evil. His own soul, if he ever believed he had a soul, contaminated by evil. A contagion he would never have believed could touch him.

He knew then this was why he was here. Anselm had told him but he couldn't until now understand. All that he had seen, all that he had experienced, was being drawn from him, sucked out of him, towards the gaping circle of light emanating from below. From God knows where. If God indeed knew, if God indeed still existed.

Beside Anselm, the figure in the jewelled robe began to intone some words, a travesty of a priest at prayer. At first he was unable to make them out: sounds murmured into the sulphorous air, at the edge of hell. They seemed oddly recognisable from all myth and legend; yet it would be so. The imagination of man created its own nightmares and when these came to reality, they were inevitably limited by that imagination. Harkness was aware of this just as he was aware that whatever he was seeing and experiencing was only an infinitesimally small part of that very reality.

The words became clearer now.

'. . . Yod, Tetragrammaton, Elohim, Eloah Va-Daath, El Adonai, Tzaboath, Shaddai . . .'

On and on went the incantation, and as it did so, a feeling of expectancy filled the cavern. The cowled figures shifted and trembled in the great light. The eyes of the speaker were no longer on Harkness but directed towards the source of the light, the great pit in the centre of the cavern. The walls

302

surrounding them seemed to shake. Anselm, whose face Harkness could see, was exultant, expectant, eyes wide, waiting . . .

Something was coming from the pit.

A strange sickly odour mixed with sulphur pervaded the air. It was so thick now as to make breathing difficult.

Not happening! This is not happening, Harkness told himself, repeating it over and over. It's a kind of hypnotism, a trance state, unreal, born of a perversion of the imagination.

Drained of memories, unable to move, his mind sought other explanations. Anselm had said it: Nothing is what it seems. All this is from some medieval nightmare, the vision of a Breughel or a Hieronymous Bosch painting. The primeval fears and nightmares of men throughout the ages brought to a living nightmare.

Then, from the depths of the pit in front of them, came a great sound, a roaring screaming sound.

The villagers threw back the hoods of their cowls and stood, moaning with anticipation. The jewelled figure backed away, into darkness, as if its task was done. Anselm stepped forward, the daemonic priest, hands flung wide, ready to embrace whatever was coming. He was muttering to himself now, first something that sounded like the Lord's Prayer backwards.

'. . . patris nomine in . . .'

The words were lost in the sound and the roaring from below.

Harkness tried to turn away but found he still could not move. He tried to shut his eyes but was unable to do so. It seemed every muscle in his body might be paralysed.

God, let me move . . . let me turn away from this . . . this thing. Nothing to do with me . . . no responsibility of mine . . .

He concentrated on trying to look away, trying even to cover his eyes with his hands. Whatever obscenity was coming, he had no wish to see, no curiosity left. His hands moved. An inch or two, no more. He was unable to move them further. His eyes remained open wide, staring at the pit. He braced himself preparing for some ultimate terror.

Anselm, taking over the incantation, was muttering loudly now: 'Excubitores, in nomine Gabreli, fas mihi tangere limina illa . . .'

His voice rose in pitch until he was almost screaming. The cavern became hot – a deep scorching heat, searing the skin. Pores opened, the flesh becoming damp with sweat. Sweat ran from the hairline, down the cheeks, on to the body. The heat made clothing unnecessary. Reacting to this, the villagers were casting off their robes. All of them with the exception of Anselm, Harkness and the wearer of the jewelled robe were soon naked, bodies gleaming in the light. Fat gross bodies, and thin emaciated ones; old and young, ugly and unpleasant: all of them twisting turning, rubbing against each other, clutching obscenely at their nearest neighbours irrespective of gender. As if attempts at sexual acts of varying degrees of perversity would encourage the rising from the pit of whatever was about to appear.

In the centre, a ball of light was forming, its essence drawn from below.

Slowly it took shape.

The activity of the villagers increased. Some were now writhing together on the ground, in frenzied sexual activity, dirt of the soil clinging to their bodies. Others leant on the walls of the cavern forcing themselves on each other.

Although Harkness's eyes were fixed upon the centre of the pit and the ball of light, he was conscious of all that was going on around him. As if his consciousness was able to embrace a three hundred and sixty degree angle; as if a bacchanalian orgy, a moving, living frieze, was mounted on the walls surrounding the chamber.

In the centre of the ball of light, a figure was created from the pit below.

Harkness braced himself for some unimaginable horror.

And was astonished as the figure formed and fear fell from him. In its place there was contentment, a lulling, soothing sense of ease. An odour of great sweetness was in his nostrils.

The figure was beautiful: a young man of surpassingly handsome features and perfection of body. Indeed, the features were so delicately moulded as to be almost feminine in their perfection of form. Golden hair shaded the eyes. Tall, but not too tall, over six feet in height. Naked and yet without regard for nakedness. Standing now on the lip of the pit, gazing with a calming benevolence on them all.

The villager's activity ceased. They stared, all with a degree of awe, at the figure before them.

Anselm was on his knees, staring up open-mouthed at the androgynous figure so close to him that he could reach out and touch the feet. The wearer of the jewelled cloak had drawn back into the shadows as if distance provided a more complete view.

The figure threw back its head, the gold hair sweeping away to reveal a broad forehead, the eyes still in shadow. The lips, full and red, seemed to twitch in amusement at the effect of its appearance.

Harkness looked up into the eyes.

The odour of sweetness became overwhelming. Too much. A sickly quality now.

As he stared at the eyes, the heat went from the cavern. A chill swept up from the pit. The eyes were deep and dark and icicle cold. One look from them went deep into the marrow of Harkness's bones, creating a sudden piercing agony.

Half-remembered images came to his mind. Dante's seventh circle of hell . . . ice and everlasting cold . . . the Devil, the Fallen Angel . . . God's beloved who betrayed him . . . Lucifer, Lord of Light . . . father of all evil . . . cast into one pit . . .

A fly buzzed around Harkness's face.

. . . other manifestations of Lucifer . . . the Lord of the Flies . . . Beelzebub . . . Asmodeus . . . the demonic equivalents of the angels of the elements, Samael, Azazel, Azael, Mahazeal . . .

The ease and contentment had gone, in their place an overpowering terror. The sickly odour turned putrid. Harkness told himself, This is some nightmare, some unreal vision. *Nothing is what it seems* . . .

The golden figure smiled now, almost coyly. A twisted, contemptuous smile. As if to say, 'You have raised me up. Now you must satisfy me . . .'

A scream from behind Harkness.

305

He found he could move now. Half-turning, he saw the girl, Abbie, naked, thrown down from the side of the cavern. She screamed again and lay on the ground, body gleaming, flesh shuddering. Thrown forward as a first sacrifice . . . or was the sacrifice in her arms? A baby, barely moving, was held tight to the girl's breast, tiny eyes flickering in the light.

Then, terrified for herself, Abbie was holding out the baby to the golden figure from the pit, nipples erect, presenting the infant to the Demon.

Harkness knew then with a certainty he could not explain that the infant was Abbie's own child. He felt the nausea rising in his throat. The girl was prepared to sacrifice her own child to survive. That was what it was all about . . .

Why?

He stared again at the figure, dazzling in the light.

Abbie was scrabbling forward in the dirt, holding out the child.

The flies buzzed around his head, increasing their pitch. As if he might be the only threat. The thing was afraid of him!

All the evil he had seen drawn from him was to nurture this figure from the pit. Necessary but dangerous. And now that everything had been drawn from him, he felt cleansed.

Yet his mind was spinning. He was dazed, frightened, on the edge of insanity.

Something had to be done. What? Why him?

He felt the small circular tube outlined against his pocket. The vial given to him by Haydock, the dead priest.

Ridiculous! A vial of water against this.

The swarm of flying insects multiplying . . .

His hand went into his pocket. There was a metal cap on the vial. A plug of iron. And so-called holy water. As if he could believe in such a thing.

Yet could he believe in all that he was seeing now? The golden figure from the pit? The sudden swarm of flies? The girl holding out her child to be . . . what? Devoured? Cast away? Certainly that.

He gripped the vial.

The icy cold bit into his arm.

306

The golden figure wavered in his vision, trembled, something seen through a wall of heat. And yet all he could feel was the cold.

Anselm, on his knees, turned away from the light to stare at Harkness. Another kind of fear on his face.

Harkness drew his hand from his pocket, fingers around the glass vial, thinking, if all this can be, then the priest's vial of water can also be. His hand was heavy as lead. As the iron plug on the end of the vial. Iron and water.

The flies were thick in the air in front of him, darkening his vision. Must act before he could no longer see. He lifted his arm and threw the vial towards the figure at the edge of the pit. He could see it describe an arc, curving through the air. Falling into the golden figure.

All he knew then was the explosion, a blast of light filling the entire cavern.

He could feel himself being blown backwards towards the wall of the cavern. Dark rocks rising in the air. A tremendous blast of sound on his eardrums.

Then, blackness.

Braden 1988

Chapter Thirty-Five

Harkness grinned, his face crinkling like parchment. His eyes stared past Braden to the black-leaded stove.

'She says . . . she aye says I'll not talk about it. But I do, and I don't care! It's her that worries, Lizzie, the cuckoo in the nest.'

He laughed and the sound turned into a catarrhal gurgle. His face turned scarlet as he tried to bring the cough under control. It took him a minute to do so.

Then he said, 'Is the snooker on yet?'

'Not yet, Mr Harkness. What happened after the explosion?' Braden said.

The old man looked up, puzzled. 'What explosion?'

'In the church. At Calderon.'

'Oh, aye, that.' He smiled again and looked up at Braden. 'I don't know.'

'You mean you can't remember?'

'Mean, I don't know. Didn't know anything until I woke up in hospital in Warwick.'

Braden felt frustrated, let down. Like watching one of those plays on television that had no end but simply came to an abrupt and unsatisfactory termination.

'And that was over a week later,' Harkness added. 'You sure the snooker's not on yet? That's a smashing wee player we've got up here. Comes from Stirling . . .'

Lizzie Harkness or Graham came back into the room. 'The snooker won't be on until tonight.' She looked at Braden. 'Has he said anything?'

'A great deal.'

311

'It's not good for him.'

The old man twisted around in his seat. 'Away! I know what's good for me. Don't need you shovin' your end in.'

'You need me to do everything else for you,' she replied. Her rebuke seemed to spur the old man on.

'You want to know what happened next?' he said to Braden. 'Told you – hospital. Didn't know how I got there at first. Then they told me.'

He took a deep breath before going on. 'They found me the next morning, lying in the road outside Anselm's churchyard. So they told me. Right there, in the centre of Greater Calderon. Out to the world. No visible injuries, no' a mark on me, just in a kind of coma. It lasted over a week. I told you that, didn't I? Over a week.'

'What caused it?'

'How the hell do I know! They didn't. Thought I'd had stroke. But, when they did a brain scan, they could find nothing. Then they thought, maybe I'd just fallen down. But there wasn't a mark on me. Except . . . except, for a time . . . quite a time, I couldn't walk. In that place for two months, I was. By the time I got out, I was finished. Compulsory retirement. Medically unfit. You know what they called it?'

'What?'

'A nervous breakdown. Me? A nervous breakdown. Fuckin' rubbish!'

'Watch your language,' his daughter said.

He ignored her. 'Never had nerves, me. Never. Never had a breakdown. Some of it was my own fault, mind. See, I was stupid. Daft enough to tell them things.'

'What things?' Braden asked.

'What I've told you. What I told you happened to me in that place. In the village. The moths in the room. What happened under the church. Told them I saw . . . I saw the devil. Wasn't clever that. Should have known they wouldn't believe me. Should have known they'd think I was ravin' . . .'

'And you were,' said Lizzie.

Again he ignored her. 'But you, you believe me, don't you, Mr . . . Mr . . . ?'

'Braden.'

'You do believe me?'

312

Braden thought of Jennet Agram, and of the murder of Gideon.

'Yes, I believe you,' he said, hardly convinced but telling himself that the old man had to be humoured.

The old man started to laugh again. Was it laughter or a kind of low cackling sound?

'See, Lizzie, says he believes me. Plays up to me. As if they could believe that story! As if anyone could. See, Mr Braden, nothing is what it seems. Now there's a wee truth for you: Nothing is what it seems. Even if I tell it. Even if I believe it. Anybody told me that story, I'd think they'd lost their marbles. Makes me not sure about you, Mr Braden.'

Braden thought, A story . . . made up by an old man? But in such detail? Not from the imagination of a tough old policeman, even one approaching senility.

'What about those cases of yours you told me about?' Braden said quickly. 'The murdered children. The woman gang-raped. Swanson . . .'

Harkness scowled. 'They happened! All true.' The scowl turned to a frown. 'I remember them all. But . . . but I don't remember them too well. Like I mislaid them in my memory. Lost them, like. How could that be?'

'Unless you lost the horror of them that night below the church in Calderon?' Braden came in quickly.

The old man stared at him, trying to smile. But the smile was uncertain.

'You're trying to make me believe what I've told you.'

Braden tried another tack. 'Jennet Agram would believe you.'

The old man's mouth dropped open. His eyes wandered now, as if searching for something to reassure him.

Lizzie said, 'You're upsetting him!'

'Maybe I'm helping him.'

'That story's not real,' she insisted, her voice sharp.

'He believes it.'

'He made it up. He has to have made it up!' She glared at Braden impatiently. 'What kind of fool are you? Demon, indeed. The Devil rising from the pit. Fairy tales, to frighten children.'

313

'Or something evil, terrifying enough to make men lose their senses? To damage them, make them lie to avoid facing what they can't face?'

And then Braden thought, What am I saying? Am I become as mad as Harkness? Or am I playing a kind of devil's advocate . . . how appropriate . . . for the sake of some sensational tabloid news article? No, it wasn't that. He really wanted the story to be true. As if it might satisfy some deep atavistic instinct within him.

'You're as mad as he was,' Lizzie Harkness said, as if she could read his thoughts.

'So he did believe in that story?'

Hunched over now, the old man said, 'Nothing is what it seems. Nothing can be what it seems. It's all in the mind. Has to be . . .'

'What happened to the others? The villagers?'

'Who knows? Nothing, they told me . . .' the thin lined hands dotted with kidney spots, twisted around each other. 'They . . . they were all there. Afterwards. Except . . . except one.'

A memory, something he'd long forgotten.

'The priest, Anselm. Father Anselm. If he was a priest. He'd . . . he'd disappeared. Aye, they told me that. Gone. Gone from the village. They never found him.'

Again looking up at Braden. 'Never. Not to this day. Told me before I left hospital. Blakelock had taken over then, not that he ever found out anything. But he came to see me in hospital, asked me if Anselm could have been the man who killed Gideon. Because he'd disappeared. Because they found out he'd not been a priest for years. Been . . . what do they call it . . . struck off, unfrocked? Anselm lied to me, you see, all that bit about the Latin Mass . . . that's not why he'd been struck off. Blakelock knew. He'd found out . . .'

'What did Blakelock find out?'

'Blasphemy – that was why Anselm had been unfrocked. Something about gross and unnatural practices. Could have been jailed but the church had hushed it up, years before in the late fifties. I would have got to that, if I'd had more time to investigate. Blakelock got it, though. Only thing he did get. Had to ask me if I thought Anselm had killed Gideon.'

314

'What did you tell him?'

'Told him, of course he had! With the others. The whole village. They were all guilty as hell. And not just of killing Gideon.' Harkness started to chuckle again. 'Of course Margaret Campion was shocked when she heard about Anselm, Blakelock told me that. She'd entertained him, treated him as her priest and confessor. Oh, she didn't like it at all. She told Blakelock she thought Anselm might well have killed Gideon. Not that she'd ever considered it before. But the woman felt . . . felt betrayed, like. Can't blame her. Pretty woman too.'

'They never caught Anselm?'

'Never found him. That one, he must have run a long way. Might still be running yet. After how many years? Ten?'

'Twelve.'

'That long, eh?'

'About Anselm – it was never reported in the press at the time.'

'What was there to report? No evidence. Always have to have evidence. Oh, for a time I think they said they were looking for a man to help them with their enquiries. But they wouldn't name him. The Catholic bishop wouldn't like that. An unfrocked priest still running a parish, and all sorts of terrible stories about him . . . were they true, were they not? Nothing what it seems, eh?'

Braden looked up at the daughter who was standing at the kitchen window staring down into a drab, dimly lit backcourt.

'You father's pretty lucid now.'

'Aye, now. When he wants to be,' she replied. 'He keeps saying that thing: nothing is what it seems.'

'Don't talk about me as if I wasn't here,' the old man said with a flash of irritation. 'Talk to me, not to her. She knows bugger all.'

'That's nice, that is!' she said, thin-lipped. 'It's time for his meal. Have you anything else to say to him?'

'Leave the lad alone,' Harkness retorted, chewing his lower lip in a kind of frustration. 'He might want to watch the snooker. He might want to hear me tell some stories. What he came for, isn't it?'

315

He swivelled around to look at Braden again. 'I was in the police, y'know. All my working life. One police medal, four certificates of commendation. And then they got rid of me over that villain, Ronnie Swanson. Him and . . . and the things happened at Greater and Lesser Calderon. But I told you about that, didn't I?'

He turned back to contemplate the black-leaded grate.

'Met a woman there. No, not there, in Warwick. Jennet, lot younger than me. But she was . . . something. She could have . . . could have put me right. Better than this one, and she's supposed to be my own flesh and blood.'

'Huh!' said Lizzie. 'That's what I get for twelve years of looking after him.'

Braden ignored her. It seemed the only thing to do.

'Jennet Agram sent her . . . her best wishes to you, Mr Harkness.'

It seemed to him then that the old man's eyes misted.

'She would.'

'I have to go now.'

'Aye. Everybody has to go that comes here. Nobody every stays very long.'

'The man's been here for nearly three hours,' Lizzie Harkness said.

Again Braden paid no attention to her. He rose to his feet. 'One other thing?'

'Aye?'

'The figure in the cavern. The one next to Anselm. The one in the jewelled cloak . . .'

Harkness coughed. 'That was the leader. Aye, he was. Him and Anselm.'

'Who was he?'

'Never did know that. Never. Failed there, I did. Part of the unsolved mystery, eh? Like whether it ever really happened or whether I dreamt it. Y'know, I dream a lot of things now. Lot of dreams. Difference is, now some of them are better than real life.'

He lapsed into silence. Braden thought, 'An old man in a dry month, waiting for rain.' Who'd said that? T.S. Eliot in *The Wasteland*. Maybe all our lives come to this, a wasteland.

'Goodbye, Mr Harkness,' he said. 'Thank you for giving me your time.'

'Aye. You believe me, eh?'

Braden had to reply, 'Yes. Yes, indeed.'

'You're a liar like the rest, but you're a polite liar. Anyway, what does it matter?' A petulant look came over the old man. 'Whether it happened, whether it didnae, what does it matter? Doesnae bring Gideon back to life. Doesnae mean anything . . .'

'See what you've done,' Lizzie Harkness said.

'I'm sorry.' Braden turned back to the old man. 'I am sorry, Mr Harkness.'

'Aye. Has the snooker started yet?'

It was past ten o'clock when Braden went out into Tassie Street. Yellow street lamps cast circular pools on cracked paving. At the end of a street was the main road, neon-lit and bright. Braden wanted to drive away out of this city, head south quickly, back to England, to Warwick, put distance between himself and the man who looked even older than he must be. Harkness was only in his early seventies, surely, and yet he appeared to be well into his eighties. Rational one minute; the next, eyes wandering, mind trying to follow but too often unable to keep up. Only when he told his story of the investigations of Calderon did he seem lucid and clear-headed. Except for the contents of his story. The madness of the witches' Sabbat and the conjuring up of . . . something. If indeed it happened.

Nothing is what it seems.

Braden, climbing into his car, felt exhausted. He drove into the centre of the city, found Glasgow's Holiday Inn on the banks of the Clyde and booked in for one night. Holiday Inn? Not quite the kind of holiday he was used to.

That night he slept and dreamt of masks, cowelled faces, dark crypts, jewelled cloaks . . . but of any linking events, he had no memory.

Chapter Thirty-Six

The next morning, he wanted the Harkness story to be real. It made everything so simple. Childhood values did exist. Black and white. Biblical evil existing and there to be fought. No grey areas any more.

The question was, who had won in Calderon? And could a vial of Holy Water really cleanse the universe?

Braden was driving south on the M6. He had left Glasgow early in the morning, thinking about Harkness's story.

The sophisticated city boy, he told himself, wanting to believe in the Devil. Not as some abstraction, some perverse anti-social action; not as premeditated murder, torture inflicted on others; the horrors of the Holocaust and the countless minor holocausts that occurred every day in secret cells throughout the world. Yes, these were evil, but if he were to believe in all that Harkness had told him, they were manifestations of a definite and enduring entity. Harkness, who'd been a hard, practical policeman, a cynic, probably an atheist, had told the story; had, if he were to be believed, lived the events in Calderon.

Yet . . . nothing is what it seems.

Was it illusion?

Rationale told him it had to be. His intellect insisted it had to be an illusion. Why then should he want it to be true? Because he would have a marvellous newspaper story? No, not that. The story would be at the least laughed at; at the worst, dismissed as a piece of cheap sensationalism. Yet perhaps, deep down, it proved what he wanted to see proved. If the Devil existed, then so did God.

As he drove, he wondered at what he'd got himself into. All his adult life, he'd been an agnostic. Now he was looking for proof of the existence of a deity, on the M6 heading south on a wet morning.

He had to get back to practicalities. Joshua Gideon had been murdered twelve years before, by person or persons never discovered. But there were people alive who could know the truth. Jennet Agram? Maybe. The villagers in Calderon? Again, maybe. There had been a priest, frocked or unfrocked, at Calderon. Father Anselm had disappeared yet might well still be alive. Had he disappeared because he had been involved in the killing of Gideon? It might still be possible to find him. Margaret Campion was almost certainly still alive, and a comparatively young woman. In her forties anyway. Did she still live in Calderon? There were others too. Mullion, the innkeeper. The girl, Abbie. Did she really have a child? It had only been mentioned in the cavern in the depths of what might simply be Harkness's nightmare. Anselm had a housekeeper too, Drewitt had mentioned her . . . what was the name? Mrs Gavel, that was it. Would she be still alive? Caroon, too, the ageing thug. And the baker, Numbles? No, Numbles had been killed by a car after talking too much. An accident? There were witnesses. Even Harkness hadn't gone into that one. And there was the man in the jewelled cloak. Who was he?

So he still had leads to be followed. The story wasn't over yet.

Braden put his foot on the accelerator. He'd been coasting along at just below fifty. He took the car up to seventy, anxious to get to Warwick.

The rain had stopped and patches of blue were struggling to come out from behind the clouds when he arrived at the council estate in Warwick. It was nearly one o'clock in the afternoon. Jennet Agram was on her knees scrubbing the steps to her flat, a bucket of warm water by her side. The blonde child was leaning against the side of the house, sucking an orange.

'Mrs Agram?' Braden greeted her.

'Miss!' she said without turning around. 'You're back, Mr Braden.'

320

'I'm back.' He was staring at the child who stared back at him and then grinned. There was something familiar about her he hadn't noticed before. He couldn't quite be sure what it was. He hadn't felt it when he'd seen the child previously.

Jennet Agram put down her scrubbing brush, glanced at Braden and then rose to her feet.

'You saw him.' It was a statement not a question.

'I saw him.'

A distinct tremor in her voice. 'How was he?' Then before he could reply, 'Better come upstairs. Like some tea or food? You've had a long drive.'

'Tea would be fine.'

She turned to the child. 'Janey, you've had your lunch. Go and play with Isabel.'

The child pouted, torn between curiosity about the second visit of Braden and going off to find her friend. A look from her mother gave her no choice. She went. Braden followed Jennet Agram upstairs and into the sitting room. He sat staring at a one-bar electric fire while she made him a cup of tea and brought it to him on a tray with some small sweet biscuits.

'Now tell me how Harkness is?'

He hesitated, undecided as to whether or not the truth would be best.

'He's . . . all right. Looks older than he is. And at times, he's inclined to wander in his mind.'

'Yes, it would be so.'

'He . . . he remembered you. Fondly.'

She smiled, a small, soft smile. 'Yes. Well, I'm glad.'

'You should visit him.'

Her eyes flashed. 'No! It's too late. Maybe twelve years ago, but not now. Not after Calderon.'

Braden shrugged. 'He told me what had happened at Calderon. Or what he thought had happened at Calderon.'

'And did you believe him, Mr Braden?'

Again he hesitated. 'I don't know. He . . . Harkness didn't seem at all sure himself. He couldn't quite distinguish between reality and some kind of nightmare.'

'It is difficult.'

321

He took a mouthful of tea. It was hot and sweet, with an aftertaste he couldn't quite define.

'It's herbal,' she said.

'Miss Agram, what did happen at Calderon that night? Walpurgis Night.' *No No HallowEen not 30th April*

'Harkness told you.'

'But was it real? I told you, he wasn't sure himself.'

'You have to make up your own mind, Mr Braden. How can I tell you? I wasn't there.'

'But you must have some idea?'

Her turn to hesitate. 'Whether it happened or he dreamt it happened doesn't matter. The effect was the same. For Harkness. Also . . . Anselm was displaced. For which we have to be grateful to Harkness. And whatever was going on in Calderon was stopped.'

'But who killed Gideon? If it was the villagers, who led them? Who was the man in the jewelled cloak? Harkness never found out.'

'Perhaps that's your job, Mr Braden.'

Braden took a deep breath. And a chance. 'Or yours, Miss Agram?'

She shook her head. Her eyes had misted over. 'Harkness did my job. He did the cleansing – with my help. Not that he was aware of it. I warned him about Calderon and I knew he wouldn't listen. He would do what was necessary. He would close the Entrance. He did it.'

'What kind of help did you give him?' Braden said, almost contemptuously.

'Spiritual strength, you might call it, as well as the physical kind. That was something else too. You know, Mr Braden, everyone talked about my affair with Joshua Gideon, the murdered man. A lecher, a practitioner of certain arts, a man of ambition. Why did I, knowing what I did, sleep with him? Even Harkness never asked that question. Even you . . . and I thought you might have come around to asking it.'

'All right, why did you?'

'I thought Gideon might destroy the coven in Calderon. I thought I could influence him to do just that. I was wrong. Gideon wasn't interested in destroying the evil in the village – he wanted to use it for his own purposes. He wanted to

322

displace Anselm; he wanted to wear the jewelled cloak. He wanted to open the Entrance as they did that night.'

'You believed in it then? This Entrance to . . . what?'

'You know all about it. You're simply afraid to admit it. Part of you wants it to be a dream, part of you wants it to be a reality.'

'That's not important. Go on,' Braden insisted.

'Anyway, when Gideon would do nothing, he was killed because of his own overwhening ambition. They were too strong for him. Then Harkness came to investigate. All I had given to Gideon, I gave to Harkness, physically and spiritually. And, you see, as a policeman, it was his job. He did it the only way that was open to him to do it. Go to Calderon now, Braden. See the people who still live there on the edge of a hell they tried to use for their own ends. They've seen what they shouldn't have, tried to bring about what no man should attempt. They're like sleepwalkers. They live out their lives knowing that at the end they may be faced with damnation. They live without hope, and that's a terrible thing.'

'You and Harkness brought this about?'

'And I have to live with it. The knowledge of what I did, what I had to do. Through him.'

Braden drained his teacup. 'I see. Or think I see.'

She smiled then. 'I did what I had to. Even though I lost Harkness, I did love him. In one night it can happen. It was all we had, that one night. Oh, I had a kind of solace. Paid in full. Not with money . . .'

She was staring at him, her gaze deep and intense. He knew then why he had felt the child was familiar to him.

'She's Harkness's daughter? Your child, Janey.'

She nodded. 'Everything in life is circular, Mr Braden. Everything turns back on itself. The circles close. You'll see.'

'Harkness doesn't know?'

'If it would have brought him joy, I would have told him. But it would only have confused an already confused mind. He'd been through all that happened in Calderon. It had nearly destroyed him. Would this have helped. No. Not him, not the child. It's enough that she exists, his gift to me.'

She stood up. 'Time you were going. You'll want to go to Calderon again, this time to see for yourself. Discover for

323

yourself. No driving through this time. You know now what the town was like twelve years ago. Find out what it's like now. Another circle to be closed. You'll close that circle. It's time. Whether you'll get your newspaper story or not, I don't know, but you have to close the circle. And, if you write about it . . . and you're free to do so . . . I would only beg you not to mention Janey. Certainly not as Harkness's daughter.'

Her gaze was intense, penetrating. 'The child is not relevant,' he heard himself say.

'Good. Now go to Calderon.'

Outside the house, as he climbed into his car, he saw two children playing further along the street. One of them was Harkness's daughter.

He drove out of Warwick, heading south, to Greater and Lesser Calderon. Now the sky was darkening again. He told himself it was bound to do so. Going to that place. To see for himself, knowing the story. Or most of it. To close the circle. Whatever that meant.

Outside Warwick lightning slashed across the sky. Again it was bound to do so. All the Hollywood special effects in place.He felt chilled to the marrow.

Chapter Thirty-Seven

Braden had built up in his mind a picture of Calderon from Harkness's story that was different from the impression he had gained on his previous brief visit. This impression was of two dull, drab little villages. If Lesser Calderon could be called a village in its own right. In a county on the edge of the Cotswolds, with its surfeit of picturesque old-world hamlets, the Calderons were like the outer suburbs of some large semi-industrialised county town. Slough came to mind. The first impression was reinforced by this second visit. On this dull day even the Edron Hill seemed grey, lacking in greenery, unimpressive. Everything seemed far removed from the nightmares of Harkness's story, and yet . . .

He drove through Lesser Calderon quickly. Nothing there but the shell of the church with its Norman tower and blackened walls, and the few shabby houses.

He came to the sign 'Greater Calderon', and just beyond it the turn-off leading to Calderon House. He hadn't noticed the driveway on his previous visit, but he could see now it was almost invisible, banked as it was by high hedge-rows.

Greater Calderon came up in front of him, grey and damp as before. Braden drew the car up in front of The Goat and Compasses. He thought at first the centre of the village was deserted. Then he saw a woman scurrying in the rain, dragging a boy in his early teens by the hand behind her. A pale, thin-faced female, wearing a cheap plastic coat, unkempt hair, straggling from under a thin rainproof square, she was hurrying to take herself and the boy to shelter. Ignoring the newly parked car, the woman and the boy ran through the doorway of the inn.

Braden climbed from the car and followed the woman into The Goat and Compasses. The low ceiling caused him to stoop as he entered the tiny reception area. Behind the narrow counter, the woman was ridding herself of the plastic coat. The boy had disappeared, presumably into the nether regions of the inn.

Braden said, 'Good afternoon.'

She looked up, eyes dull and uninterested.

'Yer?'

'Is Mister Mullion available?'

'Dunno. Just got in.'

'You work here?'

'Yer.' Long pause. 'You want a room?'

'No. I'll settle for a drink.'

She indicated with her head, the archway to his left. 'In the snug. What you wantin'?'

'A lager.'

She nodded and disappeared. He wandered into the snug. Apart from another low ceiling, he could see nothing 'snug' about the place. It was a small dusty bar, cubicles against the wall on one side. Above the bar-counter were a number of dull horse brasses, some of them hanging loose and crooked. Two shaded and one unshaded electric light bulb lit the place badly. Behind the bar, a gallery with a few bottles, also dusty, three with optics, and two beer handles. Hardly a great selection.

The woman appeared, bent down and produced a glass from under the bar. She poured the lager in silence. Braden had deliberately seated himself in the farthest cubicle from the bar and she was forced to come around the counter and cross the room to serve him.

'You've worked here for some time?' he said as the woman placed the glass on the wooden table in front of him.

'Yer.'

A thought came to him. 'Your name is Abbie? Abbie Silver?'

She stared down at him. 'So?'

326

The dark child-woman who had attempted to seduce Harkness, it had to be her. Twelve years older and it was showing. Braden thought, it has been a hard twelve years. She would only be in her middle twenties and yet she looked well over forty. The once raven black hair was now limp, lifeless and streaked with grey. The eyes were dull, lacking in intelligence, wandering; the skin dry and blotched.

'I recognised you from his description,' Braden lied easily. 'Harkness. I visited ex-Superintendent Harkness the other day. He told me about you. The girl at the inn, Abbie.'

First a flash of pure terror. The pale face grew even paler. She was motionless.

'Have to go . . .' she muttered.

'Not yet.'

She was used to doing what she was told.

'The night it all happened . . . you were there?' Braden said.

'Wha' night? Don't know what you're talkin' about.'

'And the boy, twelve years ago. He would be the child . . .'

Panic rising in her. 'What do you want, mister?'

'Harkness saved the child's life that night, didn't he?'

She continued to stare at him, eyes wide.

'If Harkness hadn't done what he did, the child would have been . . . where?'

'No! No, never 'appened . . .'

'They tell you to say that?'

'Yeah . . . no, no! Christ help me, I don't know.' Tears now, adding to a growing hysteria. Thin body moving now, twisting as if the memory was embracing the very flesh. A hand running through the streaked, straw-like hair.

Braden pressed on. 'The place below the church, wasn't it, Abbie? Everybody there and Anselm in charge?'

'The other was . . . was in charge. Left it to Anselm to spell the thing. Safer that way.'

'The other? You mean what he conjured up?'

'That was to come . . . to be conjured. The other was . . . the one who knew.'

'The other was the one in the jewelled cloak'

She nodded. 'But it . . . it didn't 'appen. It were . . . dreamt . . .'

327

'It was real, Abbie. It was real.'

'No!'

'It *was* real,' he insisted.

She shook her head, muttering something. He could only hear some words. 'God forgive us . . . sins now an' . . . at the time . . . of our death . . .'

'Be quiet!'

The voice came from the door of the bar. A man had appeared. His short stocky figure, once broad-shouldered, was thinner now, shoulders stooping. There was little hair on the head which, instead of being smooth, was wrinkled, ridged and pitted. The eyes were deeply sunken, the other features in shadow.

'Mister Mullion?' Braden said.

'My name is Mullion. Who are you and what do you want?' His voice was hoarse.

'Eric Braden. I'm investigating the murder of Joshua Gideon.' It sounded more impressive than saying he was writing an article for a newspaper. And it was not untrue.

'History, Mr Braden, and long since finished with. The police closed their files years ago.'

'The police never close files on a murder case.' It sounded like a line from an old movie. But then, the old clichés were the best. Braden added, 'I told the woman, I've just come from talking to ex-Superintendent Harkness.'

Mullion's eyes, almost visible now, were searching the room as if expecting to see Harkness in some corner.

'He must be dead a long time.'

'No, very much alive.'

'He'd still know nothing!'

'He remembers a great deal – about what happened that night below the church.'

'He was ill, a sick man. Mind blank. Nothing happened.'

'You were there. Harkness identified you.'

A silence. Mullion seemed to become aware of the woman still standing between them.

'Get the hell out of here, woman! You've work. Do it.'

She went out quickly, used to peremptory commands.

328

'She was there too,' Braden went on. 'With her child. I wonder who the father would be? You? Prepared to watch your own child being sacrificed?'

He'd taken a chance. It was worthwhile. Mullion snorted. 'Me! You'd be joking. Me touch her! Abbie's a . . . a thing to be used. Gideon used her. Only the likes of him *would* use her. And maybe your Mr Harkness, eh?'

Braden said, 'It would be Gideon. His child. Another sacrifice from the would-be usurper. That would complete one small circle, wouldn't it?'

He thought, Jennet Agram's closing of circles.

'You're too clever by far, mister,' said Mullion. 'An' too late by twelve years.'

'Not me, Mullion. Harkness always had a reputation of never giving up.'

'So what can he do now? Or you, for that matter? It's done, over, long finished. If it ever happened.' Mullion sounded as if he was trying to convince himself.

'There's no limitation on punishment for murder.'

Another short silence then Mullion said, 'There's no end to punishment.'

Braden gazed at the innkeeper's face. It was in full light now. The eyes were still so deeply sunken as to be black pits but the rest of the face . . . The cheeks, nose and forehead were scarred by deep fissures, as if sliced deep by a honed knife, criss-crossing the flesh. Between the fissures, it looked as if the skin had been seared and scorched by great heat.

'We see our punishment every day, mister, every time we see a mirror. And still feel the pain of when it happened. Some here in Calderon more than others, according to their share of the blame. Y'see, we can still feel the pain of it. So your law is welcome to put us on trial for murder. It might even be a relief. Aye, after that night, a relief . . .' He tried to smile. 'If it ever happened, of course.'

'You all say that!' Braden burst out. 'And then deny it ever happened. Will nobody admit it happened?'

'Admit it? That'd be madness, to *admit* it.'

Braden was silent. He knew Mullion would say little more, had gone as far as he would.

'Might as well go now, mister. You don't cause us any other pain or concern. We had it all. Now we have only to think about when we die. If there be immortal souls, where will ours go?'

Two more questions came to Braden. 'Who was the one in the jewelled cloak?'

'You don't know that? Then you've got something to find out, haven't you?' Mullion tried to smile. The fissures deepened and he winced in pain.

'What happened to Anselm?'

'When you raise up what he raised . . . what you bring up has to take something back with it. If you look, you'll find. Now, I'm telling you, get out of here. Do what you can with the law. You'll do no more harm to anyone here than they've already done to themselves.'

When Braden came out of The Goat and Compasses it had stopped raining. There were still clouds across the sun but patches of blue had appeared in the sky.

He gazed across at the church. A Mini-Minor was parked at the kerb. A figure had opened the door from the inside and was standing in the portal. A figure in black. Braden felt a damp chill run through him.

A priest.

He crossed to the church gate. The figure turned and gazed at him.

'Good afternoon.'

The man had a pleasant round face above the Roman collar. He was around fifty, with a distinctly Irish accent.

'Can I help you?'

'This is your church?'

The face smiled. 'God's church. Our Lady in the Wold. But I *am* its priest, Father Duggan. You are?'

'Eric Braden. I'm a journalist. Doing some features on old churches in the district.'

'Ah, indeed, how splendid. The secular press does so little on such themes.'

'You live in the Alms House behind the church?'

'Eh, no, I live in Lower Duthwaite. An absentee priest, I'm afraid. But then, the congregations are rather small. I officiate at three such churches.' The priest suddenly frowned. 'You have picked this church particularly to write about?'

Braden was finding lying easy. 'This church? Er, no, should I?'

The priest stared at him with a penetrating gaze. 'It's possible. There was some scandal, years back.'

As casually as possible: 'Oh, what would that be?'

Father Duggan cleared his throat loudly. 'A deal of pagan practices still around in these parts. Some evidence that the church itself was used by these foolish people. Such a pity. Such a beautiful example of the Norman style. The church was shut for a time. I believe the bishop himself had the church re-sanctified.'

'You mean, exorcised?'

The priest's forehead furrowed. 'You'd not be printin' a thing like that?'

'No, of course not, Father.' This time he was determined to be truthful. There was no need to bring that up when he wrote the story. *If* he ever wrote it.

The priest's frown disappeared. 'That'll be fine then.'

'May I see inside?'

'Well, now, I usually lock it up. Not that I should, but these days . . . ach, it's a nasty thought. So much petty thievin'. Still, I'm off to Douthwaite. But I'll be passing by again in a couple of hours. I can lock it then. When you're finished, you'll just pull the door shut?'

'I will indeed, Father.'

Braden watched the priest drive off in the Mini-Minor before entering the church.

If it had once been, as Harkness and Drewitt described it, garishly decorated, twelve years had dulled the garishness. Or perhaps discreet redecoration after the exorcism? Braden was sure that's what the priest had meant when he'd talked of re-sanctification. It was now a typical small Catholic place of worship. A gold cross above the altar, everything readied for the sacraments. Not that Braden knew much of the Catholic religion, or any religion for that matter. Church of England briefly as a child, and then the settled agnosticism.

He walked down the aisle and around the altar, looking for a door he knew would be there. It was. It led to a narrow passage and two more doors. The one on the right led down to the crypt. He went down.

He found damp stone walls. Some ancient grave stones, the inscriptions unreadable. A stone knight at rest, lady by his side, dog at his feet. And seemingly no other exit or entrance.

He walked around the walls, searching, feeling the stone with his hands. If there was no other doorway, or sign of one, then there was no story.

It took him twenty minutes to find it – an outline's break in the cement between the stones – and another five minutes to find out how it opened. There was a rusting iron lever just above ground level to the right of the outline. He tugged it upwards. No movement. He tugged again. And again. Bracing his feet against the wall, he tried a fourth time. There was a grating sound as the lever moved upwards, and a louder growling sound as the section of wall rolled inwards.

The doorway to the cavern was open. Braden stepped in and on to the top of a flight of stone steps leading downwards. The air was heavy, stale, an unpleasant odour of – what? 'Corruption' came to his mind.

He climbed slowly down into darkness.

Chapter Thirty-Eight

With one hand on the wall, Braden cursed himself for not having had the sense to bring a torch. He was feeling in his pocket for his cigarette lighter when he realised the darkness was lessening. First he could make out the walls on either side, no longer stone but with every appearance of having been carved out of the very rock itself. And yet, he told himself, it shouldn't be rock. Calderon was supposedly built on marshland. Unless the church had been erected on a subterranean outcrop from the Edron Hill . . . that had to be the explanation.

The lessening of the darkness was caused by the rock itself. It was emitting a phosphorescent glow and the further he descended the lighter it became.

The steps came to an end and he found himself standing on a ledge looking down some six feet on to the floor of what appeared to be a circular cavern, some forty yards in circumference. The ledge ran around the entire cavern and across from where Braden stood, there was a dark recess which might be another doorway.

It was exactly as Harkness had described it. Brackets which could have held torches were on the walls above the ledge. Not that they were necessary. The walls glowed here with an even greater intensity of phosphorescence than the passageway. And, in the centre of the cavern floor, was the rough outline of a circle, like some giant, begrimed metal cylinder capping a well. Scrawled on the surface of this was a cross in flaking paint and other kabbalistic symbols.

There was something else, too, at the side of the cap. At first it looked to Braden like a bundle of old clothes. Yet under the cloth there was a shape, a form, like a recumbent body.

Some yards from where Braden stood, another flight of steps had been carved from the stone leading from the ledge to the floor of the cavern. The steps were eroded by dampness and use. Braden picked his way carefully down, and moved across to the shape on the floor. With his foot he gently turned the bundle over.

And learned what had happened to Anselm.

Perhaps the sealed cavern, perhaps something in the soil, had resulted in the partial mummification of the body. There was still flesh and skin, dry, shrunken and wrinkled, under the tattered clothes. The mouth was now a black hole, what remained of the lips twisted into a grimace of horror. The eyes were gone. Black sockets only stared up at Braden. Under the tattered cloak, there were shards of a Roman collar around the neck. And, around the collar, was a chain from which was suspended a crucifix, the figure on the cross upside down. It was all as Harkness had described.

To confirm the identification there was, in the claw-like left hand of the corpse, a small leatherbound volume, open at what had been the fly leaf. The paper was torn and gave the appearance of having been gnawed by some small rodent. Yet still visible in faded yellow ink was the name 'Anselm'.

Braden lifted the book and flicked through torn pages. Symbols and signs had been hand-written between an ancient Latin text. What had at first seemed to be a leather binding felt damp, ridged, unlike real leather. Something else perhaps? The skin of some animal. Or the skin of . . .

Braden dropped the book and turned away, feeling nauseous, and thought: Another part of the circle closed.

He stared at the huge metal cap. It was so much larger, close up. He knelt beside it and placed his hand on the metal. He was relieved to find that it was ice cold. Yet there was something, a tremor, a slight, almost imperceptible throbbing. He withdrew his hand quickly and stood erect, at the same time backing away from it. Wanting to be away from it, out of this place. This *terrible* place.

334

He looked down at the body. It should be reported to the authorities, a twelve-year-old corpse. Dead these long years, with no visible sign of cause. Except for the rictus of fear on the face. How had Anselm died? A stroke, a cerebral thrombosis? Heart attack? A minute pin head of dried blood clogging an artery? Could they still tell after so many years? Or something else. Could a man die of absolute terror? Or perhaps of something else? Something beyond nature. Does the soul exist? And, if so, can it be extracted from the body, sucked out, causing instant death? Leaving only this lump of mummified flesh, the refuse of mortality.

If he reported this Braden too would have to explain how he had come here, come upon the body in this secret place. There could be other consequences. Some fool might, out of curiosity, remove the metal cap. And only God or something else knew what might result from that. The church would certainly be threatened. Another re-sanctification or whatever they called it? An inquest and inquiry into the death of Anselm? After twelve years. In a vast tomb dedicated to the . . . the thing he had worshipped.

Braden made his decision then to seal up the cavern again and go without informing anyone. So much easier that way. No delays, no inquiries, no questions to which there were no logical answers. Whatever had killed Anselm could not be brought to justice. Or perhaps the killing itself had been a kind of justice. Better to leave well alone. Anselm's tomb for twelve years would remain his tomb for eternity. And if, in some hopefully distant future, the body were to be found, who would be able even to identify it? Not from the tattered book at least. Braden put that in his pocket, to be destroyed.

He climbed up on to the ledge and moved quickly back up the stone steps, feeling easier the further he was from the corpse and the metallic circle. Thinking: Call yourself a newspaperman! What would some of the more lurid tabloids make of such a story? A Sunday article in which no one would believe. Wouldn't dare to believe. A story his editor would dismiss out of hand. No, if he wrote of the Calderon murder, there would have to be omissions. Large omissions.

Back in the crypt again, he tugged at the concealed lever and the stone entrance moved, with a grinding sound, back into the wall. With his foot, Braden kicked dirt and dust over the marks on the stone flags made by the movement of the hidden door. With his hands he pressed dirt scooped from the crypt floor between the stones of the wall and those of the door.

Hands and face begrimed, he went up into the church. At the rear of the building he found a small washroom and removed the evidence of his work in the crypt. Then he went out of the church, carefully drawing the door to behind him, and walked out into patchy sunlight.

Almost finished, he told himself. One more visit – the story from the point of view of the lady of the manor. What had Margaret Campion made, twelve years ago, of the disappearance of her priest?

He climbed into the car and with relief drove out of Greater Calderon.

He turned off the road at the rutted driveway that led through trees to Calderon House. This was the track Harkness had driven to talk with a dying Church of England priest who had given him something he had dismissed as a religious trinket. That trinket, the vial of Holy Water, had later saved his and other souls, may even have saved Calderon. That same night Harkness had driven back with Margaret to watch Haydock's church burning.

It seemed to Braden that on this, his second visit, all the Calderons were filled with the shadows of the story he had heard from Harkness.

He drove out of the trees and the house was in front of him. It was as Harkness had described it: a plain Georgian house with little exterior embellishment. Yet the simple clean lines and the large windows had a kind of charm, marred only by an air of decay. Ivy swarmed uncontrolled up the walls. And where there was no ivy, there was a patchy peeling of stucco, revealing segments of brick and plaster. The large windows too seemed to have been unwashed for some time. The lawn in front of the house was unkempt, overgrown by weeds. Even the gravel around the entrance was patchy and, in parts, revealed areas of mud.

After parking, Braden walked to the door of the house and rang the bell. As he waited, he became aware that the sky was darkening, the day dying. Although he had no sensation of cold, he shivered.

The door was opened by an elderly woman in an apron.

'Sir?'

'I'd like to see Miss Campion.' Was she still 'Miss' or had she married? In twelve years much could have happened to an attractive woman.

He was reassured by the housekeeper. 'May I tell Miss Campion who is calling?'

Braden handed her his card which had merely his name and home address on it. He added, 'Please tell her I'm a journalist, writing an article on the Calderon murder twelve years ago. You might mention to Miss Campion I have already interviewed ex-Superintendent Harkness.'

The woman's face was expressionless. She nodded and took the card.

'Will you wait in the hall, sir?'

He waited, studying an ancient, stuffed bear and admiring the sweep of the staircase, probably the house's most attractive feature. And the portraits on the walls. The Campion family throughout history.

The housekeeper returned. 'Will you come this way, sir? Miss Campion is in the library.'

He followed the woman across the hall.

'You're lucky sir. She don't usually see anyone these days.'

'Why is that?'

'I suppose . . . her not being in the best of health. Through here, sir.'

He was shown into the library. Leatherbound books lined the shelves. There was one large window, a log fire burning in the wide fireplace, and a high-backed chair turned towards it, away from the door.

'Come in, Mister Braden.' A calm strong voice came from the chair. Roedean English with no trace of a local accent. 'So you're from a newspaper and you want to know about our old murder case?'

Braden took a step forward, suddenly hesitant without knowing why.

'Doing a series of articles on famous unsolved murders,' he said, feeling ineffectual. Why was he bothering this woman who probably knew less than he did now about the murder of Joshua Gideon?

'And you've seen Mr Harkness? You know, I wouldn't have thought he'd still be alive.'

'Oh, he is, he is.'

'I'm glad. He was an interesting man. A strong man. But, perhaps, out of his depth . . . Come and sit round here, facing me, Mr Braden.'

He walked around the high-backed chair and sat in its twin, facing her. And looked into her face.

The shock was like a bolt of lightning.

Chapter Thirty-Nine

The face was not that of a woman in her forties but something else; something unexpected and terrifying in its aspect. On the brow the skin was like parchment stretched thinly across bone. Where the flesh was thicker, wrinkles and crevices were etched deep. There were also gouges, like scars folded in upon themselves. It was the face of an old old woman.

The eyes, almost hooded, noted his reaction.

'You look disturbed, Mr Braden.'

'No! No, I . . . I didn't expect . . . no, not at all.'

He was trying to regain his composure, without success. Was this the woman Harkness had talked of? Was she the victim of some horrific illness? Alzheimer's? Presenile dementia? The physical indications were there but there was no obvious lessening of mental ability. The voice was clear and logical in its greeting of him. The eyes, under the hooded brow, bright and alert.

She cut in on his thoughts.

'You're a polite liar, sir. This aspect of what was once a reasonably presentable woman . . . your friend Harkness was responsible.'

The marks on her face were familiar. Lesser but similar marks had been on Mullion's features. The deep scarring, the scorched look . . .

'Oh, yes, I was there that night, Braden. I was at the ceremony.' A statement with no attitude of the confessional. *Non peccavi* Lacking a sense of sin. A simple admission.

He should have known, seen in the evidence in the portraits on the walls of the hall. Every subject, from generation to generation, portrayed in a heavy brocade cloak or cowl. So theatrical, it was almost ridiculous.

'The one in the jewelled cloak?' he said.

'Adapted from the regalia of the Grand Masters of a sect of the Knights Templar. A family heirloom, fourteenth-century, from the reign of Philip IV of France. A cruel man but, by his lights, right to expel my ancestors in 1312. We were indeed indulging in . . . esoteric practices.' She took a long deep breath. 'Oh, you mustn't think my appearance denotes great age. I'm no Ayesha in Rider Haggard's *She*. This is simply a result of Harkness's . . . enthusiasm? And I was only carrying on the esoteric practices of my ancestors. Moving further forward. With the help of the villagers of Calderon.'

She believed it.

'Witchcraft?' he said, thinking about the scene in the cavern as described by Harkness. Could it be taken seriously? He had already accepted that an entire village could behave like that in a Hammer horror movie. This woman believed it, as had the hard-headed policeman. As if reality were no more than a scene from a bad horror film. He could only suppose human behaviour en masse lacked originality. Reality was as false as fantasy. Or it was all a dream?

'We never called it witchcraft,' she replied. 'I never considered myself a witch. I was no old hag on a broomstick, more a practitioner of the occult sciences, experimenting in . . . possibilities.'

'Like raising Lucifer?'

'You believe in the Devil, Braden? If you do, how very broadminded. So few people do nowadays. I prefer, myself, to call it the conjuring of . . . entities from other dimensions.'

'You were behind it all? Anselm was working for you?'

'Questions, questions! But, yes I suppose it can be put like that. There was a continuous line of experimentation, from the fourteenth century until twelve years ago. Anselm was an enthusiast . . . a seeker . . . with some expertise. Of course he needed me. And I could distance myself from inherent dangers by placing him before me.'

'You killed Gideon?'

The tight, scarred lips creased into a caricature of a smile.

'We all did. It was necessary. The man wanted to take over. He had just the degree of knowledge which can be dangerous. To others. To himself. Of course his death brought us a bonus – Superintendent Harkness. Without him the ceremony would never have been possible.'

'You're blaming Harkness?'

'Oh, yes. You see, this man they sent us, this policeman . . . he was the repository of so much evil. The things he had seen had left their mark, the things inside him, the . . . the evil, thereof . . . oh, Mister Braden, evil permeated his very soul.'

Braden shook his head. 'The man was just a policeman investigating the evil done by others.'

'It's not like that. Evil infects those in contact with it,' she insisted. 'Even when the receptacle is not aware of his own infection. And we were able to draw it from him, channel it, feed it to the One who came . . .'

'He wouldn't know what you were doing!'

'Not consciously. But subconsciously he was drawn towards us. All his life, of his own free will, he sought out what we call evil. What ordinary man does that? What other policeman found himself investigating so many of the more extreme manifestations of that evil. You, Mr Braden, the normal rational man, the humanist, would deny such evil exists – despite thousands of years of evidence! Despite your being surrounded by it! But Harkness knew, albeit subconsciously. Yes, Harkness was responsible, was the receptacle. When we tried to frighten him off . . . he would force himself to go on.'

'He was investigating a murder . . .'

'. . . that he knew no one person had committed. Oh, how Harkness was drawn to us! As he was drawn to Jennet Agram, although she was on a different path. I think she knew his life gave him the experience, the power to raise . . . what we wanted to raise.'

'But he destroyed whatever you . . . you raised up.'

Her thin, claw-like hands gestured impatiently. 'Did he? Or was it Haydock who destroyed it, with his holy water? From beyond his own grave. Perhaps, too, the influence of Jennet Agram helped.'

341

'Harkness believed that, by throwing the vial of water, he destroyed . . . whatever it was,' Braden insisted.

The white head nodded. 'He would have to believe that. And anyway, he cleansed himself that night.'

'As if the experiences of evil were sucked from him? He said something like that.'

There was a silence now, Braden staring at the young/old woman, trying to understand. As if, he thought, as Jennet Agram had said, the circle was now almost closed. No, there was nothing else. The circle must be closed now. He was surprised, awed almost, at his own adoption of belief in the story, now that the pieces had come together.

'Will you take some tea, now, Mr Braden?' Margaret Campion asked.

'I . . . I don't think so.'

'I assure you I'm quite harmless now. De-clawed. No longer able to test people with plagues of moths. Sherry wine perhaps?'

'Thank you, no.'

'You need worry about none of us here now. We missed our chance and I received this for bungling.' She indicated her face. 'It all ended that night. Of course, it was dangerous then but it would be impossible now. You found Anselm's body?'

'How did you know that?'

'It was inevitable you would look for the place under the church, and find it. And the body. You see, no matter who is responsible, when you invoke whatever we did, when you raise It up and then bungle the raising, and send it back, It does not go empty-handed. Oh, it damaged us all, as you can see, but It took Anselm. Took him where is an interesting philosophical question on which I do not propose to speculate. Won't you please have something? At least a small whisky?'

'I should be going back to London.'

'Of course. There's no need for you to stay. You must know almost everything now. As Jennet Agram would say, "The circle is almost closed." Isn't that what she would say, Braden?'

He nodded, feeling cold now.

342

'Strange,' Margaret Campion went on, 'I don't think I ever met her but we seem to know each other. Opposite sides of a coin, you could say.'

'Thank you for seeing me, Miss Campion.' He rose to his feet.

'It's of no consequence.'

He went to the door, aware of the depth and softness of the carpet. Everything seemed easier now.

Her voice stopped him at the door. 'Over for us, Mr Braden, but others carry on. In small quiet places, in the night. Looking, as an American wit once said, for loopholes. And there are those well qualified to carry on. By reason of knowledge. Or of birth.'

He turned. She had swung the chair round and was facing him, gashed, aging face pale but eyes aglow.

'Goodbye, Mr Braden. Have a good journey to London.'

He drove away from the house, down the driveway, on to the road and through Lesser Calderon to the main arterial road. He drove south into the darkness of approaching night. Going to London; going home.

Thinking: about evil, about his coming to believe in abstract evil. Was there such a thing? True, factual evil . . . the Holocaust, child murder, many of the crimes Harkness had investigated throughout his career . . . all that he knew existed. But evil, as an abstraction or a separate entity, how could he believe in such a primitive, such an ancient idea? Yet, if one believed in God, should one not as easily believe in the antithesis of the Deity?

His mind rebelled against the thought.

But Harkness maintained he had seen something rise up from the cavern below the church. The down-to-earth, logical police superintendent believed. As did the villagers of the two Calderons. As did Margaret Campion.

Illusion. Mass hypnosis. There were all the logical explanations. And what had he been told? That he wanted to believe in what they had seen. Believe in the Devil, he could then believe in God.

In two and a half hours he let himself into his Chiswick apartment. In the morning, he would return the car to the London branch of the firm from which he had hired it, and go into the office to write his story. But what story? If published it would be considered a wild piece of sensationalism. It probably wouldn't do the circulation figures any harm, but, as a writer he'd be laughed at. What would his friends think? Hammond the accountant would laugh and say: 'Forget it! If it raises the circulation, that's what counts.' Judy, if she read it, would think what?

First time in days he thought of Judy. Should he be glad that Calderon and Harkness and all the horrors he'd heard of had taken her from his mind? The pain of her going had returned, but only momentarily. Was he over that? He tried to picture her in his mind as he made himself coffee, and found he was having trouble doing so. There were too many other images. Jennet Agram for one, and the ravaged features of Margaret Campion.

He drank his coffee and went to bed. Early, very early. Nine o'clock. He lay in the darkness unable to sleep . . . nothing new about that. There'd been so many sleepless nights over Judy's departure. He found himself wishing she was with him again but not with the same painful longing as before. He needed someone now to be with him, a warm body by his side. Perhaps Jennet Agram would have been a better companion. She at least would have understood. After a time his thoughts turned to Harkness and the Calderons and other twelve-year-old nightmares. Could Margaret Campion have been right? Had Harkness been drawn to Calderon by something other than his investigation? Was the seed of so much evil within the policeman as much as within Anselm and the others?

After a time, a very long time, he fell asleep.

When he woke, dawn was breaking, first light filtering through the cracks in the curtains. He felt a strange serenity then. Perhaps because it was over. Perhaps from something else. An achievement. A belief where there had been no belief, a faith where there had been only a void.

He rose took a cold shower, dressed and drank a cup of hot coffee. Telling himself it was crazy to find himself embracing religious belief.

He drove his hired car to the London office of the rental firm and handed it over. He retained the receipt, another expense for Jordan to moan about.

In the office, he started to type the Calderon story on to the word processor. Jordan came in just after he'd started and stood behind him.

'You're back.'

'Looks like it.' He continued to type.'

'Story had better be good. With a decent sex angle.'

'You mean, an indecent sex angle?'

'That would be better. But does it work? Do you know who really did it?'

'They all did.'

'What the hell does that mean?'

Braden explained.

Jordan frowned.

'You can't do that. God, the whole village could sue us! One guy trying to sue us, that would be no problem. But a whole village?'

'We'd just have to prove it was true.'

'Can we do that?'

It wouldn't be easy.'

'Damn it, Braden, I should never have listened to you and this stupid idea . . .'

He swung around in his chair. 'Not my idea. Yours! You gave me it.'

Jordan shook his head violently. 'No, no. Don't tell me that. I'm the bloody editor. If I say you gave me the idea, then you did.'

'Not me this time, Louis. Look for another whipping boy.'

'Well, then, somebody else gave me the idea. You don't think *I* thought it up?'

Braden felt a strong desire to giggle. 'No, I'd be surprised if *you* thought it up.'

Jordan glared at him, aware that other members of his staff had arrived and were listening, amused expressions on their faces.

'Not funny! All right, it wasn't you. I remember who it was . . . that fooking Alec who runs the clippings library. His idea. I'll speak to him later. Yes, I will.'

345

He went, grumbling, behind the glass and wood partition that was his office.

Braden stared at the screen of the word processor, puzzled. Alec in the cuttings library . . . *his* idea? Alec, who had put him on to the Calderon story? Why that one? Out of all the unsolved cases in the world, why Calderon?

Braden took the lift to the basement. Been here before, he told himself. Only this time the questions are different.

Deep behind the shelves and drawers, Alec sat on a high stool at a high desk, head down, back towards Braden. Working on something like a Dickensian clerk.

'Alec?'

'You're back, Mr Braden.' It was said without turning.

'From Calderon. Your idea, Alec.'

'Uh?'

'Mister Jordan, the editor, says so.'

'Aye. Might have mentioned the general idea to Mr Jordan.'

'But not to me, Alec.'

'For all I knew, Mr Jordan might have told you himself.'

'And you led me to Calderon.'

'Seemed like a good idea.'

The hunched back was beginning to irritate Braden.

'I learned something in Calderon, Alec, and from Harkness – there are no co-incidences.'

A pause, then Alec turned on his stool and faced Braden.

'Fair enough. I wanted it brought out, the whole story about Calderon.'

'Why?'

A tired grin spread over Alec's face. A seamed face, yes, but not that of an old man. In his early fifties, no older.

'You know my name?'

'Alec . . .'

'Second name. No? Nobody bothers, do they? Just Alec. Short for Alexander. Short for Alexander Gideon.'

It would have been easy to say he should have known, but no, only now did he make the connection. In hindsight, he remembered that Joshua Gideon had a younger brother, Alexander Gideon, the one who had gone away.

346

'They killed my brother, see?' Alexander Gideon said. 'All of them. Oh, I knew that, but I wanted it brought out. I wanted everyone to know what that damned place was really like! I wanted some justice for my brother . . .' The circle was closing, Braden thought.

He said: 'Your brother was one of them.'

'Maybe. But it's the blood, Mr Braden, that tells what a man should do. I wanted it brought out, so I got you sent there.'

'Jordan isn't sure whether he'll publish the story. Doesn't like the idea of accusing a whole village of murder . . .'

'He *has* to publish. Has to!'

'Alec, it doesn't matter. They . . . they've been punished. More than any newspaper story could punish them.

The old man stared at Braden again in silence, for a full minute. Perhaps longer.

Finally he broke the silence. 'You think that?'

'I've seen it.'

The stars were unwavering. 'Maybe. Maybe you'll be right. And there's something else.'

Without looking away he reached behind him, and taking a small clipping from his desk, handed it to Braden.

'From this morning's *Glasgow Herald*.'

It was a tiny paragraph. The headline was DEATH OF FAMOUS DETECTIVE.

It simply recorded that retired Superintendent J.B. Harkness, formerly of Scotland Yard, had died the previous day after a long illness. It referred only to his work in London on the breaking of the Swanson gang. There was no mention of Calderon. The man was dead, why bring up his failures?

Braden felt cold and couldn't explain why.

He looked up at Alexander Gideon.

'It's over,' he said.

'Is it?' said Gideon.

'What else . . .?'

'His child is still alive.'

'His daughter? He lived with her . . .'

'The other daughter. Jennet Agram's child.'

'What about her?'

347

Alexander Gideon looked away. Over Braden's shoulder. Into the distance.

'The child takes over from the man. In time.'

'Takes over what?'

'You know, Mr Braden. You been told.'

The evil thereof? Margaret Campion's phrase. The child had been conceived before the ceremony under the church. And if the evil had been in Harkness then . . .

'It's never finished, you see, Mr Braden,' Gideon said. 'It goes from generation to generation.'

The evil thereof . . .

The circle could never be closed.